Consideration Of Tragedies

Pat Kane

Copyright © 2022 Pat Kane

All rights reserved.

ISBN: 13: 9798369882436

DEDICATION

I dedicate this, my first book, to my wife, Margaret.
Thank you for putting up with my typing.

CONTENTS

Prologue
1. The Son
2. The Freemans
3. The New Beginning
4. The Van Man
5. The Mysterious Mr. Wright.
6. The Mother's Passing
7. The Sell Up and Moving On
8. The Baker
9. The Emergency Conference
10. The Barflies
11. The Researchers
12. The Wroxham
13. Nada
14. The Magazines
15. The Humph's Research
16. The Gangster
17. The Post
18. The Cleaner
19. The GNC
20. The New Task
21. The Trip
22. The Humph's Day
23. The Introductions
24. The Viewings
25. The After Shock
26. The Reports and Invoices
27. The Investigations
28. The Researcher's Findings
29. The Journalist
30. The Specs
31. The Boss is Back
32. The Good Fings
33. The Introduction of Fran
34. The Odd Date
35. The Busy Bar
36. The Attraction
37. The Telling Off
38. The Goodnight
39. The Pockets

40. The Late Invite
41. The Guns Problem
42. The Briefcase
43. The Concerned Baker
44. The Den
45. The Power Punch
46. The Tale from George
47. The Close-Encounters
48. The Meeting of Mrs. M
49. The Injured Idiots
50. The Black Coffee
51. The Day Trip
52. The Trio
53. The H-Files
54. The Gruesome Find
55. The Raid
56. The News
57. The Irritating Barflies
58. The New Staff
59. The Guinness
60. The Discussions
61. The White Corkboard
62. The Godfather
63. The Algorithms
64. The Big Surprises
65. The Tale of Kumar
66. The Demise of a Drunk
67. The Temp Tenant
68. The Revelations
69. The Truth is Hard
70. The Fraudster
71. The Initials
72. The Old 'Acquaintance'
73. The Judge
74. The Hard Work…
75. The Smiling and Touching
76. The Cosy Chat
77. The Link
78. The Hart to Hart
79. The Bar Buzzed
80. The Alley
81. The Experts
82. The Team and Listening

83. The Set Up
84. The Travelling Monies
85. The Middleman
86. The Shots in the Dark
87. The Recordings
88. The Phone Calls
89. The Warehouse
90. The 16th Floor
91. The Interrogation
92. The Search for Ambrose
93. The Oops
94. The Rag Journalist
95. The Decision
96. The Prodigal Returns
97. The Wine Taster
98. The Explosive Meeting
99. The Boss Mug
100. The Sad Judge
101. The CBCT
102. The Nervous Alan
103. The Weird Calls
104. The Bouncing Accounts
105. The Daylight Robberies
106. The Good and Bad Results
107. The Discovery
108. The Tudor-Style Pub
109. The Attempted Assassination
110. The Strange Guinness
111. The Truth
112. The Intrusion
113. N/A
114. The Bruised Alan
115. The Infiltration
116. The Real Evidence
117. The Fronts
118. The Friends Bridge
119. The King is Dead
120. The Auld Fella's Visiting
121. The Truth and Nothing But
122. The Pre-Post-Mortem
123. The auld Fella and Gloria
124. The Grab
125. The Metal Box

126. The son and Dad Chat
127. The Gang Chat
128. The New Mob
129. The Interpol Confirmation
130. The Funeral
131. The Attack
132. The Superintendent
133. The Booking
134. The Long-Awaited Trial
135. The Super's Round
136. The Last Task?
137. The Conference Preparation
138. The Society of Justice
139. The Bottles
140. The Afters
141. The Last Bastard
142. The Lady Theresa
143. The Future Plans

ACKNOWLEDGMENTS

A big thank you to the Scribophile members who critiqued this book making it possible to publish.

A special thank you to Randall Krsak and Anastasia Mosher for giving up your precious time away from your own projects and family life to assist in editing.

An extra special gratitude to Yvonne Kavanagh and Christine Smith. Two fantastic tutors who opened my eyes to writing. So, all your blempt.

                          Cheers.
                          Pat

Prologue

July 2003.

Somewhere in mainland Europe, a late participant joined a small conference via speaker phones. Waves rushed softly then crashed against beached rocks.

A man panted before speaking. "I do apologise to the society. Family matters. Did I miss much?"

A croaky voice said, "Not at all. Anyway, we have discussed your recommendations of two recruits. Her Ladyship has made some good points."

"Yes, I think your second choice may have a cross-over affect with your favourite recommendation. Some past events in their lives have a connection. Does that worry you?" came a soft, well-spoken woman's voice.

The family man's sharp intake heard. "My connection, and indeed, another member's more so, does have important implications to the tasks we may request of him. My second choice will be restricted to data collecting rather than actions. Although that person does have vast knowledge in academia topics."

"I agree," a marbled tone said. "I too have a connection with the second, albeit academic and I thank our esteemed member for his recommendation."

"I must thank the Society for Justice for their patience." A distinct European brogue interrupted.

"Your first choice, dear friend, suffers in silence. His mind has not settled. He had shown some latent development but has regressed. I, above all, have faith in him as long as our society is in full agreement."

"I trust your choices," the lady said. "Though I doubt that their paths will cross, the second choice will be good for our society. We do need more intelligence operatives."

"Permit me to contact other members that could not attend this short conference and inform them of our decisions," the marbled voice said.

They agreed.

"Very well. I will also draft and send an introductory letter to the two assets with a brief outline of why we wish to recruit them."

A short lady-like cough interrupted him. "Do not tell them too much. If they do agree to at least stick to our rules, we can send them a trial task leaving the ball in their court as to how they perform it."

Agreements once more echoed followed by phones disconnecting.

1 THE SON

Dublin, May 2004.

Chris Freeman turned slowly in his bed. "Ooh. Stiff again."

He eased his scarred right leg out and sat up. Resting his hands on his knees, he turned to a framed picture on a bedside locker. "Morning, Mary. What will the day hold for me today?"

Pushing his feet into flip flops, he gradually stood. Legs straightened, he walked to the bedroom door, removed an Arsenal FC bathrobe from a hook and put it on.

A phone buzzed in a pocket. Taking it out, he viewed the caller. Tapping speaker he answered. "Talk to me."

"You sound narky," a strong Dublin voice said.

"I'm not a morning person, Dad."

"You dropping by this morning?"

"I'm in Dublin. Have an appointment with the specialist." Chris opened the door and walked along a short corridor.

"Oh, okay. Head or leg?"

"Head. I don't need glasses yet, but the headaches, though not frequent as they were, are really heavy." He turned into a bathroom and placed the phone on the sink.

"What's that noise?"

"Dad, I'm only out of the scratcher. You do call at the most awkward of times."

"Oh, I get you. Your mum is going for another check-up on Friday."

"I'll be back Thursday. I've to read through the latest research findings." He flushed.

"They look good, but you have the last say. We have a new chemist and researcher starting Monday. He comes highly recommended."

"That's Mum's end. Her judgements have been great so far. Anyway, I've to get ready. Can't eat because having blood tests too."

"Okay, son. Good luck."

Chris tapped off. Stripping, he went to his walk-in shower, turned it on and stepped in.

Showering had been a chore and a half up to recently. Physiotherapy had been hard, but it did the job on his damaged leg. His rehabilitation had been slow over the two years, both in mind and body. Not being a mummy's boy, but Margaret Freeman nursed her son's traumatic demur back to almost his old self.

Now it was her turn to be cared for. Though liking Dublin, he hated being away from his parents for too long. Margaret was always strong;

the driving force behind her husband and their multi-million pharmaceutical company, Ostrofman. The news of her contracting cancer had urged Chris on to find remedies to ease and perhaps cure her.

Dried off, he looked into mirrored doors over the sink. His short, dark hair still dripped. His grey eyes stared back at him. Rubbing his stubble, he opened the unit doors, took out his shaving gear. He kept himself well-groomed. At meetings he felt self-presentation was more important than demonstrating company results and products.

Casually dressed in a short-sleeved blue shirt and jeans, he relaxed on the balcony of his three-bedroom apartment drinking bottled water. North Dublin's Malahide was a pleasant coastal village. A place to get away from after company meetings and tours. Delegates can be such a pain in the arse. Checking his watch, he took another slug then left for his check-up in Blackrock Clinic. No driving. The local Dart train service ideal for travelling to the South Dublin town.

**

Dr. O'Reilly looked over his glasses at Chris across his office desk. "We'll have your blood tests back by Monday."

Chris rubbed his right knee. "Will I ring? I'm away next week to Germany for a medical conference and touring our centre there."

"I'll call you. Now, you don't have a tumour. But there are some abnormalities in parts of you brain. Your sight is perfect, hearing excellent. The headaches should lessen. You have come on leaps and bounds since the accident." He leaned over the desk. "I notice you're rubbing your knee again."

"It's getting there. Back training. Putting pressure on it can be sore when kicking."

"Martial arts—that would keep you fit. Though you're only twenty-four, ease down on putting too much reliance on the right leg. So, we'll chat Monday afternoon. How's Margaret?"

"Mum is doing okay. Has tests on Friday." Chris eased out of the chair.

O'Reilly stood and walked towards the door. "Give her my love and tell Ben I was asking for him. Your parents have done well and I'm glad to see you're getting back on the straight and narrow."

They shook hands.

"Cheers, Doc."

**

Chris was lost gazing at low tide of South Dublin bay through the train window. It had been a hard two years. Though back working as CEO of his parent's company, he needed answers to something else. Something that had changed his free spirit. His sporting days were over. Some confidence had been knocked out of him. No more amateur theatricals. He had enjoyed them at Trinity College. Him and young law student Luis Mendez, Dublin born to Spanish parents, had earned praises. But both preferred the real world rather than acting.

Chris breathed heavy waking from his daydreaming.

Think I'll have brunch in town.

Taking out his phone, he tapped in a text.

He got off the train at Tara Street station and walked across the River Liffey's Butt Bridge towards Brady's in Marlborough Street. The small bar, renowned for hospitality, chat, and banter, wasn't busy. But the rush at lunchtime would see regulars vi for their normal seats.

Chris climbed onto a high stool at his round pedestal-table. Though his name wasn't on it, anyone looking for him would expect to see him seated there.

"Chris, hi. What'll I get ya?" Emmet Brady asked from behind the counter.

"G'day. Eh—" He looked to his right wrist. "Midday, just a coffee and plain chicken sandwich, please."

Chris looked along the bar and waved at two regulars. He stared up at the TV. He had time to think before the rush and Guinness. His family had been using the pub for generations; of course the bar had different names. Ben had told him it was known as the TV bar by locals back in the 1950s. It was the first pub to have a television. Unfortunately, his Great-grandfather was temporarily barred after throwing a bottle at the screen when showing Queen Elizabeth's coronation.

To his right the front door open.

Eyes naturally looked to his table. "Chris, good to see you."

Chris shook the smaller man's hand. "Luis. You didn't text back. How are you?"

"Grand. Was at the Four Courts. You're looking good. How's your parents?" Luis sat opposite.

"Fine. Mum's having more tests on Friday."

Emmet arrived with Chris' order and placed them on the table. "There you go. Hi, Luis. What'll I get ya."

"Hi, Emmet." He looked at Chris' fare. "Same as him, please. Aunt's in later."

"Oh no." Emmet left them.

"Cata's coming?"

"Yeah. Her and Fernando are on some mission for a few days. Anyway, you—over for tests too?"

Chris spooned a little sugar into a large mug and stirred. "Yeah. No tumour. Get blood results on Monday."

"Well that's good news. And the headaches?"

"Sometimes bad, but not as often. Apparently, when I'm stressed, or something irks me, they start. Doc said that's not unusual."

Emmet placed Luis' order down. "Enjoy."

"Cheers," Luis said.

The two ex-amateur actors chatted about their jobs and health between mouthfuls. They weren't close but kept in contact if about their hometowns. Luis career choice was criminal law, something Chris had always asked him about. How could he represent someone that had obviously committed the crime and fight to get him off. They had many heated arguments on the topic of defending the guilty.

Chris cared about people, innocent people. Like those mowed down two years ago by a careless hit and run driver. Especially his new bride, Mary. She would never be forgotten. Always in him, and along with his mother, urged him forward.

Luis had called for two Guinness after their meals.

A few more lunchtime drinkers arrived and nodded or said hi to the pair.

"What would you do if the company was sold?" Luis asked.

"Sold? We're in the process of taking over a German company and expanding. Dad's talking about Sweden."

"Really? Wow. It'll be worth some money in the future. But if it was sold, what would you do?"

Chris leaned back. "Ask your Uncle and Aunt for a job—or buy this pub."

"You, a P.I? A barman perhaps, but I can't see you chasing crims. The way you think about them, they'll have no chance in court."

They chatted over one more round before Chris decided it was time to go. No toilets on the communal train.

2 THE FREEMANS

England, May 2004

On Thursday, Chris had returned to his empty five-bedroomed house on The Warren, in Royston. It was meant to be a family home in a rustic small town. Big garden for his children to enjoy. Room for his and Mary's parents to stay over. A home for celebrations. And being close to the main routes between London and the company's headquarters in Cambridge, it was ideal.

But there was no Mary, there wouldn't be any children. He hated the place. The only solace being the Green Man pub around the corner.

He pulled a back-barstool to his favourite position at the counter. Rubbing his eyes, he yawned.

"Travellin' again, Chris?" Owner Seth Green remarked behind the counter.

"Aye, Seth. Dublin. Can I have a pint of Extra. Is Agnes on?"

"So you want a chicken wrap?"

"Ah, she is. Yes, please."

She was his favourite pub chef. He wouldn't be there daytime for food if Agnes Peters wasn't working. He sipped the strong beer.

"Knew it was you, Chris." Agnes placed a full plate in front of him. "How's all?"

"Good, thanks." He smiled.

"Liar. Can always tell."

He picked up the chunky wrap and bit off a morsel. "Well—" He chewed and swallowed. "'Scuse me—speaking of liars, any word of Noel?"

"Couldn't care anymore. Showed up last month, stayed a few days and off on his travels again—worse than you."

They laughed.

Her hubby loved baking but was never satisfied at opening his own place. His cousins had bakeries; it was a family thing. Chris and Agnes had something in common, they were alone. At least she had children to comfort her when Noel went of discovering new recipes—or so he had told her.

"You're looking well, Agnes."

"Go off with you. Just like your dad—charmer. How's your lovely mum?"

Chris chased the food down with a sip of beer. "I'll see her tomorrow. She's having tests."

"I couldn't believe they've lived here for years; I mean in England. You wouldn't think they'd left Ireland. And owning that company."

"It was hard work for them. Mum was great, Dad told me. He was happy to work for a company instead of owning one."

"And you—what do want?"

The question hurt him. The wrap stalled at his mouth.

Agnes, I want you to stop asking the same fucking question.

"Might buy this place."

"I 'erd that. Not for sale." Seth pulled a tap.

"Nah, too big. Something smaller. Perhaps Dad's old stomping ground in Clapton." He chewed.

"In the Smoke. Beer's crap. No special like our local brews," Agnes said.

"I'll order some."

Perhaps one day he would buy something like this. But Chris had remarked how big it was. Not his thing. He was like his father. Ben preferred the comfort and comradery of a small pub, bit of a sing song and banter.

Agnes was called to a table. "Good to see you, Chris. Keep well." The small woman walked away.

Chris's eyes followed her.

Jesus. The size of her compared to Noel.

**

The Freemans lived in a renovated farm cottage on the outskirts of Stevenage, a few miles south of their son's home. Chris took after his mother in looks and height. He being six-two, his friends had wondered how Ben, at five-seven, could've fathered him. The answer laid with Margaret. Five-eleven and dark features. Her family came from Galway, but she was born not far from Ben's Clontarf area of Dublin.

Ben was perhaps a charmer in his college days. Loved singing and played the piano well. He could have made a career out of it but for Margaret. He was caught by her during their second year at Dublin's Trinity. They progressed with the same degrees and Ph.D.'s. There were two paths lined up for them, marriage and start their own company.

They sat in their back garden in the late May sunshine with Chris.

"So, Mum, how'd it go?"

She needed the sun. Her face was pallor. "Painful." She touched her chest. "No need for chemo just yet. Don't want the fucking thing anyway."

Yes, Chris took after his mother.

Ben poured more red wine into their glasses. The awning fully pulled over the patio.

"How's your head, son?" she asked.

"No tumour. Just some strange growth. Doc claims it's from the accident. Eyes and hearing perfect."

"That's good news. And your leg—you're limping again."

"Was training this morning. Oh, Luis was asking for you both."

"How is he?" Ben sipped. "Fighting the good fight for the guilty as usual?"

"Got it one, Dad."

"Oh, you two stop. He's doing free legal aid. It's not his fault. When he's established I'm sure he'll get the real innocent cases." Margaret always saw the brighter picture. Hope for people.

Ben preferred to fight for people. Get the proper affordable products out there to ensure they stay healthy or ease their pain.

Chris was in between, a bit of both. The way genetics was meant to be. Blame the parents before society takes the rap.

Though they all had degrees, Chris provided the latest technology for the company. He was back researching, throwing ideas at the company's renowned and trusted engineers. Each time his mother was on his mind. She was touching fifty. Why should she die? There's loads more work left for her to do.

"This new researcher starting Monday, what you know of him, Mum?"

"Well, Cambridge education. Top honours in chemical engineering. His thesis on chemical restructure was impressive. Alan Bradford should be a good recruit to our research department." She took up her glass and drank.

"I'll talk with him when back from Germany. Is he local?"

Margaret looked to Ben. "I don't know."

"Bristol. Has digs in Cambridge. He might suit the German company," Ben said.

"Fucksake, Dad. Let's suss him out first."

Chris hadn't lost his Eastend upbringing. Though well-spoken for a blow-in Cockney, the Dublin born man still preferred real people. He could mix with all classes just like his parents.

Ben looked sharp at him and shook his head. "Just like your mother."

"I'm over here—yoo-hoo." Margaret smiled.

They laughed. It was them. The way they always were and hoped to be for years to come.

3 THE NEW BEGINNING

October 2004

Chris had travelled extensively between mainland Europe and the UK over the past months. Conferences taking up more time than he would have preferred. The new researcher was shipped off to recently acquired German company to head up its research department. Chris didn't like him. Too in your face and boring. Quoting facts on this and that akin to a snotty nosed bookworm.

Reads all, does fuck all.

Chris understood the man was well educated, knew his stuff hands down, but not his cup of tea.

Margaret had improved and spent more time with Ben at the company's headquarters due to unwanted developments.

Concerns had grown over quantities of product that had escaped final approval for public use. The medication had been specifically researched and established for the African market. Once a product has passed all tests, it's packaged and given a batch number.

Accordingly, the next shipment is tested and given a new batch number and so on.

It was the third batch that had caused the concern. Children had died, where as previously there had been no problems. A chemist in charge of the final testing and computer referencing was found to be liable and discharged pending investigation.

Alarm bells went off.

All production had stopped while each item was retested. The German company appeared not to be involved.

Ben and Margaret went out to view the latest asset.

She was impressed with the new recruit's research regarding cancer. She became fervent with his findings. Results from the labs were excellent. So much so he convinced her human trials could commence soon.

The Freemans sat in their hotel suite before dinner.

"I want to test the medication," Margaret said.

"What? No way. It barely passed the tests on rats." Ben fiddled with a cup of coffee.

"Darling, this could be it. If I wait another year or two, it could be too late." She rubbed his cup-hand.

"Something you're not telling me?"

Margaret never asked questions of his late 'committee' meetings. They trusted each other.

"I've started already. Two days ago. One tab a day for a month."

Ben jumped for the chair. The cup smashed on the floor.

4 THE VAN MAN

Cambridge, February 2005.

Many Society of Justice operatives needed disguises. Julius Sigerson had changed his name for the latest task. He had become *John Brownlow,* a delivery van driver with impeccable credentials. He had driven throughout Europe and UK, a perfect candidate for the job he began six months ago.

The character orientated task neared fruition. A task that needed meticulous planning and establishing a real persona vital for further missions.

Altering and adapting to new identities, playing a different role to one's normal make-up, wasn't easy. Individual candidates handpicked for each assignment based on their unique specialities and similarities to the character to be accepted. Some had multiple talents. Like others', Julius' experience of gadgetry played an integral part in his task.

Brownlow loaded the last box into a van.

Mr. Toplan, Ostrofman Pharmaceuticals' warehouse distribution manager, held his right arm. "John, are you sure you won't reconsider? You have become part of the structure—in fact, on your first day, you appeared to know your way around."

Bulky Brownlow looked down to the smaller, white-coated man. "Mister Toplan, I'm a quick learner and grateful for the job. But I did warn you that it was only for four months. I extended by two months, altering my planned India trip."

Only because the subject changed his plans.

The rear doors of the chrome-blue Ford transit clunked shut. Brownlow walked to a nearby grey steel fire escape, picked up his large travel backpack and returned to the van.

"I know you have another driver to replace me next Monday," he said.

Mr. Toplan rubbed his hands together to warm them up. "Yes. But you will be missed even so. Perhaps when you return from India, think about coming back. In the meantime, when returned from Hamburg, drop into my local Saturday night. We'll have a few drinks as a thank you."

Brownlow opened the driver's door and climbed in. "I sure will. I'll tell Herr Müster about the replacement."

He pulled the door shut, fastened the belt, turned a key. The engine shook into action.

The van slowly moved from the company's carpark then right onto Cambridge Science Park road. So began the first leg of the long trip to

Hamburg.

He tapped a rhythm on the wheel to music from the radio. *All in place. Last few days then hopefully a long well-deserved rest. May return to Benidorm for a few days as well for some rays.*

**

The driver's side window of the transit whirred down. Brownlow handed his false passport and driving credentials to a Dunkirk customs officer.

Emotionless, the official looked at the documents. "Is this a short round trip to Hamburg, eh—" He rechecked the name. "Monsieur Brownlow?" His breath floated as he spoke.

The officer looked up from the paperwork to confirm Brownlow's ice-blue eyes, trimmed light red hair and heavy beard.

"Yes, it will be a few days before returning." His Norfolk brogue distinct.

The officer looked again at the documents. "Okay. Drive safe." He waved the vehicle on.

**

The van cruised through the Normandy countryside heading for the quickest route to Hamburg via Antwerp through Duisburg. Brownlow stopped in the small town of Lotte, Belgium, for a snack at Pizzeria Roma.

No one knew him as Julius Sigerson; that name was for more personal endeavours. The previous month, the landscape was a winter wonderland. Flat grasslands and coniferous trees glistened in morning sunrises. Now, travelling was faster as speed restrictions loosened due to late seasonal rising temperatures.

He read a local paper's sports page during his thirty-minute stay, then paid for the meal before setting off on the next leg to Bremen. Establishing his regular stops and people he met on the rest-breaks secured his identity. Would he be missed if anything went wrong?

Listening to a variety of radio stations kept him alert and distracted from the ultimate task rehearsed in his mind.

His last rest stop after a five plus hour drive was at Mevlana Holzkohlegrill, Hemelingen, in Bremen. Although he ate there on his way to and from Hamburg, staff remained somewhat aloof to all customers. The lamb chops with fries sustained him until his late-night snack near his guesthouse in Hamburg.

**

Brownlow drove along Brandstücken, north-west Hamburg and turned left into GEHE Pharma Handel GmbH car park. He glanced at the dashboard clock: 4:00 p.m. Vans and trailers parked in order delivering or collecting goods. He stopped the transit at a vacant space in front of a loading bay. Gathering the goods itinerary, he climbed out of the van.

Walking spritely towards him, wearing his customary pristine brown work clothes, came the efficient Herr Müster. His coat correctly buttoned and with two pens clipped to a single breast pocket. A dark, perfect thin hairpiece shone on his head.

With clipboard carried sergeant major style under his left arm, he came smartly to attention in front Brownlow. His toupee slipped right.

"Herr Brownlow," he began in a high-pitched voice. "You are remarkable. Never late—excuse me." He unashamedly adjusted his hairpiece.

They walked in step to the rear of the transit.

"Well, you Germans respect time-keeping." Brownlow opened the van. "It is a shame I couldn't fully learn your lingo though. This is my last trip, Herr Müster."

The store manager raised his eyebrows. "How disappointing. For an Inglander, you have been zee best punctual driver."

"*Danke*," Brownlow said. "I believe the new driver starts on Monday. I am off to India next week for a few months."

"*Wunderbar*. Frau Müster and I ver der some years ago after our two *kinder* had left for university." His chest proudly stuck out. "Zo, vat have you got for me today?"

Not intentionally mocking, Brownlow stepped sharply to attention for the manager to look at the load. "All yours."

"*Gut, gut.*"

Müster waved a hand towards two dungaree-wearing subordinates. They immediately rushed forward with a large four-wheel trolley.

The manager and Brownlow smartly stood back from the transit as the men unloaded the boxes onto the trolley.

"Are you staying for the match, Herr Brownlow?"

Brownlow furrowed his brow. "Match?"

"*Ja*. Bayern against Arsenal."

"No way. Firstly, I don't like football and secondly, I will be heading back tomorrow after breakfast."

"Zo, dis would be goodbye, Herr Brownlow." He ticked off the items as they were loaded. "Now I vill sign yours and you vill sign mine, *Ja*."

After both had checked the dockets, they shook hands. As Brownlow climbed onto the driver's seat he watched Herr Müster turn sharply and march behind the trolley.

He chuckled as Herr Müster adjusted his hairpiece again.

He reminds me of someone.

The van moved slowly from the car park to a nearby guesthouse on Notkestraße, the Chateau Marciella. Because the guesthouse only catered for B&B, he ate a late dinner at Bistro Samarkand near the impressive Volksparkstadion, home of Hamburg FC. He finished off his last night in the guise of John Brownlow in the Bahrenfelder Sportsbar.

**

John Brownlow locked the Ford transit in the Mevlana Holzkohlegrill car park. He shuffled the large backpack on a shoulder and headed to Bremen Hbf station. The 12:09 p.m. to Hanover waited for passengers. He entered a train carriage washroom. Removing the body padding took a while. Staring wide-eyed to a mirror, he removed blue contact lenses and spent some time rearranging his clothing. He stuffed the wadding, clothes along with his wig into a plastic bag.

A little over an hour later, clean shaved and thinner, Julius Sigerson emerged from the station. He took a taxi to the Mercure Hotel on Willy-Brandt-Allee.

"*Danke.*" He handed the driver a crisp twenty Euro note. "Keep the change."

The driver stared wide eyed at the tip for such a short ride. "*Danke.*"

Julius removed a small bag from the backpack and walked to a private parking area at the rear of the hotel. Looking left and right, he bent down, retying a shoelace. Holding a two inch square device and small camera under the chassis, they clicked firmly behind the left front wheel of a grey Mercedes. The job done, he stood and continued walking towards Rudolph von Bennigsen Ufer.

The long road was quiet, hardly any traffic or people rambling to take in the view of the adjacent one and half mile long manmade Maschsee Lake. Resting between leafy trees, a few benches welcomed lunchtime chats and others preferring the solitude of a book.

He crossed the thoroughfare to the pavement. Reaching a pedestrian crossing island, about two-thirds along the extended road, he took out two objects. He had time and privacy to switch on the flatter of the two one-inch devices. Taking out his phone, the screen showed the front view from under the Mercedes.

All good.

The inch oval magnetic pad clicked to the island's red and white traffic sign. He tapped an app on his phone and connected all devices. Pressing a button, a pale-blue light flashed; it would change to red when connected with its partner later that evening. Turning, his step quickened back towards the train station past the hotel. The information so far had been dependable. All was going to plan.

A night of football beckoned.

**

Julius made good time and checked in for a one-night stay in the Novotel Muenchen Airport. A taxi brought him to Bayern Munich's stadium an hour before kick-off. Connections had secured a seat mixed in with the German club's officials and Arsenal executives. Not wearing colours painted him a neutral football fan. The Olympic stadium full and loud as most German fans out chanted the English side's supporters.

His operative coldness had been temporarily dropped as he uttered encouragement to Arsenal. His shoulders and legs jerked with every ball at a Gunners' feet.

His head dropped.

Bayern took the lead in the third minute. Julius kept up his interest as Arsenal later scored and held onto their precarious one all draw until the fifty-eighth minute.

One would think he had planned the timing and scene. Beeps distracted him from the on-field action. *Balls.*

He pulled his phone out from an inside pocket and switched the screen on. A speedy road twisted and turned as the Mercedes bobbled towards its unplanned destination. His eyes fixed on the progress. He pressed a button. He jumped as Bayern's Pizarro's goal brought a rapturous roar around the stadium. It had drawn attention from his concentration while looking at concrete and tree branches twisting before the screen went blank.

He quietly left amongst cheering Bayern fans and headed unnoticed to the exit.

**

The following day, Julius boarded a 12:45 p.m. Lufthansa flight for Heathrow. He moved into a window seat, placed his small backpack underneath, and buckled up. He needed to relax after a couple of hectic days.

Twenty minutes later, the landing gear rose.

Two yellow-shirted stewards guided a serving trolley along the narrow aisle and stopped beside his row.

"Something to eat, drinks?" An effeminate blond male smiled.

"Hi, yes please. Gin and tonic with lemon and ice." Julius returned the smile. "Oh, could I have a newspaper as well?"

"Certainly, sir. English or German?"

"Both, *bitte*."

Within a minute Julius rested the transparent plastic cup of gin and small can of tonic on the drop-down table and received his change. He briefly read the front page of *Das Bild* and turned the pages until a large headline drew his attention; *Tragischer Unfall*. The photo directly underneath showed a crane lifting a car from Das Maschsee lake, Hanover. He read the report.

He poured tonic into the cup, took a sip of the diluted gin, followed by a satisfied deep breath.

Fuck him.

Opening a laptop, he began to type:

Subject dispensed with.

John Brownlow will remain a mystery.

**

Mr. Toplan reported his concern of Brownlow's delay returning from Germany. Head office contacted Thames Valley Police.

A week later detectives arrived at Ostrofman Pharmaceuticals' warehouse responding to a missing driver report.

"Mister Toplan, you can confirm that the transit abandoned in Bremen belongs to your company?" Trainee DC Robinson passed a photo of the chrome-blue Ford transit to him.

Toplan moved uneasy on his office chair. "Yes, it's the same reg. But what happened to John Brownlow? No phone call, so I went to his flat and no answer. His bicycle is still here." His teary eyes stared at the snap.

"We were there this morning and forced the door. It was clean as a whistle. Nothing disturbed. Fridge empty. A couple of brown government envelopes on a counter. Bed made up. Couple of shirts and a pair of jeans in a wardrobe." The detective took back the photo. "Are you sure he lived at that address? I mean, not even a cup in the sink or towel in the bathroom."

"Yes, yes. I pushed a note into the letter box."

"We got that. It was still on the floor."

"John had made the delivery. Mister Müster confirmed that when I called him last Friday."

"Okay, Mister Toplan. If you hear from him or if someone contacts you, let us know," Robinson said.

The DC's sergeant tipped his shoulder.

"Oh, yes. Sorry, Mister Toplan. Do you mind if we keep this picture of Brownlow?"

"No—I mean yes. Keep the copy." He remained in shock scratching his head.

The detectives headed to their car.

"He shouldn't be hard to spot," the DC said. "I mean, he is distinctive and large, Sarge."

"You have much to learn, young Pete." The sergeant open a door and climbed into the driver's seat.

The DC sat in the passenger seat and buckled up closing the door. "I know that, Sarge."

The sergeant nodded to the paper in the DC's hand. "Brownlow has chubby features, but that's probably the heavy red beard and mop of hair. Easily cut and shaved."

Pete stared at the image. "Yeah. I getcha. Best start on finding out about his relatives and friends. And that trip to India."

5 THE MYSTERIOUS MR. WRIGHT

With a backpack on his back, Mr. Ambrose Wright pulled his medium size suitcase as he walked from a hired Toyota RAV4. His stride slow, not just due to the sixteen-hour plus flight from London Gatwick. The consultant, in what remained a mystery, breathed in Lake Victoria's freshness before entering the four-storey Pinecone Hotel, close to Dunga Bay, Kenya.

The air appeared scrubbed clean after rain, perhaps like a mixture of flowers and woodsmoke from evening campfires. It was pleasant compared to the smell of burnt garbage and taste of overpowering gas fumes when he had stepped off the plane at Kisumu airport.

The lobby sparkled bright and cheery with a long grey marble reception desk. Though not small, Ambrose struggled to distinguish a dark head that appeared to float along the counter. When nearing, a petite dark-skinned women, bearing a wide smile and a smart cream blouse with a green trim, rose from a swivel chair.

"Welcome to Pinecone, sir."

"Thank you." He leaned right. The backpack slid off his shoulder. "I am Ambrose Wright. I believe you have a suite for me."

The receptionist tapped keys on a laptop. "Ah, yes. Mister Wright. You requested a low floor with a lake view. Yes, room one twenty-two. Oh, one moment." She searched under the desk and produced a large brown envelope. "This was delivered this morning for you. Here is your card key. Will you sign the registration form, and may I have your passport, please?"

"Certainly."

Ambrose removed the passport from an unzipped pocket on his pack. He looked at it as if making sure it was his. He passed it to her and took off his sunglasses. Taking the package, he shoved it into the bag, and filled in the form.

The receptionist confirmed the image likeness: dark short wavy hair, tight beard, and glasses over hazel eyes. "Thank you, Mister Wright. I will make a copy of your passport and you can collect it when you wish. Here is a key to the room safe and on this is the Wi-Fi password." The smiling receptionist moved a card to him. "You can take the elevator on the right or the stairs on the left. Enjoy your stay."

"Thank you. Eh, which is the closest to my room?"

"The stairs."

**

Ambrose closed his hotel suite door. A living area extended through open double doors to a bedroom and a king-size bed. A chunky dark grey three-seater leather sofa faced its matching twin armchairs. A knee-level teak veneered coffee table sat in between, and a flat screen TV centred on a cream wall facing the bed.

A home from home.

He was there for two reasons; one insignificant, the other concerned an act of justice.

He placed the suitcase on the bed and backpack on the sofa. Taking out a litre bottle of water from the backpack, he poured some into the supplied kettle and switched it on.

With his clothes and toiletries neatly put away, he opened the balcony door. A cool breeze ruffled curtains against a desk. Once again, Ambrose breathed in Lake Victoria's freshness. Its waters waited for both business and pleasure.

Picking up the backpack, he sat at the desk and took out the envelope and a laptop. Plugging its charger into the mains with an adaptor, he switched it on. As it connected to the given Wi-Fi code, he made a cup of black coffee.

"*Mmmm*, not bad."

He tapped in his password. The screen flicked to a page and his fingers worked the keys. While reading the information contained in the envelope, he spotted what was required for five days on the water. Under advisement, a fast three-seater Sea-Doo Jet boat ideal for solo fishing on the lake.

Another sip of coffee passed his lips. He angled his watch arm.

Almost six o'clock. Couple of hours sleep, shower then have a ramble, old chap.

He set a time on his mobile and lay on the comfortable bed.

**

Ambrose never looked like the typical well-to-do tourist in their knee-high socks and sandals. He preferred walking in flip-flops, cotton trousers or shorts and short-sleeve top. That night called for pale blue trousers with deep pockets and a white shirt. Though carrying the brown envelope, he ignored warnings of 'watch your wallet and pockets' when visiting unfamiliar places. He remained aware of anything to be caught off guard, a trait that had served him well so far.

The area no different from other so-called deprived tourist habitats. Three to five-storey apartment buildings attempted to hide small, rusted tin huts.

He enjoyed a fish dinner in a local lakeside diner, one a common tourist would miss out on. He rambled in his usual casual fashion from the Ui café.

Passing locals smiled courteously as if thanking him for discovering local cuisine.

On a sturdy jetty, he observed the lake beyond a small marina left of a Kisumu pier. Nearby, rubbish smouldered in a rusted oil drum.

He removed contents of the envelope and took a mental note of the photo of a Sea-Doo jet boat alongside a larger Jeanneau – Merry Fisher 585 Legende. Taking out a lighter, he set the papers alight, dropping them into glowing embers in the drum.

He stretched his tall build and breathed the air. His eyes concentrated on the emptiness around as darkness provided cover. From a pocket, he took a small device and boarded the Legende. Below deck, he opened a hatch. His hand stretched to fix the device securely to the steering mechanism.

Moments later he walked back to the small-town centre arriving at the exclusive Gecko Club bar. Sitting outside, he ordered a bottle of his favourite tipple, *Luis Montfort* red wine, and relaxed until the early hours enjoying local chat.

Tomorrow fishing.

**

Ambrose waited at the yellow and white Sea-Doo. Its matching windshade, pulled half down, fluttered on angled chrome steel bars. Jerome, a middle-aged marina attendant, fixed two fishing rods to their holders. He moved necessary tackle, a basket of food and refreshments to the back seat.

"Thank you, Jerome. As this is my first day, I doubt if I will stay out too long." Ambrose boarded. "Just to get the feel of the waters, old chap. I may go for a drive later."

"Yes, Mistah Wright. Good idea. Anyway, the Sea-Doo is yours for five deys so hold on to the keys." The chubby local eyed a group of men approaching. "Eh, you can leave the rods but take the baskets to the centah when finished for the dey. I will refill them daily for you."

Ambrose palmed a large note to the man's free hand.

"Mistah Wright, there is no need to —"

"I insist. Any tips for me?"

"Thank you, sah. It is fairly calm todey but tomorrow the lake maybe a bit choppy. It is wise to hitch to one of the buoys." He smiled broadly while untying the mooring then pushed the small craft away from the jetty.

Ambrose pressed the starter and turned it left along the waters. He looked back. The attendant acted subserviently to the group as they boarded the Legende.

**

The Sea-Doo rested a discrete distance from other fishing boats. Ambrose removed surveillance items from his backpack. He had leisurely cast the rods when a cackle of laughter came from a small receiver beside the food basket. He switched on his earphones then looked through a scope.

"Oscah, you must be careful sitting at da back," a voice said.

"What do you mean, man?" A high local tone replied.

"It is okay when not moving but sit at da side or beside da wheel when da boat is moving," the voice advised.

"Okay, man, tuh. Why you worry, man. Just fish, da watah is calm." Oscar leaned back. "Give me anudder beer, man."

Hum, the information is spot on so far. Demands attention.

As he slipped onto the back seat, Oscar's rotund body appeared to ease the boat lower into the water.

He likes to relax at the back and drink. Not much into fishing.

"Juli, what time are we meeting da Arabs tonight?" Oscar sipped from the bottle.

"At eight, Oscah. I had wondahed why you chose da Pinecone." Juli cast a rod. "Now I know. It is nice and discrete."

Oscar's two companions were of similar build; thick set, broad shouldered and shaved headed. Hard to tell them apart if they were wearing similar clothes. But their blue and orange shirts separated them at least in appearance. Juli wore the blue.

"Yes, man. Maybe we should have brought them fishing." Oscar cackled again. "If we did not like da deal, dey could practice der swimming techniques."

Jesus. He's a nasty piece of work.

Ambrose put the scope on the seat and poured a Luis Montfort into a glass. His toes tapped the wheel while pulling off his yellow vest to collect some rays on already tanned hairy legs and torso. He removed the earphones and turned off the devise.

Fuck them. Rough waters tomorrow, according to Jerome.

**

Ambrose remained a master of surveillance. His late-night walks proved to be the best times for his actions and bugging an outside hotel bar was easy.

The air remained fresh around the exterior hotel bar. Crickets clicked their attractions as he played with his laptop alone at the last table. He pulled out one earphone and signalled to a barman.

The tall local man's teeth shone bright matching his white shirt and shorts as he approached. "Good evening, Mistah Wright. How are you this evening?" It was the young man's usual greeting.

"I am good, Maurice. May I have a large cold beer for a change. Too much wine already." Ambrose held up a hand. "Oh, who are those interesting but noisy people near the pool?"

"Well, it is not really my —" A crisp note passed to his right hand. "Tha – thank you, sah. The noisy tall fat man is Chief of police." He leaned to the table. "The other two at his side are *Wafanyabiashara*, henchmen. The two facing them are not staying here." He looked left and right. "I believe they are Arab businessmen."

"Chief of police staying here? Must be an important meeting. You are very observant."

The young man displayed a nervous smile and went to the bar.

Ambrose adjusted his earphones and played with the keys observing the meeting.

"We must finish this tonight. We have to leave first thing in the morning, Mister Kihika," the younger of the two Arabs said.

"I must be guaranteed full payment before da children are moved to da cargo boat. When I have received da money, da okay will be given." Oscar's arrogance visible.

Ambrose saw the young Arab move to Oscar. His older companion's hand rested on his shoulder.

"When our partners forward their share tomorrow, we will send the full amount as agreed. We will probably be in flight." The elder's left hand combed his greying goatee.

"Yes, I can wave to you from my boat." Oscar's cackle annoying.

A shadow distracted Ambrose. "Ah, thank you, Maurice."

"Did you catch many fish, Mistah Wright?"

"Three small Nile perch. Are there really some that are six feet?"

"Yes, sah. An American boasted last year of nearly catching one."

"Well, he would, wouldn't he."

They laughed.

Maurice was called to another table leaving Ambrose to enjoy the cold beer and conversation.

**

Next morning, Jerome had left another full basket in the Sea-Doo.

Ambrose, in shorts and an unbuttoned Hawaiian-style short-sleeve shirt, started the motor and eased further into the lake. The Legende was already hundreds of yards from shore when hungover laughter pierced his ears.

Jerome was correct. The waters are a tad rougher today.

Brisk winds and heavy 'traffic' on the lake buffeted the waves. He stopped the engine and the Sea-Doo bobbled making it harder to loop a mooring rope around a buoy. After two attempts to settle the craft by holding the weighted object, he succeeded securing the rope. He readied the two rods. When cast, he continued to listen and viewed the antics through the scope. Oscar was doing some sort of silly tribal dance on the equally unsteady craft.

Ambrose raised his eyebrows and shook his head. *Do not rock the boat. And don't forget you are not wearing lifejackets.*

An hour passed. After some unsteady foot moves and carefully placed empty bottles, Oscar finally sat at the back.

"Man, dis is boring. Has da money arrived yet, Juli?"

Ambrose saw Juli, Oscar's head henchman, look at a phone. "No, sah."

"Tuh. Move this boat from here now. Quick now, man. Give me a beer."

"But sah, it is getting very choppy," the pilot said.

"Just do it man."

The engine spurted into motion. Oscar adjusted on the cream padded back seat.

The Jeanneau picked up speed. Oscar tottered as it lightly bounced on the swollen waves.

Ambrose eased a hand to the seat beside him fingering a gadget. His right index rested on a red button.

Now.

The Legende suddenly veered right. Juli fell to the deck.

The other henchman grasped a rail.

The pilot's hands yanked the locked wheel hard but the engine roared.

Oscar's legs shot up high. The beer bottle flew from his hand. Yells on the deck attracted other boat crew to watch helplessly.

The boat continuously circled. Oscar's head jerked violently backwards. He plunged towards the blades.

The pilot tumbled to the deck.

Consideration of Tragedies

In Ambrose's ear phones, Juli's scream echoed when seeing Oscar's right hand, minus an arm, fly upwards and landed beside him. The chief's head bobbled on reddened waves; mouth wide open; free from his shoulders.

Seconds later, Ambrose pressed the button again and another. He put down the scope, lifted the mooring from the buoy and observed smoke rising from the Legende's bow area.

**

At his table, Ambrose waved Maurice over.

"Good evening, Mistah Wright. How are you this evening?" Maurice retained his greeting.

"I am good, despite what happened. I couldn't continue fishing when I saw the commotion."

"Yes, it is sad." Maurice placed a bottle of Luis Montfort and a clean glass on the table. "I know the pilot. Luckily, he only has a broken an arm."

The chief deserved it. Pity about the pilot's injury.

"Ah, I know what you are thinking, sah." Maurice uncorked the bottle. "The death of the chief may be even celebrated."

Ambrose's eyes widened. "Oh." He leaned closer. "I understand he was not liked."

"I cannot say much, Mistah Wright." The young man poured into the glass.

"Thank you, Maurice."

On his laptop, he finished his personal report.

**

Days later, Mr. Ambrose Wright eased into a first-class window seat of Qatar Airways flight 1335 and fastened a seatbelt. Within twenty minutes, the return flight to London Gatwick had retracted its landing gear.

He accepted a glass of Luis Montfort from a flight attendant.

A blonde stewardess leaned to him. "Would you like a paper before falling asleep, Mister Wright?" Her perfume and sultry voice lingered.

"Thank you, eh—" He eyed the tag on her burgundy jacket. "Janina. What a lovely name."

"Here you are, Mister Wright and thank you." She eased back. "Anything else?"

"Just ensure I do not miss my top ups before dinner."

He had the row to himself and eased back to open *The Standard*, a weekly Kenyan national newspaper.

He took a sip of wine and read:

The Standard
8th May 2010
Oscar Kihika, Chief of police in Nyamira County, Kenya, died tragically in a fishing accident last weekend in Lake Victoria. 54-year-old Mr Kihika was fishing with two friends when the boat's steering mechanism suddenly spun out of control of the pilot. One friend said Mr Kihika was sitting on his usual seat at the back of the Jeanneau – Merry Fisher 585 Legende and fell backwards holding a fishing rod.

Mr. Kihika's injuries were so severe that he wouldn't have survived long in the water. The survivors claimed the steering mechanism remained stuck for almost thirty-seconds until the pilot gained control. Investigators reported that, although not a common occurrence, the operator and passengers could be ejected overboard resulting in the boat continuing to spin until the fuel ran out.

The Chief of police was accused of corruption in 2008 by journalist Michael Nyauri. On 29th January 2009, Mr. Nyauri's decapitated body was found near his home. Although not accused directly, relations of the journalist had blamed Mr. Kihika of being involved. Funds destined for refugee families and children in need of medical treatment had been filtered by unknown sources. He was suspected of having links with European criminal underworld.

Mr. Kihika has no surviving family but retained land and large mansion near the Bomet county border.

Known as the circle of death which involves the propeller still turning as the motor stays on and steering wheel locked. Experts in such accidents have revealed that injuries by propellers, including amputation and bleeding are rare in forensic information. The most frequent situations surrounding boat-propeller-related injuries are concerned with water skiing, falling, or being thrown from the boat.

An investigation was performed immediately by an engineering team. They studied the mouth of the pump and the dynamic characteristic of rotating propeller blades. They could not determine if the burnt mechanism was radio-controlled.

A spokesperson for the police commissioner confirmed that no further investigation will be taken and Mr. Kihika's death was officially ruled as an unfortunate accident.

Ambrose took another sip. *It was well that my gadgets melted.*

He turned the page. *Interesting. Children rescued from a container before loading onto a cargo boat.*

He raised his glass. *Well done someone.*

6 THE MOTHER'S PASSING

Cambridge Addenbrooke's Hospital, 1:30 p.m. August 10, 2011

Ben held Margaret's hand. His watery eyes gazing at her angelic face hidden by an oxygen mask. Her breathing soft as annoying beeping continued from monitors.

"What will I do if you go, love? What is the point of all our work if it can't save you?"

There was no reaction from her. Eyes still shut. Fingers soft but rigid.

They were strong together. Now Ben Freeman was a lost soul. The man that loved life, humanity and people was now drained, alone. It wouldn't be long the doctors had told him.

A knock on the private ward door disturbed him.

Gloria Kelly, a close friend to both since the accident, entered. "He's not answering."

Ben looked away from his dying wife. "Chris hates hospitals. He won't come."

"God, this will haunt him, not being here."

"His head isn't right again. He blames all at the company for this. In a way I suppose he's right."

She closed the door and went to the other side of the bed. "I'm going to miss her too. She really helped me." She looked across to Ben. "The two of you did. Thank you." Gloria unashamedly cried.

Margaret didn't shake. Her fingers slowly moved in Ben's hand. He smiled to her.

The beeping stopped as a long green line displayed on a monitor.

Margaret Freeman had passed.

**

Royston, 2 p.m.

Chris paced his large garden like a caged tiger. "Bastards, bastards." He had no thought of anyone hearing him.

His arms flayed around at invisible foes; kicks aimed high at their heads. Then he slumped to the pristine lawn, his fists pounding the hard ground. "Bastards."

George Inglis, his best friend, and ex-brother-in-law, walked towards him from the kitchen door. He knelt beside him. "Chris, please come back in." He eased him up. "Come on, old mate."

George kept an arm around his taller pal's shoulder as they walked back to the kitchen.

Consideration of Tragedies

"She had improved. Why did she start taking them fucking tablets?" Chris bawled.

"I don't know, mate. It was your mum's choice."

Chris sat at the oblong kitchen table. "I can't do that fucking job anymore. I mean, recruiting, getting the best chemists." He stared at George. "You know the auld fella got rid of the second fucker. He had signed off on another dodgy consignment — That's his second time. Luckily we got them back."

He picked up his bottle of Pils and finished it off.

"I remember you telling me about him and those poor kids in Africa dying." George went to the fridge and took out two more bottles. "Here."

Chris took one and twisted the cap off. "Bastard chemist."

George sat. "And the other guy simply packed up and joined another company?"

"Yeah. Mum believed in his new fucking remedy." Chris' fist smashed onto the table. "He treated her like a lab rat. Now she's gone. Man, she was so stubborn."

"Well, he wasn't to really blame then. Don't forget, your mum was a chemist too." George sipped.

Chris' shoulders shook as tears flowed. "I should've been there."

**

Margaret Freeman had been laid to rest in Almond Lane Cemetery, Stevenage. Tearful floodgates remained as colleagues, relations and friends walked away from the graveside. Family friend Gloria linked Ben and Chris as they stayed.

Ben broke from her arm and knelt. "Why did you do it?" He thumped the wet earth. "Why?"

Gloria turned to Chris. "What is he talking about?"

She had become close to the family since being one of the injured during the hit and run.

"Mum tried more unapproved meds for her condition. Then she worsened. It shouldn't have happened. She had improved without the extra meds."

They bent and stood Ben up.

"Something must be done. This sort of negligence can't be tolerated. The courts are useless. The victims of crime should be compensated in kind—and more."

Their heads hung low over the grave once more.

**

Chris had approached Seth Greene about hiring his large lounge for the afterwards. He was happy to do so.

The Freeman's were a small family. Ben was an only child and Margaret had an estranged brother. Something Chris had always wanted to improve on.

Though family members were rare, they had a vast range of friends and colleagues. Seth had to hire extra staff to cater for the large turnout. Foreign dignitaries and their partners conversed with local friends of the Freemans.

Chris had enough of the shaking of hands and pats on his back. He went to the bar and sat at the counter. "Seth, give us a Southie, please—two cubes."

Seth handed the tall glass to him seconds later. "You don't look well."

Chris' eyes widened. "He says at a funeral reception."

"Oh, you know what I mean. At least it made you smile."

It did. Chris sipped his favourite tipple.

Seth nodded towards the back of Chris. "Here's your dad."

"Get him a Guinness."

"Son, I don't blame you coming out here." Ben sat on a barstool.

"Well, you know me. Prefer real people, not hangers on. Don't know where I got that from."

Ben grinned. "Both of us."

They were father and son, but different. Both detested boredom, even when relaxing. Chris the sporty type; Ben playing and singing at a piano. Workwise, they got stuck into whatever projects demanded to completion.

Seth placed two Guinness in front of them. "I knew you'd be wanting one, Chris. On the bill?"

Chris thumbed-up.

Father and son raised their glasses.

"To the best mother and wife," Ben said.

They slugged a quarter of their pints.

"I've had time to think since your mum died. How about we sell the companies?"

Chris sat straight. "Really? When and to who?"

"Ah, I see you have no objection."

"Well, I—"

"Think of getting out?"

"Yes, Dad. Those other deaths and near misses, too much hassle for me and the company."

Ben breathed deep. "We'll share your mum's stakes."
"She's probably clapping up there now. So, together we have eighty-two percent—you sixty of that."

"That's about right. Always good at the maths, eh."

"What are we worth?"

"Frightening to think about it. Never thought of selling before." Ben took another long mouthful. "Billions."

Chris almost choked on his pint. "Fuck me pink."

"Exactly."

They swallowed more Guinness.

"Two more, Seth please," they both said.

7 THE SELL UP AND MOVING ON

Within six months one of the largest pharmaceutical companies was sold to German and Swedish interests for an undisclosed sum. The Ostrofman name still flew, and the Freemans retained small percentage of shares. Their comfort ensured for their remaining years. But what to do with them.

Chris had stayed in the background as his father took care of the final selling. He had more pressing things to do health wise. His head had been all over the place. He had visited Dublin more often and met with Luis a few times. At some of those drinking lunches, Cata and Fernando Lando, Luis' aunt, and uncle, turned up.

Chris became interested in their selective P.I business. In other words, they were a word of mouth agency, no cards pinned to police station notice boards. He did some minor work for them, mostly research due to his vast knowledge in the tech world. They were European based with links to Euro and Interpol. This suited Chris. A different world away from touring companies and lecture halls.

His new multi-millionaire status hadn't changed his normal welcoming standing. Though bouts of aggression had been shown through frustration with his headaches. He had become somewhat withdrawn since his mother's death, but this new outlet had him back to drawing boards. The items developed were not for the general market, but for him and the Landos.

He and Ben had met in Dublin more than in the UK. His father had become semi-reclusive and rarely talked Ostrofman. As years stretched, Ben had become more reliant on Gloria. She had grown to be a family member more than a friend. An observant Chris had a feeling that friendship may develop into something else.

It did.

**

Ben didn't first ask Gloria to marry him in the summer of 2015. He had asked for Chris' permission to do so. She was only four years older than Chris.

Like father, like son they had moved on. They sold their UK homes. Ben and Gloria settled in Florida while Chris bought a pub in Clapton and small properties in Lanzarote. It had choked him returning to the island, but Gloria urged him to believe in his own abilities to carry on living.

Chris opened a P.I side-line employing the semi-retired Landos. Nothing too heavy, finding people that deserved to be found. Some divorce work. His reputation grew within the community of Clapton. He brought the pub back as a local favourite in 2013. Ordinary, hardworking people steered clear of once infamous haunt of dealers. The Clapton Bar had been known locally as the Junkyard for obvious reasons.

Gone were the doormen. He believed they not only deterred unwanted custom, but also passers-by who might have entered.

"Must be a rough place now. I mean why are they there for," Ben had said before Chris bought it.

It was August 2013. They sat at the front oval window. An area Ben once enjoyed Sunday afternoon dominos.

"Look at this place, Chris. Even Jack won't come in here anymore."

Chris rubbed his smooth chin. "Granted it needs work. I'll get George to do a rocky and give the job to Steve Urban."

Ben shook his head. "I don't know. You shouldn't have bought it. Look at those idiots at the bar. What – It's ten past three and their pissed."

Two large buffoons almost slipped off their barstools while arguing.

"Lads, please. No more. I want you both to —"

Buffoon one threw a punch connecting with the elderly barman's forehead.

Chris stood.

Ben held his arm. "Chris don't get involved."

He shrugged his dad's weak grip off and walked to the bar. "Same again, please."

"Oi, fuck off, mush," buffoon two said.

"I wasn't speaking to you. Of course, if you work here, that's different." Chris planted his left foot to worn alcohol stained carpet.

"Sir, please. I don't want trouble," the barman said.

"I just want the same again—"

Buffoon two swung a punch at Chris.

He twisted his shoulder avoiding the fist and simultaneously kicked the wobbling stool away.

Buffoon two's head cracked onto the counter. His pal was sharper and leapt at Chris.

Again, moving swiftly back, Chris slammed a fist into the back of his assailant as he passed by.

"I believe there's a side door, barman."

"Ya-yes. But—"

"Just open the fucking thing." Chris gripped the stunned idiots' shirt collars.

"You can't do—"

"I can. I own this shop. Now, open the fucking door."

"Oh—new owner, yes, yes." The barman went through the opened counter to a small back hall.

Chris dragged the idiots up and pulled them towards the opened door. He threw them into an arched alleyway.

"Don't come back." He punched them out and turned to the barman. "I hope they remember what I said."

He walked back into the bar, picked up the two stools and smiled. "Nice one. Oi, where's my drinks. Send them over."

The barman rushed back to pull the order without a word.

The only two other punters sat open mouth opposite the counter.

"Barman," Chris shouted when seated beside Ben. "Give them two the same again."

"Yes, sir."

"Cheers, mate. Well done," one of them said.

Ben tapped Chris' shoulder. "They'll be back."

"Couldn't give a fuck. Closing this when we leave. Won't open until it's refitted."

The barman came to the table with their drinks. "You must be Mister Freeman."

"No—he's Mister Freeman, I'm Chris Freeman."

The barman's brow raised.

"Serve them two, get yourself one then sit here."

"Sure."

The Freemans didn't speak as the barman worked. Soon he sat opposite them.

"Right, Stan isn't it?" Chris asked.

Stan nodded.

"Okay. I believe you've been here about a year. Now, I'm closing the pub for renovations." Chris read Stan's sadden face. "You'll be paid. And I believe the other two barman left yesterday with till money."

Stan gulped. "Yes, how did you know that?"

"When I came here two days ago for a final look. I planted a cam just beside the TV when going to the gents—fucking mess out there too." Chris took a mouthful. "Now, they're due on at five, right."

"Yes."

"They've had their pay, so they're fucked. I'll make sure they won't get a legit job behind any bar again. I didn't just buy the lease, I bought the lot—site, rights to the alley way and courtyard."

"Wow. Really? Well when do you think it will open again?"

"Well before Christmas for sure. I can get you part-time in the

Pembroke, I know Bill well."

"And you're offering to pay me as well." Stan drank.

"Ah, that's on condition that you take up the soon to be offered job. I don't want lazy barmen working here." Chris grinned.

"Thank you, I will."

The pub reopened at the end of November without Stan. The poor man was found two days later badly beaten not far from his home opposite Hackney Downs park. He later passed away.

8 THE BAKER

Near Chelmsford, March 2012.

Noel Peters wore his customary grin as he cracked open another two eggs onto a hot flat-plate cooker to join sizzling sausages and thick cut slices of bacon. His last day as a breakfast chef in The Rose Café.

"Hey, Noel, you'll be wasted in Paris. Those Frogs don't appreciate good English breakfasts," a burley truck driver said.

"No way. No more greasy roadside cafés for me." Noel brushed his dark two-week-old stubble and winked to Rose. "Big Dave, yours's up. —Rose, what's Rodney's?" He shouted towards the counter.

"He wants his usual. Scrambled and two bacon, Noel," bespectacled Rose hollered above the din.

"Hey, Joe. You want extra for that long-haul?" she asked.

Joe patted his oversized belly. "Yeah, go on. Noel, another egg, mate."

"Will you get past the weight allowance over there?" Noel bellowed over the crackling.

His attention was drawn through a steamed-up window. A large grey van pulled left off the London Road into the café's uneven car park and stopped near waste bins.

"John's pulling up," he said. "We need more sausages and bacon. Scramble's up, Rose."

She took two heated white plates filled with hot breakfasts and brought them to Joe and Rodney. "Plate's hot." She turned. "I'll bring yours now, Big Dave." She looked to a disgruntled customer. "They were here first, Father."

The elderly priest threw his arms up in submission.

Rose arrived back with his and Big Dave's plates. All threw various welcomes to John Carr as he entered the roadside café.

"Usual, Rose please." John sat opposite Big Dave.

"So, John, what's the load?" Dave cut into his bacon.

"Furniture," John said. "You foreign this week?"

"Yeah, mate. Back to Hanover. Business picking up again. Ostrofman is hiring." He chewed. "You interested?"

"Not really. I'm staying a home bird now."

Noel's ears twitched toward the conversation. "Alright, John." He waved from the blistering cooking area.

"Yeah, Noel. When are you off to Paris?"

"In three days. Tuesday. Last day here today." He raised both hands. "All teas are on me."

Muffled and egg-filled cheers brought a smile to Rose's wrinkled face. "You're not getting a bonus."

All laughed as she placed steamy white mugs of tea in front of the customers.

Noel placed a red mug on the counter. "Here ya are Rose, John's tea." He looked up at a clock on a wall behind the counter. 7:30 a.m. "Due for collection later so I'm emptying the waste, Rose."

"Okay, luv."

Noel walked out of the side door of the bungalow café carrying a blue bin to a waste container. Looking around, he took from a pocket a small white tub labelled *Zolpidem*. It dropped from his hand into the larger bin with the café waste. On the way back, he tapped John Carr's van and returned to the kitchen.

**

The café thinned out leaving the regular priest. This allowed Noel and Rose to sit and enjoy a well-deserved break.

"You'll be missed, you know." Rose sniffed.

"Here." Noel handed her a serviette.

"Thank you." She patted the tears. "I suppose you won't stay long in France either."

"Well, cooking is not really my thing, though I love this place. Your customers were here before me and will continue to turn up."

"Too true, Noel," the priest shouted over. "But feck ya anyway."

"You're always on the move, Father." She shoved the serviette into her pinny.

"I go where I am needed most. It's God's will." He sipped his tea.

"More likely the Bishop's," Noel said.

"Yes, Father. How many times have you returned to Holy Name parish?" She collected the mugs and plates from the table.

"Ah, I love Chelmsford." He chewed a biscuit. "Seven."

"Seven?" Noel stood to assist Rose.

"Yes. The countryside reminds me of good old Tipperary." The priest looked through the wide window reminiscing. "Did you know that I was in the Vatican twa—" He jerked back from the window.

Blue flashes zipped past as sirens screamed along the road out of Chelmsford south-west towards Margaretting, the nearest village.

The priest's right hand made a quick sign of the cross. "That's not a sight seen every day."

Rose placed the dishes on the counter and headed to the entrance. Noel and the priest followed.

She opened the front door. "Wow." Two more squad cars and a fire engine flew by.

Noel and the priest joined her in the empty carpark catching sight of emergency vehicles speeding to Three Mile Hill.

"What the fuck."

Rose and Noel raised eyebrows to the priest.

"Really—Father O'Brien." She scurried back to the café.

"Well, sorry. But it's quite unusual." He turned to Noel. "It's my birthday today. Imagine that, Noel. Pensionable." He adjusted his white collar and sighed.

They walked to the priest's bicycle.

"Fucking Irish. First born gets the farm, the next becomes a priest and the next can do what they like," O'Brien said.

"Father, you need to get out of the priesthood." They hugged and laughed.

"All the best over there in French land." O'Brien shook the taller man's hand and straddled the bike. "I may be needed at whatever has happened. Good luck, Noel."

**

Days later, Noel briefly chatted with a porter at Chelmsford station about an accident that held up trains on Saturday morning. When his train arrived, he sat at the window seat on the London express and opened a local newspaper.

12th March 2012
Doctor Giles Brotherton, 72, retired London Bridge hospital consultant, has been tragically killed near his home in Margaretting, East Anglia. Dr. Brotherton had been on his regular morning stroll along Parsonage Lane, a small one lane right of way, when a van hit him near the level-crossing just after 8 a.m. The 07.59 train from Chelmsford was delayed for two hours as the scene was investigated. The van driver was taken to Broomfield hospital, Chelmsford and is suffering from head and leg injuries.

There were no witnesses to the accident; however, Mr. Albert Jones reported the accident when he approached the crossing on the other side. Police are waiting to interview the driver to determine what had happened. There were no other vehicles involved.

The train slowly moved off. His blue eyes watched trees gain speed past his reflection.

Consideration of Tragedies

Hope John was alright.

**

Sitting at a table outside the Cafe Lamartine on the corner of Avenue Victor Hugo, Noel cringed at unwanted news in an English paper.

14th March 2012
John Carr, the van driver involved in tragic accident near Margaretting, East Anglia, was interviewed yesterday in Broomfield hospital, Chelmsford. Mr. Carr, 42 from Chelmsford, told investigators he had become weak and blurry-eyed as he neared the Parsonage Lane level-crossing then lost control of the van. He was unaware that the van had hit retired London Bridge hospital consultant, Giles Brotherton. The driver has an impeccable driving record and has never been involved in an accident of any kind.

"I deeply regret what has happened and my thoughts are with Dr. Brotherton's family," he said from his bed.

Mr. Carr is due to be released from hospital tomorrow.

The front of the delivery van was completely crushed along with extensive damage to the steering, brakes, and dashboard. Investigators are keeping an open mind as to how the crash occurred. Mr. Carr's medical tests have shed no light on as to why he had become suddenly weak.

**

Rome, June 2013.
Noel had been well-travelled since the Rose Café. A year later, he was far from the sweet-smelling countryside of Essex. Another gorgeous June afternoon and he walked along Rome's Via Vittorio Emanuele Orlando. He strolled into the cool air of a shopping mall to Dagnino's, a busy eatery.

A man called out from his shop door. "Ciao, Noel. See you later for my favourite cannoli."

"Ciao, Giorgio. I will save your favourite table." Noel waved.

He moved between round tables and black chairs that appeared to take over the mall.

Dagnino's was the mall. The top-class eatery drew people, young and old, to the interior shopping area. The famous aromas wafted outside testing the resilience of passers-by; few resisted.

Noel fitted in well, even in shorts and multi-coloured t-shirt. The

Rasputin look-a-like's talents with flour and a variety of ingredients welcomed by all. Even Italian ministers and papal dignitaries were drawn to the take-away or stop and eat premises.

The gruff speaking Englishman had a working knowledge of Italian to instruct his subordinates in the kitchen. All produce freshly made on site. Take-away orders catered for. His specialities cannolis and his greatly sought after rum cake.

The cake consisted of three layers of sponge soaked with his unique rum-flavoured syrup, filled with layers of vanilla and chocolate pastry cream. It's mouth-wateringly decorated with frosting and adorned with crushed peanuts or sliced almonds around the outside.

Regular customers and staff waved or called out his name as he made his way to the double doors of the kitchen-cum-bakery. His working hours varied. That day was spare, but a special order needed his expert attention.

"Ciao, Noel," echoed throughout from most. All dressed in their netted hats, white coveralls, and latex gloves.

Noel merely waved as he walked to the staff area and changed into his working clothes from a designated locker.

In the kitchen, his dark beard and wrinkled eyes set him aside from the staff.

"All, listen up." Though many didn't speak English, they recognised his first instruction.

Those that didn't understand the language, or his Yorkshire version of it, were told later by the few that did.

"Your favourite minister, Giuseppe Galiano—" He paused to let the grunts and moans settle.

"He has asked for a couple of his favourite rum cakes. Tadeo told me the minister is flying to Munich tomorrow for a conference and wants to show off our cakes."

He waited again for the air to clear of dislikes and bad wishes.

"Non credo che l'arsenico sia consentito nelle ricette di torte." A cake decorator, Gianni's comment about being sorry arsenic was not permitted in cakes, brought riotous laughter.

"Okay, okay." Noel swayed his hands for calm. "We will make three." More laughter erupted. "I do not think so, Gianni, *due.*" He showed two fingers. "Now, back to work— *Pronto.*"

Noel arrived in Rome three months previously with outstanding credentials from Paris, Madrid and of course London. Manager Tadeo knew it would be hard to hold on to the marvel. Noel preferred to travel and gain more knowledge of the baking world.

Tadeo had often queried the Yorkshire man's ability for keeping the family business alive in England.

"I have a staff and cousins that own small bakeries in Yorkshire and London. Alas, I'm separated now, so more free time. They look forward to my new recipes." Noel had told him.

A couple of hours later, two rum cakes were ready. Noel alone checked the crushed almond adorned finish on them. Health minister Giuseppe Galiano was highly peanut intolerant; therefore, the second choice of decoration had to be used.

"Right, I'm off to the Druid's Den if anyone wants to try the Guinness," Noel announced before leaving. "See you tomorrow and Gianni, make sure the cakes are packed for your favourite minster's flight."

Shouts of Italian expletives rang in his ears for the last time.

Noel Peters didn't turn up at the Druid's Den. The baker never showed up anywhere since he walked down Via Vittorio Emanuele Orlando.

After Gianni boxed the cakes, he brought a waste barrel to a back alley and tipped it into a waiting garbage container. Empty packets of raw shell peanuts dropped to join the rubbish for collection the next day.

**

Julius Sigerson's eyes widened when reading an article at a Benidorm bar.

June 2013,
Giuseppe Galiano, 52, Italian health minister, died suddenly on a flight from Rome to Munich yesterday afternoon. Controversial Galiano was to attend a WHO conference in Munich tomorrow. Initial reports state that the minister may have suffered a reaction to peanuts, which he is highly allergic to. He had recently attended a clinic in Milan when he accidently ate a favourite cake that had minute traces of peanut additives not shown on the ingredients label. It was proved that similar brands of cake do have a warning of containing peanuts.

Galiano had been under investigation two years ago due to alleged connections with uncertified and untested cancer treatment drugs that resulted in some research laboratories being closed in Germany, the UK and Africa. Reports of side effects and some deaths, mostly involving children, are reputedly connected to the untried drugs. Arrests occurred last year in Kenya and neighbouring Tanzania of medical staff at two centres where the children had died.

Nearby passengers told of Mr. Galiano coughing continuously then struggling to breath before flight crew members could render assistance.

On landing, it was discovered that the minister's epi-pens had been mistakenly packed in his suitcase. His secretary wasn't available for comment.

Galiano, recently divorced, leaves behind two children in Calabria. A post-mortem will be held next week.

Julius grinned and raised a hand to a barman. "*Por favor,* I see that you have *Luis Montfort,* may I have a glass of the fine red wine with my food order?" he asked in Spanish.

"Certainly, sir, but I am afraid that you must buy the bottle. We do not sell that wine by the glass," the tall barman said.

Julius nodded. "Very well. It's hot today, so, time in the shade would probably be best."

He opened his laptop and typed:
Subject dispensed with.
Noel Peters has disappeared.

9 THE EMERGENCEY CONFERENCE

Somewhere in Europe, February 2018.

Her Ladyship coughed lightly during a phone conference. "Apologies, I didn't take the flu jab before Christmas. As you are all aware, there is a leak in our ship. One operative has reported a journalist becoming *too nosey* and due to his speculative articles, suggests action taken soon."

"Agreed. I hope you keep warm and well," a marbled voice said. "Another has come to my attention. A rather intrusive solicitor has been gathering information from sources in the UK and Europe. There could be a possible link. Although he currently does not pose a threat to our operatives, the solicitor has a connection with previous *accidental departures*."

"I agree. Further research has come to light regarding trafficking," a distinct brogue uttered. "As you are also mindful of, anything to do with underage sex will not be tolerated. This solicitor is currently being watched. He may need to be *distracted* from further investigations that could interfere with our society."

A sea breeze echoed through the speaker as family man spoke. "I can *disrupt* the solicitor directly if an emergency occurs. I believe he has indulged in the sickening vice. I for one was appalled by the photos an operative recovered."

"No. His observance must be continued. I'm sure there are more links to his activities," a croaky voice said. "You have played your part. You have contributed much towards our cause for many years. Best that you remain as you are and act when required. Enjoy your family."

"Ah, you know me well." Family man's laugh echoed. "Okay, my resources are always available. So, perhaps we should start recruiting younger operatives. I have a few in mind."

"We know that." Ladyship coughed again. "Excuse me. Perhaps we should stick to not involving family members as littles as possible. I feel it is time to think about retiring operatives."

"Yes, Ladyship. They must *tidy up* their lists before so. We can ease operations from the end of the year. Unfortunately, justice would be suspended for a time," the marbled voice suggested.

The distinct brogue butted in. "Draw up the list of operatives currently under obligation to complete their tasks and send them letters ASAP with an explanation for their sudden *retirement*."

"Good idea," Family man said. "Also, get in touch with sleeping operatives declaring them null and void with full explanations as to why."

Her Ladyship almost had the last words. "Ensure that all current tasks be completed. I think that will be all for now. I hope we can all meet up soon under different circumstances."

"I reckon you have a place picked out already," Family man said.

The phones clicked off.

10 THE BARFLIES

Clapton, East London, June 2018.

Chris Freeman walked with an almost undetectable limp and stood aside on a pavement. He waved a delivery truck on its way from an arched alley towards Amhurst road. He turned, rubbed his clean shaved chin admiring new exterior paint job of his pub. Two central red pillars supported an overhanging front façade displaying *An Fáilte Tavern*. A half-oval glass front being the main attraction with 'Welcome' displaced on doors left and right.

A wide smile appeared on his face. *Nice one.*

Down the alley, he walked through the pub's side door then to the cellar to sort the newly delivered supplies.

Thursday afternoons in the Tavern remained slow. The early-June sun mirrored gold leaf outer lettering from the glass at an angle across polished wooden floor. The light rested on tables and firm upholstered tanned seating opposite the bar. It reflected off Arsenal FC memorabilia behind the bar and a few hanging on the walls in between original artwork.

Two barflies chatted on barstools at the far end of a long counter. An ideal area to spot the next arrival through one of the two squeaking entrance doors. A TV broke the relative quietness along with muted clattering of empty beer barrels below.

The right door opened with its recognisable creak. A tall prospective customer entered. The regulars' heads automatically turned from their quiet discussion over newspapers then returned to their conversation.

Chris appeared like a jack-in-the-box through the beer cellar hatch behind the bar. "Hello, sir. What would you like?"

The customer, temporarily startled, looked out of place, and lost. Fully suited and a necktie undisturbed against his white shirt on the hottest June day so far.

"Hello, I'm early for an appointment next door." His announcement sounded purposeful. He placed a brown briefcase on the floor and smoothed his reddish hair.

The barflies cast inquisitive eyes towards Chris then to the customer.

"I wonder would it be possible to have a pot of tea." His grand, marbled voice out of place in the Clapton establishment.

"Of course, sir. Anything else? A sandwich perhaps?" Chris epitomised the pub's name.

"Eh, yes. Eh, could I have ham and cheese—oh, and a little mustard if possible, please?" He stared across the bar. "I say, are they fresh?"

"Sorry?"

He pointed to a display on a shelf. "Those buns and cakes?"

Chris turned to a small plastic dome. "Yes. Raz, our local baker brings in a few each morning, 'cept Sundays. Do you want one?"

"Too tempting." He patted his stomach. "Local you say. Where is the bakery?"

The barflies continued to hold an interest.

"Down Mare Street. Out the door, left. He's been there since—" He turned. "Vince, how long has Raz been here?"

"Since about two thousand and four," Vince Zachary said.

"There you go. It's a family bakery. Well, his kids are gone now but still lend a hand when home." He looked to the display again, brows raised. "Are you sure I couldn't tempt you?"

"No honestly. The sandwich will suffice."

The two barflies looked away.

'Suffice?' Vince mimed.

"Okay, sir. Take a seat anywhere and I will be with you shortly." Chris remained the gentleman.

"Oh, would you like a paper? *The Times, Mirror,* or *Gazette*?"

The man's brows furrowed. "*Gazette*?"

"Yeah, the *'ackney Gazette*. Local paper," Vince offered.

"Oh, yes. That would be rather handy. Get to know more of the area." The customer chortled.

Chris took the *Hackney Gazette* from a small wire newspaper stand on the counter. His eyes caught a headline. *Clapton Winning The Fight Against Drugs*.

He rolled his eyes and handed the paper to the man.

"Thank you."

"*De nada*," came Chris's normal reply.

The man wore a startled look. "Pardon?"

"You're welcome—It's nothing—in Spanish." He nodded each phrase.

"Oh, I see."

The barflies continued to observe like schoolboys, tilting together over the bar tittering.

The forty-something customer chose a seat at one of the two central brown-bricked pillars. Tan-leatherette stools, showing signs of wear, usually occupied when the bar was full, or a person didn't want company. He leaned on a wide, circled ledge to get comfortable. His attention turned to the pages of the local paper.

"Cut it out you two," Chris whispered to his regulars.

He placed a small teapot under a water boiler.

"Well, you know—it's fucking roasting out," Vince quietly remarked.

"Sayeth the guy in full uniform delivering letters all morning." Mike

Orpen's Bristol accent remained separate from his dark fellow barfly.

"My issued shorts are in the wash. Anyway, Muscles, I start on the shaded side of a road." Vince took another mouthful of ale. "You must've shut early today. Or did the women lose interest in lifting your *barbells*." He laughed.

"Fuck off. I do have staff at the gym. Anyway, I had to organise for the shoot outing on Saturday." Mike sipped.

Chris cut the freshly made sandwich into four even triangles and placed them in a weaved oval basket on top of a red serviette. "Where is it this time?"

"Out Enfield way. Only six members." Blue-vested Mike returned his glass to a bar mat.

Vince grinned. "Can I come?"

"There's only one thing you're good at aiming at," Chris suggested.

He placed the basket on a tray next to a small teapot, cup, small jug of milk. He added a serviette-covered cutlery then, beside the sandwiches, poured salt and vinegar crisps from a bag.

"Hey, mate—" Vince began. "Some of those letterboxes can be nasty. One has to be quick, or you could lose a finger or three."

"Nice one, Vince." Mike gently thumped the postman's left shoulder.

"Ouch." Vince rubbed the offended shoulder. "Christ, that hurt, mate. I work out Saturday morning, not now."

Chris threw a warning glance at them before walking through the bar opening to the pillar. He placed the tray on the wide ledge. "There you go, sir. Enjoy. Anything else, just ask."

The customer sat straight and smiled. "No thank you, this looks good." He looked towards the inattentive barflies and leaned to Chris. "Excuse me, there is something. I wonder could you help me?"

Chris rubbed his head. "Sure, what do you want to know?" He moved to a stool.

The man stretched out a hand. "My name is Humphrey Barrington."

Chris, being usually courteous, shook it. "Hello, Mister Barrington. I'm Chris Freeman. I own this famous establishment."

"Hello, Mister Freeman. Famous, you say." His brow rose.

"Well, it has been here forever—I mean, I'm from the area. Me and my Dad enjoyed a few pints here." Chris turned to the oval front. "I used to join the auld fellas over there for dominoes back in the day."

"That is interesting. And the name, An Failty Tavern." Humphrey tipped some milk into the cup before stirring the contents of the teapot.

"No, no. It's pronounced Ahn Falt cha. The welcome—it's Irish. Hold up, I'll join you. They can be boring at times." He ticked to the bar and stood. "Never busy at this time and them two know where everything is."

He returned to the bar.

"Getting comfortable, Chris?" Mike sniggered.

"Keep the customers happy." He looked at their half-full glasses. "If you want anything, get it yourself." He eyed them. "Leave the till alone."

He took a bottle of Pils lager from a bar fridge, picked up a cold glass and went back to the pillar.

"Okay, Mister Barrington—"

"Humphrey, please." He smiled.

"I'm Chris. What can I do you for? What would you like to know?" He poured into the glass.

"Well, Chris, the office next door through the arch. I was led to believe it fronted to the footpath. I have made enquiries regarding renting the premises. But I do not wish to run a back-alley business." Humphrey enjoyed a quarter sandwich.

Chris shuffled on the stool staring at the man as if trying to read him. "It does have a street front but closed a while now. What type of business, Humphrey?"

"Well, I was, still am actually." Another nervous chuckle.

Chris rolled his eyes.

"I'm in a joint law firm in Cambridge, but I have grown tired of corporate law and the odd good old pals' lawsuits. This area is growing socially and, although not involved too much with criminal law, I feel that I can offer a service to all sections of the law here." Humphrey paused for another morsel. "Yours is the third establishment I have visited over the last month. Just to get a feel of the area and I—"

A pain rushed through Chris' head.

It's happening again.

He held up a hand and interrupted him. "Hold up—get one thing straight. This is a mixed community." He directed Humphrey to the barflies. "Look over there. Vince, obvious is black, was born and raised here."

Vince turned and nodded at the mention of his name.

Chris continued. "He actually went to Cambridge. Mike, Mister Wonderful, is an ex-army captain. Has his own gym and gun clubs, he's from Bristol."

Mike waved.

Humphrey shifted awkwardly. "Don't get me wrong, I am a man of means. In other words, I want to share my knowledge within this community without people breaking the bank. Now, in your opinion, would I be wasting my time?"

"I was born in Dublin, dragged up here in Clapton. You only see three people here from different backgrounds. So, what do you hope to achieve?" He winced as if reading the newcomer.

The doc said the headaches may return. Why now?

Humphrey drained the last of the cup, poured the remainder from the teapot and took a third quarter.

Chris continued to study him. He was good at it. *Fucking cheek. Who does he think he is? Man of means indeed. Something weird here.*

Humphrey had hit a nerve. Had he somehow set off Chris' headaches?

Chris boldly moved an arm around his shoulder. "Listen." The word sang. "I don't normally brag — Not the type. But let me put you *wide*." He saw Humphrey's question. "Wide — Fill you in — explain."

"Oh, I see. Sorry."

Chris shook his head. "That's okay. My auld fella and Mum started a business in Dublin and brought it here and to Germany. I have degrees in physics, chemistry, and technology, some say bolloxology as well. I speak a couple of languages." He smiled and took a sip from the glass. "I'm a multi-millionaire, perhaps on the verge of billionaire." His eyes read Humphrey. "No joke. Ben, my dad, told me." He stared at him. "Did I say I don't brag?"

Humphrey adjusted timidly again and coughed. "Sorry."

"Dear old dad sold the company for oodles of money. This—" He stood, waving his arms around.

The barflies stayed interested.

"See this. Hobby—just a hobby." Chris' nose wrinkled. "I don't go around the playboy world on super yachts or private jets, although I have them. Did I mention that I don't brag, often?"

Humphrey nodded rapidly.

Fucking hell. Is this guy for real?

"Clapton is me and if you want to be part of it—" Chris stuck out a hand. "You better buy a round for the lads when you move here." He leaned into him grinning.

"Move? Oh, I haven't thought of that. Yes—yes." Humphrey's expression changed from one of worriment to elation and firmly shook Chris's hand.

"One more thing, well, a few." Chris' head tilted left and right.

Humphrey waited, open mouthed. The last quarter in a hand waiting to be devoured.

"If you use this establishment for various reasons, you must be willing to sing a song." Chris stared. "Wear Saint Paddy's day funny green hats." He thumped the ledge. "And be a Goonah."

"What's a Gooner?"

Chris jolted back.

"Oooh—to be a Goooonah," sang from the bar. "Goonah—Arsenal

supporter." Vince punched the air.

"Oh, but I am a season ticket holder. I know Mister Wenger very well. He and I discussed his future before he—-"

"Okay, Humphrey, no bragging, we will have no name dropping here." Chris pointed to the retired Arsenal manager's central photo hanging proudly amongst several others above a rotating fan behind the bar.

Mister Wenger? Arsene, surely? Something wrong here.

"Oh, I say." Humphrey looked to the bar. "And that's you and your two pals. Who are the others?"

"You will meet them I am sure." Chris turned to the barflies. "Say hello to Humphrey Barrington Esquire, lads." His mocking obvious to them, but not to Humphrey. He wasn't *wide*.

"Hi, Humphrey Barrington. That's a mouthful." Vince raised his glass.

"Hello, Humph." Mike shortened the customer's name. "Come, join us."

"Well, I shall be going soon." He looked at his watch. "Oh, why not then. Still have ten minutes."

Chris, sharp-eyed, and quicker mind, tipped Humphrey's watch arm. "A Ulysse Nardin? You had better choose another timepiece if planning to stay around here," he whispered.

"I say, I can handle myself. I was an instructor in the Territorials." Humphrey smiled.

"Good to know." Chris, brows raised, led Humphrey to the bar. "You'll have something in common with Mike here."

Humphrey shook the barflies' hands and sat on Mike's left side.

"Humphrey was in the TA, Mike."

Chris left the newly extended barfly club to get to know each other. His cheerful expression slipped. He appeared disturbed; distracted from the company. Something about the new customer had hit his suspicious mind. His head ached.

He looked at his watch and observed the barflies' almost full pint glasses. "Just popping into the office, lads. Give a thump on the bar if you need anything."

**

Chris opened a door behind the bar, entered his compact office and pulled a string. His head hurt again. *Must go back to the doc.*

A small fan hummed into action. A modest, barred window permitted some light onto his desk. A glass wall-cupboard reflected a five-drawer high grey cabinet. On a table-stand opposite his desk, bottles of spirits and upturned glasses rested on a tray.

Leaving the door open a crack behind him, he moved to the more comfortable of two chairs and opened his laptop. It whirred into life.

Why would a wealthy solicitor be interested in Clapton? Why did he not know what a Gooner was? It's sung at all matches. And the scar under his watch.

He tapped a password on the keys then typed into the search bar: 'Humphrey Barrington, Cambridge.'

He stared at the results and moved the cursor then clicked. *Interesting - it appears that my possible new customer has travelled extensively and has had his fingers in many pies. Let's see.*

Chris liked researching. It had been an important role in his parents' company and his part-time P.I service.

He slowly scrolled the information. *Chadwick, Darling, and Barrington – Corporate Law Foundation. He must have joined last. How can they represent fabulous clients? Actors, government ministers. Ah, a trade minister. I remember him. Johnston—lucky to hold his job after a sexual discrepancy while at a trade conference. They look after an orphanage. That's a plus for them I suppose.*

He opened a new window and typed: *Undercover, 2012.*

"Ah." Green hue from the new page brightened his face.

When I investigated Agnes Peter's concerns about her hubby. Fifteen years ago, in Germany. Jesus, more connections to that country. Yes—Dad walked around with Johnston in our labs. He was a junior minister at the time. Let's see. Ah, yes—two soldiers claim a night out with the minister turned nasty.

"Fuck me pink."

Humphrey was there too. What's going on? I still can't understand Agnes' theory about 'Boys' club. She did my head in.

He closed the laptop. His head in thought. Staring at a framed family photograph, he took his phone from a trouser pocket and typed a message.

**

At the bar, the 'new club member' remained all ears, telling little of himself but learning more from Mike and Vince.

"If you move here, do you want to join my clubs?" Mike asked.

"Perhaps the gym, just to try it out." Humph's chest extended.

"Don't you like guns?" Vince sneered.

Humph stirred. A large shadow across the floor distracted him. "I have used them, of course, but not a great fan of them."

A door creaked open.

Humph glanced up. His expression changed, checked the time, stood, and picked up his briefcase. "I'm afraid I must be going now."

At the same time Chris appeared from his office.

"You off now, Humphrey?"

"We call him Humph now," Vince retorted.

"Oh, here he is," Mike announced.

A rotund man approached the company carrying magazines.

"Yes—eh yes, Chris. The appointment you know. I will drop in again soon and give you an update." Humph hurried.

He caught the new arrival's eye.

Chris drummed the counter. "Okay. I'll open a tab for you."

Humph stopped. "Oh, I do beg your pardon—" He hurriedly searched an inside pocket. "I do have a forgetful nature. Have a habit of writing things down."

"You're off the hook this time. On the house. See you again soon, Humph." Chris waved.

"So kind and so embarrassed. Thank you, Chris." He managed a bow before rushing to the exit.

**

Outside in the late afternoon sunshine, Humph had a spring in his step and a satisfied smile as he walked past the Tavern and the busy Marino Café towards his parked car. His meeting proved successful; he gained a new premises for a growing enterprise. An organisation that would, not only bring him closer to the community, but uniquely attach him to events Clapton had unwittingly welcomed over years past.

"Now where to live?"

11 THE RESEARCHERS

The Tavern door slowly shut.
"Who's he?" the large new arrival asked.
"Hi, Alan. That's Humph—Humphrey Barrington Esquire," Vince offered.
"You're early for a Thursday, Alan. Usual?" Chris lifted a pint glass.
"Yes, go on." Alan Bradford sat close beside Vince. "Had department meet today. Lunch meeting, so got the bus back after."
"Do you want to sit on my lap?" Vince nudged him. "Fucksake, move up."
The barstool creaked as Alan jerked to the right. He placed the magazines on the bar-counter. "Cheers, Chris."
Mike grinned. "Hard day at the lab?"
Mike never understood the 'white collar brigade', as he named them. Always working strange hours and endless meetings with apparent secrecy between salad lunches and iced spring water.
Alan ignored his regular badger. "Well, Vince, another nice day for postmen."
"Yes. So, how was your save the world day?" Vince tolerated Alan; they all did in their own way.
Alan had become a Gooner barfly purely to join something and cheered for Arsenal when the crowd did. He wasn't' the greatest conversationalist unless someone had shown a real interest in his research studies, which were rarer than Tottenham's league titles. He found Clapton a place to be unseen within a diverse community. His fourteen years in the area had been mundane compared to his unrehearsed past. A past mixed with euphoria and disgrace; a past that remained private, even after a few pints. So far.
"Lay off you two." Chris returned with Alan's change. "Oh, I see you have this month's *Strange and Curious* and *Unsolved*."
Alan tasted a mouthful of ale. "Yes." He turned the magazine covers over beside Chris's half-full glass "Haven't really read them yet."
"You must have been sitting at the back of the bus again eyeing all the lovely—" Mike began.
"Give it a rest, Mike." Vince sympathetic to Alan, sometimes. "That record is well scratched."
"No, Muscles. I only bought them in Mare Street. Prick." Alan did retain some non-alcohol assisted bravado.
Chris' clapping echoed. "Ooooh, good man, Alan. Let him have it."
The company laughed. Their bar banter infamous, and that was a mild

session. A stranger would envisage more than a verbal row ensuing from the counter when voices raised. But time and culture had been changed since Chris bought the once notorious gangster pub. There was never a quiet discussion at the far end of the bar, Goonah Nuts' Corner. The GNC displayed on a plague over their heads.

"We still on for Saturday, Mike?" Alan diverted the conversation.

"Yes, early start. We have the area for two hours, so we meet at the club and make sure all weapons are clean. Tell more tomorrow night."

Alan relished research. "I read about the longest shot. Over two miles using a McMillan Tac-fifty." He began enthusiastically.

"Yes, Sherlock. A Canadian sniper in Iraq last year. The Tac-fifty is designed for a hit up to four and half miles." Mike equally passionate about their only real common interest outside of Arsenal.

"Will you be getting one, Mike?" Vince had no interest in guns, only his partner Ilsa, the Gunners, and the Gym.

"Must be joking. Sherlock, take the flow while I go to the gents."

"Really?" Chris' eyes rolled.

"A man's got to do." Mike headed to the end of the pub.

Alan a mine of information. Enquiry his thing, either as head of the research dept. in the Institute of Cancer Research, old unsolved crimes, or strange deaths.

"It's a great rifle. The Mac is rumoured to have hit targets nearer twenty-five hundred yards." Alan took a gulp of ale.

"Wow." Chris leaned heavily on the counter, grey eyes showing miniscule interest.

Mike chuckled entering the gents.

"There is one problem though, the handguard generally comes off-centre, which does influence accuracy the further out you go—" Alan rambled on and on about the long-range weapon.

Chris and Vince continued displaying uninterested grins, nodding occasionally.

The expert at last paused to wet his excited dry mouth again.

"Really? Fan-tastic." Vince's view equalled Chris's interest.

Alan continued enthusiastically. "Overall, the average precision shooter can expect high accuracy, maybe even two miles and beyond—" His words tapered off as his audience raised their eyes and glasses.

The gents' door opened. Mike returned to the bar wiping excess water from his hands on his shorts. "Finished, Sherlock?"

"Christ, change the fucking subject. You two talk as if you're secret assassins," Vince pleaded.

Alan huffed and took another mouthful of ale.

"Same again, and another for Sherlock." Mike shuffled on the stool.

"Oh, how's your dad, Chris?"

"He's good, thanks for asking." He took three glasses and put them under their relevant taps. "Just sent him a text. Supposed to go to Dublin in two weeks for a few days. He and Gloria will be there for a week—anniversary. Three years."

"That's good." Mike finished his glass.

"Florida, eh. Fantastic, and a young wife." Vince couldn't resist.

"Watch it, mate. We have known Gloria for years. My mum would have given her blessing for the marriage—if able." Chris's eyes fixed on Alan as he placed the full glass in front of him.

Vince raised his glass. "Here's to Mister and Missus Freeman."

Two more glasses rose.

"Thanks guys," Chris said.

12 THE WROXHAM

June 9

Humph had taken time out from his research. He rested alongside others on a hotel's double-decked terrace mesmerised by a bank of swans dipping for food on the River Bure, a stunning stretch of the Norfolk Broads. The ambience, fragrant potted plants, sunshine, and comfortable Rattan furniture on the boardwalk-type walkway. A perfect setting to relax while on business or pleasure.

Many eyes, mostly male, followed a woman down steps to a lower terrace.

"Excuse me." Her sultry, college-trained voice distracted Humph.

He breathed in a pleasant perfume. Looking up, he squinted to view a small silhouette holding a shoulder bag and a half-full glass of orange. "Yes, how can I help you?"

"Would you mind if I sit here. I was sitting in the shade, and it appears this the perfect spot for the sun and the view," she said.

A cream peaked cap covered almost curly fair hair and shaded her face.

He placed his newspaper on the table and stood. "Of course. The company would be an extra attraction on this pleasant day." He pulled out a chair for her.

"How sweet, thank you." Her loose pale-blue blouse revealed more than expected as she sat.

Humph smiled, politely averting his eyes.

"Eh, are you a guest here at the Wroxham?" He sat.

"No and yes. I did stay but leaving today. How about you?" She took a gentle sip.

"The same, almost. I arrived to stay for one night. A short business trip. Oh, how rude. I'm Humphrey—Humphrey Barrington."

He extended a hand. Hers soft with short unpolished manicured nails.

"Hello, Humphrey. I'm Fran. How do you do?" She removed a phone from the bag and placed it on the table. "Expecting a text or call."

"No problem." His gaze fixed to her round face. "You look familiar."

"I've heard that before. Someone once thought I was Barbara Windsor's daughter." Her eyes indicated the loosened blouse. "It is lovely here, isn't it?" She crossed her shapely legs showing more thigh below dark-blue shorts.

"Eh, yes—yes, it is." He had trouble concentrating.

"Hope you don't mind me asking, but would your business be water based? You know because you are here at the Broads and wearing a fisherman's hat."

He tipped the forgotten head covering. "Yes, Fran. Some research involving—" He looked at an occupied table. "Yes, the food. They make their own excellent pastries and cakes."

"Oh, I see. They do. So, I guess you are planning to help them branch out." She played with her glass then took a longer mouthful.

Humph picked up his almost empty teacup. "Blast, it's gone cold."

"Would you like another or a drink perhaps?"

"No, please, allow me. What would you like?"

"Are you sure?" Her eyes peeked over her shades.

Humph nodded shyly.

"I'll have a scotch and orange with ice, no straw, please." She smiled.

"How unusual. I thought you were drinking orange juice." He left for the hotel bar.

Fran took up the phone and played with a few keys:
He's gone to the bar.
She read the reply. *What's the room number?*
264 but not yet. Watch for him coming back and call me.

**

Inside, at a long rosewood bar, Humph caught a barman's attention.

He leaned on the bar-counter. "Yes, sir, what would you like?"

Humph looked at the wide choice on glass shelving along a mirrored wall. "Eh, first, a scotch and orange with ice."

"Ah, for the lovely lady on the terrace. Very unusual drink. Ask her about Canada. And for you, sir?"

"I beg your pardon."

"Oh, you are not together. She is leaving and you arrived today." He shrugged. "I like detective programmes."

"Oh, very clever. I will. I'll have a bottle of German Pils, please."

"Certainly, sir."

The bar sleuth walked to a glass-door fridge.

"The cakes," Humph said.

"Would you like some?"

"No, well not yet. I believe they are made here."

"Yes, sir. Nigel Peters is our famous pastry chef. His family are renowned and have many small bakeries further north. I believe that a cousin has another in London." The barman placed the drinks on the highly polished bar-counter. "Would you like someone to bring them out to you?"

"No, I'll manage. London, you say. Where in London would that be?"

"I've no idea. Oh, you're in luck." He nodded over Humph's shoulder. "Here's Nigel now."

Consideration of Tragedies

Humph turned and almost bumped into an equally tall man wearing a black and white checked apron.

"Nige, this guest is enquiring about your bakeries."

Nigel stopped. "Indeed." His Yorkshire accent distinct.

"How do you do? Yes. I've heard of Peters' bakeries. I do believe you are welcomed on the continent too." Humph said.

"Well, yes. A cousin worked abroad. He used to send fantastic recipes. Haven't heard from him in years though."

"And London, where is the bakery?"

Nigel took a step back. "Are you interested in buying or supplying?" His eyes sharpened.

"Oh, please don't get me wrong. I will be moving there soon and have found a fondness for rum cake, which you are famous for."

Nigel breathed easy. "Ah, Cousin Raz is in Clapton."

"Raz?"

"Short for Raymond or Rasputin. He used to look like him." Nigel's laugh brought a few stares from guests.

"Oh, I see. A fine coincidence indeed. I shall look out for the bakery. Thank you." He turned to the barman. "Oh, could you charge this to my room. Two six four."

"Certainly, sir." The barman collected the receipt from the till. "Just sign this."

Humph penned his signature. "Good talking to you both."

He picked up his drinks and returned to the terrace.

"Nosey fuck, eh Nige," the barman said.

Nigel nodded and took out a phone.

**

Outside, Fran put her mobile on the table.

"Here you are, Fran. It appears you have made an impact with your drink." He placed their drinks on coasters.

"And I thought it was me." She tittered. "Thank you, Humphrey."

"Humph. I was recently baptised again in a Clapton pub."

"Cheers." She raised her glass. The phone stuttered on the table. "Oh, excuse me, Humph. I must take this."

**

Fran walked to the privacy of the rail overlooking the river with the phone to her ear. The swans went about their own business.

"Yes, wait five minutes and do it. Remember to slip the other bug into the case through the side. He must feel safe if finding it," her voice almost a whisper. "Okay— Yes, the handles are standard. Christ, we discussed how to replace it before. That's why you have the rivetter." She listened to the long reply. "Just sandpaper under the grip of the new one to age it, not much though. Test the bug in the handle and let me know if it works, text me. Thanks, Max."

She turned and returned to the table.

"Sorry about that, Humph." Fran's blouse widened as she bent over to sit.

At another table, a women elbowed her partner reminding him who he was with.

"Eh, no problem. Why are you here, Fran? Business or pleasure?"

"Now Humph, what sort of question is that for a lady?"

His face reddened. "I apologise. Were you ever in Canada?"

"Humph, what did the barman tell you? You're not good at chat up, are you?" She crossed her legs.

"No, no. Don't get me wrong. I didn't mean to be forward, it's just that he—"

"Oh, stop it. Humph. You're digging the hole bigger."

Their laughter turned a few heads.

She changed the subject back to the cakes until the phone shook again.

Fran smiled apologetically and read the text. "Nothing important, Humph. Now, were where we. Oh yes, Clapton and cannolis."

14 THE MAGAZINES

Alan relaxed on Saturday morning in his first floor two-bedroom apartment off Clapton Square. A short walk from the Tavern. He hadn't many interests, but cooking was perhaps his favourite pastime. According to his figure, his culinary skills bypassed dietary recommendations.

He remained house-proud. The apartment smelled of fresh lavender and everything in its place to be found when needed. His research material filled bookcases along the living room's main wall behind a desk and chair. A forty-inch flat screen television sat right of a balcony window.

His bedroom bright and spacious with a king-size bed waiting for extra company. He preferred virginal-white theme with double built-in wardrobe and dressing table on top of a pale grey laminate flooring making the room appear large.

The spare bedroom contained a regular double bed, single wardrobe and dressing table and chair, again white themed. The kitchen small with all appliances needed for his gastronomic habits.

He moved to the area for many reasons: cheaper accommodation, easy access to public transport and to disappear in a crowd. His time in Cambridge resulted in first grade degrees in the biosciences leading to outstanding appointments to pharmaceutical companies both in the UK and Germany. He attended a variety of conferences worldwide; however, Alan was driven to remain in research.

He had a lot to make up for.

Alan pulled on his brown leather recliner release and stretched his rotund six-foot to the maximum. Picking up the copies of *Strange and Curious* and *Unsolved*, he flicked through their contents and stopped. He remained intrigued with unsolved crime cases and strange accidental deaths. He had often chatted, when permitted, in the company of the GNC why so many cases haven't been solved.

Putting his regular reads aside on the coffee table, he picked up the extra magazine; a small headline had drawn him to the newly published *Why and How*.

He read between sips of coffee:
Brian Purcell:
After years of investigation on my part, I was asked to include this article to these pages merely to ask why such incidents are classified as accidents. The following is a copy of an article I wrote concerning an outrageous tragedy.

Billionaire's Son Mowed Down on Honeymoon.
Brian Purcell
22nd August 2002.
Tragedy struck renowned industrialist Benjamin Freeman's family yesterday when newlywed son, Christopher, his wife Mary, and another tourist were involved in a hit and run on the holiday isle of Lanzarote. Tragically, Mary Freeman later died from her injuries.

Witnesses claim the victims had just stepped onto a crossing as a delivery van slowed to stop, which is normal courtesy throughout the island. A white Seat Ibiza hit the tourists at speed and pulled away towards Puerto del Carmen. A taxi gave chase after the driver had informed the emergency services.

The newlyweds lay unconscious as onlookers and the van driver assisted them until the ambulance arrived. The third victim, Ms Gloria Kelly, remained conscious and appeared not to be severely injured. One witness claims that two ambulances arrived twenty minutes after the accident had happened. All three were taken to Hospital Insular de Lanzarote in Arrecife.

Guardia Civil reported that the car was probably hired meaning a tourist may have been involved in the accident. They are currently checking all car hire businesses.

Benjamin Freeman built his pharmaceutical and technology empire from small beginnings in Dublin, Ireland, expanding to England, Germany, and Sweden. He was unavailable for comment on the tragedy; his wife is currently undergoing treatment for a cancer condition. Christopher Freeman had recently joined the board as director when completing a Ph.D. degree at Trinity College, Dublin.

The Freeman's arrived in Los Pocillos, Lanzarote, eight days ago to enjoy their honeymoon. Christopher remains in a critical condition and relatives have flown to the island to be at his bedside. Ms. Gloria Kelly, on holiday with friends, remains comfortable; she received injuries to an arm and face.

The local police are urging anyone walking or driving in the area at that time and may have seen the Seat, to pass on their information directly or to their complex reception desks.

Alan closed the page, momentarily stunned, then finished his coffee. "Fucking hell." He rarely cursed or swore, even to himself. "I never knew, none of us. Chris has never talked about his past."

He pressed his feet against the cushioned end and the recliner closed with a thump. *I'll keep schtum. Won't mention to Chris. Perhaps his pal George will know what happened afterwards.*

He hurriedly opened the page again and continued to the end of the article:

The next article is equally intriguing. When experts arrived at the scene of a collapsed house. In next month's issue I will ensure that your interests will grow further due to questions asked at the time. Plus, how a pharmaceutical mogul couldn't save his wife.

Alan's face had whitened.
 Next month's issue? What did Purcell find out?

15 THE HUMPH'S REASEARCH

Humph returned to his two-bedroom lodge on Saturday after a detour to Chelmsford and interesting stayover near the Norfolk Broads. In his fusty study, labelled black file containers cluttered on shelves. Discoloured folders lay scattered on a teak desk alongside a stained mug and assortment of pens and pencils. A laptop blinked as he clicked on new online pages of information.

Licking excess cream from his lips, he placed a half-eaten éclair on a plate.

Ah...I knew it.

His eyes widened at the screen.

Professor Joseph Cole, 78, died yesterday after years of battling cancer. The renowned biochemist's research was instrumental in the production of new cancer relief drugs; however, they never led to the cures he had hoped to achieve within his lifetime.

Forced to retire through ill health 4 years ago, many believe his retirement was due to some private issues that may have involved students as far back to his undergraduate days at Cambridge.

Humph scratched his red hair.

That guy was involved with the professor?

He scrolled further through Cambridge university articles and came across a snippet:

Police were called to student accommodation on Mill Road in the early hours of Saturday. Local residents grew concerned about screams coming from the premises at around 2 a.m. and called the emergency services. A man was escorted to a waiting ambulance and taken to Addenbrooke hospital. Another two men were taken to Parkside police station for questioning. A local said he saw one man covered by a blanket, wearing only shorts and sandals. A police spokesperson said the incident was domestic and would not comment further.

Humph typed *Cambridge voting registry - Mill Road 2000-2010* and keyed in a code. He stared at the results and penned notes of his findings.

Coincidence? I think not. The professor was no angel even in his younger days. Must confirm those names though.

He closed the laptop, pressed keys on his mobile phone and listened to the ring tone.

"Hi, this is Barrington. Could you do me a favour —" He listened to the muffled reply. "I want to confirm a few names and dates — I'll text them to you — No hurry. Could you send me all the information you can via email, relevant documents et cetera — Thank you and you. Pardon? — Well, drop around and I'll give you a spare key. Drop into letter box when done. I can't be here while you play and clean up afterwards." He hung up and smiled.

He finished off the cream éclair and opened his laptop then typed his password and searched.

Houses for rent/sale in Clapton, London.

16 THE GANGSTER

In a large warehouse somewhere on south London docks, voices echoed around a table under a low hanging light bulb.

"You need to stay clear," the larger of the five-man group said.

"Fucksake, Specs. We do what we can. The less I'm told the more I can deny." Detective Chief Inspector Travis King pulled hard on a cigarette. "Your dealings stays out of my manor. Some are getting suspicious."

Hugh 'Specs' Morgan's chair crashed sideways as he stood. "Listen mush, you get enough readies from us." Thuds vibrated throughout the empty warehouse as his fist pounded the table. "This has to go down in Wick. That fucker owes me. We are going to do his shop as a warning."

King threw his hands up. "Okay, okay. But you listen to me, you tow rag. Anyone gets hurt, I'm on your back."

Specs' coarse laugh was joined by two 'assistants'. "Leave off, Travis. You? Do you know I keep some records for tax purposes?" His laugh grew louder. "Listen, he done us, you as well, don't forget. Ten grand, not bad for a couple of days sitting at your fucking desk."

King lit another cigarette. "That's a good one, Specs. I can see it now in your red ledger – 'DCI Travis King—paid ten grand, five grand, et cetera.' Fuck off."

Spec's nodded to a gorilla-like assistant. He pressed his phone and the conversation played back.

King leapt at the corpulent ringleader, but a second wiry assistant was fast. He kicked behind King's left leg and grappled him to the dust-covered floor.

A younger clean-cut young man stood motionless watching the actions.

"Now, mush." Specs right foot connected with King's groin.

"Oooh. Fuck you, Specs." King held onto his treasury.

"Don't play silly buggers with me. You've been on it for years and other stuff." Specs moved from King's body.

King remained doubled-up. His face twisted in pain.

"Your boy here has more sense." Specs patted the young, thin Detective Constable on a shoulder. "When are you getting married, Ding?"

DC Bell helped his superior off the ground. "October."

"There you go, King. This lad knows what he wants. Are you going to ruin his plans? I mean, you're good at that. Fucking up your own son. Poor Harley. Packing him off to Hendon. I think you were jealous. And what about goody-goody Robinson? That Detective Sergeant may be a problem."

King grimaced but managed to stand. "He's clean. Under the watchful eye of Pockets."

"Yeah, the *real* pain in the arse. You need to steer him away as much as pos. Give him something interesting to cling to." Specs turned to Bell. "Would you rather be under DI Macken, AKA Pockets, or this arsehole?"

Bell grinned. "Too much detective work under Macken."

"There you go, King. Diplomatic too. This guy could take over from you someday." His laugh joined by his assistants again.

"Now, you two coppers get yourselves sorted. Get me the info on the jewellers and leave the rest to me." Specs nodded to the 'Gorilla'. "Belch."

A thick brown envelope left a trail across the dust-covered table. King waved a hand for Bell to pick it up.

"A down payment. The rest when the job is done. Now, jog on."

King's lips tightened as he and Bell walked out a side door and climbed into the DC's car.

King slammed the passenger door. His hands bounced on the dashboard. "We're fucked, Tony."

"There must be a way out, Guv. That recording. I mean, my name and voice on it too. Why did my old man have to be pals with that fucker?" Bell started the engine.

"Drive." King scowled at Bell.

17 THE POST

June 22

A letter box springing closed served as an alarm to many. One pair of ears remained alert to someone saying, 'Good morning, postie'. Feet pushed into flip-flops and moved quickly to the front door.

The post hurriedly checked and sorted. He was not looking for a certain envelope; quite the opposite, he didn't want to receive it. Heavy breathing announced his dismay. There it was once again after almost a year. Though expected, inwardly, he had hoped another operative would receive the next task.

He sat at a desk and reluctantly tore the brown official envelope open then removed a single page:

Hello my friend,

This is perhaps the most important to date. Although not concerning atrocities on their part or indeed any unjust decisions the subject may have benefitted from, the subject has come to our notice. We have discovered outside interests in past tasks completed by you and other operatives from unexpected quarters.

We have discussed this problem at length and are obliged to offer the immediate task to you. Your methodology is left at your doorstep. This is quite unusual due to its urgency, and we implore you to reply forthwith for acceptance or refusal. If not performed soon, any delay will no doubt have a domino effect on others that have been investigated by the subject. Many under the subject's microscope are innocent of any crimes and are merely means to enhance further investigations on matters already undertaken by our operatives.

Enclosed are the details. Reply in the usual fashion.

God bless you.
Mors meritas (MM)

His fingers withdrew the remaining contents from the unsealed white envelope. Notepad on hand, coded initials of places, signs representing areas and numbers for times and dates were jotted down. A therapeutic way to remember details. With all the necessary information registered, he picked up a disposable lighter. Igniting the corners of the pages and envelopes, he disposed them into a metal litter bin. The flames rapidly turned the contents to ash.

He pushed a button under the desk. A hidden drawer slid open. He

Consideration of Tragedies

removed a mobile, and quickly pressed the digits.

"Hello, I wish to place an ad — Yes I have an account," a disguised bass said. He pressed a six-digit password. "Thank you — Yes, I know it has been a while, but it is the same reply. Okay—it's *Notification: En Casa. Permission is granted for the settlement in due course. Do not worry. MM.* in the usual format — Yes, many thanks, goodbye."

**

Mike Orpen's bike leaned against a red brick building as he unlocked a steel door. He easily pulled it back and locked it open to a fixed wall receiver. He wheeled the bike through a short corridor and pressed alarm keys. Footsteps echoed behind as he pushed two doors open.

"Mornin', boss," a toned five nothing woman said.

"Helen, good to see you. How was Majorca?" He placed the two-wheeler in its normal resting place.

"Hot. Good to get back to cool weather." She handed over the post.

"Oh, thanks. What you mean cooler weather? It's warmer this morning."

"Sorry, boss." Another staff member walked through the corridor. "I can't go tomorrow."

"Okay. Listen, will you do me a favour then and lock up later. I have things to do after lunch." Mike made his way to his first-floor office.

"Sure thing."

Mike closed the office door and looked out to the large gym through a full-glass wall. Clocks on two walls displayed 06:58. He sat at his desk and flicked through his post, opening each of the five envelopes and removed their contents.

"Bill—bill—application—application—what the fuck." He re-read the last letter and leaned back, breathing heavily.

His chair swivelled around to view members preparing to use apparatus. His tanned face now lined with worry. He remained committed to whatever he started; but his past was the past and now, the ex-army captain had to rethink his options.

He slammed the unwelcomed papers on the desk. "Why can't people mind their own business?" His office didn't reply.

Picking up the office phone, he pressed the keys. Almost immediately someone answered.

"Yes, hello, can you put me through to Serious Crimes please — I don't know who. King? Yes, Chief Inspector King — Oh, okay. When will he be in — Not sure? Oh, thank you. I will call again on Monday when he's back." Mike replaced the receiver and leaned back again.

18 THE CLEANER

Chris did much of the bar-area cleaning. Work on the pumps ensuring fresh flow of beers. He placed varieties of full bottles in the low glass door fridges spanning the wall behind the bar.

The usual 9 a.m. bang on a front door disturbed him. Dim light lit the bar area as he pulled gently on the door blind to reveal a woman blocking the morning sunshine.

The upper bolt slid down smoothly. He opened the dead lock.

"Missus M, looking gorgeous as usual in your flowery pinny."

The portly, cherub smiled on entry. "What's that smell?

"I just emptied forgotten ashtrays into the waste. You don't mind bringing out to the bin?"

"I want a raise—or you can marry me." Her soft lady-like Irish accent a pleasure to hear.

"And when will you divorce me?" He closed the door behind her and pulled the blind down.

"Ooh, locking me in again? The divorce will be after the honeymoon."

"Done. How's the hubby? He singing tonight?" He continued their usual banter while walking to the bar.

She went directly to a cleaning closet next to the office and rolled out her personalised trolly. Mrs. M came with the pub. Originally from County Tipperary, her and hubby Tom were regulars. Even at almost seventy, she kept the pub clean as a new pin.

"I didn't see the post." She brought a bucket behind the bar to fill.

"Got it, read it, dumped it."

"You mean shredded. They're great yokes. No more crumbled paper around for me."

"Your fav barman will be in charge for a few days," he said.

"Rory? Why? You off to Lanzarote or some such place I suppose." She removed the bucket from the sink and returned to the main floor. She squeezed excess water through the mop bucket.

"The Shelbourne in Dublin. A large double room with king-size bed." Chris stretched his arms wide. "I will be all alone. Dad will be too tired to stay at the bar when Gloria is finished with him." Bottles clinked quietly as they were replaced on the shelves. "Private jet. Plenty of room on that too. You want to join me?"

Her mop squelched and splattered across the wooden floor. "I've a hair appointment."

"I'll bring a hairdresser specially for you."

"Getting my new dentures, the next day." Her large behind waddled jokingly as she moved in rhythm with the mop towards the entrance.

"You don't need them. It'll be something different for me." He quickly moved his lean six-foot frame as a wet cloth splatted a pillar.

"I've nothing to wear—shite." She hung her head. "I shouldn't have said that. Will you behave and let me work."

They both laughed. "Carry on, Missus M. Give me a shout before going." He disappeared behind a door leading to a private area above.

**

Chris stepped into the bathroom of his apartment rubbing his face. His grey eyes stared back at his youthful image above the sink while turning on the cold-water tap.

He ran a hand through his short dark hair.

A few greys. Never mind.

After sluicing water over his head and smooth face, he quickly dried with a towel. He filled a small watering can and moved into his spacious living room. The Den. It was more than a den, the large area served as a study, dining room, TV room. A couple of two-seater sofas stared at each other as two easy chairs guarded an unused ornate fireplace. He liked his comfort.

He stepped through one of the two long windows to the roof of the bar's entrance. An array of flowers displayed in artificial baskets along the roof parapet welcomed the early morning watering. Two white wrought iron chairs and small table provided outside comfort for a couple in the private area. Beside a window, pushing a button, a retractable red and white awning strained open above him.

He sat on a chair and pressed keys on his mobile.

"Dad — Sorry to wake you. Oh — Okay you were up. Good flight? — Thanks for letting me know you were arriving sooner — Yes, I fly out tomorrow and stay at the apartment. Missus M can't come." He laughed. "I know, she's gas — Yes, I'll tell her hi from you. I'll probably stay three or four days. — Meet? No, not at the hotel. How about meet at Brady's — Yes, old habits. Listen, I'm still having those headaches and weird dream-like visions. — Okay, Dad but you need to tell me more — Okay. Give Gloria my love. See you."

19 THE GNC

June 22

GNC members never entered at the same time. However, regulars conceded that Goonah Nuts Corner remained for the Arsenal Supporters Club alone. Any stranger sitting on one of the stools would soon feel uncomfortable and move elsewhere or leave the Tavern.

Chris wiped the counter.

Alice, a part-time bar help, sorted clean glasses. "Here's the first. Bob the Builder." She took out a cold German Pils bottle from a low fridge. "Alright, Steve. Usual aperitif?"

"Cheers. Great weather. A belter on the site though." Steve Urban, the local builder claimed his customary area at the bar. "Hi, Chris. How's your dad?"

"Fine thanks. He arrived in Dublin early. Heading off there tomorrow." He looked towards Alice. "Rory and Alice, will take care of you lot."

The petite long-haired brunette smiled. She learned fast to give as well as take at the bar since starting there over two years ago.

"Double," the Clapton born bargirl said.

"No, just the Pils." Steve handed her a crisp tenner.

"Not you, Steve." She went to the till. "Double pay, Chris."

"I suppose so." Chris conceded. He always did.

The two front doors squeaked almost simultaneously. Alan entered the left and a young couple through the right. He nodded to them when passing and claimed the next vacant GNC barstool.

"Hi, Steve." He used proper names, mostly. "Pint of usual Alice, please."

"A gentleman as always, Alan."

"Evening, Sherlock." Steve's right hand slapped on Alan's back.

Alan shook. "Lucky I wasn't sitting. How's work? Busy?"

Both similar build, though balding Steve had less stomach than Alan.

"Yep. You off shooting the bad guys tomorrow?" Steve almost emptied the bottle.

"Please, don't get him started again. Alan here was only short of describing a rifle manual a while back." Chris walked to the couple for their order.

"Yes, Steve. I won't stay long tonight, early start." Alan handed over a five pound note. "Thanks, Alice."

The bar doors' hinges had been being well-used. Friday nights entertainment varied, but that night, two young guitar playing singers were due to perform for the first time. When punters entered, they headed to their normal seats or near as possible. It wasn't long before the window seating held familiar posteriors with their partners occupying the outer stools. Not all customers would stay the distance. Many reached their limit around eleven o'clock making room for late comers.

A door squeaked again.

Steve looked at his watch, and without looking up, announced the arrival. "Here he is."

One particular member of GNC had a regular time.

Alan was slow and looked around. "Ah, George."

George stopped at the first pillar. He exchanged unheard niceties with a seated middle-aged couple then walked towards the end of bar.

"Alan, Steve. How goes it? Hi, Alice. Usual, please," came his breathless opening.

"Evening, mate." Chris welcomed his life-long friend.

Besides as being ex-brothers-in-law, they had attended the same Clapton schools. A couple of inches difference in their heights, Chris being the taller. George remained groomed as if coming straight from the barbers and a tailor. The joker of the pack bore a welcome grin enhanced by his trimmed fair beard.

"How's Uncle Ben?" George had always known Chris's father as Uncle Ben.

"He's good. He and Gloria are in Dublin. So, heading off there tomorrow."

Alice placed George's first drink on a coaster; sparkling water.

"Cheers. There you go." George handed her a fiver.

Steve raised a hand for his first real ale pint of the night.

Alice brought back George's change.

"In the box." He pointed to a yellow container.

She dropped the few coins into a Cancer fund box chained to the bar near Alan.

More repartee passed between the few GNC members when two more entered together, Mike and DS Pete Robinson.

The DS waved to a table.

Mike claimed his stool.

"Hi, Muscles," Steve remarked. "Pete."

"Steve, George." Mike paused. "And Sherlock. Alice, gin, and tonic please. No ice or lemon."

Alice nodded. She tolerated Mike but didn't enjoy his company as much the other members.

Chris, ever observant, returned behind the bar with empty glasses. "Gin? Are you ok?"

"I'm good." Mike looked at faces waiting for a story. "I am, really.

Nothing to worry yourselves about." He looked at their wide-eyed faces again. "Fucksake."

"Why should we worry about you, Mike?" Pete Robinson retained a copper's nose even off duty. "Move up, Alan."

The larger member duly bounced his stool to the right, followed by Steve. Pete pushed a seat in between him and Mike. The traditional seating positions formed.

"Think I'll close early. You lot are grumpy tonight—'cept you George." Chris winked, knowing what was coming.

"Oh, yeah. Old school unite." Steve quipped.

"Yeah," followed Alan.

"Shut up, Sherlock." Mike had to have a word in.

"Lay off Alan. He means no harm," Steve fired back.

So, it had started; the predictable Friday night GNC debates. Unanswered questions flew around the area in between orders of drinks and crisps. As the pub filled, more Goonah Nuts arrived with peripheral members.

"Watchya Vince, Ilsa, and here's Joanne with, eh—" George stopped and moved left to his usual spot beside the bar counter entrance hatch.

Chris winced and rubbed his head. He looked to the entrance. Humph. Coincidence?

"Who's that with Joanne?" George asked.

"No way," Mike said aloud. "Humph."

"Who the fuck is Humph?" Steve slapped Vince's back.

"Hi Steve, Sherlock. Alice, usual for me and gin and tonic. Hi, Pete. Shove up a bit, please." Vince spoke hurriedly. "George."

The group welcomed Vince's partner and politely shifted their stools left and right.

Alan put his hand on the remaining vacant stool claiming it for Joanne.

"Thank you, Alan, you're an angel," Joanne said softly.

She removed the stool and placed it beside Ilsa.

"Move up, Sherlock," Steve insisted.

Alan duly obliged, again.

"Humph," Vince started. "Did we make that much of an impression on you?"

"Not at all, Vince. I mean." Humph confused.

"Don't mind him, Humph." Mike took his side. "Everyone, this is Humph, a prospective new member of GNC."

Alan moved to an empty stool allowing Humph between him and Steve.

"Welcome to Clapton," Steve said for the group. "I'm Steve. I hope you're not a Yid spy. This is a Goonah pub."

"Oi, language, Steve," Chris shouted from the behind the bar.

Steve bowed his head to Arsene Wenger's picture.

"He's a Goonah. Season ticket holder, in fact," Vince announced.

"Impressed, Humph. I run the pub supporter's club. Welcome again. What's your poison?" Steve cordially asked.

"No. Chris," Humph shouted. "Same again for the group as promised."

"I was joking, Humph. I didn't think you would remember to come back."

Chris rubbed his head. Something about this fella.

"It's only about two weeks ago. I would've come sooner but business prevailed. Now, please, I insist."

Various forms of gratitude were thrown at him.

"Okay." Chris turned to Alice. "Their usual."

He came from behind the bar and tapped each member. "This is George, Joanne, Ilsa, you know Vince, and Mike, this is Pete, Steve and Alan."

"Hello all." Humph turned sharply to a noise.

Chris saw Humph's fear in his eyes. "Don't worry about them. That's Duo. They're setting up for the music. Well, enjoy the night and—" Chris turned and cheerfully continued. "Spend, spend, spend. Alice and Rory don't work for nothing." His loud announcement was followed with a variant of cheers.

Chris tapped barman, Rory's, shoulders as he reported for duty.

**

Singing voices outdid GNC banter. The regulars were used to the unorganised weekend competitions as the bar corner lost out again. Their conversations became personal, chatting about the shoot, Mike's Gym, and Chris's upcoming trip. He remained alert to most bar-side conversations.

"So, Steve, before I visit the estate agent tomorrow, have you any recommendations? Shall I buy or long-term rent?" Humph managed to straighten on the stool, with help. "Thank you, Alan. Not used to sessions like this."

"Nor is Alan. Well, Humph. Oh, excuse me." Steve turned to Rory. "Irish, give us three more here, mate, before I head."

"Steve, please not for me," Alan said.

Humph held the pint glasses before him. "Or me. I have this and a full one already."

Steve had a barrel inside him that could retain gallons before releasing before going home. "Okay, but one for me and Alan. I insist."

Alan nodded in submission; his limit had now been passed.

Consideration of Tragedies

"Well, old chap." Steve leaned into Humph. "Property is on the increase around here. I've done loads of work locally. Perhaps long-term rent for now."

"Yes, good idea—hic. Oh, excuse me," Alan said.

"Here you go." The Galway twang clear from young Rory.

"Cheers, Irish. Keep the change."

"Thanks, Steve." Rory clanged the tip-bell twice.

Steve lowered down a third of the pint. "Hey Alan, there's a flat in your place. I recently did some renovations there and number seven, the Square."

"That's right, at the end of my floor. Very nice two-bedroom apartment." Alan confirmed eyeing Humph.

"I must mention that tomorrow," Humph said.

**

Chris chatted with George.

"Flowing tonight, Chris," George said.

"Certainly is, Bro. Must be Humph's influence. Two rounds." He leaned on the bar. "My head is at me again."

"Listen, did you go for your visit?"

"Yeah. Last week. Doc asked if I had any fainting spasms."

"Have you?"

"No, mate."

"You still working out and jogging? If so, you better cut back." George sipped from his glass.

"Yeah, not much though. The headaches are like a sense, tension about things. I don't know."

"Talk to your dad. Right—one more and I'm off."

Chris went to the taps.

**

Rapturous applause welcomed Duo back after their short break to begin their closing session.

Pete headed to the gents.

He washed his hands as the door opened.

Standing at a urinal Vince remarked. "Can't wait for the season to start again."

The door burst open. "Any room for a small one." Steve's curtain call before heading home.

Pete shoved his hands under an auto drier as Vince zipped up.

"Off then, Steve?" He asked knowing the answer.

"Yeah. That fucker Humph asks loads of questions. I thought he was with you, Pete. A copper."

Vince dried his hands. "He's alright. A new Goonah member and a pal of Wenger no less."

"Maybe he could bunk in with Alan," Pete suggested while leaving followed by Vince.

"Good one, Pete. Night you two," the big man said.

**

At the bar Mike pocketed his mobile. "Smoke, Joanne?"

"No thanks, Mike. Perhaps later."

He moved off the stool.

"When did he start smoking again?" Ilsa asked.

"He takes an odd one when drinking. More when worried."

Mike headed to the front. Outside, a few punters chatted holding glasses, adding to climate change. He walked to the privacy of the arch, lit a cigarette, took out his mobile and texted. A minute later he read the reply and texted again. The written conversation went on until he flicked the half-smoked cigarette down the alley. He trudged back to the bar.

"Chris, gin and tonic." Mike's abruptness drew attention.

Still paying attention to customers, Chris looked after Mike's order.

**

Humph slanted right. His hand tapped Alan's knee "He's a character, is Steve."

Alan smiled. He didn't mind who leaned into him, especially after going past his pint limit. Real company had been hard to come by. He had a moment to think back to that Thursday.

"Yes, Humph, excuse me, have we met?" Alan's eyes widened to focus. "It could be the extra bitter but I'm—hic, sure I've seen you before."

"No." Humph sipped, removed his hand avoiding Alan's eyes. "I don't think so." He quickly changed the subject. "We could be neighbours soon." Humph smiled and turned looking at the delighted drink-assisted punters singing and swaying to the music. "It's so vibrant."

"I suppose so." Alan was used to being ignored. "Where are you staying?" He looked along the bar.

A few stools away Mike gulped down his drink. He had a quiet word in Joanne's ear before passing Alan.

"See you in the morning, Mike." Alan waved.

"Sorry, Sherlock. Have to cancel. Something came up. I'll try to re-arrange for next month, okay. Have fun you two." Mike hurried to the exit.

"I say, rather strange rushing off like that. What did he mean us two have fun? I thought we were." Humph chuckled.

"Don't mind him." Alan returned Joanne's wave. "Always passes remarks to wind people up. You were saying where you're staying."

"Yes, Alan. I believe not too far from your place or Pete there."

Chris looked up from the sink. How does he know where Pete lives?

"It is rather convenient, Clapton Square. Just until next Saturday." Humph sighed. A movement at the end of the bar distracted him. "I meet with the estate agent on the corner, Montrose, tomorrow at eleven."

"See you all." George disturbed their chat as he patted the men and kissed the women's cheeks. "Enjoy Dublin, Chris."

George idled to the entrance saying goodbye to familiar customers.

Chris tipped Rory's shoulder. "The place is thinning out and head not the best, so I'll get packed and to bed. Up early tomorrow. Pay Duo, do the till, lock up. Text me when you're gone. Night, Alice." He slipped away through to his private stairway.

His staff were reliable due to being paid over the odds.

**

Chris closed the extra thick fire-door behind him.

I keep feeling as if I'm being called to something.

His head hurt again. He wouldn't be disturbed unless for emergencies. Steve had done a good job on the renovations including soundproofing his living area from the lively carry-ons below. In the Den, he opened a window allowing a cool night breeze then returned to his packing.

When finished, he sat on a high-back barstool at his small private bar and poured a cold Pils into a chilled glass. His phone announced a message. He went to his laptop and typed a password then scrolled the screen pages, Stapleford Aerodrome.

20 THE NEW TASK

Camouflaged against a moonlit night, a figure removed a homemade key-tool from a small hip bag and opened a stairwell door. A landing light flickered in time with padded footsteps as they quickly reached the first floor. They moved to the door of a vacant apartment at the end of a long balcony. His eyes glinted in the moonlight when looking right and left. He was alone. The same tool slipped into the lock, quietly opening the door.

He stepped into the freshness of a newly painted interior. Pressing a mains switch off before climbing stairs, he stopped at a small shower room. His head jerked in surprise. A LED head-torch highlighted his blue eyes behind a dark ski-mask in a mirror before aiming the beam at an electric shower unit. His fingers went to work.

The panel opened silently. He armed a small rubber and plastic electrical device fixed to the water on-off dial. Replacing the panel, he concentrated on the top of the facing shower wall. A cordless drill whirred softly as three screws fell to a gloved hand. The white plastic vent cover swung down on the remaining fitting. A homemade miniature camera fitted nicely into position before replacing the covering. Pressing a button on a remote control, he viewed his image on a mobile phone. The intruder then slipped quietly away via the same route.

Further work remained. Easily scaling a wall in the complex courtyard, he landed cat-like in a patioed-garden, went to a basement door, and entered a refurbished premises. He performed the same procedure as the previous apartment before stealing away into the brightening morning.

21 THE TRIP

On Saturday, Chris steered his mid-grey Subaru Legacy off Ongar road into Stapleford aerodrome carpark. Stopping the car at his permanently reserved carport, he climbed out. Stretching his arms to release stiffness, he eyed his watch: 08:30 a.m.

Right. Loads of time for on-board breakfast.

He took a large holdall from the boot and walked towards the runway acknowledging 'good mornings' and waves from staff.

Jonesy, his regular pilot, and Sam, his not so regular stewardess, waited at the steps of his family's white Embraer Legacy 500.

"G'morning Jonesy—looking gorgeous as usual, Sam. Starving," he chirped when reaching the top.

"I suppose you want breakfast." She knew his routine.

"Yep." Chris poked his head into the flight deck. "How's the weather stats, et cetera?" He peered through the windshield.

"Clear skies all the way to Weston aerodrome. Due to depart in—" Jonesy glanced at his watch. "Twenty-two minutes."

"How was the flight from Dublin last night?"

"Not too bad, Chris. In fact, travelling from Florida to Dublin wasn't as choppy as normal."

"Nice one. Cheers. Right. Breakfast." Chris eased into his padded single seat in the twelve-seater cabin and buckled-up.

22 THE HUMPH'S DAY

Humph walked into Montrose Estate agency at 10:55 a.m.
A receptionist opened a door to the main office. Humph passed her onto a dark blue thin pile carpet.

A small, bespectacled balding Mr. Montrose stepped from behind a desk and stretched out a hand. "Mister Barrington, welcome. Please, have a seat," He directed Humph to two easy chairs.

"Hello. You can call me Humph, Mister Montrose." He sat.

"Andrew. Something to drink. Tea, coffee perhaps?"

"No thank you, Andrew."

"That will be all, Miss Preston," her boss said.

She closed the door as Montrose moved to a tall chair behind his desk. His feet rested on its foot-rail

"So, Humph, you are interest in property in Clapton. Would you be renting or purchasing?"

"Well, I thought of long-term rental for the moment after discussing with my newly acquired acquaintances in An Fáilte Tavern last night. Perhaps a two-bedroom apartment within this immediate area."

"Ah, this is a community of fast flowing rumours. You must have been in the company of Steve Urban, Alan Bradford and, of course, Genial Chris Freeman."

"Why yes."

Montrose leaned back into his chair. "I have four suitable properties within the area: Cricketfield road, Clapton Square, Churchwell Court and Amhurst road. Steve has worked on all four. Two, Cricketfield and Amhurst, have been viewed and almost sure of going next week; however, you can view them along with the other two on Monday."

"That would be super. I have a limit in mind, but the budget can be moved if, what Alan described last night as the 'wow' rental, comes into effect."

"Oh, dear Alan. I should hire him. But be wary if renting Churchwell, you may receive many invites." Montrose rocked as he laughed. "So, Humph, would ten Monday morning suit you? We could meet here, drive to Amhurst then Cricketfield returning here for a short walk to the last two."

"Yes—perfect. Ten it is." Humph rose and shook Montrose's hand.

They moved to the main shop.

Montrose held the front door open. "Until Monday, Humph."

**

Humph walked up Mare Steet buying groceries and some essentials. A door opened releasing the aroma of freshly baked bread from Pringle's Bakery.

He stepped inside as a women held the door for him. "Thank you," he said.

She smiled. "Can't resist it, eh?"

Raz stood as a white-coated rugby player behind the counter. A white hat barely covered his mop of greying hair. A welcoming smile grew beneath his salt-and-pepper trimmed beard.

"Yes, sir. How can I help you?" His Yorkshire brogue distinct.

"The aroma drew me in. Couldn't resist." Humph chuckled.

"It's purposely done, sir. Now, what would you like?"

Humph's eyes widened as a child. "Are those cannolis and rum cakes?"

"Yes, sir. A family trademark of sorts." Raz leaned into the counter indicating the sizes. "Made to order, large or small. I put a couple on show, and they will be gone before lunchtime."

Humph's lips visibly watered. "I'll take one of each small ones before the rush."

"Good choice, sir." Raz opened a white box and used tongs to carefully place the small cakes inside.

Humph's eyes watched the cakes being packed. "Very friendly area. Opening a solicitor service up the road soon."

"Ah, the solicitor friend of Wenger. Nothing is secret around 'ere."

"You look familiar though. Have you worked abroad?"

Raz's hoarse laugh loud. "I don't like planes. People always get me, and Cousin Noel mixed up. God knows where he is now." He handed over the cakebox. "None of the family have heard of him for years though. Where would you have seen him?"

Humph handed over a crisp ten sterling note. "Rome, some years ago."

"Eh." Raz took the note and fiddled nervously with the till. "Rome, you say, I didn't know he was there." He returned to the counter and palmed Humph's change.

"Well, you did say he wanders around. Thank you. I hope to come again."

"Yes, please do and if you would like an order of those cakes, don't hesitate."

"I am looking forward to them. Cheerio." Humph stepped out onto the busy street as eyes watched the direction he walked.

Raz took a mobile from a pocket.

**

Humph returned to his rental abode, sat in front of his laptop, and stared. Taking out a notebook, under 'L' he read his password and typed. Much research still needed. The dossiers almost completed to forward his reports. Ensuring the viability of the information would be useful to him while living and working in the area.

He pressed a button on his digital voice recorder:

"For my safety, copies of this will be forwarded to my old firm in my name. I need to discover more of the gun club. Perhaps joining would bring me closer to members of concern.

"My main trepidation; however, is being discovered. My initial introduction, though brief, to some persons of interest two weeks ago has extended my research. I must maintain discretion; do not become too involved with them, namely, Inglis, Orpen, and Urban.

"Bradford is a tad suspicious of me. He may have remembered meeting me at the pharmaceutical site noted in his file. Need to stay close, though his interest in me is purely sexual.

"The baker, Pringle, is an interesting character. Where is his cousin? My client appears reluctant to offer his obvious knowledge of the parties in question. Take a note of the concern. I do believe he has connections to this community.

"I must note that the bar owner, Freeman, can assist me via small talk but do not overdo it. His apparent links through the sold industries with some parties may invite more information. He would be a convenient source for conformational purposes. His obvious connection to all parties may bear fruit in the long run. Has he stopped his P.I side-line?

"I will use this weekend merely to put together the smaller pieces of my research thus far. I might add, it is interesting to note that all have something of a dark background. I have itemised in each portfolio; therefore, will draw on conclusions of possible interconnections with each or perhaps all parties.

"Footnote: As advised, look into DCI Travis King and suspected involvement with a local entrepreneur."

Humph paused and reached for his briefcase. When clumsily opening the flap, something rolled across the laminate floor. He watched the small object stopping at a chair leg. Standing, he picked it up.

"A bug. Surely my client trusts me."

He placed the recorder down and rushed to the kitchen sink, turned on the cold tap. The water splattered over the object. He put it on the counter and pounded with a rolling pin, rendering it useless.

The recorder's red light blinked while he hurriedly emailed copies of his portfolios to a secure address. He pushed each hardcopy into pre-addressed large envelopes and shoved them into his briefcase.

He looked at his watch. "Post office would still be open." He headed to Mare Street with the envelopes safe in the briefcase.

23 THE INTRODUCTIONS

The Tavern's GNC was oddly less vibrant on Saturday night. Steve had held his usual spot with his wife, Ellen. She chatted with Ilsa and Joanne while Vince and Pete dealt with Steve's views of who should Arsenal be buying for the new season. Alan had tried his best, though unsuccessfully, to offer his ideal players up for discussion.

Alan turned as a front door squeaked.

Humph walked in wearing newly bought blue-jeans and pale-orange shirt. He tried his best to at least appear cosmopolitan.

"Good evening all," he said.

"Watchya, Humph." Steve nudged Alan. "Move up."

Alan duly obeyed.

Steve introduced his wife Ellen to Humph.

"Where are you from?" She asked.

"Cambridge. I'm moving here though." He adjusted on the seat.

"Pint, Humph?" Alan remained unconcerned.

Humph thought for a few seconds as Alice waited patiently. "Oh, go on then." He looked along the bar. "Quiet for a Saturday. No Mike or George."

"Well, George wouldn't come in if his pal was off. Chris. We were just discussing Mike's absence. Though he did call off today's shoot," Pete offered.

"There you go, Humph." Alice presented the pint in front of him.

"Thank you, Alice—Alan." He acknowledged with a smile.

Alan's eyes widened. *Perhaps I'm wrong about him.*

Alan leaned to him. "Would you like a home cooked meal sometime?"

Humph's brows rose. "Actually, I would."

"Monday evening? We could meet here first?"

"That would be great, Alan." He fingered the 'on' switch for the recorder in his left pocket.

**

The evening moved slow with many final fantasy buys for Arsenal completed, fashion items discussed due to Humph's attire, along with cake prices.

Humph turned to Steve for further info with even less success. Ellen was more forthcoming when her husband went for his odd smoke.

"Oh, they're punctual is Alan and Mike." She tilted her mature body closer. Her right hand tipped Humph's knee while brushing her platinum hair with the left.

Alan looked away.

"My fella is punctual too. Leaves early mornings and never home before seven. Are you going to join Mike's Gym?" Her voice soft and sultry.

Humph's neck strained and eyed the front door nervously. "Well, actually I was thinking of joining the gun club too." His laugh anxious.

Her hand grew tighter. "I hope you do, Humph. It's good to have new blood." Ellen teased and withdrew her grip as Steve opened the front door.

"Watch her," Alan whispered to Humph. "Steve can be the vengeful type. Still suspects that a postman delivers more than letters and she receives very personal training in the gym."

**

The remainder of the night stayed jovial. Around 11:30 p.m. with no information coming his way, Humph bid all goodnight and returned to the apartment.

He removed the recorder from his pocket. "Damn." He stamped childlike.

The recorder's battery had exhausted; his night out proved to be a waste of time. He shoved it back into the briefcase and retired to bed.

24 THE VIEWINGS

Montrose stopped his car at its parking spot behind the office. He and Humph emerged into warm sunlight carrying similar brown briefcases.

"You can leave your briefcase in the car," Montrose suggested.

"Well, there are rather personal papers in it. Very private. Clients, you know."

"I understand."

They headed to Churchwell Court. "So, Humph, I've a feeling you were not impressed with them."

"Not really."

Montrose searched a keyring for the stairwell door key, opened it then led Humph up to the apartment.

Inside, Humph inspected all the rooms, paying particular attention to the kitchen area and bathroom.

Montrose opened a balcony door. "The balcony is just right for one person."

Humph breathed deep. "I like this. This is favourite so far."

"Great. So, let's move on to the next one." Montrose led the way.

At the entrance to the Court, they turned left for a few paces then up steps to a main door.

Humph looked down at a grey roof at ground level covering the basement area. "That's interesting."

"Yes. As you can see, all the other houses still retain a separate basement entry with just a small front garden. George Inglis did an amazing job with the design." Montrose's hand waved over the area. "The entire garden was excavated, covered with a flat roof allowing for extra space to the apartment — come."

"He did." Humph looked along the long row of houses. "Mister Inglis lives along here too."

He followed Montrose through the main door. In the small hall he pointed to another. "That door leads to a larger rental upstairs."

Through the apartment door, they walked down to a large reception area containing another staircase.

"Upstairs is an ensuite bedroom. Down here is another ensuite bedroom, this living area and kitchen leads to a patio garden. No mowing involved." Montrose chuckled. "As you can see, the basement extends to what was the front garden."

Humph nodded at each displayed for him.

"Oh, mind the floors, the mats could still be damp." Montrose stepped over one.

Humph, as in the previous apartments, inspected all the kitchen cabinets and bedroom closets. In the downstairs ensuite, he tested the toilet flush and shower pressure. On leaving, a damp mat slipped slightly under him.

"Careful, Humph. Now, upstairs," Montrose said.

"So far so good. I like the light from the extension to the front level and the idea of solar heating. Impressive." He followed.

"Yes. That needs to be switched over if you move in. There are also some kitchen appliances to be attached to the mains."

Elsewhere, their conversation played through earphones as eyes watched a small screen. Their footsteps clearly heard heading to the main bedroom.

Humph and Montrose simultaneously placed their briefcases on the bed.

"This is it." Humph breathed in fresh air. "Wow, a balcony from the bedroom."

Humph nodded continuously while inspecting the built-in closet and the balcony. "Ah, the small ensuite."

They picked up the briefcases.

Humph walked into the shower room closing the door behind him. He tested the toilet flush and sink taps flow. Turning to the shower, he pulled the folding door open. His treasured briefcase almost glued to a hand. Tentatively standing on the damp mat, he leaned forward.

Somewhere else, a finger rested on a button while eyes spied Humph's left hand turning the shower water-on dial. The switch clicked.

Crackling sparks flew from the shower unit and vent. His body became a conductor between the shower unit and mat.

**

Outside, Montrose heard taps running and toilet flush. "What do you think?"

The reply came as spine-chilling screams.

He moved to the door. "Humph, Humph."

Muffled squawks joined jerking thumps. An unpleasant stench wafted under the door.

Montrose shoved it open, turned and fell to his knees retching. Fumes of melted flesh and burning hair engulfed the bedroom as he crawled towards the balcony. There was nothing he could do but call emergency services from his mobile.

"Hello — I need help — A man has had an accident in a shower — I don't know — The smell is awful. Sorry, seven Clapton Square beside

Churchwell Court — Yes I will do it now — Please hurry."

Shouts from outside the apartment door alerted him. He ran to the fuse board. The trip switch hadn't clicked. He turned the power off then opened the door.

"A man—I can't do anything. An ambulance is on its way. He was going to rent the place," Montrose said to a couple.

"Oh, the smell." The man covered his face with a hand.

The astounded pair assisted dazed Montrose back into the bedroom.

A young woman caught the fleshy aroma and put her hands to her face. "Oh, my God." She gagged.

The man gingerly looked behind the shower door. "Fucking hell." He jumped back, turning, almost stumbling in shock. "It's terrible. Poor man. How could that happen?"

Montrose couldn't move, his body shook. "He's new here. Knows no one except from the Tavern. He was moving here—a solicitor. New offices and all. Christ." His words jumbled.

The couple shrugged, almost throwing up.

Sirens alerted them to head for the main front door and wait on the steps. The ambulance and police car arrived simultaneously. Onlookers gathered quickly or peered out of opened windows and doors. Children ran to the park railings opposite, and dogs barked excitedly.

Montrose quickly explained to the attendants what had happened when leading them to the scene. One policeman followed while another talked to the couple on the steps.

The estate agent remained distraught, struggling to explain to the officer. The attendants entered the shower room and emerged seconds later shaking their heads. A younger one threw up.

Humph wasn't fully charred; his head, left arm and legs were black and dark red, almost purple. His trousers and shirt burnt into his body. The briefcase and contents mere flakes.

A policeman led Montrose outside while the attendants organised the respect of the body.

Montrose sat on the steps hugging his briefcase and cried.

25 THE AFTER SHOCK

June 25

Steve rarely drank Monday to Thursday nights, never mind late afternoons. His right hand shook as it approached another glass of Jameson.

Ellen rubbed his back.

The TV and radio turned off. The bar scene represented a silent movie.

Rory pulled another pint for quiet Vince.

Humph had merely walked into the pub on a Thursday lunchtime a few weeks previously. Now, those that had barely knew him, paid their respects—sort of.

"I fucking put that shower in myself." Steve grabbed the glass, downing the whiskey in one.

Ellen tried her best to calm him. "It was an accident, love, please. It wasn't your fault."

Mike walked in signalling for a drink.

Equally tall Pete followed. Their faces saddened.

"Nothing for me, Rory. I'm on duty, mate." Pete patted Steve's shoulder. "Your phone's off. I offered to take your statement and a list of properties with that type of Sherwin's Shower units."

Steve nodded and signalled for another whiskey.

"Not now, of course. You can either drop in tomorrow or arrange for me to pick them up. All up to you, mate."

"Never had an accident—none of my employees or me. Never. Everything is checked and passed, wiring especially." Steve hardly moved on the stool. Eyes fixed to the bar counter.

"I talked to Sherwin's. They admitted having a problem with that model, but it had been rectified and recalled all faulty versions. Please, Steve, you have to understand that it was not yours or your workers' fault," Pete said.

"Who was the man? Who was Humph?" Steve's shoulders flexed.

Mike paid Rory. "C'mon, Steve. Finish that off and get home with Ellen. At least gather what Pete wants. Help the investigation clear this mess up."

Steve took a deep breathe. "You're right, Mike, not always, but this time you are." His head jerked up. "Shit, the trip-switch mustn't have been connected. Fuck." His powerful fist echoed off the bar.

"You told me that most shower units aren't always connected to the main board," Mike said.

"Yeah, okay." Steve lowered the whiskey and reached into a pocket.

Consideration of Tragedies

"Go ahead. It's okay, Steve." Rory waved his hands.

"No, I'll pay now," Steve said.

"I rang Chris and told him what happened and who was here. He really sounded sick. Drinks on the house for GNC he said, until he comes back. In other words, no invites to any outside the group." Rory returned Mike's money.

"Well, fuck him anyway." Pete's laughter escalated through the small gathering.

Even Steve managed a chuckle.

"Pint, please Irish," Vince said. "Put on his tab."

"Whose?"

Vince nodded towards the creaking door.

"Okay. Not a word yet, unless he's heard the news," Rory said. "Afternoon, Alan. Usual?"

"Yes, Rory." Alan's eyes widened. "Hi, Steve—Ellen. Unusual for you two to be here at this time."

"Yeah, Alan, just off. Business to attend to." Steve rose as if carrying a hod of bricks. "Bye, mates. C'mon, girl."

Ellen patted Pete's shoulder and smiled. "He'll be okay later."

Alan had spotted the empty whiskey glasses. "Summer cold eh, Steve. Have a hot shower. Do you the world of good."

Steve stopped, took a deep intake, lips tightened, then breathed. "Good idea, Alan. Will do."

The couple left the Tavern without another word.

**

Before sitting, Alan caught the remaining stares. "What? Did I say something wrong?"

"Here you are, Alan. It's on your tab. Take a mouthful before I explain," the genial Irishman said.

Alan shrugged and did so. "Now, why have I a tab?"

"Because you were the closest to him," Vince offered.

Alan's face distorted. "Closest to who? Nobody sits close to me." A smile grew on his chubby face.

"I'm off. Catch you later." Pete tapped Alan's shoulder and quickly headed to the exit.

"What did I win?" Alan took another mouthful.

Vince nodded to Mike.

"There's been an accident," Mike began. "Humph has died."

Alan slid. Stool, pint glass and his knees hit the floor.

**

Alan slowly focused to view three faces leaning over him beside the long seats.

Rory smiled. "Lucky his head landed between your knees first, Mike," he said. "You really do like him."

"And facing down." Vince beamed.

Mike gave them the middle finger.

"Oh, no. What happened?" Alan's eyes flickered recognising them.

The long seat squeaked under his pressure to get comfortable. His hand rubbed a knee. "Ooh."

"I gave you bad news and you passed out. Can you remember what I told you?" Mike asked.

"I have a tab?"

The onlookers laughed.

Alan remained bewildered.

Vince retold the news. "Okay, you're sitting comfortably now. So, Humph had an accident while viewing a place near yours. Number seven Clapton Square."

Alan's hand covered his face. "Oh my God. Really? How? When?" The questions aimed at each of them. "Is he okay?"

"Early today. Turned on the shower, was electrocuted." Rory finished the tale.

"No way." Alan's eyes widened. "And I told Steve to have a shower. What must he think? Jesus."

"It's just you. He'll understand," Mike suggested.

"Your round again." Vince held out a hand to pull Alan up.

"What's this tab about?" Alan said.

26 THE REPORTS AND INVOICES

June 26

DS Robinson sat in his second-floor office and studied a preliminary report of the accident.

He made two copies of the information: filing the original and placing the copies into large envelopes. He left the office for the Tavern.

**

Behind a desk, Detective Inspector Bertram Macken's fingered through a file. He hardly had time to react to a hard knocking on his office door.

DCI Travis King from Special Crimes entered without waiting for a response.

Macken's brows furrowed. "Travis, and it's not a pleasure as per. You want something?"

"Okay, Pockets. There was a death yesterday in Clapton Square, electric accident. Now, I know it's not my routine thing, but I believe the unfortunate man was a well-to-do Cambridge solicitor planning to open a business here. Then, wallop. Dead. Perhaps something that you could look at."

They weren't the best of work colleagues; in fact, they couldn't stand each other. King believed that Macken was too smart to be true. Macken suspected King of getting to where he was by not displaying hard policework.

Macken leaned back, putting extra distance between him and the unwanted DCI. "Where's the report?"

"Your pal, DS Robinson has it. The builder is a mate apparently, and well, you know," the thin, tall DCI revealed.

"You can't stand him either. What is it with you, King? Why do you mistrust real coppers?" Macken's eyes flamed at the DCI.

"Yes or no to a superior."

"Playing that card, eh. Okay, Guv. I'll have a word with DS Robinson. Need a favour back though."

"What is it?"

"Sign his promotion papers next time they come up." Macken held the stare.

"I'll think about it when I get the results from you." King grasped the door handle.

"Oi—wait, Guv. What's the latest on the robbery?"

"Nothing new but the guard remains critical." King left and the door slammed behind him.

"Fucksake. How do bastards like him get there?" Pockets Macken said to the walls.

**

Mike had left the gym early again and headed to the Gun Club on East Barnet Road. Closing the grey building's alarmed doors behind him, he proceeded to a strong room. Normally, hardly anything rattled him; however, it had been a bad week, with bad news, and bad luck. He stared at an inventory list, focusing on dates, the monthly check due soon. Two weapons remained unreturned.

He removed his mobile and perused the news links again; probably for the hundredth time:

The security guard remains in a critical condition. Thames Valley police are still searching for the brown Vauxhall mini-cab seen pulling away at speed with three occupants toward Hackney Wick after the Jewellery store robbery last Friday.

"Fuck fuck fuck." He threw the inventory across the room, then, gaining some composure, pressed digits on his mobile and waited.

"Pete, Mike here. Listen, I've a bit of a problem — No, not money, all good that end. It's personal. Very personal — Yeah, I can meet you there later, but the gang will be around — Okay."

He pressed red and placed the phone into a pocket.

27 THE INVESTIGATIONS

Thursday night at the bar Pete turned when a door squeaked. Mike acknowledged a few customers as his flip-flops echoed on the wooden floor.

"Warm night again. Usual, Alice. Cheers." Mike strained a smile.

"One more too." Pete sat back. "So, what's up, Mike?"

"There are two weapons missing. Well—" He tilted. "They weren't returned." His voice low.

"What you mean *not returned*? Who had them and how the fuck did you not make sure you had them?" Pete's eyes pierced Mike. "Oh no." His elbows rested on the counter. "They used your guns. What were you thinking of?"

Pete thumped the counter.

Alice jumped.

He wiped his wet hand on a beer mat. "Thanks. Add to the tab," he said.

She moved discretely away used to keeping her distance during whispered words.

"I reported them missing from my car when checking it while at Barnet a couple of hours ago. I said I forgot to put them back. I went to the boot—gone. I've forwarded them details of the Glocks plus serial numbers." Mike lifted his pint glass and took a long mouthful.

"That may not be enough. The guard died an hour ago."

Mike's glass almost slipped through his hand. He swayed, barely managing to hold onto the bar.

"You okay? Mike. Mike." Pete held his pal's elbow.

"Sorry. I-I don't know what happened."

"I do." Pete took a sip. "And you can expect visitors very shortly. I will have to call it in that you admitted your mistake to me. Now, fucking now, all your members are suspect. You didn't think of them. Some are buddies."

"Shit. Was he married? Family?" Another mouthful disappeared. "I won't grass though."

Pete raised his voice. "Won't grass? You had better give them something. And no, he's a refugee but it still doesn't make it right. Mister Wonderful fucking-tough-guy."

Alice's eyes warned them to lower it.

Pete held up his hands to her.

"Okay, okay. I deserve that. I'll contact those members. Make them see sense," Mike offered.

Pete picked up his pint and took a swallow. "I'm off. Get it sorted." He eyed the clock. "I'll have a word with Pockets tomorrow."

The door squeaked. Pete eyebrows raised. "I don't believe it."

**

DI Bertram Macken, AKA Pockets, swaggered into the Tavern, noting everything and everyone about him. His hands remained in his off-the-rail trouser pockets. Elbows held back his unfashionable short grey jacket. His face scornful when seeing two persons of interest chatting at the bar.

Pete nodded towards Macken's pockets. "I see you have no intention of buying, Guv."

"My two at-the-moment fav people. Pint of best, Sergeant—" His hands reluctantly left their comfort zone. "As I'm off the clock."

He planted himself on a free stool between them.

Pete used the imaginary pen sign to Alice.

She ticked beside his name on the tab book and pumped liquid into a pint glass.

"So, Mister Orpen, as I was leaving the nick, I heard your name mentioned regarding misplaced weapons." Pockets looked up.

Alice placed the pint glass on a beer mat.

"Thank you, my girl."

"You're welcome." She smiled.

"Fucking scary, Bert," Mike looked at his pint. "I hope they hadn't been used for a crime."

Pockets' laugh was hoarse even for a non-smoker.

Pete turned facing the bar as if drawing a line between their conversation.

The DI stared at Mike. "How many legs do you think I have, Mister Wonderful?" He took a long mouthful then continued. "You did well reporting them missing before the guard died in hospital. Now, I know you have told the DS here what really happened; however, I would like you to make a voluntary statement tomorrow ASAP with all the facts, times, every-fucking-thing." He took a small swallow and turned to Pete.

"Now that's sorted, kind of—Pete, your pal asked me to have a word with you about some solicitor's strange and sudden death. As Irish would ask 'what's the craic with that?'"

Pockets wasn't a regular but made it his business to know the staff, customers, and Mrs. M. His strict fairness was renowned throughout the Clapton area. His memory of local occurrences, faces and names were called upon by many colleagues rather than depending on computer data banks.

Pete returned to the conversation after a swig of his tipple. "Pal me arse. Yeah, here's a report for you and the other is for Steve. Set his mind at rest. He really is broke up about the accident."

"Efficient as ever, Pete." Pockets accepted the brown envelope. "I'll have a gander later. What was he like?"

"Humph?" Mike said. "Don't really know. I mean, he came in here a couple of weeks ago for tea and an Armani before a meeting next door. He had a chat with Chris then joined me and Vince at the bar. Told us a yarn about moving here to open up an office for the community. Solicitor's office. That's all really, in a nutshell."

"Knew Wenger," Pete added.

"What? God? How did he know him?" Pockets gobsmacked.

"Apparently Humph is, was a life Gooner," Mike said.

"Coincidences I don't believe in." Another sip disappeared. "Same again, Alice. For these two as well."

She glanced at Pete.

"Yeah, go on. I'll tell him when he's back," he said.

Pockets eyed Pete. "Tell who what?"

"You don't know everything, Bert. Chris left a tab for us GN members until he comes back from Dublin. Respect for Humph. No greedies mind," Mike warned.

Pete shook his head, stared at Mike, and shook it again.

"He's lucky to have great staff, is Chris. He has either taken on a case over there, or his old man is visiting again," Pockets suggested.

"Case, Guv?" Pete took a sip. "Thought he gave up that lark."

"He has. Should've joined us as a civvy tech. Wasted behind the bar. Amazed how he gathered info on that pervo bank manager. The poor wife had no idea he had another wife in Spain." Pockets took up his glass. "Did either of you meet Chris' old man?" He emptied his glass.

"Never met him. You Pete?" Mike took a gulp.

"Yeah, in Lanzarote two years ago. You wouldn't think that he is a billionaire. I mean, just an ordinary guy and still retains his Irish accent. Cheers, Alice." Pete smiled to the busy barmaid.

"Funny that old Ben hasn't visited here for a long time." Pockets wasn't fully off the clock. A born a detective.

A few stragglers arrived for the last couple of hours as the bar conversation drifted from crime to one topic or another and a few pints.

28 THE RESEARCHER'S FINDINGS

Alan hadn't taken the news of Humph's death well. Perhaps he had proposed the date with him the wrong way. Possibly his work or the lack of a companion had distracted his normally acute memory. He had suspected something wasn't right about Humph.

He took out old research files and spread them on the livingroom floor.

Lifting a brown folder dated 'June-Oct 2009', he placed it alongside 'Jan-Feb 2009' and 'Mar-May 2009'.

Why didn't I realise I knew his face?

He flicked through the Jan-Feb files searching for relevant information. He jotted dates and names of interest in a notebook under separate headings then perused through the Mar-May and June-Oct files in the same fervent manner.

Yes, yes.

Ink flowed from a ballpoint to paper.

Leaning right, he managed to lift his bulk off the floor and placed the files on the coffee table. He went to the fridge, took out a bottle of bitter and sat on his recliner to read his extensive notes. He had realised his past may catch up with him.

Humph was there on the tour of the plant when I worked there. Had a beard. Bastard never mentioned his firm's name.

He turned a page.

Chadwick, Darling, and Barrington – Corporate Law Foundation. Even then they were investigating the three plants and GEHE Pharma for production abnormalities. Jesus.

He shifted uneasy and took another sip.

Humph was here for a reason. Was he here for me? All his notes are probably with the police now.

Alan ticked off what was considered the most valuable information. He pulled the recliner lever, jerked back, and finished the bottle.

**

Seeing a prospective renter being fried had taken its toll on Andrew Montrose. He had placed a card on his shop door the day after the incident announcing closing for two weeks due to a family bereavement. Police took his full statement.

He looked to a briefcase on his livingroom floor.

I shouldn't have this. He said there's personal stuff in it. Clients. He liked Alan Bradford. Perhaps he knows what to do with it?

Consideration of Tragedies

He dialled and waited for a reply. "Hello — Alan? This is Andrew Montrose, sorry for the early call — No, not doing so good. I closed the shop for a couple of weeks." He listened to Alan's reply.

"I have another problem." Montrose took a deep breath. "You are the only one that could help — You see, your friend carried my briefcase into the shower room instead of his. They are — Were similar. — Yes, I know but it is locked and don't want to give it to the police directly. I mean, the poor man's death shouldn't open his private life and I don't care to know any more about him." He sniffed then continued. "Could you take it off my hands? Perhaps then pass it to your police friend. — Would you? — That would be great. I'm at home now but I'll drop it around later. — Yes, thank you, Alan."

**

Montrose was good to his word. Alan carried Humph's briefcase into the livingroom as if attached with a bomb-triggering device. He placed it gently on the coffee table and sat.

He stared at the reddish-brown object's locking device wishing it open.

A Pineider Power Elegance? Has a palladium combination lock. No idea how to open these things. If I fiddle with it and the police find out. Well. Perhaps Google for a way to open it? No.

He stood and walked around thinking.

"Shit. I shouldn't have this." He stamped in frustration. "The fucker really has a lot to answer for. Sorry. Never speak ill of the dead."

What was Humph up to?

He stared at the briefcase again.

Alan returned to his previous research. He had picked up tricks in technology from an old uni pal. Having managed to get into Humph's recent phone-call list, his right index rested beside the first number. He dialled on his mobile and waited for an answer.

"Ah yes — Hello. Is this Chadwick, Darling, and Barrington? — Oh, I see. Has Mister Barrington left?" Alan listened to the long reply.

"That is awful. Has he any relatives? Me? Well — I— I." He hung up. "Damn."

He jotted down the limited information before calling another number. He listened to the automatic reply and took notes. The third and fourth numbers were discontinued.

He had an even drabber life than me.

He sat back in the sofa and pressed a name on the phone.

"Douglas, how are you? Yes, it has been a long time." Alan laughed at the reply. "No such luck. Do you recall about six or seven years ago a lawsuit

Consideration of Tragedies

regarding a product being released without full certification? — Yes, similar to a case that I was linked to years before." He listened to Douglas's detailed reply.

"Well, I was exonerated — Thank you. Anyway, the law firm for that second case, was it Chadwick, Darling and Barrington? — It was? Fantastic — No, nothing really important. The family, do you recall the name? Okay, Bryant. Fantastic. Oh, Barrington looked after that. You did? Thank you for your help. — Yes, still in London. Wow, yes that would be great. Give me notice, I've plenty of room. Byeeee." Alan eased further back into the sofa bearing a wide smile and hugging his phone.

He returned to Humph's call list. "No way." His smile disappeared as he circled a number in red ink and wrote 'Douglas' beside it.

**

Douglas Cartwright grinned, pressed a name, and waited.

"Hello, long time no chat. — Yes. I will be in your area probably in a week or so." His mouth screwed to the reply. "Well, a bit of both. They will assist each other, you know — Where would Tom be without Jerry or Santa without his beard?" His squeal-like laugh echoed around a sparsely furnished office.

"I received an interesting phone call barely ten minutes ago and due to the unfortunate passing of a mutual acquaintance. We can kill more birds with one stone, so to speak. — I totally agree. The funds are welcomed, and I am sure all parties will be satisfied in their own way. I will have to secure another to undertake our investigations, but it should be all clear to proceed with both projects." Another reply and more laughing.

"What about our friendly policeman, King? I do believe he may be due an early retirement present, but he has become a bit of an underachiever of late. His fingers are becoming very sticky from all those pies. — Yes, again I agree. Have we anyone else? — Really? You don't say. Would he swing our way? — Yes, that could work." He chuckled. "Yes, I cleaned up his bungalow after your pals' used it. Messy fuckers. We will carry on as we are, and you stay in contact as usual." He pressed off on the mobile.

Douglas the ultimate middleman. A game changer and deviously manipulative. He always covered his arse and stayed in the background. Renowned for his hacking abilities, he thrived on challenges, beat the system no matter the consequences. His family all departed, no one to worry about and no personal ties made him impervious to threats. His contacts varied from unpleasant underworld characters, banking, to religious orders and royalty. Along with the ability to swerve possible bodily damage by pleasing all at the same time, Douglas was a dangerous

man.
He fingered his notebook and stopped on 'Ostrofman'.

29 THE JOURNALIST

Honey Lane, Waltham Abbey, Wednesday June 27

Fran Wakefield furrowed her eyebrows re-reading an article headline.
 Solicitor Tragically Electrocuted.
"Bollocks."
She scratched her left ear trying to erase her mother's warning. *"Frances, you'll do damage to the drum with that habit."* She never listened.
"Fucking years of work gone up in smoke. Literally. Fuck, you, Barrington," she ranted at the paper.
She had been onto the solicitor since 2016. Humphrey Barrington's investigations had drawn her interest when she read a 'left behind' file in a Cambridge hotel.
Why was this man interested in the death of a retired doctor?
She had forsaken family tradition with the judiciary and found investigative journalism much more satisfying to her persistent behaviour. She *met* Barrington once when a person of interest was on the same radar as the solicitor. Her siblings, Charlotte, a corporate lawyer and Gerald, a barrister, gave her first-hand knowledge of Humph. Her journalistic prowess suited to gaining more information on the suspicious solicitor.
Now, all had been blown away in a shower accident.
He would have files—the police probably have them by now. Damn.
Tapping her phone awake, she pressed a name and waited for an answer. "Hello Max — Yes, it is. That guy is dead — The solicitor. Okay — Yes — Yes, blah blah, just listen for a minute." She held her breath. "Send me the recordings of his conversations — What you mean 'there's not much'? I see, well, send them all anyway — Yes, all of them." She looked to the ceiling for help. "Copy, paste the files and email them. I thought you were a tech guy — Fine, practice first then. Okay. You need to get back to updating your knowledge of IT. Thank you — And you, Max."
She collapsed back into her easy chair breathing slowly. Seconds later, she sat up, opened her laptop files, and clicked on *Brotherton*:

The Chelmsford Echo:
10th March 2012
Doctor Giles Brotherton, 72, retired London Bridge hospital consultant, has been tragically killed near his home in Margaretting, East Anglia. Dr. Brotherton had been on his regular morning stroll along Parsonage Lane, a small one lane right of way, when a van hit him near the level-crossing just after 8 a.m. The 07.59 train from Chelmsford was delayed for two

hours as the scene was investigated. The van driver was taken to Broomfield hospital, Chelmsford and is suffering from head and leg injuries.

There were no witnesses to the accident; however, Mr. Albert Jones reported the accident when he approached the crossing on the other side. Police are waiting to interview the driver to determine what had happened. There were no other vehicles involved.

She opened another document:

The Chelmsford Echo
12th March 2012
John Carr, the van driver involved in tragic accident near Margaretting, East Anglia, was interviewed yesterday in Broomfield hospital, Chelmsford. Mr. Carr, 42 from Ingatestone, told investigators he had become weak and blurry-eyed as he neared the Parsonage Lane level-crossing then lost control of the van. He was unaware that the van had hit retired London Bridge hospital consultant, Giles Brotherton. The driver has had an impeccable driving record and has never been involved in an accident of any kind.

"I deeply regret what had happened and my thoughts are with doctor Brotherton's family," he said from his hospital bed.

Mr. Carr is due to be released from hospital tomorrow.

The front of the full delivery van was completely crushed along with extensive damage to the steering, brakes, and dashboard. Investigators are keeping an open mind as to how the crash occurred. Mr. Carr's medical tests have shed no light on as to why he had become suddenly weak.

Fran leaned back in her chair.
Think I'll pay Mister Carr a visit—and as I haven't been to London for a while, see how the East End is doing.

**

Fran's red-tanked 500cc Enfield motorcycle noisily turned off Wicklow Avenue onto Cotswold Crescent, Chelmsford, stopping outside a red bricked semi-detached house. The front door opened.

A small balding man stood on the threshold.

Removing the helmet permitted her natural fair curls to spring to life. She walked up the uneven, weed covered, badly laid driveway, notably absent of a vehicle.

"Hello." The man gripped the door with his left hand. "Can I help you?"

Fran, in her figure-hugging green and red biker's jacket and black leather bottoms, stopped. "Are you John Carr?"

The man hesitant at first; his eyes fixed on her armour. "Eh—yes. What do you want?" His voice gravelled then he coughed.

She removed thick padded gloves. "I'm Fran Wakefield. I called this morning."

"Ah yes, sorry. My head at the moment isn't the best." Mr. Carr widened the entrance. "Please, come in." He stood back and motioned her inside.

She stepped into the hall. "Bike's ok there?"

"Yes, Miss Wakefield. It will draw attention to some but around here is fairly quiet—through there." He ushered her into a front room and closed the hall door quietly.

She entered a small parlour designed for intimate welcomes. A black two-seater sofa behind the door, its matching easy chair opposite next to an unused fireplace faced a triple glazed white PVC bay window. An oval knee-high glass coffee table was in front of the sofa. A forty-inch flat screen TV sat on an old drawer unit in an alcove left of the window dominated the room.

He politely directed Fran to the sofa. "Sit, please." He slowly eased in the armchair. "My back."

She nodded knowing the circumstances for the pain.

"So, Miss Wakefield—"

The journalist interrupted. "Fran, please."

"Fran, you wish to know more of the accident?"

"Well, yes. But more of the anonymous payment to you." She pulled down the jacket's zip a few inches and leaned forward. "If that's okay?"

He took a deep breath. "The police became suspicious when I received such a large sum. I mean, the insurance company compensated everything but then the cheque came two months later. Two hundred thousand pounds." His lips blew a heavy gasp.

"And the van? It just went out of control and your eyesight was blurred."

"It was a strange feeling. Black dots at first then it was like a thin fog in my eyes, and I felt woozy, then, wallop. Nothing." He began to rise. "Sorry, how rude. Would you like a tea, coffee?"

She held up both hands. "No thank you, Mister Carr. You told the police about a letter that came with the cheque. I tell you why I ask." She eased back into the sofa. "Someone else had taken a rather secretive interest in your case to the extent of amassing a large file on your accident and of Doctor Brotherton. It's him I'm interested in. His name is

Humphrey Barrington, a solicitor from Cambridge. Had he talked with you?"

"No." Carr's eyes squinted. "Never heard of him." He rubbed his eyes. "Sorry, I tire easy. It's the medication."

The journalist was good at reading people and John Carr showed truthfulness. He hardly fidgeted even though his back remained a problem. This was an honest man. Open, with nothing to hide. He didn't need to admit to the large cheque. It was nobody's business but his.

"That solicitor died suddenly three days ago."

"No. Wow. How?" Carr's eyes returned to their normal setting.

"Well, me being an open-viewed type, I think it was a planned accident. He was electrocuted while being shown around an apartment. Tried out the shower and bang, gone." Her lips tightened.

"Wow. Well, I never. Why would he have a file on me?"

"I don't know. Seemingly he has been gathering files on many people, but I want to see if there is a connection with you to the doctor and perhaps others he may know."

"I'm sorry but I never knew the doctor and glad that I couldn't see what I did. I've never worked since, I mean employed. I paint now." He pointed to seascapes above the sofa.

Fran's leather gear squeaked on the sofa as she turned to view two paintings.

"You have some talent. They are very good." She turned again to face Carr. "Sell any?"

"Why yes." His eyes brightened. "I've sold a few at the local market and a gallery shop portrays some, even my local hung a couple."

"Do you mind if I take a couple of pics? I know a few collectors." She took out her mobile.

"Not at all. I must point out that I don't do commissions. I paint what I like." He shrugged. "If they sell, well and good."

She stood and clicked the phone at the wall then looked at the results on the screen. "Nice. Are these for sale?"

"No, Fran. My wife would divorce me. They're her favourites."

"Well, you have shone some light." She pushed the phone into a zipped pocket.

"Oh, I just remembered." He straightened in his chair.

"Remembered?" Her eyes widened.

"I sometimes find it hard to recall things. Yes, a few years ago a man arrived here and offered to buy two paintings. Funny thing though, when I asked which ones, he said he didn't mind."

"That's weird," She said. "What's his name?"

Carr rubbed his chin. "Eh—oh, what was it? English or something like

Consideration of Tragedies

that. He said they were for a new premises. Wanted some genuine art, nothing established. A builder I think, or something like that. My head goes sometimes. I have his name somewhere." He began to get up.

"No—it's okay. Would you mind if I keep you informed of anything I may find out?"

"If there is something that would help me discover what actually happened, then yes." Carr stood. "If anyone else contacts me, how will I get in touch with you?"

She took out a wallet then produced a thin card. "Here." She handed it to Carr. "Call or text and leave a message. Don't say what it is about—merely ask me to contact you. If you do remember the buyer's name, let me know. Right, I'll be off—great paintings. Don't be surprised if have to you start buying more paints and canvasses soon."

They shook hands and Carr led her to the front door.

She stepped out under the porch and pushed her hands into the gloves. "Will be in touch, Mister Carr. All the best."

"Great. Drive safe."

Fran's thick thighs straddled the saddle. She put on the helmet, waved a card over the handle, pressed the starter, revved, and noisily pulled away.

**

John Carr waved her off and turned to close the door behind him. "Inglis—that's his name. George Inglis." He held the card. "Where's my glasses?"

30 THE SPECS

Thursday June 28

In a large warehouse on South London docks, Specs bore a rare smile.

"You came good, King. Nice little earner thanks to your info." He nodded to a wiry assistant. "Mouse."

King caught a bulky envelope. "You fucked up, Specs."

"Who cares about a foreign guard? Probably illegal anyway."

"You don't realise what you've opened. The guns can be traced. What a pair of idiots you have working for you."

Belch moved his gorilla frame to King.

"Leave it." Specs waved a hand to his sidekick. "He's right though. Belch, a gun club? Really?"

Specs turned. His smack to Belch's face echoed.

"Well, the usual was not available, boss," Mouse said. "I mean, this was sudden."

"He found them missing—Mike Orpen. He's reported them with all the details." King lit a cigarette and pulled hard.

Specs sat on the lone chair at the table. "Have you anything on him?" He remained calm.

"No. I don't frequent the Tavern and rarely venture near Clapton."

"Bad memories, eh. He's some tough guy, is Freeman. He finished with acting the P.I?"

"Not interest."

"I remember his old man. Shrewd businessman and clean as a whistle. Fair play to him." Specs turned to DC Bell. "Did you join the gun club?

"Yeah, need the extra practice," Bell said.

"He really is a good un, King."

King eyeballed his junior.

Bell shrugged; his mouth screwed up.

"Well, where was I—oh yeah, Ben Freeman sold his business. I should say, I have some fingers in the industrial pie. Good to have some legit businesses, eh. The next project is looming." His full chest proudly extended further.

King tossed the cigarette butt. "You're joking."

Specs eyes widened as he shook his head. "No joke. My source tells me some African country has an order from Ostrofman delayed due to money problems. Ten of boxes waiting in their premises in Cambridge."

"Listen, I've enough on my plate to deal with. The accident, missing guns."

"Shut up, you Mary. I need some more food. Making is better than buying. That young Freeman's parttime P.I business really fucked up that area for me." Specs pulled out a pruned Havana cigar.

Mouse lit it.

Specs took a long drag. The aroma wafted to King's face.

"I need to win back my old stronghold, force him out." Specs tapped the ash.

"That's a laugh." King eyed Bell. "Do you know that Chris Freeman broke Specs' two favourite dealers' legs. No bat, stick or brick. A couple of taps and they were hospitalised for weeks."

DC Bell's brows raised.

Specs hit the table. "I need to send him a message. Use the gym and gun man as a primer of sorts." He pulled hard on the cigar and eased back in the chair. "Funny how Chris didn't mind my younger bro joining the boxing club. So, I can't buy him out. The only way to hurt him is to hit his pals."

The last remark drew attention from King. "Have you heard from Lens?"

"Nah. Suppose he's happy enough in LA or wherever he landed."

Specs' phone interrupted his memory. He picked it up from the table. "Yes? — Ah, my fav info gatherer." He puffed away on the cigar. "Really? You think he'll be a problem? — Okay, I like it. I know you're into that sort of thing." His laugh erupted again. "Well, I suppose don't mock it until you try it. — Yes, I realise the solicitor did some work for you." Specs sat straight. "Oh, that's interesting. Didn't realise that you knew him. — Really? Well, I never."

He looked at King. "Can he be turned? — I know it could be hard, but can he? — He really orchestrated that. Jesus. Why didn't you tell me this before?" Specs paid attention to the long reply. "Probably my fault for not telling you the connection." He laughed. "Got his number?" He snapped his fingers. Mouse handed him a pen and paper. "Okay, got it. Cheers for that, mate. A big bonus for you if it works out. Oh, and thanks for the key. Sorry for the mess."

He hung up and clapped once. "Thing are getting rosy." Specs bore a wide grin separated by the protruding Havana.

31 THE BOSS IS BACK

Late Friday June 29

Chris hadn't announced his arrival back from Dublin. He had entered his pub via the private entrance down the alley and went straight up to his apartment. In the kitchen, he flipped open a tab container lid, filled a glass with water, and washed down two painkillers.

A private chat with his dad hadn't explained the problematic headaches.

He threw his bag onto a sofa, went to the fridge, and took out a cold Pils.

At his desk, he tapped a password into his laptop. *Diary* opened. Staring at a smiling Mary photo on the cover, he tapped the multiple pages dated from 2002. Taking a sip from the bottle, he placed it on the desk and grasped his head.

When is this going to stop?

His eyes closed tight. Seconds passed before they opened. Inhaling slowly through his nose, he held his breath for five seconds before releasing. He calmed somewhat after two more exercises.

His fingers moved speedily along the keyboard typing updates of the last few days. Emphasising the bouts of headaches. He stopped and read over.

It's been a while. Now it's starting all over again.

"Fuck it anyway."

He continued the details, taking sips in between.

Leaning back, he saved and logged off. "Shower then bed."

Alone again.

**

Next morning, Chris unlocked the Tavern's two front doors and pulled the oval window's blinds up. A stream of pre-midday sunlight brightened his pub's interior. At the bar, the morning papers folded neatly and placed into the wire holder on the counter. Beer mats arranged on each table. Outside in the beer garden, he placed matching *An Fáilte Tavern* ashtrays.

Back behind the bar, the obligatory towels removed from the taps. He was open for another day.

Rubbing his smooth chin, he checked the bar clock and looked to the entrance area.

Twelve-twenty. Saturday.

A door squeaked on cue.

"Watchya, Chris. How's Dooblin?"

"Having your usual, Vince?"

"Sure."

"So—awful about Humph. I mean, hardly knew the man but not a great way to go."

"Steve is still in bits." Vince's words remained low. "And Alan hasn't been in for two days."

"Okay. That is strange, unless he's working away again."

Vince took a sip from the glass. "Hey, is your place free to book in Lanzarote? Never there, so Ilsa would like to go."

Chris was always good at reading faces. "You've named the day." His fingers drummed the counter. "You have."

Vince couldn't hold the smile. "Yeah. October twelve." He shook Chris's extended hand. "Not a word to anyone yet."

"No problem, Vince." He looked at the pint. "That'll be—nah. On the house." He patted the postman's shaved head. "Hey, I forgot to tot up all your freebees."

"Cheers, mate. Don't worry, Rory and Alice only looked after us."

Chris brought the Tab book to the counter. An index finger moved down the list while counting the ticks beside each name of GNC members.

His eyes narrowed. "Oi. Pete and Mike had a session Thursday."

"Eh. Well, eh." Vince struggled. He wasn't a tattletale.

"C'mon, spill them."

"Okay. Pockets was in here asking questions." He took a mouthful.

"Fuck. This place has been trouble-free since I bought it. Why was he here?"

"He's on the Humph case."

A front door creaked.

Chris lowered his voice. "Case? What case? Thought it was an accident?" Recognising a customer, he smiled. "Usual?"

"Yeah, cheers. Can you eh—" The customer pointed to the TVs over the bricked fireplace and beer garden door.

"Yes, sure. Racing on both tellies." Chris leaned to Vince. "Well?"

Chris looked to the customer. "Here you go."

The man paid and took the pint to his regular seating area for the racing.

Chris fiddled with TV remotes connecting two racing channels to the screens.

Vince's lips tightened. "Some of Mike's guns are missing. Apparently used in a robbery."

Chris's eyes widened. "What the fuck. Gone a few days and all hell breaks out. Dear oh dear."

Vince shook his head and almost drained the pint. "Well, I don't know and that's all I know."

More customers arrived as the pub's phone rang. Chris picked up the receiver. "Hello, An Fáilte Tavern — Yes, speaking. How can I help you?" He acknowledged the customers while listening to the reply. "He was but I wasn't in the country when the accident happened, Miss Wakefield. I doubt if I could be much help." Another pause and eyebrows raised. "Okay, no problem but I don't want my customers interrogated. This is a pub not a cop shop. — Yes, and you." Chris gently replaced the receiver.

He noticed their enquiring eyes. "Press. Usual gents?" Chris said.

"Please," a customer answered.

"Okay. I'll drop them over." They joined the first customer as Chris read Vince's eyes.

"Another?"

"Is Guinness black?" Vince said.

Chris welcomed their laughter.

32 THE GOOD FINGS

The pub welcomed more Saturday sports regulars as shouts of 'go on ya good fing' and 'move your 'ed' became the normal quotes on another glorious June day.

Alan had turned up and joined Vince. His shoulders slouched, retaining a mournful aura.

Vince nudged him. "Another, Alan?"

"Sorry, yes please." He placed his phone on the counter. "I think I'll pack up Mike's club."

His drinking partner shot up straight. "What's up?"

"Them guns missing and the guard dying."

"How did you know that?"

Chris heard the conversation. He moved to the counter as shouts welcomed another 'good fing' winner.

He stared at the barflies. "You two keep it fucking down."

"Sorry, mate. Two more here," Vince said.

"Okay, but anymore shite about guns and such and you two are out for the night." He moved to the taps and released their preferred beers into pint glasses.

He returned with full glasses.

"Hey, Alan. Some geezer rang Pete about Humph briefcase. Did you hear anything?" Vince asked.

Alan shifted uneasy on the stool. "Well—" He looked around the pub and leaned to the bar. "Andrew, you know, the estate agent. Humph picked up his briefcase by mistake and well, you know. So, he called and brought it around to me."

Chris and Vince shrugged.

"Brought what?" Vince said.

"Humph's briefcase. It's locked. Andrew suggested I have it and pass it on to Pete. I mean, it's personal. Nothing to do with the accident." Alan looked at their faces for assurances. "Well? What do you think?"

"Christ, Alan. You shouldn't have it," Chris said.

"Andrew is still in bits. He didn't know what to do with it."

"And Pete's away for the weekend—anniversary." Vince held a tenner.

An echoed roar of an engine drew the trio's attention.

"Is that a tank?" Vince smiled.

Chris looked at a small security monitor behind the bar.

A small rider in green and red leathers dismounted a motor bike in the alley.

Seconds later, a door squeaked. Heads turned to see an attractive biker, helmet under her right arm, approaching the bar. Her walk confident yet enticing. She pulled the jacket flap open revealing a large cleavage under her V-neck grey T-shirt.

No more shouts of 'go on ya good fing', just silent stares. Even Alan's eyes guided to the stunning sight.

Chris momentarily captivated. He jolted and held his head as if someone poked it. "Gents is the racing over?" he shouted from the bar.

Coughing and muttering, the punters gradually, some reluctantly, returned to earlier conversations and 'good fings'.

Chris focused. "Yes, Miss, what would you like?"

Vince's tenner still waved above the bar. His eyes entranced by her hugging biking gear. Alan merely hypnotised.

"Hello." Her soft upper-class voice not expected. "Well, a cola, please. Is Mister Freeman around?"

"You're speaking to him." Chris stood straight. "Oh, Miss Wakefield, welcome. I didn't expect, well, you know. Hold on." His eyes displayed a sudden interest. "Alan, look after the bar until Alice comes in." He looked to the clock. "She probably won't be long."

No reply.

"Hey, Sherlock."

Alan woke. "Oh, sorry. Eh, sure thing."

Chris looked at Vince. "You've had a few. These are on the house." He finished pulling their pints.

"Cheers, Chris," Vince said.

The tenner returned to his pocket.

"Miss Wakefield, come on through to my office." He gestured to the gap at end of the bar.

Envious eyes followed.

"I'll turn the racing off if you don't want it."

No replies as they averted their eyes again.

He picked up the glass of cola and a cold bottle of Pils.

Miss Wakefield nodded to locals while walking to the end of the counter. She half stopped her stride. Paintings held a sudden interest before following Chris's hand directed towards the office.

He closed the door. "Take a seat. Well, there's only two and this one's mine. Here." He gave her the glass of cola.

She pulled the zip down. "Warm. You have a nice shop. Décor is great."

"Are you a Gooner?" he asked.

"Not a football fan, Mister Freeman."

He quickly averted his eyes. "Okay. So, Miss Wakefield, how can I help, and it's Chris. My dad is Mister Freeman."

He leaned back into the swivel chair. Taking a mouthful from the Pils bottle, he strained to focus elsewhere. Were they strangely connected?

"Eh, call me Fran." Her hazel eyes softened.

Her hands fiddled around in her bag. She took out a notebook and pen.

"I did some digging and thought that you would be a more reliable type to talk to about Humphrey Barrington's accident." She smiled.

He took a deep breath. "You dug info of me. Why?"

"Not much. Learned your family sold Ostrofman and you turned to being a P.I."

"Hobby. Started out of boredom really. But don't indulge anymore."

Bleeding journalists, but wow.

"How well did you know Barrington?"

"Only met Humph on two occasions—Thursday, few weeks ago and Friday night last." He took another swig and relaxed more. His eyes remained fixed to her almost round face. "I flew out Saturday morning."

Her next question stalled. She found her voice. "What was Barrington doing here?"

"Now, don't take me for an eejit." He grinned. "You know full well why he was here."

"Okay, hands up." She gestured the guilty sign. "He had been at odds with his partners over an investigation and pending lawsuits with a few pharmaceutical companies. He began to follow leads on certain persons of interest. I don't know names yet."

He felt her eyes studying him.

"I know your company has a great record and not involved in anything untoward, even now."

Clever woman. She knows how to research.

"Well, we still have a few shares there and in other companies, but no say in company matters. Just free access to cold remedies when needed." He raised his bottle of Pils in salute. "Of course, you would already know that."

"Cambridge keeps coming up as a common denominator along with Germany. Humph, as you call him, had shown interest in a Doctor Brotherton and a—" She opened the notebook and flicked a couple of pages. "A Giuseppe Galiano."

"What was his interest in them? Have they something in common? Mafia?"

"Not Mafia. He was an Italian politician. And yes, they're dead."

Chris' eyes widened. "Humph killed them?"

She almost dropped the cola when laughing and placed it on the desk. "No—Christ, no. Suspicious accidents. And both involved in cancer research one way or other." She leaned back. "How are you with the local police?"

"I get on well with a few."

"Are there any police that can be approached discretely for info?"

"Fran, I'm not used to all this dark industrial stuff. When head of Ostrofman, I dealt direct and not underhanded. I had sources of how other companies were doing and knew of strange deals." He swigged again. "Our research and products were private until proven safe to present publicly."

He swivelled in thought. "Alan Bradford. He may help. He had the hots for Humph and seeing him at the bar, he is really upset."

She wrote the new name down. "He's the man you asked to help out?"

"Yes. A decent sort. Always means well and tries to join in with whatever is going on with the pub."

"So, what can I do?" she asked.

He blew out the side of his mouth. "Are you around tomorrow?"

"Well, I hadn't planned to stay the night." Her eyes widened.

He looked at her. "How far did you travel?"

"Over an hour away." She ran a hand through her hair, eyeing him.

"Alan has a spare room. Buy him dinner and it's yours."

"How do you know he'll let me use it?"

"I'll have a quiet word with him."

"Okay, Chris. I'll chat him up."

Their drinks clinked.

"I may have something that will interest you."

"Oh. What can that be?" Her eyes strayed down his body.

"Humph had a briefcase. The estate agent picked it up by mistake and brought it home. Then dropped it off to Alan."

Why did I tell her that?

Her eyes widened. "Be good to get to that before the police."

"For you perhaps but whatever is in it wouldn't be relevant to the accident. Do you think if the police discover something relating to your interests, they may find more than expected?" Chris sipped from the bottle.

"They may." She looked away. "I don't know."

She's lying.

"Humph could have been onto something bigger." She shifted in the chair.

Chris retained his apprehensive look. "I don't want to be drawn into whatever you are after. Question Alan quietly. Don't push him—he's clever." His eyes withdrew from her stare. "Come, we retire to the bar, and you can small talk Alan."

33 THE INTRODUCTION OF FRAN

The punters had heeded the owner's warning. They treasured their racing too much to risk losing it. Their focus remained on the screens as Fran followed Chris's polite directions to the bar.

Alice's shoulders jerked back.

Chris realised her shock. "Hi, Alice. Fellas, this is Fran, a journalist." He guided the journalist to a spare stool.

"Hello, guys." Fran smiled waving a hand.

"Hi, I'm Vince."

Fran shook his extended hand.

Alan took a sudden interest in the more than opposite sex. "Hello, I'm—"

"Alan? Yes, I know." She released Vince's hand and held Alan's with both of hers.

"Wow." His eyes smiled.

"Now, now, Alan—remember your place," Chris said. "What will you have, Fran? On the house."

She released Alan's hand and sat beside him. "Scotch and orange, ice." She leaned to the bar. "No straw, please."

"That's a new one on me. Scotch and orange for Fran, please." He turned to her. "This is Alice, one of my top staff."

"Hi, Alice," Fran said.

"One of my top staff?" Alice lowered her stare at Chris. "He only has three and one of them is Missus M." She smiled to Fran.

"Well, one has to keep praising them," he said.

He was a natural. Though not flirting, that was not on his CV, he retained that certain Irish charm earned from his parents and generations of countrymen. A long-lost uncle, on his mother's side, was reputed to be the ultimate charmer. Chris epitomised many writers' view of wandering Irish eyes and charismatic attraction portrayed in countless novels and on screen. It suited him. Underneath that façade remained a different man. One ready to explode if he hadn't learned to control that hidden temper.

Alice placed the drink on a bar mat. "There you go, Fran."

A sudden roar from the racing lovers distracted Vince. He glanced at the bar-side clock.

"Shit, that the time? All your fault, Alan—crying on my shoulder." He stirred quickly off his stool.

Alan sat up straight. "What did I do?"

"Fuck. I'm supposed to go to her mum's for tea. Shit." He looked at Chris. "Can I?"

Chris nodded to the end of bar. "Yeah, go on and shut the door behind you."

Vince quickened his step behind the bar and out of the private entrance.

"What's that about?" Fran took a sip.

"He can get to his place quicker out back and over a wall through the courtyard. It's an important meeting if he has to go to tea at Ilsa's mum's." Chris sat beside her. "His partner. Ilsa."

"Yeah, even I would jump the wall if it was me," Alan said.

"That scary, eh?" Fran remarked.

"Listen, Alan, just as well Vince had to go." Chris signalled to Alice to pull Alan another pint.

"Fran has a few questions for you. It appears that your pal, Humph, was a bit of a Nosey Parker."

"He's not—wasn't a pal. Just met a couple of times." Alan emptied his glass as a full one arrived.

Chris moved from his stool and leaned to him. "Fran needs a place to stay for the night. I thought of you, you know, spotless nice place."

Alan eyed Fran and smiled. "Yes, of course, if you like."

"Wow. That was sudden." Fran took another swig. "I thought I was supposed to build up to ask you. Sorry and thank you."

Chris grinned. "There's a large clothes shop up Mare street if you want to have a change of clothes."

"Oh, you are a smart guy, Chris, but I was top in the Guides. Be prepared. I always have a few extras with me. They are safe and fresh in my bike."

Alice turned and attended to a customer at the end of the bar.

"Nice one. So, I will leave you two to work things out. Your bike would be safe in the alley," Chris said. "And Fran, I know I'm on duty but if you want to have a good old East London knees-up here tonight, feel free."

"I may take you up on that offer but only if Alan will be my bodyguard." She nudged Alan.

"My pleasure, My Lady." He bowed.

Chris walked to the bar entrance tapping a known customer on a shoulder while passing. "Excuse me—Alice." Chris took her aside. "A couple more on the house for them both. What?" He questioned her stare. "No, nothing's going on. I just want Alan to be comfortable in Fran's company. See you later. Need to chat with my dad."

Alice nodded and returned to the customer.

Chris had a skip in his step. Something new had happened to him, a sudden tingle down his back. He shivered and grinned when opening the stair door. His head hurt again. Thoughts of departed Mary rushed through

his mind. When the door closed behind him, he stopped, rubbed his head, and climbed the stairs.
What the hell is happening.

34 THE ODD DATE

Fran and Alan walked a little unsteadily to his apartment.
Inside, Alan showed her around.

"Wow, this is fantastic and so spotless. You would make someone a good wife." She broke into a hearty laugh and burped. "Oops, sorry no offence, Alan." She moved a hand from her mouth.

They had talked about his preference.

"That's okay, Fran. I detest untidiness. Makes it hard to find something." He opened the spare room door. "This is yours."

She placed a small holdall on the bed and sat beside it. Her mouth wide open. At last, she spoke. "Alan, this is gorgeous. I do insist that I treat you to dinner tonight. You can drop your invitation to cook."

"But—"

"No buts. Pick a nearby place. Anything and I know you're not vegan."

"Fine, there are a few nice restaurants on Mare Street. Eh, how about Verne's Bar and Grill? Only opens evening time. I can ring now."

"Yes, Alan. Sounds like a good nosh-up place. Sorry again. A few hours in East London and catching the lingo already." She fell back on the bed laughing.

"Are you okay?"

"Yes, yes. Oh dear." She sat up. "Can I have a shower. I promise you that I will be fine afterwards. A brand new Fran."

What am I doing?

Alan had an uncertain look. "Yes, of course. There are fresh towels in there, gels, shampoo."

"Great. I have my own toiletries but no towels. So?" Her brows raised.

"Oh sorry. This way."

She followed him to the bathroom, and he opened the door. "Thank you, Alan. I won't be long."

**

At the Grill, a waiter walked them to an open booth. The 'blue' theme obvious throughout the L-shaped restaurant. Four-person booths ran along two walls from a wide entrance. Around to the right, the tables stood more central on the floor. Kitchen staff hid behind double doors at the end of a service counter.

"This is cosy." Fran looked at prints of famous entertainers decorating the walls. She slid across the mid-blue upholstered seat.

Alan looked troubled as he squeezed along opposite.

"You okay, Alan? We can sit somewhere else." She looked up at the waiter. "Can we?"

Alan reddened. "Well, I would enjoy the meal better if we did." He patted his large stomach.

"Certainly, sir, madam. This way." He brought them to an open seated area near a small bar and pulled out a chair for Fran.

"Thank you," she said.

Alan breathed more easily opposite.

The waiter handed them menus. "Would you like drinks before ordering?"

"I have had enough for now, thank you. Perhaps water?" She looked to Alan.

"Oh yes, I agree. Water would be fine."

"Certainly." The waiter smiled and left them to peruse for their meal choice.

Their picks announced how hungry they were. Both opted to forgo starters and ordered the house special, mixed grill.

She hadn't questioned Alan during their meal. Her interest concerned his short tales of Cambridge, life working at home and abroad in pharmaceuticals companies.

She took a sip of water to wash down a forkful of food. "Alan, I know we said that we would stay away from Humph's interests tonight, but I have a feeling that you're hiding from someone." Her eyes moved to his face. "I'm sorry. He appears to have been on the trail of something. Oh, I don't know, underhand dealings but there are gaps."

He knows something. Or Humph knew something about him.

She concentrated cutting into a small steak. "It's my journalistic nosiness. But did you two meet somewhere before? Perhaps Humph discovered mishaps in a company."

"I have had accidents. Well, I didn't cause them. It was hard then. Many small companies had become envious of the more established—like Chris's father's company. Ostrofman led the way in many medical research projects." His fork pinned a sausage. "I was there for two years, in their German branch, just before it was incorporated into the company. I mean, it wasn't Ostrofman then, it was Kerner Pharmazeutika."

Fran's magic worked. "Oh." Her loaded fork stopped between plate and mouth. "So, you knew Chris already?"

"Yes—well, not really. I don't think he remembers talking to me years ago when I started first. Barely chatted for a minute or on a couple of occasions. Since buying the pub, he hardly talked of his involvement. Although we all know he is wealthy. Very wealthy." He nodded; eyes lowered. "But he never throws it around. Gives out the more than odd 'on the house' at times. But keeps himself to himself. Did you know he has a full members box at the Emirates?"

"What's that? An airline cabin?"

"No, silly. Emirates Stadium. Arsenal's stadium." He chewed his steak and swallowed.

They simultaneously took a mouthful of water.

"He's nice—Chris. I didn't think he was a millionaire. Though I did look him up before contacting him—selling the company and such." She admitted.

"Sorry, but can I ask you something?"

She sat up straight then leaned back. Her beige V-neck T-shirt exaggerated her breasts further. "I suppose you are entitled to."

"How much do you know of Chris?"

Fran tweaked her head left. "Why do you ask? I only did a surface research around Ostrofman, his P.I work. Do you know something?"

"Well, he was married."

"Oh." She returned to cutting into her food. "Well actually I didn't know. I kept away from his personal life."

"She was killed—his wife. A hit and run apparently. And on their honeymoon."

The clatter of her fork on the plate turned a few heads. "Fuck. Oh, excuse my language." She picked up the fork. "How long ago? How did you find out? Did he tell you?"

"I read an article by Brian Purcell in a magazine."

"Him? I know that gold digger. Always after the sensation story. Half of it is made up you know. A tow rag." She stabbed a sausage with a fork.

"Really? He's writing for *Why and How*. Each month he'll be revealing some of his past news stories."

"Huh, you mean other people's stories. He robbed articles off me. Got my big brother to sort him out." She chewed the sausage with a vengeance.

"No way." His eyes opened wide. "When? Did he beat him up?"

Her laugh turned more heads. She nodded to them. "Nosey lot here. No, my brother's a barrister and older sister has a law firm." She took another sip of water. "We took Purcell to court and shut him up. He was fined a pound. We just wanted him quiet. If he printed any more bullshit about us or robs my news stories, a larger fine looms."

"So, what you are saying is all he writes may not be factual?"

"Well—" She screwed her mouth. "Some could be exaggerated. Some could be fake news. I think someone is feeding Purcell stories and he exaggerates them. Claims he is the main investigator."

He appeared to relax. "That's a relief." He forked a mixture of meat and veg to his mouth.

She read him. "Come on, out with it."

"What?" The word disguised in munching.

"You might as well be up front now because I *would* find out if I wanted to. Whatever you are hiding." Her eyes penetrated his.

Alan was trapped by a woman. "He wrote something about the next issue being about certain problems around the hit and run." He chewed another morsel. "I really shouldn't have mentioned it."

"If it's in a magazine, someone was bound to see it—it just happened that you are that someone. Has Chris ever talked about it?"

"Not a word. We know that he's a widower and his father married a younger woman after his wife, the father's, died of cancer."

"Christ—tell me more." She moved hair behind her left ear and scratched it.

"That's all we know of his personal life."

"He has no one in his life now?" Deep breaths.

"Ah, is there interest brewing?" He smiled.

"Shut up. I'm a journalist, so naturally curious." She shifted in the seat. "Do you know that I met Humph."

"No way. When? Where?" His stomach almost straightened in interest.

"Yes, recently on the Broads. That's when he told me of the Tavern and how you all renamed him. I followed him. Well, I knew where he was going and got there a day ahead of him. I have good staff too." The last mouthful waited on her fork. "He was in Chelmsford before arriving at the hotel but didn't talk to another of interest. He was definitely onto something, but I think he was working for someone." The food slipped into her mouth.

"I wonder what he was looking for. Hey, perhaps he was working for Purcell." His large belly puffed out.

"That's a good assumption. Humph's firm represented him. It would suit that fucker—sorry."

"George."

Her eyes widened and mouth screwed. "What? Who's George?"

"George Inglis. He's Chris's best mate and brother-in-law. Chris married his sister. He would know more of what happened. He doesn't talk of Chris's past." Alan pushed empty his plate aside. "Dessert?"

"Why not. My treat." Her raised hand caught the waiter's attention.

35 THE BUSY BAR

Chris remained observant even on full nights. He smiled watching Rory carrying empty glasses as he manoeuvred between standing punters.

"Man, it's busy here tonight," one said to him.

"Sure is." Rory dodged a passing shoulder.

Safe behind the bar, he placed the glasses on a dishwasher tray. "Jesus, it's crazy out there. Did you lower prices, boss?"

"Duo are really bringing them in." Chris nodded to another thirsty customer. "Yes, coming up, sir."

At GNC, Mike was first to notice them. "Well, look at this. Sherlock has a date."

"Hi, Fran, welcome," Vince said.

Ilsa's eyes widened.

"A journalist. She was here earlier to talk with Chris." He coughed. "Hi, Alan."

Alan rocked from Steve's usual welcome thump. "Sherlock, who is this lovely lady?"

They all towered over her, even when seated.

"This is Fran. A friend." Alan took the stools.

"Move up, Muscles," Steve said.

Mike did so as the stools were placed to Ellen's right.

"That's a first." Alan clapped.

The GNC members did the same.

"For you, madam." Alan held Fran's arm.

"Thank you, sir." When comfortable, she slipped her jacket off, moving it under her.

"Ouch." Steve rubbed his side. "What's that for?"

Ellen rested her elbow on the bar. "Your straying eyes."

Alan sat on the newly delivered stool.

Chris' head eased. "So, how was dinner?" He placed their preferred drinks in front of them.

"Thanks — Yeah, it was good. Went to the Grill." Alan raised his glass. "Cheers, Fran."

"Cheers, Alan. You're welcome."

Chris shivered and brushed his head. "So, Fran, settled in then?"

"Yes." Her right fingers swept through her curls and turned to Alan. "He has a gorgeous place."

"You're staying with Alan? Do you work with him?" Ellen's ears were tuned in.

"Babe, did you not hear Vince say Fran's a journalist?" Steve signalled for another drink.

"Oh, I see—going to be in the papers then, Alan?"

"No, Ellen, we are researching for a magazine." Alan took a mouthful from his glass. "Sorry about this, Fran."

"It's okay. I'm usually the one asking questions, Ellen. It's good to be on the other side for a change." Fran toasted Ellen.

The GNC members managed to chat above the musical mixture of the entertainers, and the customers. Chris introduced Fran to all present.

She took greater interest when George Inglis acknowledged her with a nod from the end of the bar.

A giant hand tipped her right shoulder. "Sorry Miss—hi Alan. Would you mind passing my drinks?"

"Oh, certainly, Raz." He picked two pints of frothy lager and watched them almost disappear in the baker's hands.

"Cheers, Alan—sorry again, miss."

"That's ok," she said.

He towered above the punters as he walked back to join his wife, Marge, keeping guard of their precious seats at the pillar.

Fran turned to Alan. "Wow, he's tall and big."

"That's Raz Pringle, the local baker. A gent." Alan moved comfortable on the stool.

"I've heard of him." She leaned into her date. "Humph was interested in him." Her soft voice tickled his ear.

Alan tipped it. "Why?"

"I don't know, but at the hotel before leaving, the nosey barman told me Humph talked to the pastry chef. He asked questions of his family's bakeries and in Clapton." Her drink was low. "You ready for another?"

"My twist." Alan raised a hand. "Rory, same again, please when you're ready."

Rory's index acknowledged the order.

Fran stayed close. "Tell me about George."

"What can I say. He's a top architect. Best pal of Chris, which you already know."

She bent over the bar and turned her head. Brushing her hair back. Fran glanced at George chatting with Chris. His eyes caught hers and she slipped into conversation with Steve and Ellen.

36 THE ATTRACTION

At the end of the bar, Chris had time for a quick chat with his pal.
"What's she after? Your journalist," George asked.
"Something to do with Humph," Chris said.
He nodded to a waiting customer. "Same again, mate?"
"Yes, Chris and a packet of cheese and onion, please," the patient customer said.
Chris pulled the order but was drawn to Fran as if she called him.
She winked while learning more about the pub from the GN and took a curiosity in all of them.
A real journalist. Clever girl.
He smiled to her before placing the drinks in front of the customer and took a packet of crisps from a box. "There you go."
The customer handed him a tenner. "In the box."
"Cheers." Chris took the small change from the till and walked to the chained cancer charity box. He forced the coins through the slit.
He looked around the throng.
"Need a hand?" Fran said.
"It's mad here tonight. My spare, Joanne, is on hols. She sometimes lends a hand when busy." He turned to another order.
Fran tipped Alan. "Excuse me. I'll give Chris and Rory some help."
"You sure? I mean, have you done this before?" Alan asked.
"Yes. Be a dear and look after my jacket and seat."
She took up her bag and leaned on him to move from the stool.
"Yes, Fran."
Her bubbly body reached the bar hatch. "Hi," Fran said to George.
"Hello—have you got an ID?" the joker of GNC asked.
"Why?"
"You don't look old enough to be here."
She laughed. "Not good enough, that chat-up line. It's as old as you."
Chris heard the quip and clapped. "What's up, Fran?"
"You're busy so I'm offering my expertise."
His eyes widened.
Something going on with me. First that Humph character now Fran.
"Well, how about collecting empties first, we're running low. Hold up." He turned to the water taps, rinsed a cloth. "Here, just give the tables a quick wipe."
"Hum, sure thing, boss." Fran smiled.
Their eyes connected. Though the pub buzzed, a moment of silence surrounded them as if they had drifted to another place.

She handed him her bag. "Could you put this somewhere?"

"What? Oh, sure. I'll leave it in the office."

Their hands touched. They both tingled.

**

Fran took no nonsense from punters while picking up empty glasses from beer-stained tables. Most were polite as she moved from each section wiping surfaces with the cloth.

At the hatch, George watched his pal. "You fancy her."

"Fuck off."

He leaned to Chris. "You do." He tipped his arm. "Never seen you like this since, well, you know."

"Christ—every guy sees her, even you and Alan." His eyes followed buxom Fran to the front tables.

"Why did you let Alan put her up?" George touched his glass.

Chris acknowledged his pal's signal for another drink. "This your last?"

"No way, pal. I want to see if anything develops."

A middle finger raised to George as glasses clinked on the bar beside him.

Fran lifted the hatch.

"Mind that step up, Fran," George said. "You stay behind the bar and give me the cloth. I'll collect the empties in the Smokers."

Fran looked down. "Oh, I wondered why they look taller behind the bar." She stepped in. "Thank you."

She went to the tap, rinsed the cloth, and handed to George.

Chris eyed him. His lips tightened. He knew what his pal was up to.

"George said he'll do the tables out in the 'Smokers'. What's that?" she asked her new boss.

"A semi-open beer garden. Some go out front to smoke or in the alley. I get pissed off sweeping the cig butts up."

"Oh. So, who's next?" She had grown taller behind the bar. "Yes, Mike, what will I get you?"

Fran had drawn the pressure off Chris and Rory as punters called orders to her. She passed the requests to the barmen, and they pulled pints. She concentrated on the shorts and bottle orders.

"You're a natural," Chris said while passing. "If you plan to pack up the busy-body biz, let me know."

Her hazel eyes melted him.

**

George watched the 'actions' while pretentiously chatting with Vince and Ilsa.

"What do you think, George?" Ilsa asked.

"Sorry, oh yes. Eh, I don't know how good Unai Emery is. Never heard of him. Won't be near as good as Wenger though."

"No. We've changed that subject. Fran. What do you think of her?" Ilsa took up her glass of gin and tonic. "As bar help."

His mouth drooped. "Fine. She's doing great."

"You should know," Vince joined in. "I mean, you've hardly taken your eyes off."

"Shush. I'm watching Chris. Look at him." George nodded towards his pal.

The couple and Mike turned attention to Chris.

"He's caught," Ilsa said.

"Isn't he just." George took a mouthful from his glass.

"Well, I never. Our Chris." Mike took a sip.

Vince and Ilsa drank from their own.

Soon, GNC members were eyeing the action behind the bar. Rory stationed at the pumps. Chris and Fran moved up and down along the bar taking orders and serving. The attraction obvious.

Alan tipped Steve's shoulder. "She should stay here, not my place."

"Nah. They should take it easy." Steve smiled. "Ouch. What's that for?"

Ellen's elbow returned to the bar counter. "Mind your own business."

Duo announced their break for fifteen minutes.

**

Chris turned from the till. The GNC strangely silent. His eyes pierced each one.

"What's up? More drink?" He waited for replies. "What?" His hands stretched out. "I'm busy."

Their smiles and raised brows gave him the answer.

"Fuck off or you're all barred."

He was saved further embarrassment by a rush of orders.

Chris turned to Fran "This is the last big rush. Some will leave after their last drinks and a few stragglers will come in when Duo start their last session. So, we deal with these thirsty punters and I'm firing you." He smiled.

Another customer waited at the bar.

"How do you do this all night, Chris?" Fran gasped. "I need a drink." She dealt with a customer. "Yes sir, what will I get you?"

Consideration of Tragedies

37 THE TELLING OFF

The music finished along with last orders. Shouts of 'goodnight' and 'thank you' to bar staff from leaving customers woke Alan.

"Ooh." A creak in his neck caught Fran's attention.

"Here, let me." She worked her soft fingers into his neck.

"Sorry. How long was I asleep?".

"Five minutes, mate," Vince said. "We're off, Chris."

"Yeah. See you both next week. See you tomorrow, Vince." Chris walked with them to the door and held it open for them. "Still warm out. Safe home."

He closed the door and returned to the barflies. "A word, Mike."

Mike rocked a little as he followed him to the empty Smokers.

**

Alan watched the pair. "Someone's in trouble," he said to Fran. "What did I miss?"

Her inquisitive eyes stayed on them as they disappeared. "Nothing." She turned to Alan. "You missed nothing. I enjoyed tonight. It has been an awfully long time since I had one." She finished the last of her scotch and orange.

"It has been a long day. I don't normally have two sessions like this in a day. Hope there wasn't too many here when I flaked out."

Fran laughed. "You're a good singer."

"What? I didn't, did I?" His eyes widened.

"No. Just wanted to see your face."

Chris poked his head into the bar. "Rory, give them two on the house and bring me out a gin and tonic and a Pils. Have one yourself if you want to stay."

"Cheers, boss, but I'll leg it soon."

Alan and Fran stared at each other.

"Something's up," he said.

**

Out in the beer garden Mike flopped onto a padded low stool. "Sorry."

Chris stood over him, his face ready to burst. "How I didn't floor you when you entered tonight."

"I know and I wouldn't have reacted if you had." Mike's head lowered.

"I was aware of this pub's reputation from the time me and Dad drank here. Why do you think I got rid of the bar billiards? Every sort of fuckheads came here slipping this and that into palms. The alley was used for everything, sex, drugs, violence."

He pulled up a stool and sat opposite Mike. "Why? Why did you let guns go missing? And involved in a killing."

Mike shook his head. "As it happens, one of the gang has been a member of the gun club for years." He looked up.

Chris read his face. "You were paid."

Mike's silence gave him up.

Chris jerked forward but held back. "Fucksake. Ahh."

A thud reverberated a partition. He massaged his head not hearing the barman approaching.

"Boss," Rory said.

"Oh, thanks. Lock up and use the side door. See you tomorrow, mate. Cheers."

His barman didn't say a word and left them to their discussion.

Chris handed Mike the glass of gin and bottle of tonic. "Here, pour all the tonic in." He took a sip from his bottle. "Lucky for you Pete wasn't here because the two of you would be barred to show who is the boss of this pub. No tow rags anymore. Every fucker will be nosing around and the last people I want back in here are Specs and his sidekicks."

He took a longer swig.

"I gave Pockets a full statement and—" Mike jolted.

His glass bounced in rhythm with Chris's thump on the table. "He's good, we all know that. The best copper this area ever had. This is a clean establishment now; it took a lot of work."

Mike held the glass. "I know and we are grateful for being here."

"You should be. Oh, I don't know." Chris puffed. "What am I to do now? The smell of Pockets around here. Specs will be asking questions, 'what's the interest in the Tavern'." He drank again. "Did you know Pete never drank here until I bought it. Vince rarely and George too. Only home match days for afters drew decent punters. Old fellas were rare and women less."

When the bottle wasn't in his hand, both sets of fingers wiggled as if getting ready for action on a piano.

"Yes, yes. What can I say? It's done and been taken care of. I told Pockets I won't give names and—" Mike struggled.

"You what? You fucking will give them up. A guard died, shot with one of your guns." His voice echoed throughout the bar. He stood and paced around.

Am I losing it?

Mr. Wonderful Mike, AKA Muscles, cowered again. The loud mouth of the local was unusually lost for words. No smart arse quips.

"King—has he been around?" Chris finally broke the short silence.

"No. Pete reckons he is more interested in Humph's death. Asked Pockets to look into it."

"Why? It was an accident."

"I don't know." Mike drank more.

"Jesus. It's King. He doesn't want Pockets getting too close to the shooting."

Mike saw the look in Chris's eyes. "I'm sorry, mate. I never realised this would affect the bar." Mike shifted on the stool. "I've never seen you like this. I mean, I don't blame you. I saw you throwing hard geezers out of here single handed when you first opened." He swallowed his remaining drink. "You kept a cool head. We didn't tell you at the time, but we were impressed. We recognised your stare at unwanted people entering. They just turned and left. Word got around about you."

Chris breathed easier and calmed.

He put an arm around Mike's shoulders. "This was my dream. To own my old man's local and bring real life back to it. Community. Done and dusted, mate. I want to keep it that way. I'll sort Pockets out and we'll discuss King. The DI detests him." Chris stood with bottle in hand. "Now go. Use the side door."

38 THE 'GOODNIGHT'

Fran and Alan shifted on their stools as sullen face Chris directed Mike to the private entrance. The latter strained a smile across his tanned features.

"Sorry, guys. Got a bit animated," Chris said. "Night, Mike."

"Cheers, Chris. Night Fran, Sher—Alan." Mike's shoulders sagged as he disappeared through the bar. The side door slammed shut behind him.

Chris's stare told the last two to say nothing. "Nearly done? Thanks for the help, Fran. How's the neck, Alan?"

"Still a little stiff. Never did that before."

"Vince told me you dropped when hearing of Humph's death." He walked behind the bar and rinsed a few glasses.

Alan screwed his mouth. "Oh, well. It was the shock."

"Like it, Alan. A big shock for all of us—but more for Humph, eh." Chris was pissed off. He looked up from the sink. "And Fran, what did you think of GNC and An Fáilte Tavern?"

"Oh, I don't know. Very, eh, lively. Specially the after entertainment."

Chris raised a finger to her and lowered his eyes. "I may explain some time, but for now, off you trot." He waved a hand to the side entrance.

Alan assisted Fran off the stool and held her jacket.

"Thank you, kind sir."

She eased into the warm coat.

He linked her arm walking through the bar.

Fran stopped, went up on her toes and pecked Chris on a cheek. "Fantastic night. Will I see you tomorrow?"

"You will because I'm taking your bike into the back hall. So, unlock it."

"No need. It won't start without my card. The alarm will go off."

"I know, and I want to sleep."

"Point taken."

She released her arm from Alan, took out a card key flashing it at a spot on a handle. "There you go, boss. See you tomorrow."

Chris kept an eye on them as their steps echoed through the archway. He wheeled the bike into the small hallway.

39 THE POCKETS

Sunday July 1

Chris shaved and showered then made a Sunday morning fry-up before opening. Mrs. M had come and gone with her usual smile. By 11:00 a.m. it was warm again, so sitting outside on the roof in shorts, vest and flip-flops made sense. He perused his phone for news and messages between mouthfuls of sausage, eggs, and bacon.

'Hey Girl Don't Bother Me' announced a phone call.

He recognised the caller. Pockets. "Hey, Bert. It wasn't me. Maybe someone looking like me, but I wasn't there, right." He listened to the reply. "Don't you lot take Sundays off? — Okay, drop around in half an hour. Ring the side doorbell."

Chris shook his head staring at the phone. *This place must be bugged.*

He finished breakfast and carried the dishes through to the kitchen.

In the bar he busied himself with laying out the beer mats on all the tables and setting the Sunday papers. The *Avon Calling* ring tone told him someone was at the side door. He glanced at the monitor to confirm the DI was the culprit.

Pockets Macken appeared unusually unshaved. His hands remained in his trousers.

"Where's your coat?" Chris remarked.

"I'm only around the corner and I do take it off now and then. You gonna leave me standing here?"

"Get in." Chris patted Pockets' back.

Pockets edged past in the hall. "New bike?"

"Not mine. I care for my customers safety." Chris eased the door shut and they moved to the bar.

"Glad you called. I've a bone to pick with you." He pointed to a barstool at the hatch. "Sit. Pint?" He waved a glass.

"Yeah, go ahead."

Chris rested the glass under an ale tap. The liquid poured slowly as he took a can of cola from a fridge and filled a cold glass.

He placed the pint down. "There you go." He sat beside Pockets. "Cheers." Chris took a long mouthful of cola. "Now, the scourge of Clapton, what can I do you for?"

"This Barrington fella, it appears he'd been asking a lot of questions. King wants me to look into his death." Pockets played with his glass, turning it left and right.

"You going to drink that? Get to the point and stop fucking about."

They were on equal terms, both showing regard for the other's station.

"Okay." Pockets took a mouthful and licked his lips. "Barrington had a falling out with his partners months ago over a lawsuit. Seemingly, he'd settled out of court for a client without the partners' knowledge. They got rid of him, but he still traded under their banner. Now a company, one that you were involved in, is being by sued his ex-partners."

Chris leaned back. "Which company?"

"Ostrofman."

"What? Why would anyone sue them in the first place?" He rubbed a hand over his face.

"I know, they're clean. Always upfront." Another mouthful of ale went down. "I met with the present CEO, and it has come to light that an Ostrofman product had been 'diluted' and rebranded by a sister company in Germany. It reached some shelves here before being taken off after two weeks."

Chris' brow raised. *I thought that was stopped and filed.*

"A woman died two days after taking the recommended dosage for a cancer treatment. The diluted product had been somehow contaminated."

Chris' fist thudded the counter.

Pockets jerked. "I'm sorry to bring it up, Chris, but your dad is good, and I know what you two went through before your mum died." He rubbed Chris's back. "Barrington was researching someone or perhaps more. Why here in Clapton? Come on, mate. I need help with this."

Chris breathed slowly and calmed. "I'm out of that game." He turned sharply.

"You are best for this. You still hold a licence don't you? You know your old companies. Who the fuck was he after?"

"Humph has—had means. It wasn't money. He wore an Ulysse Nardin watch. Christ, I wouldn't even buy one of those. Anyway, I'm out of the P.I. biz."

"Just snoop. Use your specialised skills."

"What if I do some digging, you know, ask a few old colleagues." He checked the bar clock.

Pockets lowered the remaining ale. "Who's upstairs?"

"No one. Let's stick to what we are talking about." Chris knew he wouldn't let up. "Okay, The owner, she's a journalist, is staying at Alan's. I couldn't leave such a classic in the alley, the bike."

"Sherlock's? Come off it."

Chris got off the stool and grabbed Pocket's empty glass. "True. When I've found out more about Humph, I'll let you know about Alan's mystery guest." He waved the glass under the tap.

Pockets nodded.

"Your bestest pal gave you the file on Humph." Chris placed the full glass on a beer mat.

"Cheers. Yes, King's up to something."

"Something else on your copper's mind? We have Humph, King and you haven't mentioned Mike yet. How many free pints do you think you can get out of me?" He sat.

"Hands up." Pockets showed his palms high. "I know Mister 'Wonderful' Mike Orpen had nothing directly to do with the robbery, but you're right about King. He's trying to lead me away from that case." A sip moved the ale down the glass. "I tell you what we'll do. You get info about Barrington, and I mean real stuff. That will leave me free to look into whatever that fucker King is up to. The father of his driver, DC Bell, was a good pal of Specs."

Chris's eyes widened. "No way."

"Yes. Some say Specs was *too close* to both parents. They were chums before marrying. I think the lad is looking for an easy track to promotion, like his boss."

"One favour, keep Pete out of this for the moment. A promotion is coming up. King is hell bent on keeping good coppers down the ranks."

"Pete does deserve it. What about you? You must be well overdue." Chris finished his cola.

"Desk job? No way. Audrey would like it of course but there is a need to keep the younger ones on their toes and on the streets. They learn nothing about people behind a desk." Pockets finished his pint. "I admire you, Chris. Loads of dosh and working in this area. I know you don't need to. Why?"

"Done it all. The world. This is perfect, real people instead of those annoying meetings and sycophantic suit-types. I still like to research, though. Real nosey, should've been a copper." He chuckled.

"You were a good P.I, though part-time. Let's get those fuckers. Your lot, the whatever suit-types, and my lot, the bent bastards, and Specs-types."

Chris smiled as their glasses clinked. "Another? How's the missus anyway?"

40 THE LATE INVITE

The afternoon had been relatively quiet. The good weather drew families and couples to parks and other outdoor activities. Pockets made an early exit before getting too comfortable with on-the-house ale.

Fran arrived to collect her bike.

Chris assisted. "So, Fran, did you learn enough from Alan?" He guided the machine into the alley.

"You're holding back something." She zipped up her jacket. "I must tell you this. I heard Humph talking about you."

His brows creased. "What you on about?"

"I bugged his briefcase."

"What?" He grabbed her left elbow, looked around and leaned to her. "You need a licence for that. You're nuts." He chuckled.

"Well, I sat in good company last night then." She forced herself free. "I can't talk now about it, but we need to get that briefcase open. He was going to use you for info. He suggested you would be a great source due to your pub."

He let out a heavy sigh and paced under the arch. "Okay." He raised his eyes to the Tavern's security camera then turned his back. "I'm onto something but working with a good cop. Humph is complicated and others, not so nice as me, are more than interested in him."

"Who? What do you mean?"

"Go home, do what you have to do, and come back tonight. It will be early closing. I'll sort out the briefcase with Alan."

Fran's shoulders straightened. "Really?"

"Yes. You scratch my back and I'll—forget it. We work together on this, you get your story, I get my quiet pub life back. End of." He smiled.

"Okay. No strings, just chat about Humph et cetera."

"Yes but forget about the et cetera. At, say, seven."

"Fine." Fran once again straddled the bike and donned the helmet.

The camera didn't pick up her pursed lips disappearing behind the black visor.

He winked and cringed as the engine reverberated noisily out to the road.

41 THE GUNS PROBLEM

Alice's nod ensured Chris that all was under control behind the bar. Closing the door in his office, he pressed a name on his phone.

"Pick up," he said into the phone. "Ah, Alan. — Yes, it's me. First, thank you for assisting Fran — Thank you. Now, listen, it's eased off here so I'm going around to pick up the briefcase." He listened to Alan's worries. "No, I know a guy that can open it, okay. — Shut up and listen. Humph made recordings and apparently, he had an interest in you — Fucksake, not that kind of interest. Investigations." He shook his head. "Also, he may have been looking at others here and around the area. Fran has agreed that we look at the contents, determine what's relevant, then hand over to Pockets." He raised eyes to the ceiling listening to Alan's muffled moaning. "Right, we'll tell you and others if there is info about them — yes, and you. I'll be around in about ten minutes."

**

Chris didn't linger at Alan's. He sauntered back to the Tavern through the private side door. With the briefcase in a black refuse bag behind him, he peeked into the bar. The pub had a few customers.

"All good, Alice?" He saw Mike at the bar. "Watchya, Mike."

"Yes, boss." She eyed Mike. "Boring really."

Mike didn't get the hint.

"Okay. Back down in a jiff. Tot up your end and you can leg it when I'm back." He was gone and didn't hear the 'thank you' or see her smile.

He left the package on the kitchen counter and returned to the bar.

"Okay." His quick hand clap echoed. "All done, Alice?"

"Yes, boss."

"Great. Off you trot. Enjoy the sun while you can."

Alice picked up her shoulder bag and said her goodbyes to the few remaining customers and Mike.

Chris checked the till count and turned to the bar. "Any thoughts, Mike?"

Mike remained in a dream world twisting his almost empty pint glass left and then right. "Sorry?"

Chris leaned on the bar facing him. "About our little chat?"

"I was in the club earlier. The guys will lock up. I got the address of that member we talked about."

"Ah, good. Because Pockets was here and we had a nice chat about what could be our mutual problems." He bent closer, though no one was nearby. "I know of Specs and—"

Mike sat straight. "What? He's involved? Fuck." He finished off the pint.

"Hold on, relax. It's King. We—Pockets and I, concur that King gave him a file on Humph to keep him busy. Keep the best DI away from your gun problem." He went to the beer taps, took up a pint glass and let the ale flow in. "By the way, you're off the hook. Pockets realised you wouldn't be involved directly."

He placed the full pint in front of Mike.

"Cheers. So, what's going to happen now?" Mike's right hand almost wrapped around the glass.

"Well, I'll keep my eyes open. You keep me informed of everything relating to the robbery, no matter how small. Give me the address of your 'member'."

Mike looked around the bar and slid a folded note from a shorts pocket. "There you go. He's not in this parish. He's Shoreditch. You back in business?"

Chris eyed him and unfolded the note. "Specs' area. Still close enough. I'll tell Pockets. Oh, any word on a young DC Bell?"

"Have a Tony Bell in the gym." He took a sip. "Joined about two months ago."

"Hum. Has he shown interest in the gun club?" Chris was distracted and turned to the front door. "See you, lads. Cheers." The door creaked shut behind the customers.

"Do you know what? He has. I believe he filled in a form last week. Helen mentioned it." Mike stared at Chris. "You don't think he's the same Bell?"

"Check his forms tomorrow and get back to me. This will blow things wide open for Pockets if he's the DC. He really would love to have something on King." He went through the counter hatch. "Could be nothing. He could be just a cop that wants the easy track."

Mike winked. "You *are* back in business."

Chris didn't reply. Empty glasses clinked as he collected from a table. A front door creaked, and Rory walked in.

"Nice timing. Heading upstairs for a while, Rory. If it gets busy, give me a bell," Chris said.

"No problem."

Chris disappeared toward his private apartment.

42 THE BREIFCASE

Chris pulled the reddish-brown briefcase from the refuse bag and laid it on the coffee table. His hand caressed the smooth double gusset Tuscan leather. A release button rested between two combination dials on the flap. Its palladium hardware protected any valuable items from rust or mould.

Wow, even I wouldn't have bought one of these.

He examined the strap handle on top before turning the dials hoping to accidentally find the combination. Chris eased back on the chair.

It's heavy. Maybe a laptop and files inside. Strange scratches on the handle's rivets, though. Humph wouldn't have misused such a valuable briefcase if he bought it.

He rubbed his chin as framed wedding photos smiled at him.

Birthday?

He looked to the photos. *What you reckon, Mary? Would he use a birthday for a combination like you? Too obvious. Parents' birthday? Home number and something else?*

His eyes willed the lock to open.

Can't be more than four numbers. Alphabet? I can't keep fiddling with it. Okay, I could simply move each dial until hearing a click. Nah. Must be something closely connected to him—or not. I know fuck all about Humph. Defo nothing to do with Arsenal.

He rubbed his chin.

What do I know of Humph? He's a solicitor. Worked for a company. C'mon Chris—you're good at conundrums. Didn't Humph say he can be forgetful.

He stared at the briefcase again. His shoulders jerked when it hit him. "Chadwick, Darling and Barrington. C D B. Three four two. Humph—H is eight."

His fingers worked the first dial: three, four. Then the second: eight, two. He compressed the button. Nothing. Chris tried two, eight on the second dial. Click.

Bingo. What a brain.

He held the flap back to reveal a brown file and a laptop. In the smaller compact pockets were pens, a mobile, note pads, business cards, a digital voice and telephone recorder and charger. No bug.

He took out one of the black moleskin note pads. Flicking the pages, he saw names, phone numbers, dates, references to each marked in red ink.

"I don't believe it." Chris' hands raised. "Passwords. He was forgetful. What a plonker."

He removed the file. His eyes widened at the name. *Chris Freeman.*
Inside, photos of him, the pub and a few references to his father's companies outlined in red. *Fran was right.*

His eyes trained on the recorder.

He stood, walked to the desk, opened his laptop, and slipped the recorder into a USB port. His own pre-programmed scanner ensured that the new device had no viruses. He took up the plugged-in earplugs and listened to the last messages. His mouth and eyes wide open as he lightened to Humph voicing opinions about certain characters. He stopped the device and removed it, resting the earplugs on the desk.

A lot of rushing around, water and thumping. Fran must hear this. Perhaps there is something on it compromising me in all this. Using me, indeed. Cheek.

He logged onto *Diary.* His fingers engaged in vigorous typing. Bringing all facts and 'need to knows' to his private pages.

I may hold back further. Plenty of time. Just make a note.

He continued updating.

43 THE CONCERNED BAKER

Finished his short investigation, Chris returned to the bar.
He went to the till. It rattled open.
Rory stood beside him out of earshot of Mike. "You okay, boss?"
He sighed. "Yeah. Just tired. Fran will be here later." He glanced at the bar clock. "Oh, pretty soon actually. Didn't realise the time. So, could you manage alone for a couple of hours?"
Rory stood back; smiling eyes widened.
A large shadow caught Chris' attention. He turned to a customer. "Raz, what can I do you for?"
The baker's face was drawn, worried. "Can I have a word in private, Chris?"
"Sure. Come through to the office." He waved to Marge sitting at a pillar.
She smiled and nodded.
"Do you two want a drink?" Chris asked him.
"Please, the usual." Raz stepped behind the bar.
"Rory, give Marge a glass of Pinot Grigio." Chris pulled an ale tap. "Go through, Raz. I'll bring this in."
Chris joined the baker in the office handing him his pint glass. "Sit, please."
Raz moved to the second chair.
Chris sat observing his furrowed brow.
"Who the fuck was this Humph character?"
Chris jerked back. "Wow. What happened?"
Raz took a long mouthful and wiped his beard. "My cousin in The Wroxham called me a while back you know, Nige."
"I know Nige, great baker." He managed a smile.
"Well, Humph was there asking questions. Then he turns up at my shop praising this cake and that as if he knows me. Asks about Noel too."
"Listen, I can't tell you much, but you remember Alan's 'date'?"
Raz nodded.
"Well, she's a journalist looking into Humph's business. Something fishy about him. Blowing hard about Arsenal yet not knowing what a Gooner was."
"I see. Are you doing your P.I thing again?"
"Eh, not really."
"I don't wish ill of the dead, but Humph annoyed me asking of Noel and Rome."
"How is the big guy?"

"We haven't heard from him in years. Just the odd recipe emailed up to about four years ago, I think. Supposed to have gone to America from Paris but turns up in Rome. Then no more news or recipes. It's funny how you met him before opening this shop."

"That was years ago, before the company was sold. Weird. You in touch with Agnes?"

"Yeah, a while back. She hasn't heard from him either."

"And Humph asked of him? Leave it with me and I'll tell Fran."

He stood.

Raz followed suit. "Cheers, mate. I won't tell Marge yet. Get back to me if you find out more."

"You hiring me?" Chris chuckled.

"I didn't mean—"

"Get outa here." He followed Raz to the bar.

"You're a gent, Chris. Cheers again." Raz's long strides had him sitting beside his petite wife in seconds.

A front door creaked open.

Chris checked his watch. *Right on time.*

44 THE DEN

Chris' wide smile must have been obvious as Fran approached the bar. "On the button, Fran," he said.

She removed her shoulder bag. "Oh, I see you do wear a watch."

He eyed his right wrist. "Had to keep an eye on the time. Was expecting company."

"A Rolex, no less. Did you get that down Cockney Hooky Street?"

"Off the Trotters? No fools and horses here, Kid. So, you watched the telly today. Repeats."

"Just trying to get in with the local lingo, Guv."

"That programme was based around Peckham, no way genuine Cockney. One has to be born near the sounds of Bow Bells." He organised her drink.

"I didn't know that. I thought all East-Enders were Cockney."

He placed her preferred scotch and orange on a mat. "Cocky, yes." He managed a quick wink across to Raz.

Chris leaned forward to Fran. "I've a surprise for you upstairs."

Jesus, that came out wrong.

Her eyes widened. "Wow. This is quick."

He smiled. "Naughty. Something about your investigation. Show you later."

Fran looked around observing the few customers. "It's not busy."

His hands raised high. "Okay. Come through." He turned to Rory. "If there's a mad rush, bell me. Wipe that smile off."

Ice crackled in her glass as she picked it up.

"Take your time, boss." Rory wiped a glass.

Fran reddened as she passed through the bar to the office carrying her drink and bag. Chris followed.

"No, through here." He held the private stairs door wide.

"Oh, privileged I'm sure."

The door closed softly behind him.

"Nice, isn't it." Her small sultry figure teased to the top step.

"I do have eyes. Nice shorts. Turn right."

She stopped on the landing in front of a white panelled door displaying *Conference Room*.

"What do you do in there?" Her voice playful.

"Used for club meetings and small party gatherings." He stood on the penultimate step.

She stepped into the Den. "Wow. Impressive. And I thought Alan's place was cool. But this—" Her eyes focused on an object resting on the coffee table. "The briefcase."

He reached her side. "Sit, please." His hand directed her to a sofa.

Taking two pairs of surgical gloves, left over from his P.I days, he pulled the coffee table nearer. Chris handed Fran a pair and sat opposite on the other sofa.

"Best put them on." Chris slipped his hands into the gloves and unlocked the briefcase.

"That was quick," she said. "I didn't see the numbers."

"And you won't. Where do you want to start?"

Fran's hands and eyes itchy with anticipation. "I don't know." She looked up. "Notebooks?"

"Good choice." He handed the first one over.

He watched her eyes and expression as she read through it. His concentration slipped to her body as she breathed slowly, delighted at what she read. Something about the woman had affected him. Not her perfume or bubbly body, an aura seemed to surround them. Her purple V-neck sweater bulged in the right places.

"Excuse me. Need a drink." He stood but she hadn't looked up.

Safe behind the private bar, he took a Pils and glass from the fridge. "What do you think?"

"Wow, Chris. He was mad. Imagine keeping all the passwords in this." She looked up. "Did you open the laptop?"

He shook his head.

Fran reached into the briefcase.

"Are you going to tell me?" He poured the lager into the glass.

"Tell you what?"

"Where the bug is."

"Two were planted. I figured if Humph found one, he wouldn't be concerned about another and keep chatting."

"He found it. So, where is the real one." Chris walked back to the sofa with his cold pint glass. "No, let me guess." He sat. "Clever." He smiled. "It's in the handle."

She sat straight; his eyes wondered. "How did you know?"

"Scratches on the rivets."

"Would you have a—"

Chris raised a finger. "Yes, I have a hand rivet tool."

He went to the kitchen area, pressed a button under the counter rim and a panel slid open. He removed the tool from the assortment of items neatly stored in the compartment.

"How come you have that?"

"Ah, come on—P.Is always have spare tools."

"So, you're not finished."

"It's not under my name. Had a couple doing most of the running around." He returned to the task. "Now. Let's see what we got."

The handy device pushed a rivet through and released one end of the leather strap handle. The minute bug fell to his open palm. "You want this for anything else?"

She stayed wide-eyed at him "Why don't we leave it in it? Battery's good for years."

"Good idea. I mean, we'll be handing it over. Never know what we pick up in the evidence locker." He grinned. "Now, I have freshly made salad, cold meats to enjoy while we look at the laptop or listen to the recordings. Your choice." He walked to the kitchen.

"Laptop."

"I charged it up and haven't looked at it, so all new to me too." Taking off the gloves, he removed food containers from the fridge to the breakfast counter.

"We can sit outside or here. Again, up to you. Have more gloves in the box. Don't want our dabs on everything."

"Outside?" Her head turned to the open window. The lace curtains gently fluttered.

"Yes. Table just for two and shaded."

Her interest whetted, she stood and peeked through the curtains. "Very nice. Yes, outside would be cool."

"Okay. Put what you want on a plate, grab your drink and we'll start." He pointed to the plates and cutlery.

She looked up to the canopy. "You like to let the world know you follow Arsenal."

He smiled. "Oh, the *Gunner* sign. And why not."

As they settled themselves outside, Chris positioned the laptop so they could both view the screen.

"It looks nice out here and still warm." She fingered the top of her V-neck.

He opened the laptop. "You have the password, so, off you go."

Her digits typed rapidly, and the screen started showing a large manor. She looked at him for permission to search.

He nodded.

They sat eating, chatting, and often gobsmacked at what they observed.

Fran's hands covered her face at times viewing some disgusting material.

They realised Humph was working for someone. But no information or file found of the person. Amazingly, for such an educated man, the solicitor wasn't IT literate. He had many files and sent them via email to another address.

"I thought he was looking into industrial espionage," she said.

"Obviously there are several investigations. Many appear linked. We should copy onto a hard drive then hand the laptop over." He forked the last mouthful from his plate.

She stood and collected the dishes.

"What are you doing?"

"It's okay. Just clearing the table."

"I suppose we can move all this inside." He took up the laptop, notebooks and laid them on the coffee table.

He watched as Fran ran the tap and placed the dishes in the sink. He hadn't had real company for years. Joanne used to stayover after a late closing or three, but they had a mutual agreement; no strings attached. The travel agent had one concern regarding men, getting Harley back and disregard the age gap. Chris knew that; therefore, they both served a purpose for each other when needed.

Now something unusual was happening. Fran was different. Not pushy like some frustrated vixens coming on strong in the bar while their partners ventured out for a smoke and the like.

The cold water rinsed off the suds. "You're quiet." She took out a plate.

"So, are we finished with all the info from this? It is shocking, I know. Nobody wants to be reminded that underage sex and child trafficking is still rampant."

She dried her hands and sat opposite him. "Did you listen to the recordings?"

"Some. I think you should do that. After all, you planted the bug." He glanced at her. "I can put them onto the hard drive too."

"Yes. That would make sense." She rolled her eyes. "I'm actually waiting for my tech guy to send them to me. He's hopeless."

Chris worked his magic expert skills, transferring relevant files to a hard drive. He placed a personal password into it.

**

An hour later all necessary work was done. Chris leaned back in his chair and cracked his fingers. "I deleted my info from the laptop."

Fran nodded. "Very clever. Are you sure it's gone?"

"Yes. No info of me." He stared at the screen. "Did you ever get a feeling about a name? I mean not familiar but a name that hits you. 'Where did I see that before' sort of name?"

"I know what you mean. Who is it?"

"Douglas Cartwright." He purposely drew her attention to the name. "I've been all over the world and met hundreds of people and never met again, you know, business investigating. Important ones I note but this name rings a bell." He stared at the monitor.

"It'll pop out at you. Perhaps during the night or at a match." She took up a notebook flicking the pages. "Here."

He took the notebook.

"Told you. But there's more about the name." His lips tightened trying to squeeze out a forgotten memory. "No, gone. Forget it. Listen, we pack this up, shove it in my safe for later."

Her eyes brightened. "Later?"

"You know what I mean. We get back to the bar." He checked his watch. "Christ, ten to nine." He looked at her. "Front door or through the bar."

"What do you mean?"

"Your entrance." He walked to the bedroom carrying all the material.

"Shall I link an arm?" She collected her phone and placed in the bag.

"Bar and no linking." Came the muffled reply from the bedroom. "Just getting something decent on. I mean, shorts, T-shirt, and flip-flops not good for an owner of a top-class joint."

"Okay. I'll use the bathroom if you don't mind."

"All yours." He closed his bedroom door.

45 THE POWER PUNCH

George almost fell off his barstool at the sight of Fran walking through the bar from the office area.

Chris grinned. "Close it, George."

His pal's mouth shut tight.

"Hi, George. Nice to see you again." Fran slipped past him to a stool beside open-mouth Alan.

"And you, Alan. Hi, Mike." Chris walked to the spirits' shelf. "Usual, Fran?" He grinned.

"Of course. You are really getting to know me." Her fingers ran through her hair.

George coughed, spluttering drink over the bar in front of him.

Chris turned to the sound. "Now look what you made George do, Fran." He picked up a cloth. "Can't bring him anywhere."

He wiped the counter and handed George a tissue from an ever-present box on the bar. Sunday bars shut at 10:30 p.m. so no mad rush to the bar yet.

"Sorry, mate." George wiped his face and threw the tissue in a waste bucket inside the bar.

Fran tittered, along with Alan.

He leaned to her. "Any luck with the briefcase?"

"Couldn't open it," she said.

Chris winked when handing Fran her drink.

Alan's demeanour faded to despondency. "Oh. Rather hoped there would be something exciting in it."

"Never mind. Probably nothing anyway." Ice rattled as she shook the glass to ensure a good mix.

"I'll give the briefcase to Pockets." Chris looked right.

George stood and headed for the gents, phone in a hand. Fran noticed the sudden act and took a sip while staring at Chris.

He shrugged.

Seconds later, a door quickly creaking open drew his interest.

Two men burst in. Specs' sidekicks, big Belch, and wiry Mouse. They focused to the end of the bar. The few regulars fixed their eyes at the unwelcomed pair.

Rory fingered an old baseball bat under the counter.

Chris didn't wait and limped from behind the bar as they approached.

Mike jumped from his stool; fists clenched.

"Oi, Orpen, outside," Belch roared.

Chris' hand rested on Mike's shoulder forcing him to his stool.

"Yes, gents. How may I help you?" Chris' soft smile affected their immediate intent.

"None of your biz, mush." Mouse moved to Mike.

Customers rose from their seats and approached the *discussion*.

Chris raised both hands in front. "Now look what you've done." He stood an arm's length from Belch. "They are about to leave. I'm losing punters. If that happens, how will I pay my staff? Will you two help out or leave?"

Alan stood in front of startled Fran.

George emerged from the gents eying the confrontation.

Belch didn't take the advice.

Chris raised his left arm in front of the bulk, fist folded.

"Really, mush? You think your hand is going to stop me getting past you?" His laugh matched Mouse's.

Chris fixed his good leg firmly on the floor.

Belch took one step forward.

Only an inch from the big man's face, Chris' fist smashed into Belch's jaw.

He tottered back, knocking Mouse over a small stool. The power punch copied and studied from Chris' boyhood hero, Bruce Lee. A punch many fans thought was a film stunt.

George joined his pal as Mike walked to the fallen pair. He dragged Belch by his black t-shirt towards the side door. Alan arm-locked Mouse. With George's assistance, moved the struggling intruder outside.

"Cheers," Chris said to his other customers. "What a pub, aye."

Fran sat stiffly. Her eyes barely moved throughout the short movie-like scene. Alan had blocked her view of the magic punch.

Chris twirled a finger. "Rory, drinks all round." He followed the exodus to the alley.

**

Belch and Mouse struggled to free themselves from firm grips. They were dragged and roughly dumped under a courtyard lamp.

Chris stood over Mouse. "That's my pub. These are my customers, friends. I couldn't give a toss about your chicken-livered boss. Times have changed." Chris nodded to Mike.

Mike's right foot crunched into Mouse's jaw.

Alan turned away from the sight.

George 'bravely' stood beside Chris.

"Now, mush." Chris leaned over Belch. "You go tell Specs I'm not King. This place is clean, and your type aren't welcome." He read the big man's fear in his eyes. "If I see a stray match, smell of petrol or any harm come to my acquaintances, even by a real accident, well, I know friends of friends that would eat Specs for breakfast and have you for dessert."

Another nod and Belch recoiled from Mike's kick to the groin. The sidekicks' whimpers echoed.

George cringed at the scene. He looked out of the alley, then quickly eyed down.

Chris grabbed groaning Belch up. "Now pick up your pal, fuck off, and cry to Specs. You haven't got far to go because he's parked outside PP's bookies."

The four waited as Belch struggled with Mouse through the archway. Chris followed down the alley raising a finger towards a blue Ford.

Specs slammed the steering wheel, mouth moving rapidly expressing unheard words towards him.

George's head remained down.

46 THE TALE FROM GEORGE

Chris walked into his office as the others went to the bar.
He sat, head in hands. *What the fuck has just happened?*
He looked at a small cut on his middle knuckle. Taking a tissue from a box on his desk, he cleaned the wound.
He threw the tissue into a metal wastebin.
Jesus. What must Fran think?
Chris stretched his fingers, stood, and went to the bar. He smiled at the seated punters apologising for the disturbance and congratulating them for their bravado.

**

Fran watched him.
There's more about this man.
His unfussed manner deserving of the customers' gratitude for changing the once outlawed pub.
"That's only the third time in my four years here Chris has cleared the pub of trouble," Rory said.
Fran jerked. "Sorry, what?"
"Chris. There has never been a huge fight in here since he took it over. So I've been told."
She glanced over at Chris again.
"He earned respect of the locals, and they came flooding back. No more brawlers knocking over drinks. No rucks outside after closing. The two other incidents were drug related." Rory noticed her looking at the bat. "Sorry." He placed it under the bar. "Never used. It would probably split."
"Drugs, you say." She took a longer mouthful eying Chris.
"Yes. Both times two guys came in trying to deal. The place was packed. But Chris spotted punters shaking heads at the dealers and he removed them on his own. Days later, two others came in. They didn't see Chris, so they began pushing a few auld people near the door. He snuck out the side door as I picked up the bat. He came at them through the front door, dragged them out to the alley. I saw it on the monitor. He battered them, without a bat." Rory spotted Chris's hand wiggle for another round of drinks.
"He doesn't need a doorman, even when he's not here. The auld customers take care of all that." Rory began making up the orders. "Sort of gratitude towards him."
She played with a curl hanging above her eyes.

**

Chris reached the bar. "All done, lads? You okay, Fran?"

"Yes. I've never seen anything like it, Bruce." She rubbed his left hand.

"Funny. Pussy cats really. They work for Specs Morgan. He was outside in his car watching so had to put on a show for him."

"He'll retaliate. You made him feel small. Is it Bruce Lee or Bruce Wayne?" She looked at him. "The latter had loads of money too. You're the Batman." Fran turned to Rory. "And Robin here was ready for action."

"Nice one, Fran." Chris patted nearby George on the back. "Cheers, mate and you too, Alan."

Alan sat without a word. His hands shaking too much to pick up a glass.

Fran held them down until they eased.

"I was never so scared. I mean, I'm no hero but had to stand in front of you, Fran." He turned; face still pale. "Will they be back?"

Mike stood beside him and patted his back. "Well done, Alan. Proud of you, mate."

Customers stared wide eyed at the bar. A pin could be heard.

Mike had praised Alan Bradford, Sherlock, the man of ridicule and put-down comments. His smile disappeared while looking at the stunned silence.

"What?" he asked.

All stood and claps echoed.

"Fuck off." Mike reddened at the praise and sat on his stool.

Rory placed his pint in front of him as the clapping eased.

Chris's arm moved around Mike's shoulder and leaned in. "I was going to bar you for a while. You know, keep the trouble away. Show Specs that this is my pub. But what you just did changed that. Well done." Chris straightened up.

"I'm sorry, mate. This is down to me," Mike said.

Mr. Wonderful, AKA Muscles, was like a whimpering pup. The pint glass shaking in his hand.

"They won't be back. Now, drink." Chris turned to the customers. "When leaving later, make sure you leave all together just for tonight."

'Cheers, Chris', and other various forms of 'thank you' were expressed to him.

He breathed, relaxed, and went behind the counter. He viewed their faces. Many remained calm and returned to their conversations without a care. Fran, Mike, and Alan chatted about the events. But George, the joker of the GNC, remained quiet, gazing at his glass.

**

Chris moved to the far end of the bar to keep way from their little chat. Alan and Mike bonded of a sort. Rory ensured all were taken care of.

Fran caught Chris's glance and the tic of his head.

She realised his hint and moved beside George. "Are you okay?"

He woke from his trance. "Oh, Fran. Yes. Just not used to that sort of thing."

"Chris handled it very well."

"Yeah, he did. Never allowed any trouble to get out of hand here." He took a sip from the glass.

"He wasn't always calm and collected." George took a longer mouthful. "Great guy though. Always caring. Probably too much."

"What do you mean? I think he's a gentleman. One wouldn't think he came from around here. And no way acts as if he's loaded," she said.

"That's him alright. He can take the floor or stand in the background. He hardly brags about himself, but he withdrew years ago after the accident, well one would." George fixed on Chris.

She noticed the unusual change of look. Another viewpoint needed. "What accident?"

"Sorry, he never talks about it. No one here knows the details." He stopped and breathed deep. "They know that his wife, my sister, died, but not aware of how." His head hung low.

"Oh, dear. I'm sorry that I asked. Forgive me. We drop the subject." Her voice comforting.

"No, it's cool." George faced her. "A tragic accident on their honeymoon. Two thousand and two. A car drove through a pedestrian crossing mowing them down with another woman." His lips visible tightened. "Gloria. It's funny how life can turn out."

"Chris' step mum?"

"Not then. She stayed in touch with Chris' family afterwards. Uncle Ben, Chris' dad, paid for Gloria's care, then later, treated her and her pals to a holiday as compensation of a ruined holiday."

"Wow. You can see where Chris gets his caring qualities from."

"I suppose so. Me and sis were always close. He and Mary were childhood sweethearts. Well, I knew him from school. I never had any real mates, until we began to hang out at our houses. Went to Arsenal matches. Our families became close. He grew closer to Mary, though." He stared at Chris again and took another mouthful. "Rory." George wiggled a hand for another drink.

"And me too, Robin." She winked at the barman.

George continued. "We boxed you know. Same weight before teenage years but he filled out more than me then I took up football. Chris was good at it too but preferred boxing. Started moving like Ali and Bruce Lee—as you saw. Show boating. I recall him battering an Irish boxer to within an inch. He said something to Chris. He never told me what it was. He packed up after that."

Fran's hands covered her face. "Jesus. You wouldn't know. I mean, look at his nose, thin, unbroken. No punch-drunk voice. Duh, duh." Her words brought a welcomed smile to his face.

"Yeah. Good at ducking and diving. Just as well, brilliant brain. His business acumen comes from his mother's side you know."

Fran straightened on the stool. "Really?"

"Oh, yeah. Margaret Devereux was the original driving force behind a small company in Dublin. Talking about her has just given me a thought. The Devereuxs are a close family. That's why Chris has property in Lanzarote and elsewhere. They all have. She was the brains behind the company. Seemingly a family trait, business shrewdness."

"You must have been shocked too though. I mean your sister dying as she did."

He gulped. "I flew out next day. She was dead before the ambulance arrived. Took about twenty minutes to get to the scene. Fucksake. It's less than ten from the airport in a taxi." His drink arrived. "Cheers, Rory." He downed a mouthful of ale before it had settled in the glass.

Fran looked to Rory.

His eyes and screwed mouth suggested George was acting weird. He returned to serving others.

She noticed the barman's expression.

George is hiding something.

"But Chris, was he badly hurt?"

"Well." George's head went side to side. "Yes. His right leg was crushed. Unconscious for two days and in intensive care for about a week before being flown home. Christ, he hardly moved in the wheelchair at the funeral two weeks later. Like a zombie, he was."

"My God. What about the driver? Was he caught?"

"No. Whisked away somehow. A hired car."

"No name? Investigation?" She was doing well. Rubbing his back, keeping her voice soft and caring.

"Foreign I believe. A tourist type. I never told Chris, but he may have been German. Strange thing was his name."

"You know the driver's name? After all those years?" Her eyes widened again.

George cleared his throat. "Well, no. I don't think he hired the car.

Cartwright was on the hiring documents. Strange when thinking of it now. Wasn't supposed to—oh, forget it."

Drink loosened his tongue.

Fran's wide stare tried to catch Chris's attention.

My God. That's the connection. Douglas Cartwright.

She continued questioning George. He appeared relaxed when revealing more about his sister. How she teased her way into his best friend's life, even at eleven, Mary had that mature act under control.

"When Chris went to study in Dublin, Trinity College, Mary wanted to move there. No way. She was two years younger and still at school." George signalled for a whiskey, his favourite tipple when pints filled him.

Chris spotted the conversation was ongoing.

Fran's shoulders shrugged in reply to his furrowed brows.

"Last freebies now people." Chris called out from the other end. "Don't forget, leave together."

Hands lifted glasses high announcing their last preferred orders.

Rory placed a whiskey in front of George.

"Same again." George said.

"Sure, and same for you, Fran?" Rory asked.

"Yes, please."

"Chris moved well today though. What he did to those guys." Fran reminded George.

He took a deep breath and flexed his shoulders. "Stiff. Yeah. After the accident he was reduced to a shell. Took his mother's belief in him to wake him up from self-reclusion. Her Uncle Phil helped out with his head. Got him fit, did some tai chi and martial arts. Chris got stuck into the company, bringing it world renown."

"His mother, how bad was she. The cancer."

"Broke Uncle Ben. Gloria had become close to Margaret through emails, Skype. Margaret liked her as a sister. Invited over. Got her a job in the offices of Ostrofman. Although older than Chris, I think Margaret was aiming Gloria toward him. But he looked on her as an Aunt and friend of Ben." He downed the first whiskey in one.

"You really admire them, the family."

"Yeah. They had everything but couldn't save Margaret or get the ambulance quicker to Mary. What if Chris had been first to be struck down?"

Then she saw it. The sudden suspicion of contempt on George's face. His eyes narrowed towards Chris once again.

She rubbed George's back. Her fingers witnessed the tension bottled up inside him.

"He's a good man. A best mate." She took up her almost empty glass.

The smooth liquid calmed her too.

George wiped his eyes then finished off his pint. "I'll be off soon."

Her smile eased him.

"You're a good listener and I was aware you didn't ask too many questions." He faced her. "You fancy him." His fingers drummed the counter.

Fran straightened again; caught off guard.

"No." Her eyes lied.

"Yes, you do." His signature smile appeared. "Take it easy with him. He's hard to please and I know his eyes look very pleased when you are here."

He had brightened. As if the chat had got something off his chest. He looked to Chris and raised his whiskey glass in salute.

Chris thumbed-up.

47 THE CLOSE ENCOUNTER

Chris and Fran sat at the bar after all customers had left.
"Go ahead, Rory. Take tomorrow off, full pay," Chris said.
"Really? Why?" Rory gathered his jacket.
"You were typically ready. Well-done, mate. Now go."
Rory winked at them. A smile grew as he turned to the side door. "Night."
"Night, Robin," Fran said.
Chris leaned back. "Robin? Ah, okay." He checked all the doors and went behind the bar. His eyes and grin asked the question.
"Okay, one more, then taxi." Fran beamed.
"Well, tell me. George appeared a bit under the weather. Not like him. The joker." He handed her the drink before totting up the till.
"He's a lifelong friend, right?"
His brows furrowed. "Why do I think something nasty is coming?"
"George has sister issues."
He stood silent for seconds, mouth agape. "What do you mean?"
"He talked of the accident. And knows more than he told me tonight." She scanned his shocked look. "He mentioned Cartwright."
"What? How did he know that name?"
"According to him it was on the hired car documents. I think it just slipped out."
"He's right. I knew I saw it before." The till rang shut. Chris picked up a bottle and poured more than large Southie into a tall glass on top of ice.
"George was fond of your mother and suggested that she was grooming Gloria for you."
"Strewth." He took a sharp intake of breath and puffed. "I knew that too. I was reclusive. Fuck the world." He moved back to the seat.
"Something else, and it's probably just my nose." She realised his look. "He said 'it wasn't supposed to happen'."
He sat in silence listening to the ice cracking, working the distinct aromatic Southern Comfort to his nose.
"Chris?"
Tears dripped onto the bar. His shoulders shuddered.
She moved her left arm around him.
His head dropped lower.
What am I doing?
"I'm sorry. I shouldn't have said. You know," she said.
"He was jealous of Mary. She took me away from him. Me and George did everything. Boxed, fished in Chingford, football. Then I saw girls.

Mary." He took a sharp mouthful.

Her arm slipped away. "He said she was going to Dublin after you when you went to Trinity."

"Yeah. That was Mary. He came over you know. To Dublin to visit. I didn't see Mary until coming back for holidays. Hardly saw George. Fuck." His eyes shot at Fran. "George. He did it. It was the wrong one." He rubbed his head.

"No, Chris. He wouldn't kill his sister. Chris, stop that thought."

"It was meant for me, not Mary. The driver fucked up. Oh, my God. After all those years. Why didn't I see it before?" His mouth screwed; teeth shown like an angry dog. Ready to burst.

"No, no, no, no. Chris. Don't." Her hands didn't cover his large ones as they tried to fix them to the bar.

His breathing quickened as if after a long run. Short spasms jolted his shoulders as her hands held firm.

"You have to think this out. Perhaps it was just the way he looked at you tonight when I talked to him. He hardly smiled. Kept on about Mary, your mother and Gloria. Hardly mentioned you except when you were younger. He praised you." She eased her hands from his.

He turned to her. "I'm going to check passengers' names and the regular hotel we used for meetings in Lanzarote during that time."

"Why? How can you do that?" Her eyes begged him to relax.

"George had maintained that he flew out next morning after the accident. I have connections over there that will confirm my suspicions."

She shook his arm. "What are you thinking?"

"I think that he sent Specs a text message tonight." His eyes widened to her. "At the bar, before he went to the gents, he was looking at his phone, got up, went to the gents. Then seconds later, in pops trouble."

"No way. But they were looking for Mike." She took a mouthful.

"If they wanted Mike, they would have waited for him to leave. They're taunting me."

"But there must be more to this. Why was Humph interested in all this? Don't do anything yet. We need to find out more." She shook him again. "Chris, you must remain as if you don't suspect anything. We could be wrong."

He looked into her eyes.

"Please. You are a good man. You still have fond memories of your wife. Chris, please. We will find out more. It could be deeper or nothing at all."

His right-hand caressed Fran's face and worked around to her neck.

He leaned forward and their lips locked in a long embrace. No resistance. He stood and carried her to the seating. Stools kicked away as he gently laid her down. Lips locked again. Their hands lost control and hurriedly removed unwanted clothing.

"Can't find the taxi number," he said.

"What taxi?"

The leather upholstery squeaked in rhythm to their passionate frustrations. The first furlong was slow, riding in tempo, then quickening the pace along the home straight towards the finishing line. A dead heat for the 'good fings'. They breathed deep, eyes smiling at each other.

"What would you like for breakfast?" he asked.

"More."

48 THE MEETING OF MRS. M

Monday July 2

Fran walked back into the bedroom from the ensuite. A borrowed shirt hung loose as she knelt on the bed, leaning over to kiss his cheek.

"I'm awake. Just resting my eyes." Chris turned.

Their lips met again.

He reluctantly pulled free. "What time is it?"

She turned to the bedside stand.

Chris's eyes woke. "Mmmmm."

Her hand pulled the shirt down lower covering her modesty. She picked up her watch. "It's eight."

Chris stretched, showing all sinews and ribbed torso. "You haven't met Missus M yet. Well, she'll be here in about an hour. So, breakie first then bar cleaning."

A pillow landed on his face. "You bar clean, I'll breakfast." She slid out of the bed.

**

On a three-rung step-up, Fran just about reached the top shelf behind the bar. A familiar rhythmic banging on the pub's front door distracted Chris from her.

"Do you want a hand?"

"Go answer the door." She stepped down.

When the blind pulled up, his smile greeted Mrs. M. He opened the door.

She brushed past him. "Why are you so happy?" Mrs. M hurried to her station and stopped. "Oh, I see why."

"Hi, I'm Fran. Heard all about you, Missus M." Fran walked around the bar, hand extended.

Mrs. M shook it and glanced at Chris. "Oh, I'm blown out now am I?"

Fran smiled at him. "You have a lot to explain, Mister. To both of us."

"You tell him. I like you already, Fran." Mrs. M's eyes widened. "Oh, you're the new barmaid. I was here when you saved them all. Very proficient."

"Thank you, Missus M." Fran's tongue poked to Chris.

"Okay, ladies. Work."

"Feck off." Mrs. M turned to Fran. "Cup of tea?"

"Oh yes, please."

"Young fella, do the honours." Mrs. M went to the closet.

Consideration of Tragedies

**

While working, they chatted about Chris, the pub, Clapton, Mrs. M, Fran.

"What's he really like?" Fran asked.

Mrs. M pushed the trolly back into the closet.

"I'm here, ask me." Chris's head popped up through the cellar hatch.

"You wouldn't tell the truth." Mrs. M gathered her large bag and sat at the bar. "Do you know he wanted me to go with him on his private jet to Dublin—alone. Well, what does that say about him?"

"A fetish?" Fran winked to Chris rising above the floor.

"Older women? A P.I moll? I think it's my pinny." Mrs. M sipped another cup of tea.

"Mmmmmm."

"Down boy. Do you think you will retire though, Missus M?" Fran asked.

"Someday. I may give up the offices this year, though." Mrs. M shifted. "Needless to say, I won't be going back to Montrose's places after what happened to that poor man."

Fran threw a glance at Chris.

His head shook quickly.

"Yes, I understand. How long have you been here in England?" she asked.

"Well, Fran, me and Tom came to Clapton in, eh, nineteen seventy-three. Had Thomas in Tipperary, our eldest." Mrs. M's voice softened. "Sadly, he passed away soon after his only son was found in a lake."

"Oh dear. I'm sorry to hear that." Fran rubbed her arm.

"Thank you. We have three more born here. James, Melisa, and Oisin." Mrs. M smiled.

"Do you get home at all?"

Mrs. M looked to Chris as he placed bottles into the fridges. "He sends us home." She leaned closer, watching him. "He's great. Pays for the flights and we *were* on the private jet."

Chris managed a secret smile.

"Have you much family left there?" Fran poured more tea into their two cups.

"Oh, yes. And I have a brother over here. He's a priest. Marty. Always giving out about not being the eldest and forced off the farm to wear the cloth. We met up for his seventieth in March. He won't retire."

"Really?"

"Yes. Been all over. Refused to go back home to a parish. He's mostly around Chelmsford way. Loves it there."

"Oh. That's interesting."

Chris stood and stretched. "Marty's a nutter."

"Excuse me, pup. That's my brother your slagging." Mrs. M moved from the stool. She tilted to Fran. "He's right though."

"You pair are suited," Fran said. "Like Aunt and nephew."

"She's lovely." Mrs. M winked to him. "Now you can keep away from me, thank God. Peace at last." Her laughing faded towards the front door. "See you tomorrow, young fella. Enjoyed our chat, Fran."

She waved as Mrs. M closed the door behind her. "What a character."

"She is," Chris said. "Thank you."

Her head shot back. "For what?"

"Everything. You've opened my eyes." He sat beside her and kissed.

He broke for air. "I have a plan."

Fran looked waiting.

"We hand DI Macken, Pockets, the laptop, and throw all our findings together. Leave out the George thing for now."

"Okay, I'm with you on that. So, you really think there's a connection between what Humph was looking into and the gangster fellow?" She rubbed his bare arms.

"I do."

"Yes, makes sense that Humph has files on pharmaceutical companies and Specs is a dealer of sorts." She glanced at the clock. "I really should be going. Enjoyed yesterday, last night, this morning, Missus M." A kiss broke her laughter.

Chris breathed again. "Keep digging. We both have copies needed. I'll ask Alice and Rory to work extra. Think there's a thing brewing with them two. So, I can do some investigation. Phones have ears. As you well know."

Her chin lowered in guilt. "Do you want me to come here tonight?"

He puffed. "Can we take it easy for the customers?" He played cautious for himself.

Her smile answered.

"Right, taxi for you." Chris used the pub's phone to call a regular service. "Two minutes. You got everything? Toothbrush?"

She patted him. "I'll bring a spare next time."

They stood and walked to the front. He pulled up the blind. "That was quick." He thumbed-up to the driver. "Well, call me tonight or if something comes up."

He held the door open for her to pass.

"See you, young fella."

His eyes said it all. Sixteen years of being almost faithful to Mary's memory, his heart was moving to another.

**

Chris sat in his office, pressed a name on his mobile and waited.

"DI — Yes. Have some info and developments we need to discuss — no, not on phone. Can you drop in here later — Okay, well, Rory is off so I've arranged for Alice to stand in — Seven will be fine." He listened to Pockets long reply then hung up.

He opened Google maps on his laptop, typed in Humph's home and his old firm's address.

Handy. Not too far from each other.

He pressed another name. "Alice, my fav staff member — Tonight double but be here around six — Well, I have to eat." A few unseen nods. "Now, regarding tomorrow." Chris moved the phone from his ear. "Treble and paid leave for both of you for a day during next week — Yes — You pick it but not weekend. Yes, all day rates." He listened again to a calmer voice. "You're a star—and tell Rory beside you, so is he." He clicked off.

He breathed hard.

She's a tough negotiator.

49 THE INJURED IDIOTS

Specs stamped up and down his Shoreditch office.
"You two have had time to reflect on what the fuck happened or didn't happen, last night." His bulk twisted to face Belch and Mouse.

"Boss, it came from nowhere. A flash, thump and I toppled over onto Mouse." Belch rubbed his unshaven chin.

Mouse nursed a broken arm in a sling.

"One punch? You're having a laugh." Specs stomped to a chair behind a classic imitation mahogany desk. "I don't know the geezer who wants him hurt or for why, but Freeman showed me up. One fucking punch?" He took a Havana cigar from an ornate box, trimmed, and lit it, slowly taking its aroma. "We leave him, and his pub. Stay away from it and forget about Mr. Wonderful, for now."

Another pleasant puff of smoke wafted across the desk to them. "We don't need any 'Nosey Parkers' right now. King and his boy, Ding, are getting info on that pharmaceuticals. We may be able to move on it next week, so, you two, being out of condition, need to ready the others." Specs eyes glared at them under his bushy brows. "And don't fuck this up. Meanwhile, get in touch with who-you-know to find out who texted me yesterday. He's good at that, is Douglas."

The pair struggled in their own way to leave the office.

50 THE BLACK COFFEE

Alice had moaned about missing a day of sunshine. Luckily, Tuesday was a free day from her part time care-centre work. She pulled a tap

"We should have a chat about upgrading you two," Chris said.

"Well, you could hire another real part-time spare because it's hard to change things and arrangements to come in." She handed a pint to a customer.

"Thank you," he said.

"Good idea, Alice," Chris agreed.

The door squeaked and hands disappeared to the haven in his trousers.

"Well, here's the DI. So, all yours for a while. Any rush, buzz me." His smile always weaken her.

"Yes, boss. Hi Bert."

"Alice, good to see you." Pockets looked to Chris. "Thank you. I'll have a pint, please."

"Come through." Chris directed Pockets to the office. "Thanks." He took the pint off her and followed the DI.

**

They settled in the office.

"So, Chris, how are things moving?" Pockets took a welcomed mouthful of ale.

"Something, well, 'someone' has come up. A journalist, Fran Wakefield, has been on Humph's tail for a number of years. She was a tad annoyed at his sudden death and came asking questions." He poured coffee into his 'Boss' mug from the prepared maker.

"Never heard of her." His eyes read Chris's. "So, can she provide anything on the mysterious Mister Barrington?"

Chris rubbed his chin. "Well."

"Come on, Chris. We have an agreement."

"I want the three of us to work together."

"Oh, I don't know. It depends on what she has and—"

"She bugged Humph's briefcase."

The news shot Pockets back in the chair. "What the fuck. Did she have authorisation?"

Chris's lips tightened as he shook his head.

"This is no use. Can't be used as evidence in anything." He took a longer mouthful.

"True but listen." Chris's hands conducted the conversation. "Links are appearing to form a chain, knotting in parts, but they can be straightened. King's DC Bell, what's his first name?"

"Tony. Is he taped too?"

"Shite. That's the first link for you. Mike dropped in earlier and confirmed King's new sidekick joined his gun club over a week ago."

Pockets sat dumbfounded. He tightened his grip on the glass.

"That's not good for King and Ding." He saw Chris's question mark. "Ding, Bell."

"Oh, connected. It's been a busy few days." He took a sip of black coffee. "We have Humph's briefcase."

"Fucksake. Anything else?" Pockets eyes widened. "What's in it?"

Chris almost dropped his black mug while laughing. "You're gas. Okay." He sat straight. "A laptop, notebooks, a phone, and wait for it, a digital recorder."

"No way."

Chris picked up the briefcase handing it to Pockets. "I locked it again. You and I have to do this together."

"Sorry, I don't read crime suspense tales. Just tell me." Another mouthful of ale disappeared.

"Humph posted files to his old firm and I know you like the Smoke, but country air will do you good. Give you inspiration towards retirement."

"So, you're gonna flash your P.I badge again? When do we leave?"

"Tomorrow. My treat. I'll drive." Chris drained his mug.

"Off the books, mind. I'll put in for day's leave."

**

Chris and Pockets discussed the trip in his office.

Pockets' phone rang. "Sorry, Chris, just a mo."

He stood and walked to the private entrance and answered. "Yes? — I'm off duty — What? Where?" He paced the small hall. "Fuck. You sure? — Really? First thing in the morning. Hold up." He thought for a few seconds. "Okay, just give me the file in the morning with a brief. I have just booked a personal day so will get back to you late tomorrow evening after looking at them."

He walked in his familiar stooping style into the office.

"I don't believe in coincidences. There's an ongoing case, well, actually stretches back over twenty years. It concerns—" He fidgeted. "It's the sort of case that makes me vomit. Child sex." He almost knocked the glass off the desk when reaching out.

Chris paid attention.

"I've just received news of five bodies found in a derelict building site north of Cambridge. Builders discovered them as they were demolishing outhouses." He looked directly at Chris. "One is a Peters. Noel Peters."

Chris's chair swivelled left and right. "Raz's cousin?"

"Unbelievably, wallets and ID were recovered. The other is Lens."

"Specs' younger brother? But wasn't he shipped off to America or somewhere? I remember him as spotty little kid, blind as a bat."

"Worse eyesight than Specs." Pockets finished his pint. "This is not out there to the public. We can't inform anyone, and I realise now that Specs said his little bro emigrated."

"Hold on." Chris stood. "Are you presuming the find is related to a paedophile ring? Raz's cousin?"

"Don't tell him."

Papers and his mug jumped on the desk as Chris's fist thudded. "Raz asked me about Humph. He was talking to another cousin, you know, Nigel Peters."

Pockets shook his head.

"Nigel rang Raz telling him Humph was being nosey about the family bakers. The child sex ring, drugs and Humph. Must be all connected. Any child smuggling?"

"Not that I've heard. Anyway, I don't believe in coincidences. Pick me up at the shop tomorrow about ten."

He directed Pockets from the office. "Okay, ten it is. Pint?"

51 THE DAY TRIP

Stoke Newington police station, Tuesday July 3

DI Macken held a brown file close to him as he walked with hands in pockets to Chris's Subaru Legacy.

"Use a hand," Chris said through the lowered passenger window.

Reluctantly, Pockets slipped his left hand out and opened the door. "You're lazy."

"I'm not your official driver. Get in and belt up, both ways."

Pockets eased into the seat and shut the door softly. "Great motor."

"Cheers. Did you hand the briefcase into evidence?"

"Yeah. I'll do a report later for his highness. Hope you wiped it."

"Oh fuck. Fingerprints. Silly me."

Pockets stared at him. "Smart arse. You did."

Chris grinned. "We used gloves. Best not to wipe all prints. So, what about this building site?"

He eased the car from the kerb into Stoke Newington's north flowing traffic.

Pockets placed the file on the wide dashboard. "It's in Waterbeach, about six miles north of Cambridge. Won't distract your attention with all the details but the press has got hold of the news."

"Damn. That's awkward for you lot." Chris checked his rear-view and turned right.

"Yeah. But no details will be released until all the facts are established and relatives are informed."

"Specs? Who's going to be the lucky cop?"

"I'll do that. Want to see his mush." Pockets' shoulders flexed. "His eyes will tell me if he knew about Lens or not."

Chris smirked. "I notice that about you. The way you read people."

"I heard how you handled yourself the other night." Pockets nodded in approvement.

"Small area. Listen, I realise I was in school at the time in the early nineties, but I heard stories of corruption and fitting up black kids by Stoke Newington and Hackney cops."

"Dark times. Still some carry-ons even now. But not as bad."

"I recall a few from my school were framed. Hanging out around the dreaded Sandringham Road."

"That often happened there. About nineteen ninety-one, many cops were engaged in drug trafficking and perverting the course of justice. They used kids as sort of decoys away from themselves. Some were charged as punishment, even young women, some single mothers." Pockets took a sharp intake of breath. "Everybody knew that drug dealing went on in Sandringham. It was common knowledge that officers took money and drugs from dealers." He turned to Chris. "One shot himself you know."

"No way." Chris managed a glance at Pockets.

"Yep. DS Gary Mantra put a gun to his bastard head in January ninety-two. Happened in Barkingside station. I was in Bethnal Green at the time, just finding my feet. King was in Barkingside when it happened. Straight away the fucker transferred to Stoke Newington."

"Saw a chance and grabbed, eh."

"He sure did. They were even involved in prostitution and protection. Eight were transferred, but there were more untouched." Pockets' fingers tapped the dash. "How well do you really know Vince?"

"Why? Vince never touched anything like that."

"I know, but you met his mum, Opal."

"*Yeah*. So where are you going with this?"

"She was stitched up but reported it before it got out of hand. Led to Operation Windfall put in place in ninety-one. Its investigation went way above street level coppers. One senior officer was receiving as much as one thou a month. I mean, that was big dosh for that time."

The car stopped at red lights. "Christ. What was the outcome?"

"You must've been in college at the time."

"Well, I could have been if it was around mid-nineties."

He moved on green.

"Cases began to collapse due to those idiot bent coppers, even real cases deserving long sentences. Many judges were going mental having to release bastards. Supers wanting results to improve station stats on crime were the worse. In the long run, most of the dirt was shovelled out, some buried in red tape, others forced retirement with reduced or no pensions. Fuck them."

DI Macken was a real cop. Only gratitude taken were handshakes, pints, and respect.

"So, Bollocky King sneaked up the back-hander ladder." Chris eased to another set of red lights.

"He did."

They looked at each other; minds joined. "Fuck him."

**

Chris continued along London Road. When travelling from his customary area of work, his mind relaxed and opened to think of others. Certain places brought back memories of good times and chats.

The country air worked its magic on him again. "Royston is coming up. Fancy a snack? You can have a pint."

Pockets shifted in the passenger seat. "Yeah. We can look at the file."

The car entered the town from the south, turned right and eased into a carpark.

Pockets eyed him. "This was easy to find."

"Used to live around the corner. You might recognise the beer garden style." He smiled as they climbed out of the car.
Walking through to the main bar, Pockets nodded. "You styled your beer garden on this."
"Sure did." He extended a hand over the bar.
"My word. Chris Freeman. A sight for old eyes." A wrinkled hand gripped his.
"Seth Green. You look great and still running the best pit-stop." Their hands released. "Sorry." He turned to Pockets "This is Bert Macken. We're just up to Cambridge. Business."
"'ow do, Bert. What would you like?"
"What have you got?" Pockets wasn't used to small country towns.
Chris tipped his nose. "If she's on I'll have a pot of tea and a chicken wrap."
Seth grinned.
"Oh, eh, pint of best, cheese and pickle. He's driving."
"You're right. Let the younger ones do the driving, Bert. Go sit and I'll send 'em over."
Chris nodded to a beer tap.
Seth winked.
The visitors chose a table by a front window looking to the main street.
Pockets placed the file on the dark wood table. "Nice this."
"Gets well-used on weekends. Great capture pub as it's on the London Road." Chris faced the window.
"The Green Man. Named after the owner?"
"It's not. Just one of your coincidences."
Seth approached wearing a broad smile and placed a tray on the table.
"'ere you are Bert." He put the pint on a beer mat. "Tea and sandwiches on the way."
"Thank you, Seth." Pockets picked up the glass.
Eyes watched.
"What?"
"Nothing Pock—Bert." Chris winked to Seth.

Pockets took a long mouthful. "Wow."

"Good eh? Lucky you're not driving. Eight-point five percent that is." Chris thumbed-up Seth.

The owner returned to the bar.

"Don't serve this in your place." Pockets looked around the empty area. "Now." He opened the file. "The pictures are a bit gross."

Chris took the first two. "Jesus. The five appear to be dumped at the same time. What is it? Eight feet deep?"

"About that." Pockets pushed another to him. "See that? The digger sliced through the body, so this was the last one thrown in."

Chris eased back into the chair. "Why did they leave IDs?"

His shaking head alerted Pockets. "Probably thought leather would degenerate."

"I can't tell Raz about this. Fucksake."

Clicking footsteps drew attention.

"Here you are gents." A rotund middle-aged woman removed a small teapot from a tray. She glanced at Chris.

He managed a smile.

"Ahh, Chris." She turned to face the bar. "Seth, you old bastard."

Seth waved.

Chris stood and wrapped his arms around her, kissing a cheek. "Agnes, how are you?"

He released her.

"Well, I never. How are you, and your dad?"

"Sorry. Agnes, this is Bert." Chris's eyes welled up. "This is Agnes Peters."

Pockets held the pint glass tight. His free hand slid the file over the photos. "Watchya." Mouth agape.

"Hello, Bert. Welcome. It's Prefect." She turned to Chris. "Using my single name now. What are you doing out this way, Chris? Thought you sold the lot and opened a pub in that smoky place."

Chris sat. He read Pockets' eyes. "Agnes doesn't like London." He shrugged.

"Don't blame you, Agnes." He managed a small mouthful. "Are you from here?"

"Now, Agnes, watch it. Bert's married but looking for a nice retirement cottage." Chris poured tea into a cup.

"Go away with you, Chris Freeman. Just like your dad." She turned to Pockets. "Do you know, after my divorce, Ben, Chris's dad, tried to pair us off."

Pockets' stared.

Chris nodded.

"I didn't want anything to do with him." Her laughter echoed. "I mean, one fucking travelling husband was enough for me."

She tilted to Chris and hugged him. "Good to see you again. Now, I'll leave you two to look at Bert's retirement cottages. Enjoy."

Silence lingered. They took a mouthful of their beverages, bit into their food.

Chris stared out of the window.

Pockets gawked at him.

"Clever, very clever. You haven't lost your P.I instinct." Pockets washed down the quarter.

Chris rubbed his chin. "I didn't realise she still worked here."

"Pull the other one." Pockets shook a leg. "Coincidence?"

"Nice one, Pockets. Hands up." Chris angled over. "I met Noel a few times. One binge night in Cambridge, he told me that Agnes didn't want to have any more children. He got pissed off with her moaning about it. Blaming him. He then started to ramble the country, using his baking skills as an excuse." He took time-out for another quarter.

Pockets did the same and a long mouthful.

"They drifted apart. She put on weight, drank and that was the last straw for him. They divorced in twenty ten." Chris slurped his tea.

"Okay. I do believe there are circumstances of being in the wrong, or right place at the wrong or right time." Pockets' mouth screwed. "But, c'mon."

"It's Humph. Has to be. He's drawn all of us together with those names somehow." Chris bit hard into his wrap. "Okay. I give you that. The coincidence bit. But there must be a connection purposely designed to invite his investigations."

"That's true. But I'm a copper. I can't be seen investigating something off track." Pockets chewed his last quarter of cheese and pickle.

"And yet here we are. Asking questions on way to a crime scene, off the books." Chris drained the cup. "But I'm not. You don't have to flash your badge. I've a wallet."

"You mean at the building site? We'll see what it's like first."

"Yes. We're suited, respectable looking. Shirts and ties. I've nice white hardhats in the boot. How official do you want?" Chris grinned. "Pint?"

**

They left the Green Man with a promise to return.

"She's a bit big for you though." Pockets remarked. His grin due to the extra strength pints.

"Out of order for you, Pockets. Not bringing you north of London again."

"How far to Humph's?"

"About thirty minutes." Chris looked across to Pockets. "Something else."

"Please, whatever you know, tell me all now. Get it out of the way. No more surprises."

"Fran is meeting us at Humph's place."

Pockets puffed. "Really?"

"Well, she does know more about him than we do and deserves to learn what we have dug up." He glanced across. "No pun."

"We share everything, and I do mean everything from now on. Would probably need to go after those pints."

"Yes, Guv." Chris smiled. "Another pit-stop?"

"Keep your eyes on the road."

52 THE TRIO

The car cruised through a village toward Haslingfield Road.
Pockets eyed Chris. "Are you taking the piss?"
Chris shrugged. "I didn't know Humph's family name was a village."
"Barrington village. He's having a laugh."
A church stood proud north of a small graveyard as Chris nodded to the windscreen. "There's Fran outside those gates."
Pockets stared at the view in a green and red leather jacket. He turned to Chris. "Wow."
Chris steered left through the gates and stopped at trimmed hedging.
Fran's wave welcomed them as they climbed out of the car. Her bike parked on a green verge outside the estate.
"You're early," she said.
"What are you two up to?" Pockets blasted.
Chris hugged her and pulled away. "This is DI Macken, Fran. Pockets to his friends and others."
She extended a hand.
Pockets took it.
"I heard a lot about you. How am I to call you?" Her voice worked it's magic.
"Suppose you can call me Pockets. How do you do."
"Fran, what's going on? Humph's address is The Lodge, Haslingfield Road," Chris said.
"I know and it is," she said. "This is Barrington Hall, Humph's family's old place. It was sold years ago but he kept the lodge."
They turned and faced the predominantly white bungalow peeking over tall hedging. It laid within a large garden fenced off from the public along the main road. The hedging continued around the remainder.
"Well, Humph did tell me he's a man of means," Chris said. "Shall we?" He directed a hand to the lodge.
"Oh, we just knock, and he'll answer." Pockets lips tightened.
Fran waved a key at him.
Pockets' eyes rolled. "I don't want to know."
They followed her through a wrought-iron side gate. At the front door, she looked around then inserted the key. Her fingers jiggled it before a click brought a satisfactory smile to her face. The trio entered.

**

They squeezed into a small hall. Fran opened a door to her right and stepped in. It gave more room to shut the front door.

"No alarm?" Pockets noticed.

She turned "Eh, something happened to it outside."

"I like her already." He took out latex gloves from his jacket. "A pair each. Unfortunately, I only have one pair left—didn't know you were coming, Fran."

The livingroom needed airing. The stench of unuse lingered throughout the lodge as they moved from room to room. Chris opened a door, peeked inside. *Two single beds?*

At the end of the corridor, he opened a door to reveal a study.

They heaved as the smell of old papers burst through. Sunlight from a single double glazed window sparkled on cobwebs linking Venetian blinds.

"I say one thing," Chris began. "Humph needed Missus M. The bedrooms are spotless though."

"You say he was renting a place in Clapton? Fucksake." Pockets held a hand up. "Sorry Fran, excuse my French."

She smiled.

"Look at this place. Where would we start? I mean, what are we looking for?" Pockets moved discoloured files on the desk.

"Connections. Who hired him?" Her eyes widened and looked to Chris.

A grey safe rested under the window behind the desk. Fran searched her bag and pulled out one of Humph's notebooks.

Pockets looked to the ceiling, shrugged, and let them at it.

"Here it is, under S," she said.

"Jesus, the man was an open book." Chris read the numbers.

"What you two on about?" Pockets joined them.

"Humph wrote everything down, even passwords," she explained.

Chris knelt to the dial, moving it left and right after each number. Seventeen, thirty-four, fifty-one and sixty-eight.

"Definitely no imagination." He laughed.

Chris pulled back the thick safe door and stood.

Fran bent and removed a thin pile of files, placing them on the desk. She breezed through, shaking her head then stopped. She looked sharply at Chris.

He noticed the stare and followed her finger down a page. "Christ." He rubbed his chin.

Pockets moved irritably. "What?"

"It's a name related to—" Fran glanced at Chris for permission. She read the nod. "It's related to Chris's wife's death. The car accident."

Pockets almost fell back in shock. "No way. Chris, I'm sorry. This fucker had his nose in many arses."

Chris breathed slowly, getting his composure back. His hands moved leisurely at each hip, eyes closed, palms pushing down then out and back again.

Fran rubbed his back.

He eye-balled Pockets. "Tell Fran about the bodies." He returned irrelevant files into the safe.

Chris went outside breathing easily and walked around the lodge. Looking to the left, past a clump of full trees, a small play area caught his attention. He remembered the two made-up single beds in one bedroom.

Humph had children?

Pockets and Fran joined him.

"This is getting weirder," she said.

"Hold on, Fran. You've been on him for almost two years, and you didn't realise he had kids?" Chris said.

"He didn't. Humph never married or had serious relationships."

"The single beds are too tidy. Must have been recently used," Chris said.

Pockets became animated. "Oh, fuck. Lock that door and let's get out of here."

"Yeah. I'm with you, Pockets." Chris walked rapidly.

Fran trudged after them. "What?"

"Lock the door." Pockets demanded.

"Humph was one of them—paedo," Chris said to her.

Fran fumbled for the 'spare' key. "Jesus. No way. That fucker too." She locked the door.

Outside the gate she put the latex gloves into the carrier.

"We're heading to his old firm's place. I presume you know it." Chris unlocked the car.

"Okay, yes. I'll park nearby and wait for you." Fran straddled the bike, donned her helmet and gloves then sped off.

The car doors closed consecutively.

"Where are the offices?" Pockets clicked the seat belt.

"Parkside." Chris glanced across. "What?"

"Same road as the cop shop."

Chris shrugged. "Coincidence."

53 THE H-FILES

Cambridge

Fran sat on the bike as the Subaru pulled up behind her. Chris and Pockets got out and stretched.

"You okay to wait here?" Chris asked her. "We shouldn't be long."

"Yes. Don't like solicitor's offices."

Pockets looked at his watch. "We're five minutes late."

"Don't want to be too pushy." Chris walked to a black front door and tried the handle. It opened.

Pockets nodded to a sign with third name barely visible after it had been removed leaving *Chadwick, Darling* beside an upward arrow.

They climbed the stairs to the second floor. Pockets tapped twice on a door.

"Come in," a crackly voice said.

Chris followed him into a small reception office. He noticed brass name plates were on two oak-grained doors. A third had none.

"Good afternoon. I'm Detective Inspector Macken and this is Detective Freeman." Pockets produced his warrant card. "I believe you have post addressed to one Humphrey Barrington."

The elderly clerk struggled to stand. "Ah yes, Inspector. It was rather strange that this package arrived here. Then hearing of the sudden death of eh, Mister Barrington."

Did the bare polished floorboards or his bones creak?

"Yes, rather unfortunate accident. But these incidents still need to be investigated."

"Yes, I gather. Misters Chadwick and Darling are not available; however, they instructed me to give you the package."

Chris tipped Pockets.

"Oh, yes thank you. Just a few questions." Pockets took out his rarely used notebook and pen. "When did Mister Barrington leave the firm?"

"Oh, I would say about four, no, five months ago."

"Okay. What reason did he give for leaving?"

The clerk wore a tilted smile. "I'm afraid I have no idea. You need to ask Mister Chadwick."

A soft sound came from Chadwick's office. Pockets' eyes widened to the clerk.

"The cat." The clerk's smile remained.

The 'two officers' glanced at each other.

"Don't like cats," Chris said.

"Nor do I. That's why it is in there. Anyway—" The clerk picked up the oversized package from his desk. "Here you are, Inspector. If there is anything else, please call again. I am sure we can arrange a meeting."

"Indeed. We will be in touch if anything relevant should come up. Thank you for your help." Pockets held the package. "Okay, Freeman."

Chris' eyes examined the room before leaving the office and closed the door.

"Cat me arse," Chris said.

"Come on. Let's get out of this place. Gives me the creeps." Pockets led the way to the street.

Fran took her helmet off the handle. "They're watching you," she said. "One from each window."

"I suspect they don't want any more to do with their ex-partner," Pockets said.

"There's a lot more to this firm." Chris pressed a button on the keyring. "We won't hang around. We should head for Waterbeach. Follow us, Fran."

54 THE GRUESOME FIND

Travelling over the River Cam bridge, they entered Waterbeach near its train station.

Chris stopped the car on double yellow lines.

Fran, standing by her bike, nodded at them.

The nineteenth century pale brick building less than inviting. Its five front boarded-up windows, three up, two down, along with the hall door warning discouraged entry. A constable stood guard beside a 'Ropers Builders' billboard fixed to a high corrugated-tin fence between the derelict building and a terraced house. Two camera-wielding journalists faced him.

Fran's bike distracted a few children peeping through rusted holes in the hope of catching sight of something interesting.

Chris and Pockets donned white hardhats and approached a constable.

Pockets showed his ID. "Afternoon, Constable. DI Macken and Detective Freeman. We need to inspect the scene. Who else is here?"

"Yes, sir. SOCO are here and a construction crew." The officer lifted police tape and opened a wide steel door just enough for them to pass through.

"Who's in charge?" Pockets stepped in.

"Doc Granger."

"Okay." Pockets caught Chris's nod. He looked at Fran, her lips tight. "By the way, this is Miss Scully, a surveyor."

"Yes, sir. Good afternoon, Miss Scully."

'Miss Scully' nodded.

She prodded Chris and walked in front of him holding her helmet. "*Miss Scully,* indeed."

They went through a draped tarpaulin to the main scene. To the right, an undisturbed bricked shed. At the back, to their left, stood the shell of outhouses. Inside, what remained of the foundations, a tent restricted any hope of prying eyes and unauthorised cameras viewing the grisly scene. Three arc lamps above the canvas focused on the centre. A mechanical digger, its large steel-pronged bucket gripping the ground, waited for its driver.

Pockets flashed his warrant card again, introducing himself and colleagues to a woman clad in white overalls. "I'm looking for Doctor Granger."

Another pair of overalls appeared. "Hello, I'm Kate Granger." Her eyes blinked behind protective glasses over a blue mask.

"We've travelled from London and believe this is connected to an ongoing case."

She looked from one to the other. "I'm afraid the bodies have all been taken to the Institute of Criminology in Cambridge. Which is extraordinary, but with so many bodies, security would be better there."

"May we see the ditch?"

She flicked a look at the others. "We almost finished collecting fragments. There's room for one more."

Chris nodded to Pockets.

"Okay, this is Miss Scully. She's here to observe and nothing more."

Granger handed him a mask and latex gloves.

Chris puffed and led a disgruntled Fran away towards the house. A man wearing a red hardhat, puffed a cigarette.

"Hi, awful find for you guys." Chris nodded towards the tent.

The man tossed the butt. "Yeah. Two of my men have gone sick. The driver of the digger had to be hospitalised. I mean, slicing a skull off. Freaked out."

"Are you local?" Chris noticed a locked door.

"Yes. Based in Saint Ives." His gaze moved between Fran's body armour and the tent.

"What went on here? You know, before this closed. Who owned it?"

"Not for me to say. I'm only the foreman."

Chris looked at two labourers at the shed.

"Come on, spill them. What's over there?"

Fran realised Chris's sign to them and strolled over.

He leaned into the foreman. "You're telling porkies."

The foreman took out another cigarette and lit it. "I can't say. I mean we were just hired last week. A hurried job. We were told don't mind the house, start at the outer buildings to clear space for materials." Smoke billowed from his mouth. "Well, it makes sense now."

Chris slipped a crisp note between his fingers.

The foreman looked to his free hand. "Parkside cop shop contacted my boss. Said a solicitor firm wanted us to move quicker on the renovations here." He slid the note into a pocket.

"A twenty on top." Chris looked to Fran. "And one each for them. Give me names of both parties."

**

Chris left the foreman and approached Fran and the two labourers.

She eased the jacket flap open. The zip slid inches down. "What's in there?" She nodded to the outhouse.

"We don't know, miss," a spotty youngster replied. "Only started yesterday."

The older labourer looked to the house and grasped his foreman's signal. "We haven't been inside. Here's the key to the padlock."

"Thank you, guys." She winked. "Go for a smoke."

They walked to the foreman.

Chris followed her into the shed. He turned on his phone's torch and worked the corners and shelving on two walls.

The beam lit up a metal chest. "What's that?"

Fran knelt and pulled the lid up. "Jesus."

"What?"

She stood to let him look.

He stepped forward, ready to be shocked, then groaned. "There's nothing in it."

Fran covered her mouth giggling.

"Very funny." He aimed the light at the shelves again and stepped closer, brushing a finger over dust. "Stuff has been recently moved from here."

Fran stretched to get a better view. "Boxes, cans?"

He looked to the concrete floor and scraped over the dust with his right foot.

"This area is lighter than the rest."

Fran looked back the way they had come. "Love to get a look in the house."

He smiled.

They approached the foreman. Chris slid another twenty into his hand and was given a set of keys.

"The large one's for the main door," the foreman said. "Just close it and you'll find torches on shelves to the right." He rubbed his nose with the back of his hand. "It's not nice in there."

"Cheers, mate." Chris winked at him, unlocked the steel door, and entered.

Fran closed it behind her.

**

A thin beam of light through the top of a boarded window was enough to spot the torches.

Fran coiled back, a hand over her mouth. "The smell. Were they using this as a toilet and canteen?"

"The builders weren't. They'd only just started working on the site. No power connected." Chris took two large torches and switched them on. "Hold this, I'll text Pockets to let him know where we are."

It didn't take long. He followed her torch beam to a set of stairs. It only took a moment to realise her screwed up expression. Rubbish bags and beer cans littered the floor along with a soiled single mattress in what must have been the livingroom.

"Whoa. Man, that's rough."

"C'mon," she said.

Each stair creaked like a scene from a horror movie. She giggled when he put the beam under his chin highlighting his features. "Oooooh."

They stepped carefully over broken furniture on the long landing, peeking into empty rooms that had no doors.

He tipped her shoulder. "Awful smell along here. Only two rooms left." They looked into each other's eyes. "And the doors closed."

She giggled again. "Go on. Open it. After all, you're the man."

He pulled the handle down on the first. The door creaked open like a strained, lingering fart.

"Oh, fuck." He pulled the torch and door back.

"What?"

"They had no toilet paper." He shook his head, as if to knock the visual from his brain. "It's everywhere. On the net curtains, old towels, even stripped wallpaper was used."

"Used for what?"

He stared at her under furrowed brows. "You having a laugh? Shite. It's everywhere. The bowl is stuffed with whatever and the bath isn't far behind."

"Oh God."

He turned his beam towards the last closed door facing them. "Your turn."

She jolted back. "What? No way."

"Go on. Do some real investigating. I mean there was nothing in the other five rooms."

"Yes, but they didn't have doors."

He winked.

She let him pass.

It didn't creak like the last door. Dust vied for space in two cracks of light from ill-fitting window boards. The torch beam hit an antiquated wardrobe, dressing table and large sheet-covered four-poster bed.

"Well?" she asked. "Tell me."

"It's the honeymoon suite."

She elbowed him out of the way and moved her beam in to the room. "Jesus. Oh, my God. You have got to see this."

Fran edged further in.

Chris followed. Their beams hit all the walls as they turned. He went to open drawers. Inside, cobweb-covered straps, whips, restraints along with sex toys. He passed the bed and pulled open a drape.

"Fuck me pink." He looked up.

She stepped closer. They stood together, stunned at the chains hanging from the ceiling of the four-poster. An unhitched hammock lay on top of a stained mattress. He swung the beam around and saw more web-covered restraints screwed to a wall.

They jumped at the sound of loud banging, their beams hitting each other's face.

"Must be Pockets. You take pics, I'll get the door."

He hobbled over debris making his way down the stairs to open the door.

"What are you two doing?" Pockets whispered.

Chris pulled his left elbow. "Get in here. And you." He nodded to the foreman.

The door clanked shut behind him.

He glared at the foreman. "How long have you been on this site?"

Pockets looked from one to the other.

"Two days. The first crew were shifted. And, as I said, two went sick." He angled his head left and right, the creaks in his neck audible.

"How come you have the keys and said fuck all about what's in here?"

The man flicked a look at the stairs. "We were told to just cater for those guys." He nodded to the door.

"Yet you said there were torches on shelves and knew it wasn't nice inside."

"Yes. I put them there for safety if and when this place was to be—"

"Fuck off." Pockets blasted. "There were cops here."

The foreman's shoulder went up. "Well, I–I suppose so. But I did what I was told to do."

"Ropers Builders. Where are they based?" Chris asked the confused man.

Repeating creaking steps behind announced Fran coming down the stairs.

"Cambridge," he answered.

"Okay, cheers." Chris palmed him a P.I card. "You get in touch with me ASAP if others come snooping around. Not cops, okay?"

He looked at the card. "Yes. But this is due for demolishing next week."

Pockets looked questionably at Chris.

"Fran, show the DI upstairs." He gave Pockets his torch. "C'mon, we wait outside." He nudged the foreman towards the door.

**

Doctor Granger emerged from the tented area with her group and removed their PP. Then boxes were loaded into a department van. She signalled to the foreman.

Chris held the foreman's right arm. "Not a word to her. I have a strange feeling about this. She doesn't need to know anything from you. Let them do it the official way. Keep her distracted until the DI comes out." He passed him the keys. "Don't forget to lock up."

The foreman nodded and waved to his workmates to join him.

Chris observed their body language. Fingers pointing, hands directing and nods from all parties. The steel door creaked open. Pockets emerged sullen faced behind Fran.

"We're out of here. Something's not right about all this." He shook his head and let out a long sigh. "Back to Parkside nick. Must acknowledge my interest. Only way to get some attention." He trudged through the tarpaulin and gate. The man wasn't happy.

Fran tipped Chris's right shoulder. "I'm heading home. I'll send you the pics." She pecked his lips. "When will we meet?"

He saw Pockets pacing beside the car. "He's going mental. It's not good for him to be working off the books. How about we take timeout to research?"

"I think that would work."

"So, next week will probably be best. You can stay. Have more time to compare notes."

"I bought a spare toothbrush."

He smiled, waiting as she readied herself to travel.

"Oi, haven't got all day," Pockets shouted.

55 THE RAID

Early Wednesday, July 4

Douglas Cartwright had a middle name, precision. His hacking expertise ensured the route into Cambridge Science Park from Kings Hedge Road was clear. CCTV ignored a Medivan heading towards Ostrofman's goods entrance. The transport and six-man pillaging team stayed undetectable throughout the planned thirty-minute job.

DCI King's information proved correct. A guard walked a ten-minute route every hour. Another sat in an office drinking coffee and barely took his eyes from a book to glance at the static monitors. The guards took a long break from 2:00 a.m. allowing ample time.

Specs was warned by King, no guns this time.

The gang, wearing dark-blue overalls, black ski-masks, and gloves, stayed silent as the driver turned the engine off. Climbing out, they knew their tasks. One raider guaranteed the smooth operation from the top of the annex warehouse's grey steel fire escape. Dim carpark lamps from the next building gave enough light through the stockroom's high glass windows. Inside, boxes of Psilocybin, Mescaline, and Ayahuasca were quickly and quietly moved down to the waiting van. Perfect ingredients for what Specs called 'happy' tablets. Africa's loss will be London's drug-needing society's gain and Specs' empire.

In the comfort of his Shoreditch office, Douglas continued to ensure that all cameras around the building's immediate area showed no movement. However, the road cams were put back on until the van was ready to exit the industrial park. His phone alerted him to a text:

Ready to leave.

He switched the cameras to safe mode and texted:

All clear.

The Medivan cruised from the park back onto Kings Hedge Road. Once the vehicle was clear, Douglas enabled all cameras.

It wasn't unusual to see a Medivan arrive at Addenbrooke's hospital's helipad off Dame Mary Archer Way, south Cambridge. A refitted Sikorsky, bearing the required red crosses, waited to be loaded beside a Ford Sierra. Within twenty minutes, the craft was airborne towards London's dockland. The van and Ford headed to Dernford Lake.

**

The Sikorsky landed on the Isle of Dogs' heliport. The sun hadn't arrived during the cargo switch from the helicopter to an adjoining storage facility.

A familiar aroma of a Havana cigar wafted through the complex.

"It went smooth, boss," a tall, dark-clothed man said. "Best yet."

"We will know soon enough how smooth when they open for business. How much of a haul?" Specs took a satisfying pull on the cigar.

"As it happens, the chopper was almost full."

Specs waved a hand.

A thin, bespectacled man climbed out of a car: the chemist.

"Can you tell me just by looking at the number of boxes, what would be the profit?" Specs asked.

The chemist took a few seconds then added more time as the final boxes were brought in. "When the mix is right, possibly as much as five hundred percent more than the original cost of the ingredients—at least."

Specs eyes widened. "Impressed. How quick could you brew up samples?"

"But I didn't expect Psilocybin?"

"My source told me the three boxes were due to be shipped to the U.S. He thought they would add more to the quality." Specs drew on the cigar.

"Well, give me a few days. I'll make two sample batches—one high quality for tasters."

"You know me well, Meyer. Fantastic." Specs drew him back to the car. "I'll send two boys to you in a couple of days. You take what is needed for the samples and get back to me."

Meyer sat in the passenger seat as Specs climbed behind the wheel tossing the cigar butt before shutting the door.

"Breakfast?" He smiled to Meyer.

"Yes, Specs. Usual place, eh."

"Nothing better."

56 THE NEWS

In his office, Chris sipped coffee. He perused a list of barman candidates on the laptop. Local preferred with bar work experience and knowledge of the Tavern. Many had left their phone contact details, some email addresses.

Looks promising.

He picked up his phone and called a number. He didn't have to wait long. "Hello, is that Kumar Varma? Great. I'm Chris Freeman, I own the Tavern on Lower Clapton and I see you're looking for employment." He sipped listening to the reply. "Oh, and when do you expect to start there? — Two weeks? Okay, here's the deal. Come try out here first, say nothing, off the books and if we work well, you can make your mind up." He drank again. "No problem, I promise. How about this evening, sixish? It will suit because we only have a few try-hard karaoke singers on later. — You will? Fantastic, Kumar. See you then."

He stood carrying his mug back to the bar, switched the GNC TV on and chose *Sky News*. He barely glanced at the screen when about to open the cellar hatch.

'We will know the final haul by the end of the day,' a news announcer said.

His head hurt. He winced and turned swiftly. The scene was well-known. A three storey, light brown brick building, pristine shrubbery surrounding a grey cobbled courtyard. The camera moved to a steel fire-escape.

Ostrofman Pharmaceuticals.

He placed the mug on the counter continuing to watch the report.

'A police spokesperson gave no details of the early morning robbery only saying no one was harmed and as you can see—'

The camera scanned the building and zoomed onto poles along the road.

'There are many CCTV cameras available to check on possible movement to and from the building. How this was done remains a mystery for now as nothing was damaged either inside or out. Security was on duty and reported no incidents. An internal investigation started immediately...'

A rhythmic vibration along with 'Hey Girl Don't Bother Me'. Chris took the phone from his shorts.

"Pockets, I know. You heard anything?" He moved to a barstool listening. "How much? — Three million worth? For what?" He took a mouthful of tepid coffee. "You think so? It will take a good chemist and lab to transform them into street drugs. — They took Psilocybin as well.

Fuck me pink. I don't know—if adding that and depending on the strength, low price of six to high of, say ten million pounds. If they're adjusted, you know, recipes differed then the price could go higher—twenty, even higher." He finished the coffee. "Yep, I agree it has to be Specs. Heard he is running low — The van was burnt out near a lake? — Okay, I'll do some magic searching, so drop in on Thursday. I have a trainee starting tonight. Okay, cheers, Bert."

He rounded his tense shoulders then turned on the stool. His eyes studied the décor, walls, floors, and ceiling as if for the first time. He breathed deep and long.

57 THE IRRITATING BARFLIES

The afternoon dragged for Chris. Giving both Rory and Alice another day off was probably a mistake. His head hurt again. Opening a tab box, he took two out and swallowed them with the help of water. He needed time for research and the Ostrofman incident added more tension.

He barely talked to Vince and three other customers as he recleaned tables and checked the beer garden for non-existent smokers. He had turned Sky News off all TVs; Chris knew more than the reporters did.

A squeaking door interrupted his cleaning.

"Did you see the news, Chris?" Alan waddled breathlessly towards a barstool. "Hi, Vince." He waved to other customers.

"What's up, Sherlock?" Vince asked.

Chris walked behind the bar. "Usual, Alan?"

"Yes, please," Alan enthused. "It was Chris's old firm that was robbed. Millions worth of drugs taken."

Chris held it in.

Fucksake. He really gets on my tits at the best of times.

Vince took interest. "No way. No wonder you're quiet. Was afraid to ask why."

Same entrance sound, another GN member.

Chris looked to the ceiling.

Here we go.

"Chris, was that your old place that was robbed?" Mike blasted above the sound of his echoing flip-flops.

He ignored the question. "Usual pint, Mike?"

Mike took his customary stool left of Vince. "Yeah, hi Vince, Alan." He sounded breathless.

"Did you run here?" Vince said.

Chris placed the two pints on beer mats. "Now, before this gets out of hand and context—I know nothing more than what is on the news. I'm obviously not happy about the robbery but I don't want to be quizzed by you lot or anyone else." He put out a hand for payment.

The till almost shot off the back counter as he opened it. He placed fivers in a slot and took out their change, slamming it shut.

Mike and Alan nodded to the cancer box.

Chris dropped the coins in. "Sorry. I knew this was expected from customers." He looked hard at Mike. "But with Humph dying the way he did and guns missing. It's been a tough few weeks since back from a great break. My knee's aching and head getting worse."

The three GNs looked away from him to their drinks.

Alan glanced up. "I'm sorry, Chris. It's just the coincidence."

That word hit Chris hard.

Pockets' fav word. He's fucking right. No such thing in this case.

"I suppose so, Alan." Chris acknowledged another customer's order. "By the way, have to try out a new barman this evening. So, if you lot are here when he arrives, pay due respect. Give him a chance."

The GN barflies smiled and nodded approvement.

"Will give Wonder and Irish a break and some leeway on hours," Mike said.

"True. You know him? Local?" Vince asked Chris.

"Local. Don't know him or recognise the name. And no, I won't tell because I don't want tell-tale stories. Want to sus him out myself." Chris strained a smile, pleased to have diverted an unwanted subject.

"Local, eh. Should be a laugh." Mike lowered a mouthful.

"Jesus. I hope you mean he'll have a laugh at you." Chris' lips tightened. "Some people have very short memories."

Alan straightened from his stoop over the counter and looked sharply at Mike.

"Listen, drop everything. Change the fucking subjects and just drink and chat." Chris had shown another side to his customers.

I don't need all this grief. Head is getting worse. Wish I could finish it all.

His eyes flamed as never witnessed before. They knew of Chris's ability to nip rows in the bud, but his outward expression seemed different. He finished off a customer's order, accepted his correct cash as 'Hey Girl Don't Bother Me' played again. At the till he looked at the caller's name and answered his phone. "Hey Dad."

58 THE NEW STAFF

The door squeaked right on six o'clock. A young t-shirted man walk towards the bar.

Alan sat with Mike at GNC; his eyes widened.

Chris stood behind the bar. "Ah, you must be Kumar." He waved a hand to the counter hatch. "Come through."

"Thank you," Kumar said.

Alan continued to watch the small olive-skinned man follow Chris to the office.

Mike noticed Alan's concentration. "Talk about being obvious, Alan."

"Oh, sorry. It was his pink top that drew my attention." He saw Mike's unconvinced stare. "Well, he is good looking."

"I bet you change your drinking hours to the new barman's working hours if he gets the job." Mike looked at his almost empty glass. "Might stay for one more. Just to keep an eye on your behaviour."

**

Chris closed his office door behind the young man. "Please, have a seat."

Kumar sat opposite.

"Now, first up, I don't want to know about your upcoming job. I want to see if you are as good as your CV states, and you like this place. I may then tempt you to work here."

"Okay, Mister Freeman. I was in here a few times when home from studies. As a rule, I don't normally go to pubs just to socialise off hand. I meet up for occasions." He shifted uneasy in the chair.

"I'm not judging your drinking habits or social life. My concern is this pub. You getting to know the regulars, realise their privacy if needed, no eavesdropping, be friendly but not stern. Get to know their habits. Keeping behind the bar and tables clean. No empty glasses stacking up." Chris smiled.

"That's fine. As you saw, I managed a college bar for two years at Cambridge and part-timed in bars while studying abroad." Kumar relaxed.

"Fantastic." Chris clapped once. "But can you pull pints under pressure without effing and blinding? Turn to the bottles of spirits and pick up the right brand of gin or whiskey? Put up with some obvious banter with a smile and give some back where needed?"

Kumar fidgeted.

"I see some doubt. I know the pub you may be working in, and you won't last a busy weekend during football season," Chris said.

"I have worked in very busy bars."

Chris read the young man's fidgeting. *No you haven't.*

"But they weren't Spurs' bars and you're a Hammer. West Ham and Tottenham never mixed well. Won't go well for you if West Ham scored and you showed a smidgen of delight." Chris couldn't hold the laugh in.

Kumar was bewildered.

"C'mon—let's give you a go. Oh, fifty in the hand for this night only. If we suit each other, I'll throw you to the wolves Friday night. What say you?"

The young man bore a smile. "Yes, Mister Freeman."

"That will do for tonight. If I keep you, then you can call me Chris or Boss." Chris led him to the bar.

"Right, lads. This is Super Hammers supporter, Kumar." Chris patted Kumar's back. "He'll be temp for the night. Don't over work him."

"Hello, Kumar, I'm Mike," Mr. Wonderful opened. "Pint, please."

Chris shook his head and managed a smile. "He's commonly known as Mister Wonderful or Muscles for obvious reasons when needs must."

"Hi, Kumar." Alan offered a hand over the counter. "I'm Alan. You can call me anything, but not too early."

Kumar felt his soft hand and smiled. "Hello, Alan and Mike."

"Right. Mike's tipple is Fullers or gin and tonic. Alan's mild, bitter or a hug." Chris turned Kumar to the till. "For tonight I keyed in one two three for your till code. All spare staff use it. If this works out, I'll give you a regular one. I'll serve these two. Have a look around the pub, beer garden, gents. Say 'hi' to the few that are here while cleaning the tables for a few minutes." He went to the taps.

Alan's eyes followed the young man.

"Only one warning, Alan. Not here if he's regular and on duty. Leave him be. I want Kumar to work not get your nuts off." Chris's eyes penetrated Alan.

"I'm sorry but—"

"I know—and he is, but don't go showing him interest." Chris placed two pints on the counter and looked at Mike. "And you. I gave you the chance and you earned it. So, no more underhand slagging." He turned to another customer.

59 THE GUINNNESS

Sunday July 8

Things had quietened during the week with only phone calls and emails being the trio's main contacts. A temptation to look into Fran's background proved too much to resist. She had become more than an interruption to his mature bachelor life.

She's drawn me out, given me something to focus on and not just sex.

Her name flashed onto the laptop screen.

What am I doing?

Her family earned their wealth through the East Indian Company in the early seventeenth century. Related to Sir Henry Middleton, one of the main seafarers.

Later family members broke away becoming involved within the justice systems of the colonies and the UK.

She's brilliant, but why come into my life now?

He switched to updating his diary before going down to the bar.

A reverberating engine alerted him to Fran's return. He walked to the private entrance and peeked onto the alley.

He waved. "Hey, Fran."

She turned while removing her helmet. "Hi, Chris." She walked to him and pecked his cheek.

"Nice. Bring whatever you have with you and leave them upstairs." He reached to the private stairs door and unlocked it. He looked out again, mouth screwed, and eyes squinted. "That's if you're staying of course."

She waved a pink toothbrush and smiled while passing through the entrance.

His eyes brightened and closed the side door. "I'll be in the bar. Only a couple of customers."

"Okay, Chris."

The counter area was customer free. At the front window, two old lads chatted quietly and sometimes laughed enjoying their pints. Chris attended to the coffee maker and pottered around behind the bar.

What's wrong with me? She's becoming a distraction.

He rubbed his head and acknowledged a signal from one of the men. He began to fill two more pint glasses.

"It *is* quiet." The sound of Fran's soft voice raised the old lads' head. She waved to them.

"It is. Tell you now, I hired another barman. He worked a couple of nights this weekend. It was getting mad some nights here and Alice is really part-time." He let the Guinness settle.

Consideration of Tragedies

She nodded to the pints on the drip tray. "Oh. That's how it's done."

"Only way to pour a good pint of the black stuff. Top them up after a few minutes."

"Good you hired another barman. Can I finish them off and bring them over?"

"Yeah, give them a minute more. When the tan cream has turned dark, they're ready to top up."

"I heard about the robbery. We can chat if you like before it gets busy."

"That's a plan. I'm breaking in Kumar hard. Have him in at two then at eight."

"What's he like?" She looked at the pints. "Oh, can I top up now?"

Chris nodded. "Do it slow."

He watched her let the almost white creamy head reach the top of each glass and place them to finally settle for serving.

"Great job. Even they appreciate it."

Fran waved to the men's thumbs-up.

"Kumar's good. Dragged him away from a possible disastrous job in another footballing pub." He winked. "Can't mention their name with Wenger looking on."

"No idea what you are on about." She picked up the pints and carefully brought them to the old lads.

He again watched her talking to them.

She has it all. Charm, gift of the gab, looks, fun.

60 THE DISCUSSIONS

Chris wasn't mindful of his stare as Fran chatted with the old lads. She returned minutes later carrying empty glasses and sat on a barstool.

"They know your dad," she said.

"Yes. Played dominos with them on Sunday mornings. Noisiest crowd ever in this pub. Banging the tiles on the table, shaking the coin filled ashtrays making sure all paid for the next round." He nodded. "If old Jack there spotted a player making a mistake. Bedlam. And God help a customer with a Sunday paper. He wouldn't be able to concentrate on what he was reading." He took the glasses off the bar and placed them in the tray.

"Rough times."

"Coffee?"

"Thanks, Chris—black."

He poured two mugs, placed them on the counter with a bowl of sugar sachets.

They quietly talked about Pockets' reaction to the derelict house.

"You should've seen him at Cambridge nick. He made a show of the DS in charge. Even a DCI couldn't win with him. Pockets wanted to know why only one constable was stationed outside without a *sign in* board and why builders are still on the site. Went mental," he told her.

They simultaneously drank from their mugs.

"Then what?" She leaned forward.

"He got copies of the lot. Names of the bodies, preliminary results with assurance of receiving the full ones. Photos of the find and inside the house. The owners of the property. Everything."

"Who owns the house?"

"The local parish."

Her large eyes widened more.

The door squeaked.

"Eager chap. Tell more later," he said.

Kumar walked in carrying a small backpack.

"You planning on staying the night too, Kumar? This is Fran. You're taking her place 'cos I sacked her last week."

Kumar stopped; eyes enlarged. "I-I'm sorry—"

She shook his free hand. "Don't mind him. I packed up before he sacked me. Good to meet you."

"Thank you—you too." He looked at his boss. "Where can I leave this?"

"Hang it on a free hook in the office."

When Kumar was out of earshot, she turned to Chris. "Is he?"

The answer was in Chris's raised brows.

The young man stood behind the bar.

"You're early, but you can start with the till. Here's your own code. Remember it and when sure, get rid of the paper." Chris palmed Kumar a note.

The new barman went about his work, introducing himself to the old lads and any new customer.

Fran took another sip. "He's a gem. Is he local?"

"Yeah, well not far. Near Hackney Downs. It's about a twenty minute walk."

"Okay." She took another sip. "The Parish you said. How did Specs get involved with that?"

"Don't know. But we will find out, I'm sure."

"You're a natural P.I."

The door squeaked again.

"That's the end of our discussion. Watchya, Vince. Enjoy your break?" He announced the regular and nodded to Kumar.

"Yeah, good time," Vince said.

"Yes, sir. What will I get you?" Kumar smiled.

Vince jolted back. "Fucking hell. Where'd you come from?"

Chris said nothing; just watched.

"Me mum. Now, what would you like?"

The old lads joined Chris and Fran's hand clapping.

With his eyes still wide, Vince ordered. "Pint of Fullers, please."

The barman stuck out a hand between the taps while pulling the pint. "I'm Kumar."

"Hi, Kumar—Vince."

"Ah, the postman that we threw off the route." Kumar put the glass in front of stunned Vince. "There you go."

"They wanted me to do Nightingale apartments too. I asked for a— listen, who are you?"

"Don't mind him, Vince. He's a quick learner. A new fulltime barman. I've decided to ease back, and Alice is overworked with her care job."

Chris waved to the old lads and walked behind the bar.

"Eh, oh, thank you." Vince handed over the correct money. "Hi, Fran. But how did you know, Kumar?" He took a mouthful.

"Those guys told me about GNC." Kumar nodded to the front window. "I met two nutters the other evening and have a mate that comes here with his girlfriend. So, know of this place."

"Chris, you do pick them well." Vince raised his glass.

**

When Rory arrived, Chris introduced him to Kumar and let them get to know routines.

Upstairs, Fran snuggled to Chris under the sheets.

"Pockets is coming at seven thirty." He turned to the radio alarm. "It's six thirty. Fancy a Chinese?"

"No, you're enough."

She quickly straddled him. Her breast inches from his lips. It was hard to resist. He pecked them, rolled her over and climbed out of the bed.

"You're a tease." Her laughter was a tonic missed for years.

He ordered the delivery.

She freshened up and changed clothes.

He was soon showered and dressed in time to answer Rory's call about the food.

"Back soon. Set the plates please, Fran."

At the bottom of the stairs Rory gave him a warm large brown bag. "Kumar's good, boss."

"I guess I'm just blessed. Look after him when I'm not here. He's on a little less than you two per hour but rising him in a month if he's still here. You and Alice will get a rise then."

"Jesus. We didn't expect that."

"I told you. I'm easing back working long hours." Chris pulled two small bags from the bigger one. "Here. You do like chicken balls and chips?"

"Yeah, cheers."

"Eat in the office. If Pockets gets here before we come down, give him a pint."

Chris was gone, door shut, and bare footsteps padded the stairs.

61 THE WHITE CORKBOARD

Later, Chris left the Den windows wide open to emit the memory of Chinese chicken curry. He sat opposite Pockets and Fran at the breakfast counter. Armed with notebooks and a variety of coloured pens, they discussed their findings and marked any connections in red ink.

Pockets remained impressed with the white corkboard set up. Persons of interest names and places headed each list on the reversable board. Chris had pinned photos of the bodies on the right side, writing their names in red underneath each one. As the evening stretched, Pockets drew question marks beside the bodies extending arrows to King, Specs, and a blank photo with a large red X in the centre.

Pockets rubbed his chin. "Who is he? There's one person that has connections to almost all here."

"We have to join all the dots." Chris stood. "So, what have we learned?"

Fran took out her notebook. "Right. Humph's old firm are Ropers Builder's solicitors. They go under the corporate banner but in fact operate in the darker corners of society."

"Yes." Pockets jumped in. "Humph was actually researching them and a client—" He flicked through his notebook. "Missus Sarah Bryant. The cancer patient. This is where your old place comes in, Chris."

Chris noticed Fran's head slowly turn to the board. "Are you okay?"

"Yes—yes. Carry on," she said.

"That poor woman must have gone through hell after taking the illegal tablets." Chris opened his notes. "But I'm not convinced they are all directly connected. Sorry, Pockets, but some of this is coincidental. Others had suffered the same symptoms after taking the tabs. Missus Bryant appears to be the only one that had died."

Fran stared at Chris.

Pockets raised his hands in defeat. "You're right. Now, those bodies were dumped within three days of each other. All shot to the head close range with the same calibre, nine millimetre. Lens and Peters were last." Another page turned. "Blood stains in the pleasure room matched three bodies." He stopped, took a deep breath. "Sorry—semen was found but hard to distinguish the age. Analysis can't determine anything over a year."

Chris paced, marker in hand. "Theory. What if Lens and Peters were involved, you know, with each other? What if they used this place and kids weren't implicated?"

Pockets scratched his head. "Okay. Try this. There was a child sex ring involved. One of the bodies was a known paedo. Another ran a brothel in

Consideration of Tragedies

Cambridge. Parkside said they remain open cases. The fifth was a missing industrialist."

"Johnston?" Chris blustered out. "He packed up politics and joined the board of Kerner. We bought them out soon after."

"Yes." Pockets sat straight. "William Johnston. He's related to the paedo—fuck. They're brothers, well, step-brothers. Another step-brother, Stephen, is an MP."

Fran re-joined the discussion. "What about Humph's cottage? Children's play area, single beds recently used. And an incident in Mill Road involving a professor, students, and another unnamed man. Oh no." She looked at the report from a file. "The man was looking for his son." She glanced to her companions. "The boy was only twelve."

Chris rubbed his face.

"This was covered up. Any signature on the report?" Pockets asked her.

"It's stained—probably on purpose. DS T, something. There's an S then probably a five or six-letter surname. I can make out an A then an N." She breathed disappointment.

"Year?" Pockets asked.

"Twenty oh seven." She looked up from the file.

His lips tightened, then puffed. "DS Travis A King. Tow rag."

"Jesus," Chris said. "What the fuck was that man not into?"

"I know what to do. I need a good DS for a short while. Pete is off on hols soon." Pockets looked at Chris.

"Yeah. Him, Norma, and the kids have one of my places in Lanzarote but not until August."

"So, I'll put in a request to my soon to be retired deputy commissioner cousin for DS Harley King to be temporarily transferred to my department."

Chris broke into uncontrollable laughter. He coughed and took up a bottle of Pils taking a short swig.

Fran patted his back as he sat again.

"Is he related to the DCI?" she asked.

"His son," Pockets revealed.

"Are you for real? If he accepts the move and if Joanne knows he's back." Chris's head shook in disappointment.

"Don't you see? King will be distracted—thrown off balance. I mean, can you imagine when Harley walks into Newington station? His old man won't wait for the lift. He'll take three, four steps at a time to get to my office. His phone will be tapping into loads of numbers trying to get answers as to why his son's posted there." Pockets suddenly uplifted.

Fran was lost to the conversation. Her eyes flitted to both men waiting to be told what was being said.

"Joanne Leigh, travel agent and regular, had a long affair with Harley, and he was forced to go to Hendon or be transferred to the sticks as a local Bobby," Chris explained to her. "Do you want a glass of something? Wine? We can move downstairs soon."

"Yeah, go on," Pockets said.

Fran nodded.

Chris poured the wine into two glasses. "Harley and his old man came to fisty cuffs. Unfortunately, his auld fella won."

"He's a tough one alright," Pockets confirmed.

"Joanne went on the bottle. I grabbed her back from destruction. Steve Urban gave her the contact for our away game stays. Now her travel company is earning big." Chris passed the glasses to them. "If Harley comes back, Pockets, there may be unfortunate circumstances. Is this really worth the price of a woman's happiness?"

"I know what happened and Joanne Leigh was on the brink. So, this is your part. You must break it to her as calmly as possible. I don't know. Tell her he's up for promotion but needs field work." Pockets took a mouthful.

"I'll do it." Fran smiled.

Chris bent over the counter to her. "I believe you could. When do you reckon we can get all this in motion?" He moved from the counter. "Fuck. What about Raz? The papers?"

"Relax, Chris. The press haven't any names or how and when the bodies were buried. But it would be good to find out who the young boy was in Mill Road. If he can come forward or perhaps name names, even if he has knowledge of other children, it could help." Another swallow was enjoyed. Pockets moved his shoulders and lower back for comfort.

"I heard that crack in your neck," Chris said. "We have enough to get on with. I don't really know Harley—met him perhaps a few times. His mum must have been an angel."

"Her name was Angela. A star. She was a nurse."

Pockets related some tales about her then eyed his watch. "Pint?"

"Are you buying?" Fran asked.

"I like her, Chris."

.

62 THE GODFATHER

Chris led the way to the drinking side of the bar. Only Mike occupied a GNC stool.

"Watchya, Fran—Pockets." Mike saw Chris's expression. He didn't want to dirty his bib further. "All good? Drink?" He bit his lip trying to hold back smart-arse remarks.

"And why not, Muscles. Cheers." Pockets was about to sit beside him. "Well, I never. Young Kumar Varma."

Pockets stared as Kumar walked from a young couple's table with empty glasses and went behind the bar.

The new barman looked up when leaving the glasses in the dishwasher. "Uncle Bert." He rushed a hand over the counter.

Pockets shook it and sat.

"It's good to see you. How have you been?" Kumar asked.

Chris, GN and Rory waited for the next words.

"I'm good, Kumar." Pockets recognised Chris's inquisitive stare. "Me and Kumar's dad went to school together. I'm Kumar's Godfather."

Chris tapped Pockets right shoulder and assisted Fran to a stool beside the DI.

"He's a good lad and barman, Chris. Lucky to have him," Pockets said.

Rory's purposeful gruff smirk drew Pockets' attention.

"Ah go on witchya, as you would say. Goes without saying you're still top, Rory." Pocket's winked.

The top barman smiled. "Can't wait to tell Alice."

"Oh, dear, Bert. That shovel is working well." Laughter tears glistened in Fran's eyes.

Chris's left tic of the head told Kumar to get back to work.

"He's here to work on probation for a month. When we decide if he is suited, you can small talk all you like when biz is slack," Chris told Pockets. He twirled a finger to Rory for a round of drinks. "The DI has decided to exercise a hand and reach for his wallet. Please, no applause for this complicated trick."

The plea didn't work. A round of clapping preceded the round of drinks.

Pockets bowed to the audience and magically produced his brown leather wallet. Simultaneously, a passing ambulance's siren rushed towards its destination.

"Pockets' wallet alarm just went off."

Rory's quip took a standing ovation.

Pockets smiled and shook his hand. "I deserved that. But Muscles can get the next round."

Mike thumbed-up.

**

The bar almost emptied after closing time. Chris locked the door behind Rory and Kumar.

Chris returned to the investigators. "We've done well so far."

"Sure have. Anyway, you two look tired, I'm bolloxed." Pockets lowered what remained in his glass. "Listen, before I go, I just want to say thanks for giving Kumar a shot. Much different than he was as a kid but turned out good considering."

"What you going on about?" Chris' brow furrowed.

"Well, he spent holidays with a cousin or pal when about eleven— twelve. That's when he changed. His dad told me he went all quiet when he got home. Wouldn't go back the next year. Stayed in his room studying. Hardly mixed with school pals. Two and two."

"He never talked about it?" Fran asked.

"Not a word."

"Jesus. Best not talk within ear shot, eh," Chris said.

"He's a good young man. Trusting too. Anyway, just a thought. I'm off."

"Have you far to go?" Fran asked.

"Just a few minutes of unsteady walking to Saint John's Church Road around the corner. Usually, five but probably ten-minute walk."

"You're a good man, under the cop bravado thing." She turned to Chris. "You two really work well together."

Chris eyed Pockets and vice versa.

"We'll say no more about Kumar." Chris patted Pockets' shoulder.

Pockets put his jacket on.

Fran watched them go through to the door. She breathed easy; licked her lips and swallowed the scotch and orange.

"Mmmm."

63 THE ALGORITHMS

Tuesday July 10

Fran had stayed a few days. The Tavern's clientele observed their relationship. While Chris worked the bar and attended to deliveries, she busied herself with the investigation. She typed notes, placing new information on the board. When together, and not in bed, they rearranged the arrows and photos to indicate relationships with each person of interest.

She had to return home though. They made their way to the side door.

"I'm not going to tell Raz about his cousin," he said.

"Are you sure?"

"Yes. Best that Parkside get in touch. Humph fucked up his head already."

She released him after a quick kiss and placed her small backpack into the bike's carrier. "That's a good idea."

His eyes followed her every move. "You coming for another stay?"

She walked back to him. "Yes, please." She went up on her toes and kissed longer. "I'll have all Humph's relative recordings on a disc soon. I know it's old school but best not have them on 'the cloud'." She straddled the bike.

His eyes stayed fixed on her. "I have some serious hacking to do later."

"You should be careful."

"It's my own design. All algorithms are unique to me. I remain anonymous out there in the tech world. You should be wary. You might not have any money in your account later." Chris leaned in and kissed her.

"What?" she managed to say when getting air.

"Did you think that sort of thing was only in movies? I promise I'll look where I need to. I designed the system to track suspicious interference with our products. That's why we stayed honest, and I created an unbreakable online security system. Cannot be hacked. Of course, I disconnected the system when we sold out, but I still have the methodology." He kissed Fran's cheek to assure her. "It's so secure, that it changes each day, has a safe mode that attacks any hacker, rendering their system incurable. Drive safe, love. Call me."

Fran put the helmet on and blew him a kiss.

Chris stepped back. *Did I say 'love'?*

Fran drove off.

He lingered as if she would come back.

64 THE BIG SURPRISES

Thursday July 12

Chris got stuck into the accounts disappointed that Fran had to cancel the weekend. He entered the bar from the office.

Alice chatted with, Kumar.

The door squeaked.

Looking up from the taps, Kumar froze. Ale missed the glass he held.

"Are you alright?" Alice asked.

"Eh, yes. Just thought I knew that man," Kumar said.

Chris realised his sudden fear. "Perhaps you should knock off early. Go on. You've done well and deserve the rest of the night off."

"It's okay, boss. Really just a—"

"Go after you tilled up." Chris patted his back.

"Yes, Raz? Usual?" Alice asked the baker.

"Thanks, Alice. New barman?" the genial giant asked.

"Yeah. Almost two weeks. He's good. Hi, Marge. Hope you enjoyed the break." Alice responded to the wave from Raz's wife. "I'll bring them over."

Raz nodded and joined Marge at a pillar.

Kumar went to the office followed by Chris.

"The customers like you. Rory and Alice reported that you have learned quickly. But I saw something in your eyes when Raz walked in." Chris remained emotionless.

"It was nothing, really."

What will I do?

"Do you like working here?"

"Yes, enjoyed the couple of weeks."

"Sit." Chris smiled and closed the door.

Kumar sulked into the chair hugging his backpack.

Chris sat opposite waiting.

"The big man," Kumar said.

"Raz Pringle, the baker?"

"He's a baker?" Kumar shuddered.

Chris eased back in his chair. "You told me that you studied at Cambridge."

Kumar froze again. Beads of sweat speckled his brow.

Chris puffed.

Oh no.

"Don't move. Relax." Chris stood, patted Kumar's shoulder, and went into the bar.

"Alice, you saw Kumar's face."

"Yes, boss. Is he okay? Sorry, but he went pale."

"Can you hang until Rory comes on?"

"Yes, boss."

He nodded and went out to the alley. Head aching again, he took his phone from a pocket and pressed.

Seconds passed. "Fran, any chance you can come by? You're not going to believe what has happened — You can't? Okay." Chris listened to Fran's muffled reply. "One of Pockets favourite coincidences. Going to call him and let you know the story later."

He hung up and returned to the office closing the door. "I've a feeling you have met someone looking like Raz."

Kumar shot up from the chair. "What do you mean?"

"C'mon, sit for a while. I'm making a call in front of you, so you know I'm not messing about."

Kumar sat and hugged his backpack again.

Chris pressed another name and waited. "Pockets, how are you? Oh sorry, give her my love." His eyebrows rose. "Something has come up— yes, important info. It concerns your Godson."

Kumar's eyes widened.

"Yeah, he saw someone that has brought back a memory — Yes, it does concern what we are looking into. — No, just come here ASAP. — Six o'clock? Grand." He sighed after hanging up.

"I didn't know Bert Macken was Pockets." Kumar fidgeted. "I heard about this copper looking into a mugging in Dalston. A neighbour's son was attacked, and she said Pockets will sort it out."

"Listen. Pockets told me about how you changed after some sort of holiday. Now you almost fainted at the sight of Raz. So, I reckon something happened to you on holiday. More than just high jinks." Chris studied the young man's doubt. "We are looking into something, and I suspect you may be able to help."

"Well, I–I. It's hard, you know." Kumar's knuckles paled with tension.

"Do you drink?"

Kumar managed to lift his brown eyes. "Yes."

"What's your tipple?"

"Eh, Guinness."

Chris jolted back. "Really? Fantastic." He tried to brighten the atmosphere. "We go to the bar. Alice is sound and knows something is up with you. She's not nosey."

"What if my friends come in?"

"Do they know something?"

"Met them in uni."

"Ah, getcha. They wouldn't know. Trust me. You'll be grand."

Chris stood, put an arm around the young man's shoulder and went to the bar. "Just two things. Stay at the hatch side and if Alan comes in just be cordial—you know, 'hi' et cetera."

"Okay."

"You'll be fine. Now, sit." He reassured him and went to the taps. "Thanks, Alice. Kumar's not the best. Chit-chat until Rory comes on. I'll put him wide."

She nodded.

He looked to Raz and Marge on pillar high stools as he pulled Kumar's Guinness.

Small world.

**

Chris and Kumar chatted quietly about football. A familiar figure approached.

"Pint, Bert?" Chris asked.

"Yep, I suppose I would need one." Pockets sat on Chris' vacant stool. "Hello, Kumar. What have you been up to?"

Kumar's head hung over the Guinness.

Chris eyed Pockets and shook his head while placing the drink in front of him.

"We'll move upstairs," he said.

"But what about the stuff?" Pockets asked. "You know—the board?"

Chris shrugged. "C'mon."

65 THE TALE OF KUMAR

Chris directed his guests to a sofa. He took a Pils from the fridge and then sat on an easy chair.

"Anyone want to tell me what's going on?" Pockets asked.

Chris took a short mouthful. "When he saw Raz, Kumar suddenly paled—if you catch my meaning. Him studying in Cambridge, well, one of your famous quotes came to mind."

Kumar shook his head. "I don't really want to talk about it. He just looked like someone else."

"Your Godfather is one of the best coppers I know. We just want to help."

"C'mon, son. Tell us how you thought you knew Raz," Pockets said.

Kumar stalled, twisting his pint glass. "I stayed with a cousin in Cambridge about eleven or twelve years ago for summer holidays. We hung out sometimes in his youth club. A Catholic club. There were art classes, self-defence, pool—you know."

Pockets and Chris nodded.

Kumar took a mouthful of Guinness. "We had walks, fishing on the River Cam. One trip to a regular spot, Baits Bite Lock, we left our bikes chained at the lock. Six of us and two youth leaders." He breathed heavily. "We set up gear and fished. All was great. Sandwiches, cola—you know, fun. One leader, Jeff, was called over to the other side by a tall man. He walked over the lock gate, chatted like old friends on a house barge. Jeff, came back and asked if any of us wanted to see inside a real houseboat but only one at a time." He shook and tears rolled down his face.

Pockets took a sharp intake of breath. "You don't have to say anymore, lad."

"It's okay." He gave a nervous chuckle. "I've bottled it up too long. It actually feels good to finally get it out. I've been afraid of relationships. Mostly stayed in my room." He wiped his eyes and continued. "Nothing happened on the barge. We took turns seeing it. Given cola. The big man did rub my bum a couple of times when getting on the barge and leaving. My cousin told me he did the same to him and another boy." His head shot up. "That man in the bar could almost be the man on the barge."

Chris read him. "Something did happen, though not on the barge."

Kumar breathed deep. "Yes. A few days later, me and my cousin had permission to stay overnight at his friend's house. But it wasn't his house. He was there with six or seven men. There were two pool tables in adjoining rooms downstairs. We joined in playing. Had our first alcohol drink. It was great. The big man was there but nothing happened sexually."

Another longer deep intake of breath. "It was the following week." Kumar hesitated.

Pockets' nod encouraged him to continue.

Kumar's hand shook taking a sip of Guinness. "Another night-over, but this time we were driven to a drab large building near a church. It was different that time. There were pool tables, darts, a small bar, sofas all over the big rooms downstairs. We were given drink but felt woozy after two glasses of beer." He looked to Pockets. "I remember we were brought upstairs. Two men took us into this large bedroom. It was weird. Chains on a wall and a man cuffed to the bed wearing weird rubber outfit." Kumar breathed deep again. "I was forced down to his—you know. My tracksuit bottoms were pulled down while I did that."

Chris jumped up. "Stop. No more. We get the ugly picture. Kumar, we saw the place during the week."

Kumar sat straight.

"There were bodies found in the outhouses," Pockets revealed.

"Oh fuck." Kumar grabbed the pint and almost drained it.

Chris uncovered the board. "We need your help. Look at these photos and names."

The young man stood beside him. His eyes widened.

"Those five." Kumar pointed to each photo of the dead men. "They were there. And he does look like the man in the bar." His finger prodded Noel Peters' face.

"He's his cousin," Chris said.

Kumar moved quickly backwards almost falling over the coffee table.

"What else? Who do you recognise?" Pockets asked.

"He's police?"

"Who?" Pockets went to the board. "Him? King?" His index finger tapped a photo.

"Yes. That's the man on the bed. When downstairs he took his mask off."

Chris and Pockets looked at each other, the board and to Kumar.

"Are you sure, Kumar? It's important that you are one hundred percent sure," Pockets said.

"Yes."

Chris paced the Den rubbing his face. The company's eyes followed him.

"Bastard—I should've—fuck." His right fist pounded the counter. He turned sharply to Kumar. "Go home, pack a bag or something for at least a week's stay. Say you're on standby and I'll pick you up later."

"What's got into you?" Pockets asked Chris.

"Kumar can stay in a spare room upstairs until we know he's safe. It's clean, fresh sheets, ensuite."

"Safe from what?" Kumar asked.

"Him." Chris pointed to King's photo.

"But why do I have to stay here?" Kumar protested.

"I just want to be sure that when the bodies' names are revealed, nothing else comes out that may bring back a memory or two for DCI King."

"He's Terror Travis?" Kumar slumped to a sofa.

"You've seen him about?" Pockets asked.

"No. Just stories around the Common and Clissold Park about him threatening—" He puffed. "My type, not colour."

Pockets breathed deep and shook his head. "I've to get my thoughts around this. Keep him safe here. If I hear any whispers, I'll let you know. Okay. I'm off home." Pockets lowered his drink. "I'll give you a lift, Kumar."

"Use the side door," Chris said.

Kumar's eyes dropped.

"You'll be grand. I'll call you when I'm on my way."

Alone, Chris puffed shaking his head. He sat at his laptop, pressed a few keys, and opened his diary. His fingers hung over the keyboard while staring at a page under 'D'.

Tidy up.

66 THE DEMISE OF A DRUNK

In north Clapton, elderly Marcus Devereux staggered down wide steps to the River Lea towpath from The Prince of Wales pub. Stopping on the last step, he tentatively placed his right foot on the path followed unsteadily by the left. His shoulders shuffled, pleased that he had made it without stumbling again. He took his cloth cap from a jacket pocket, placed it on a hairless head. He turned left to walk under Lea Bridge towards his old folks' apartment.

Marcus was a man of routine, rain, or shine. Thursday his all-day drinking day, leaving at eight before the younger crowd entered the pub. He never employed friendship since retiring from an ambulance service. He preferred his own company. Truth is, nobody liked him. A family outcast almost since the end of primary school years in Dublin's northside. Now, in London's East End, nothing had changed for the unpleasant man.

His potbelly wobbled through an ill-fitting stained shirt over wrong fitting trousers. His equally wrong fitting legs managed to bring him to a pillar. He leaned to it, took out a prepared roll-up cigarette. At least he had managed that sensible task before leaving the pub. The next bit was always tricky. Lighting the thin excuse of a smoke.

His back firmly against the pillar, Marcus huffed and puffed searching what seemed an endless pocket. Nobody about to assist him. Even if there was, he would probably refuse with some colourful language. Pulling a lighter roughly from the pocket resulted in it falling to the dirt path. It bounced twice to the river's edge.

"Fuck it."

Marcus sort of straightened and staggered low focusing on the lighter.

A tall man approached. "Need a hand?"

"Fuck off."

"I'll give you one anyway."

"I said—"

Water splashed about the man's feet as Marcus' arms struggled to find something firm to grab in the river. A hat floated away as his cries for help faded.

The man continued his evening stroll up the Prince of Wales steps.

67 THE TEMP TENANT

Chris gave Kumar a key for the stair-door. "Now, when settled, come down to the bar. There's another half hour before closing. Your pals are there. Sit with them, say nothing of what's happening. During your stay, use the main entrance to come in but leave via the side door."

"Cheers for this, boss."

"You're welcome, Kumar. Please trust us. It took a lot for you to come out with what you said. Specially as your family didn't know."

**

Chris kept an eye on Kumar through the bar mirror.

Rory never asked questions of his boss. He respected him too much; that and he paid well.

Alan sat nearby. "Are you pleased with your new barman?"

Rory placed his pint down.

"Thanks. You're still the best." Alan managed a wink and paid.

Chris chuckled. "Yes, Alan. Kumar is good and how many have you had?"

Something more up with this nuisance.

"Not many. Haven't had anything to eat since din though—hic. Sorry."

"You just focus on drinking and getting home. I never knew you liked looking at your reflection so much."

Alan swayed to glance at Chris. "What do you mean? I know what I look like."

"And now you are familiar with Kumar's fine features."

Just fuck off.

Alan coughed. "I don't know what you're talking about." He looked forward. "Oh, he's with his pals. I see now."

'Hey Girl Don't Bother Me' sang from Chris' pocket. "Phone, excuse me." He held it to his ear and walked towards the office. "What? — When? — How?" He stopped at the hatch. "I haven't seen him for years. — George saw more of him than me. — Well, because of the new estate at the Lea." Chris saw the silent stares from customers and staff. He raised a hand for calm. "It's Sunday. He must have been drunk. — Can this be done tomorrow? I've had a few and not paying for a taxi to see that old bastard. Yeah, okay, first thing. Thanks for letting me know, Pockets."

He returned to his seat. "Give me a Southie, Rory."

"What's up, boss?"

"Ah—a relation, Uncle Marcus, found in the Lea tonight." He took his

Consideration of Tragedies

glass. "Cheers, Rory. You remember him."

"Yes, boss. Smelly fucker. How can I forget. I had to pick him up in the gents."

Alan's stool strained. "I was here that Sunday. You only started a short while, Rory. George gave you a hand to bring him outside. Stools were knocked over, customers near the door held their drinks and noses."

"Alright, alright. Enough." Chris took a mouthful and waved a hand to Rory.

The last orders bell sounded three times.

"Mum's drunken brother. Brilliant brain gone to waste with drink. Fuck me pink." He slurped. "Might as well have a quick wake. Rory, do the honours all round." Chris counted heads.

Alan swayed.

"I see you home alright, Alan." He assured him.

Chris walked to Kumar's table. "Suppose you heard my *disappointment*. An uncle drowned in the Lea tonight so just having a mini wake. No rush. The till will be done so you're not buying any drink." He patted Kumar's shoulder.

Back on his seat. "What a fucking week. Need a holiday."

"What, hic, happened to him? I mean, turning to drink." Alan managed another swallow.

"Short story? As you know, my parents were medically trained, as was Marcus. Fantastic medic. Worked for many emergency departments. He was searched for due to his astounding lifesaving results. He should have been a doctor—surgeon even. Finally, he worked for the Spanish emergency services. Drink took him and he was suspended many times before shifted to the Canaries and La Palma." Chris took another sip of his favourite tipple. "What a waste." His eyes raised. "A senorita fucked him up."

"Oh, Spain, hic, makes sense now."

"My mum bailed him out more times. Dad couldn't give a fuck. Same here." He drummed the counter. "Rory, again if they want one more."

Later, after two more rounds, Chris and Kumar held each side of Alan as his legs struggled to remember their way back to his apartment.

68 THE REVELATIONS

Friday July 13

Chris winced while typing the latest updates to his diary. His head pounded. *I had to bring that forward. Kumar's revelations are mind blowing. Connections. Connections.*

He had bottled up much for years. Money meant nothing, though helped his security in both health and mind.

Chris had no need for Mike's Gym. When able, he would go for a mild jog, not putting too much pressure on his right knee. His workouts were in an exercise room next to the top spare room apartment, when having time to do so.

He banged out a Zeppelin riff on his Cajon drum. A form of therapy.

He had forgotten about the temp tenant.

A knock on his apartment door reminded him. "Come in, Kumar."

The dishevelled barman entered.

"Apologies for the noise. I actually forgot you were here." Chris sat at the counter. Took up his toast. "Led Zeppelin? Bonzo on drums?" He saw his blank expression. "You want breakfast, help yourself. It's an open kitchen."

"I heard you go out early." Kumar took two eggs from the fridge. He placed them in a pot of water and turned on the gas cooker.

"Went to the morgue first thing. Couldn't face that on a full stomach." He spread the butter evenly on toast. "Have you seen death? I mean, have you seen a dead person after an accident?"

"No. I've been to funerals. Saw open coffins." Kumar took slices of wholemeal and dropped them into the toaster.

"It's the paleness of the face. Their eyes ready to pop. Lips purpled. Horrible." Chris shivered.

"Awful."

"It was. Anyway, Fran's gone off to dig up some more info on that site. If you're up for it, peruse the board. Might jog memories. I'm heading down to let Missus M in. So, don't come down. The less that know what's going on, the quicker we get to a solution."

**

Alone in the Den, Kumar stared at the board from the counter. The talk had set him free of recurring nightmares for at least one night. His revelation about them to Chris when they returned from leaving Alan home was the tonic needed. The initial shock passed. His eyes widened to the white panel. He stood, saw paper and pens on the coffee table and started writing.

Mill Road, Parkside, Brotherton, King. He circled the last two named with a red marker, adding *raid*. More names and connections. *Johnstons, Brotherton* in black *youth club, King, Peters, Brotherton* in green *Waterbeach*. He stood and pinned the page to the right of the body names.

Near the bottom of the page, he penned *Father O'Brien for help* adding *Bishop* underneath.

The memories flooded back while Kumar sat at the counter and dipped his toasty soldiers into the now cold egg.

**

Chris called Kumar down to the bar after Mrs. M had left.

"Missus M noticed that the bar hadn't been tidied as usual," he told Kumar. "You see how careful we have to be."

"I understand, boss. Eh, I remembered stuff while looking at the board," Kumar said. "I stuck a page on it."

"Go on, tell me. I'm not running upstairs yet."

"You don't have Prof Brotherton on the board and only one Johnston."

"Who's Brotherton and which Johnston is missing?"

"The Prof was at Cambridge. He was head of my study area. I was about to change my subjects when he retired suddenly. He died after an accident a few years back."

"Okay."

"He was in Mill Road when it was raided, in the youth club with William Johnston and in Waterbeach with King and Peters. Stephen Johnston was on the barge with the baker's cousin."

"Very interesting. He's still in politics. Humph hadn't sussed that out. Well done. You never saw Specs though?"

"No. They're the only faces I remember. Brotherton used to like watching. He—he would have two boys doing things to each other—you know."

"Fucking bastards, the lot of them. I don't want King's involvement to come out yet. I would say Pockets will enjoy that part. Hold on. That politician, he's on the Hackney planning board."

He held his head.

George.

Chris filled the coffee machine.

"You just potter around here. You're not officially on duty but I'll look after you. Have to show some earnings to your parents, eh."

His phone sang and danced on the bar. Chris picked it up. "Hello—

Yes, speaking. What? He was, yes. — Really? Someone saw him pushed in?" He paid attention. "What you mean no?" His head shook with each word. "Listen. I saw my Uncle's body this morning. I was told he simply drowned, and he couldn't swim. No, I won't talk about him, so Fuck off." He hung up.

His short fuse lit once again, and he stormed from behind the bar. Chris moved this stool and that beer mat. His head in a spin not focussing on what he was doing. He glanced at the clock and repeated organising the mats.

Kumar said nothing, he just sorted already arranged glasses.

"Sorry. That was the *Gazette*. Hate journalists." Chris noticed Kumar's stare. "Yeah, well Fran is—Fran."

He went to the machine and poured coffee into a waiting 'Boss' mug. "Can you handle things here? Open, et cetera while I pop upstairs."

"Yes, boss. Perhaps you can review the board."

Chris didn't reply.

69 THE HARD TRUTH

Chris didn't look at the board before cleaning the entire home and doing his laundry. Although necessary to a dwelling, he was able to calmly put things together in his mind while dusting, vacuuming, and mopping the floor.

George.

His best pal entered his thoughts often since Fran's chat with him. Chris threw questions around his head while working:

Why did George lie about only arriving the day after their accident?

Why was he staying in Costa Teguise for two days before checking into The Fariones in Puerto de Carmen the night before the accident?

He has connections in the planning department. Johnston.

"Fuck."

What's his connection with Douglas Cartwright?

He put away the cleaning items and opened his laptop. His designer software showed no security problems. He launched his protected web search engine before typing *Douglas Cartwright*.

His software flashed through data, finally stopping at an encrypted window. This indicated what he wanted was hidden in scrambled documents. He released his hacking search code; *H.GTolkien4*. It had taken seconds to reveal *Douglas Cartwright Enterprises*.

"Fuck me pink. *Enterprises*. Really?" His eyes moved over the information. *He has improved.*

He needed a code to permit printing the pages. No bother for him. It was easily broken, and pages began to slide through his printer.

Chris' tech skills played major parts during his P.I. contracts. Codes always changed after each use of satellite cams. Misdirection of where his IP address originated from always easy for him.

I can't believe this genius kept records of numbers, names, accounts and more. Well, of course it was safe enough, but he hadn't banked on me.

He opened *Diary* and typed in vital notes. Stopping and rubbing his temple helped him focus. *When would be right? Soon, but keep tabs on developments, then perhaps—*

Ten minutes later he signed out of his laptop and brought the pages to the counter.

He read and made notes. Specs and King shined through many of them. Pages concerned Humph and his old firm. Connections with Brotherton and Cambridge. Noel Peters mentioned with Lens Morgan and others. Payments to Cartwright from F. Johnston. Monies passed to King and S Johnston.

Then there it was. George's name and bank deposits to Cartwright of which a percentage was passed onto four individuals only known as SK, MD, RI and LF.

Here are interesting pages.

He perused the revealing paragraphs carefully. Although knowing that Alan researched in Ostrofman labs in Sweden, Germany, and Cambridge, Chris had learned he and Douglas were a little more than pals.

"I don't believe it. Cambridge Science Park and Ostrofman's security systems, dates, times. Helicopter. Fuck me pink."

He wore a gratifying smirk and stretched.

No mention of boys or Kumar.

**

The information called for an emergency meeting that evening while Rory and Kumar held post in the bar. Chris worked the afternoon allowing Kumar to operate his memory and prepare for his Master's degree entry to university.

The Trio read over the pages.

"Can't do fuck all with this, though it's all here. It's only data on security with no names. Who were they given to? Is this info held on someone else's laptop?" Pockets asked.

"I forgot about that." Chris shot up off the kitchen stool. At his desk, he reopened the Cartwright pages and searched for *sent files*.

"Boom." His arms raised for success before printing pages.

He logged off, took the pages, and sat opposite Fran and Pockets. He placed them down.

"You never cease to amaze me, Chris. If we can now get Specs and King's emails, were sorted." Pockets took his glass and toasted. "To you, Chris Freeman."

Fran smiled. "I know a judge."

Three glasses were raised and clinked.

"I noted Kumar's last entry at the bottom of the page," she said.

"It's a small world and I believe he is Marty, Missus M's brother," Chris said.

"You told me about him," Fran said.

"Yeah—you met him, Pockets," he suggested.

"Yes. A nutter."

Fran laughed. "That's what Rory and Alan said."

"Come to think of it, it's strange he was shifted many times. Bishop? It's not a name. Kumar thinks a bishop was involved. That's why Marty was moved around. I bet he knew something was going on with the kids." Chris thumped the counter.

Pockets announced, "Okay. We have a lot going on. We need a timetable—two actually. One for us to work to and another in order of events thus far."

"Question. Did you get the year of the burial?" Fran asked Pockets.

"Yes. According to analysis of the soil and concrete layers, they were buried no earlier than two thousand and ten, and no later than twelve. I reckon eleven would be pretty much the year."

"But why had Humph said Peters was in Rome in thirteen?" Chris threw at them.

"Well, obviously he wasn't." Pockets eyes widened. "Someone looking like him. Good baker?"

"No way. Raz hasn't a passport. Afraid of flying," Chris revealed.

"What about Nigel? You know, the one in Wroxham," Fran suggested. "He's red headed, can grow a beard."

"Why? What's his connection outside family? Only Humph mentions him as a source of info." Chris said.

The Trio puffed.

Pockets broke the short silence. "So, we have an imposter playing Noel Peters or it's Nigel."

"Another spanner in the works." Chris' mind was in full mode. "Why impersonate a top baker in Rome?"

"When was he supposed to have been there?" Fran asked.

"Eh." Pockets searched his notes. "Two thousand and thirteen."

The two men watched Fran looking through her notebook. "He worked in Roses Café in twelve before travelling to Paris."

They stared blankly at her.

"Professor Brotherton was killed in an accident in twelve not far from where Peters worked." Fran bore a smile of success.

"The van driver involved in the accident, Humph never interviewed him." Pockets checked his notes again under 'Humph'. "Nope."

"John Carr. A gentleman. I interviewed him. Sadly, I learned that he fell ill and now in a coma. He suffered from headaches." Fran's eyes shot to Chris. "Do you know that you have two of his paintings in your bar?"

Chris sat up. "The seascapes are his work?"

"Yes. Did they come with the pub?"

"No." He stared at them. "George brought them in when I opened the first night. A present."

Another acute silence.

George again.

**

Pockets left before closing, Fran went to bed soon after. Chris told Rory to have an early night.

Kumar and Chris were alone at the bar.

"What you told us has joined many dots." Chris planted a Guinness in front of him. "Also, opened paths to bring some strange accidents into the picture."

"Cheers, boss." Kumar took gulp. "Alan's strange."

Chris chuckled. "In what *ways*?"

"Well, I know Alan's gay. Like me, he doesn't hide it or flaunt it. But he seems to be hiding from something."

"We're all hiding from something." He took a mouthful of Pils. "Me? I suppose relationships."

"I thought you and Fran were an item."

"Nah. We just met a few weeks ago. You see, it's the same with any relationship. Like magnets—they attract and click."

"So, you and Fran are *connected*."

They laughed.

"Alan asked me do I know Stratford. Said I'm a Hammer, of course I do. Why would he ask that?"

"To be honest, he may be trying to make 'small talk'." Chris took a sip. "I've a Guinness delivery in the morning but I must go to Mechanic Brewery tomorrow. Can you handle it—the delivery?"

"Yes, boss."

"Nice one."

70 THE FRAUDSTER

Saturday July 14

Laurie Fowler perused a much used *Gazette* on the top floor of Stratford Shopping Centre after Friday morning breakfast. A fifth page story of a drowning in the River Lea had drawn his interest. Names sprang from the article; Devereux, Freeman and Ostrofman.

"Interesting, eh," a voice said over the elderly man's shoulder.

Fowler turned.

A small man moved to sit opposite him in the cosy café.

"Douglas. What are you doing here?" Fowler looked around. "Are you mad? Is this your doing?" He tapped the image of uniformed Marcus.

"Did you have breakfast?" Douglas asked.

Fowler agitated and took out a pill tub. "Yes, can't you see the empty plate. What do you want?"

"You need to go on holidays—perhaps not Lanzarote, though, eh."

"Why?" Fowler looked to the service counter. "Where's my water? Excuse me, miss."

A young woman turned when passing the table. "Yes, sir. Oh sorry, your water. Yes, I left in on the counter."

Her apologetic smile calmed him as she went to retrieve it.

A tall man held her arm. "Excuse me but do you do take-away breakfasts?" His free hand waved unnoticed over a glass of water.

"No, I'm sorry. Perhaps one of the eateries on the ground floor does."

"Thank you." The man tipped his peaked cap above his sunglasses and casually left.

The waitress returned to Fowler's table and placed the glass in front of him. "Sorry for the delay, sir. It's getting a bit busy now."

"Thank you very much, miss." His painted smile lasted seconds.

"What's with the tablets?" Douglas held the glass.

Fowler put a pill on his tongue, took the glass off Douglas and downed a mouthful. He removed another pill and one more sip.

"My heart and blood pressure. Seeing this and you don't help."

"Now, now Laurie. That's why I suggest a holiday." A bulging envelope moved across the table to Fowler. "Here, a get lost present from our mutual friend."

"Those bodies. Why did you phone me about them?"

"You needed a heads up. Others needed the same. Get out before King becomes nervous. Depleting funds from our mutual African minister friend was ingenious. Forcing him to renege on Ostrofman's order. Brilliant. Like old times."

"I didn't change those pills years ago. It was that fat guy, the chemist—researcher—whatever he was. You know him. I should have reported it then."

"Yes, yes. If you say so. Now go. I'll take care of the bill."

"Already paid for." Fowler shoved the welcomed envelope into his baggy trouser back pocket.

He stood holding the table as a knee buckled.

"Are you ok? Do you want some water?" Douglas handed him the glass.

"Thank you." Fowler emptied it in one go.

Carrying a shopping bag, he rubbed his beaded brow and headed for the down escalator. Although the café filled, nobody was on it as Fowler tentatively placed his feet on the top step. A passing hand forced him to lose his grip. He tumbled down the metal steps. Fowler's legs went high as his head smacked onto the pronged treads. No one could get to him fast enough. His neck cracked at the bottom as his trousers caught under the last step.

Somebody on top pressed the off button. It was too late for Laurie Fowler.

71 THE INITIALS

Chris returned from Bethnal Green's Mechanic Brewery just before midday. He carried the first crate from his car to the bar.

"Hi, boss. Need a hand?" Kumar asked.

"No thanks. I can manage."

"Guinness came. Two kegs, yeah?"

"Yes, Kumar. Plenty for now. Going to do a promo."

"Oh, they left display cards too."

Chris thumbed-up.

Two crates were soon emptied into the fridges. Kumar offered to take the remaining three full ones into the cellar. The work welcomed for both. A break from digging up the past and joining dots.

A knock on a front door alerted Chris to the time.

"Busy is healthy—look at the clock, Kumar. Bit early for a regular though." He walked towards the door. "I'll get it."

He pulled up the blinds, unlocked and opened the door. "Pockets?"

DI Macken almost pushed past him. "Did you see *The Gazette*?"

"And hello to you too." He threw after him. "No."

"Your uncle's on page five."

The *Gazette* stayed unfolded in the newspaper holder but not for long. Chris pulled it out and almost ripped through to the pages before reading an article.

"Fucking Gibson. He even has a pic of him in his Spanish medic uniform. How did he get all this information?"

"That's not a concern. I now have to investigate another suspicious death."

"I told Gibson when he called that no one saw anything. Marcus couldn't swim. He was full of drink. I didn't mention what Marcus worked at or where. End of." Chris was on verge of doing a volcano impression.

"That doesn't matter. The fact that it mentioned him being drunk on duty, temporarily in charge of Lanzarote emergency ambulance dispatched at the time of your accident, opens questions."

"For what? I pushed him in. Or perhaps George? Maybe my dad secretly arrived and did it."

Pockets led him to the beer garden and sat in a cubicle.

"Someone is stirring the shit. Getting us police to look away from recent crimes. Now that Kumar has given us fantastic info and Fran chases up her judge, we can legally get to the bastards." Pockets stared hard at him. "Sorry for bringing this up, but was your Uncle really in charge of the service on the day of your accident?"

Chris screwed his mouth. "How am I supposed to know that? 'Oh, *Hola, disculpe, pero ¿podría decirme si mi tío Marcus está de servicio esta noche, sólo mi esposa y yo hemos sido atropellados por un coche a toda velocidad?*'"

"What's that?"

"De nada. 'Excuse me, but could you tell me if my Uncle Marcus is on duty tonight, only me and the wife have been run over by a speeding car.' Fucksake."

"Okay, I get your point, Chris. Apparently, he *was* on duty."

"So, with this supposed info, you come round here suspecting that I…"

"No—no, not you, mate. He more than likely did slip under the influence. There was a disposable lighter near the edge of the towpath. His fingerprints were on it."

"There you have it. Fell in trying to pick it up. Hold up. How the fuck did the *Gazette* know he was on duty in Lanzarote?" Chris fumed.

A burning desire to get out of this new trouble brewing in his pub. It was as if the old unwanted Clapton of drug use and gang wars were waiting outside his doors. A chance to bring back the misery it had caused amongst friends and families. To renew the area with sights of dereliction to both buildings and people giving two-fingers to gentrification.

"Someone is after you," Pockets claimed.

"Specs. I know."

"No. I think someone else wants to hurt you. Or protect himself or herself from whatever you know of them."

He gazed hard at Pockets. "Now *that* I find amusing. Okay, I may be close of sorts to some customers. But I can't see how any of them would wish me harm. Most of them I never met before buying the pub. Of course, I've known George for years. I remember Steve starting out his firm when we lived here. Then there's Old Jack and the domino gang. Alan worked for us at some point. That's it."

Pockets returned his stare. "Try this for one of your 'coincidences'. Those initials you saw, SK, MD, RI and LF."

Chris shrugged.

"Marcus Devereux and Laurie Fowler could be two of them."

"Fuck me pink. Who's Laurie Fowler? But how are they connected? What about SK and RI?"

"Don't know who they are. Fowler had an accident this morning in Stratford shopping centre. Fell down an escalator. Broke his neck. He had a large wad of notes in an envelope, and he wasn't going to the post office."

"But who was he?"

"Fowler was great at moving and removing things—money especially.

Expert at tapping into funds and suddenly making them disappear only to return weeks or months later. He would deposit them into his account. Collect the interest and return the funds back. Clever man. Claimed he only 'borrowed money'."

"So, he just collected the money found on him."

"No. Someone gave it to him. Waitress said Fowler was with another man then he suddenly got weak and asked for water. Nobody saw him falling."

"What about the guy he was with?"

"Waitress gave a vague description. Tight, wavy fair hair. Stoutish, smallish, clean shaved."

Chris clapped once. "Cartwright."

"What? Who?"

"Douglas Cartwright. Must be our mystery man. Looks like he's slipped up. I didn't show you all that I had found. He's a super hacker but likes to show off, not like me." He managed a smile. "His face is online, and you know of the records of his dealings. Want a copy of him?"

Pockets sat back shaking his head.

72 THE OLD ACQUAITANCE

Monday, just after midday, tired Alan threw his car keys on a hall table and went to the kitchen. Switching a radio on, he took food containers from the fridge placing them in a line on the counter. He had no intentions of wasting his three days off work. Assured that a new filing cabinet would arrive the next day from a Stratford based store, he began preparing his lunch salad.

Soon he was perusing his favourite magazines and lost to present local news blasting from the radio.

He crunched on crispy lettuce while concentrating on forgotten crime tales.

His phone rattled on the coffee table.

"I wonder who this is?" He pressed a green button. "Hello—Douglas?" He managed to swallow a bite. "How are you? Really? When? No way— That would be great. Yes, of course— No problem with short notice." He laughed at the reply. "Have you far to travel?— Really? Chertsey is only south of Heathrow. A year there? Okay. Will I cook something?— That would be fine. I can book a table for—" He looked at his watch. "Say, seven. Great. See you later. Byeee."

He leaned back into the easy chair. *Mmmm.*

73 THE JUDGE

Monday July 16

Fran had a hectic day. Sitting at a desk in her bungalow on Honey Lane, Waltham Abbey, she finalised the draft prepared by her brother, Gerald. Putting her desk phone on speaker, she tapped digits.

"You're after something, best student," a marbled voice declared.

She smiled. "Now, dear best tutor, why would you presume that?"

"Well, it's not Christmas and our birthdays are months gone."

She pictured his smile. "Sir Patrick, I'm sending you information now." She hit *send*. "A certain DI Macken requires an *official* search warrant for emails of persons of interest."

"That's a name I haven't heard for a while. I take it that this is needed quicker than normal routes?"

"Indeed, your Lordship."

"Now I know that you're trying to get on my good side. Does the file contain all information regarding the needs to grant this emergency warrant?"

"It does."

"So, I can presume that Gerald lent a hand in drafting it."

"Oh, shut up, you old bastard and get on with it." She paused for a reply. "Please."

"That's better, Frances. I will peruse immediately, my best student. If there are no problems with the information, you will hear from me sooner rather than later."

"Like a jury, the quicker, the better."

"Perhaps. I won't delay with small talk as I know you will cut me off, as you say, ASAP."

"Thank you, Sir Patrick." She laughed.

"Now I know you really need it. Goodbye, Frances."

74 THE HARD WORK

Chris paced the Den rubbing his chin and hair reflecting on the day, talking to the walls and furniture.

"I'm going the whole hog with this. I hate to do it. I mean privacy laws and shite. But I need to get to the bottom of this."

He sat at the desk, opened the laptop, and put in his encrypted code. His list short but proved easy to link into phones.

I just want connections, not entire conversations.

The links passed to his mobile then he closed the laptop. He stripped, had a shower and shave before lounging about the apartment.

Returning to his desk, he typed more updates into the diary page. His head eased. Perhaps a release each time he made his notes. *Fuck them and their 'no records'.*

He logged off.

I'd better get dressed and organise the Guinness promo.

**

Chris sat at the roof table after dinner. Relaxing in shorts, flip-flops and vest enjoying the July evening sun.

Below, Alan Bradford kept his voice low talking to Douglas on his mobile.

Chris adjusted his earphones.

"Verne's Bar and Grill is a good place, Douglas. I made sure this time I have a table I can fit behind." Alan giggled.

"I prefer you that way, Alan. You know little me and my ways," Douglas said.

"Oh, I do." He giggled again.

Chris stretched to see Alan walk out of view towards the restaurant. *Hope they don't leave their phones on later.*

"Looking forward to seeing you again and I'm starving. Will you recognise me?" Alan asked.

"Of course. The one with the huge grin. See you in five."

The call ended.

**

Mike was the sole GN at the bar. His eyes widened to the now familiar engine roar under the arch.

"Getting serious this, Irish," Mike said.

Rory wiped the clean counter for the umpteenth time. "I'll say nothing." He leaned to Mike. "But Chris's changing. For good or bad?" He shrugged. "I can't say."

A squeak announced her entrance.

"Speak of the Devil," Mike whispered.

"Watchya, Fran." Came from a couple of customers along with nods and smiles from others.

Her popularity growing.

"Hi, Rory—Mike." She removed her biker's jacket used to the widened eyes. "Phew. I'm worn out. Is he about?"

"Chris' upstairs. Go up if you like," Rory suggested. "Drink first?" He winked.

She sat beside Mike. "Yes, please—usual. I'll text him."

A door thudded shut near the office.

"Oh, here he is."

Chris entered behind the bar smiling. "Hey, Fran. You're early. Getting looked after?"

Kumar came through the beer garden entrance.

"I am—oh, hi, Kumar." She waved to him.

"Bored." Kumar carried empty glasses.

There were nine customers and three of them in the beer garden.

"Well, I'll sack myself for the night then. Loads of biz to do." Chris opened the fridge and took a Pils.

She paid for her drink without any complaint from Chris.

He sat beside her.

She felt his nudge. "What's that for?" Her eyes widened.

"Coz you paid for your drink." He nudged again.

She tilted back. "What happened?"

"Later. Now, how did you get on with your friend?" He twitched.

"What's wrong?"

"Only my phone. Must be a text. Can't be important. Well—news?" His brows raised.

Mike moved from his stool towards the gents.

Chris stared at him.

"What's wrong, Chris?" Fran's whisper tickled his ear.

"Ooh." He looked around for eavesdroppers. "I've done something—eh, illegal."

She stared through him.

He shrugged.

"What?" Her left hand twisted the glass as the ice cracked.

Chris twitched again. "I've tapped into a few phones."

She glared at him and took a long mouthful.

Chris nodded to Mike returning to his seat.

He didn't sit. Mike took his glass and lowered what liquid was left. "I'm off, folks. See you tomorrow." His flip-flops echoed towards the door.

"See you," Fran called out.

Chris remained silent.

When the front door shut, he said, "Come up. I'll explain and show all." He noticed Rory's quick glance. "Funny. Do you want that raise?"

Rory broke into uncontrollable laughter.

Customers stopped drinking and talking to see the barman double up.

His hands raised high. "Sorry, boss. Be careful with your words."

Chris thumbed-up and smiled.

"Okay." Fran stood, took her jacket and drink toward the private stairs.

Chris followed her, wagging a finger at Rory.

**

In the apartment, after Chris had shown Fran the phone taps and told Kumar's tale, they sat at the kitchen counter.

"Jesus, the poor young man."

"I told him I'll tell you."

"What are we going to do with the taps?" Fran asked.

"I've kept records but need them legal."

"You're lucky that Sir Patrick, Judge Royston, is considering the taps."

Chris' phone vibrated on the counter. "It's Pockets."

"Hi, you're on speaker. —Fran's here. What's up?"

Pockets sighed before speaking. "The briefcase has mysteriously disappeared from evidence amongst some other stuff not to make it obvious."

"Fuck me pink. Who signed it in?"

"Bollocky King assigned Bell to look into it. Now all the stuff we needed is gone."

Chris looked to Fran.

She nodded.

"Eh, okay. Listen, we can't talk about this on the phone. Drop by when you can."

"You've done something."

"Chat soon." He hung up.

Fran sipped her drink. "Perhaps we should've held onto it."

"Nah. Whatever DCI King and co. are up to doesn't affect our investigation. They'll probably think they're safe now."

"Gives us more time." She smiled.

75 THE SMILING AND TOUCHING

Chris and Fran returned to the bar, apparently just in time.
A door squeaked open. His brows raised.
"I thought you said there would be a few in here." Douglas' smile disappeared.
"Hi, Kumar—oh, Fran. Good to see you, again." Alan almost tilted on the last word. "Very quiet. This is Douglas. Hi, Chris." He rubbed his friend's shoulder. "Anyone out the back?"
The couple settled at the empty GNC.
Fran eyeballed Douglas.
He caught the stare. "And who's this lovely 'Barbara Windsor' look-a-like Alan?" Douglas's smirk suited him. Sly.
"Oh, I thought you heard me." Alan acted subservient. Smiling and touchy-touchy. "This is Fran. A marvel of a journalist."
Douglas's brows furrowed. "Really?"
"And this lovely barman is Kumar." Alan was out of it through drink and expectations.
Kumar stood back from the bar.
Chris saw the young man's displeasure.
His head ticked left. "Go up, watch TV or study. See you in the morning."
So, this is the fucker in person. The mystery man.
"Alan, you're pissed." Chris still didn't pull punches.
"Well, we haven't seen each other for a while—oh sorry." Alan put an arm around his friend "This is Douglas Cartwright. An old Cambridge buddy."
Chris nodded and cursed behind a painted smile.
Two wankers now.
"How do you do, Douglas. It's been a rough day. So, as you are both obviously eager to renew memories past, I'll let you have one round, Alan. Don't want you struggling in the morning."
"I suppose you're right. Well, I am expecting a delivery from Stratford Furnishings." Alan turned to Douglas. "What would you like?"
"I would like a pint of Fuller's bitter, please." Douglas smiled sitting erect on the barstool.
"Me too."
"I'll get them," Fran offered.
Chris needed to infiltrate the enemy's defences and attack strategies. He watched as the friends small talked.
Alan pointed out the various photos on all the walls. He tried to put a

tale behind each picture.

Douglas turned to face the main wall and twigged Chris's interest. "Those are nice paintings."

"A gift on opening night," Chris said.

"Anyone famous?"

"No. An amateur artist I believe."

"Impressive. Fantastic place, Chris. So—local."

How can seascapes be local, prick.

Fran placed their drinks on the bar as a door opened.

Chris waved to the couples: Kumar's friends. He went to their table. "Kumar's off duty. I'll get him. You want your usual?"

They each replied, 'Yes'.

"Kumar rang us. Asked us to come over," one told Chris.

"No problem. Send him a text or call to let them know you're here."

Behind the bar, Chris looked after their order.

Kumar came through the bar.

Chris nodded all was okay.

A phone rang.

"Yes, Douglas—through that door to the beer garden," Alan said.

His friend smiled and went through the door.

"Needs to take a call," Alan told Chris.

Fran realised Chris's raised brow. "I'll look after Kumar's friends and Guinness."

Chris went to the office and looked at his phone.

George's number.

He didn't listen to the call; it wouldn't have helped officially. Then another number appeared. Douglas was calling someone else. Specs.

Something is brewing.

Moments later, he saw that George connected to the same number. Chris couldn't hold out any longer. He put the earplugs in and listened.

"— yes, mush." Specs last words of a sentence.

"I know it's usually empty Thursday nights," George remarked to Specs.

"Douglas said he's there alone. Only a few of the new barman's friends and a woman—a journalist."

"Please, don't do anything in public. There'll be a funeral for his uncle. I'm sure he'll attend and doubt if Uncle Ben would come over for it."

"Right, mush. We're getting Douglas to open the briefcase. Don't want anything destroyed yet. I was about to call Meyer, the Chemist, to see how progress was going. I want to get my food on the streets for testing. Relax."

Chris pulled the plugs from his ears. His hands worked his head. Things were getting out of control. He breathed heavily, stood, knees bent and moved his arms slowly in rhythmic Tai Chi forms. His heartrate gradually eased. His temperament calmed. Minutes later, he was ready to return to the bar.

76 THE COSY CHAT

Later that night, downstairs, Fran's bike rested in the hall. Upstairs, she snuggled up to Chris on a sofa.

He ensured his hands didn't wander too much.

"How are you now?" she asked.

"Mad. Must be, because I'm paying for my uncles cremation next Monday." He kissed her head.

"Your dad coming over?"

"No. Told me just order a wreath with a note. I called the Prince of Wales pub and emergency service head office just to mention the funeral. He wasn't liked, so it's up to them to attend or not."

She felt his heart picking up speed as he talked of them. She rubbed his legs as he let his thoughts be known.

"The problem I have now is keeping calm when seeing George." He breathed slow. "So, you have the warrant for Pockets. Can it be used anytime?"

"Yes. You say this chemist is making up Specs samples. If that is done soon, he will start messaging and Douglas will do his usual email thing. Even better when they open the briefcase."

"Yeah. Should be interesting. I wanted to floor him tonight. What an arsehole. So smug sitting in my pub thinking he's above all around him." He sat straight. "Should we bug Alan's place?"

She playfully thumped his leg. "I don't want to hear their carry-ons. Oh, what if Douglas has the briefcase now?"

Chris suddenly quietened and stared at a photo of Mary. His mind wandered.

Mary, I still miss you. I don't know what to do. Are you watching over me?

Fran disturbed him and turned her head on his lap to look up at him. "A penny for them."

He remained silent. A softness grew in her eyes. He read the messages sent and felt a warmth within him. At that moment Chris somehow knew.

I can't do it, Mary—not yet.

**

Fran left early the next morning with more than a skip in her step.

Over the following days Chris began plans for his future. He gave Rory the fulltime manager job in charge of hiring and firing. The Irishman realised the pressure Chris had been put under.

His new freedom saw him delve deeper into the wiretaps. He saw that Douglas had been a busy bee. His extended stay with Alan gave Chris better opportunities to cast an eye on the secretive shit-stirrer. He learned Douglas had many contacts that reached into government departments. Days of attentive monitoring and Chris had enough material for Fran to present to the judge for another warrant. Wiretapping.

His fingers worked hard on the keyboard outrunning his brain:

Douglas: *What's he up to? What next?*
Alan's getting to be a right pain.
What about George? Connections?
Money? Favours?
He logged off.

77 THE LINK

Chambers, London, July 17

Specs didn't need to be told of his brother not emigrating to America. Douglas had worked his conniving shit-stirring on the London gang leader along with Raz, government, and church authorities. The middleman good at turning one against the other but remained wary of Specs.

Sir Patrick Royston had been made aware of all. He perused the illegal documented conversations. Regarding Douglas as the link to all parties.

Sir Patrick peered over his glasses at Fran and Chris after each page. He then eased back into his chair and removed the glasses. The silence seemed forever as he stared at the couple opposite his desk.

He sighed. "You are a clever man, Mister Freeman. And because you are, how would I say, close to my favourite student, I won't report these. Another fact taken under consideration is the missing briefcase. Now, I can understand the reasons for both warrants. They are linked; therefore, to prevent the drugs being pushed onto the streets, I'm going to grant the second warrant."

Fran and Chris's hands gripped together.

"This Cartwright chappie is definitely the most dangerous. So, to ensure you can tie these reprobates together, I am going to issue single warrants for emails and wiretaps on each person of interest." The judge lowered his eyes to Chris. "However, DI Macken is in control and not you."

"Eh, what if I set up a base at my place—away from officialdom of the police station and unreliable officers." Chris smiled.

"I assure you that DI Macken knows how to run an op."

"I know him well, but Your Honour, I still hold a P.I. licence and have the technical knowhow to override any anti-surveillance of his work. Stoke Newington does have its ghosts." His executive charm in full gear.

Sir Patrick thumbed his nose. "I do recall the nineties corruption. Well, I suppose the less that know of this the better."

"Pockets, eh, DI Macken has called for King's son to take over DS Robinson's role while he's on holidays. They would work together until then. Also, there's tension between Harley and his father, DCI King."

The judge leaned forward and clapped once. "Right. The team will be small, and I grant permission to use your establishment."

Holding a pen, he quickly scripted a note, stamped, and signed it. "Here, this is to make you the official overseer at your home only. And make sure your licence is up to date."

Chris took the paper. "It is, thank you."

Sir Patrick waited as each warrant rolled from a printer. He stamped and signed each one.

Fran placed them into a large envelope.

"I want updates, best student. The government and police being under scrutiny again is bad for morale." Sir Patrick stood.

"So, where does that leave the children and their morale?" Chris eased out of his chair as he stared at the judge.

Sir Patrick sighed. "I'm sorry, Mister Freeman. You are of course correct. Get these bastards, and their cohorts. Thank you and God bless."

They shook hands, both reassured that justice must be done.

78 THE HART TO HART

Thursday July 19

Rory welcomed the new role of manager on his first day. Kumar's return to his parents' home the day before guaranteed he wasn't being looked for.

The regular barflies hadn't noticed Pockets entering. He settled beside Mike and Vince.

"Pint, Rory please," he said.

"Guinness promo still on." Rory held a Guinness glass.

"Yeah, why not."

Chris stood outside the office with Fran. "Will you bring these upstairs while I grab Pockets' attention?"

"Sure love." She pecked his cheek.

**

In the Den, Pockets read through the warrants.

Fran said at the kitchen counter, "You have a nice smile, Pockets. You should do it more often."

He looked to them. "Do you remember the useless TV program *Hart to Hart*?"

They both shrugged.

"An American husband-and-wife detective thing. He was rich too and a P.I of sorts." He glanced down at the pages again. "Brilliant work you two."

Pockets looked around from his stool to the board. "Won't take much rearranging. Are you sure it's okay with you?"

"More than happy and my system won't be hacked. That's the assurance I gave the judge. Oh, and I'm the detective in charge in my Den. Judge's orders."

Pockets eyed Fran for confirmation.

Her grin and nodding gave it. "Signed and all. So, how do these warrants work?"

Pockets explained, "They are individual warrants granting me leave to listen and record phone conversations from any of their phones. Read and copy each email from the named parties. Which will lead to search and seizures, whereupon they will be presented. Your Sir Patrick is well up on the law. If these were grouped warrants, they could easily be thrown out of court. But being individual, all we do is make connections to each thereby proving conspiring to criminal activity."

They took sips of their drinks as a breather.

Chris looked to Fran. "Eh, Pockets. We have an idea where the briefcase may be." Chris grinned.

"The bug." Pockets clapped. "Have you—you know, plugged into it?"

"On automatic. It's range a thousand miles," Fran admitted.

"You didn't tell me that." Chris said.

"Sorry, love. Forgot."

Pockets eyed her. "Perhaps they've shot themselves in their feet."

"Well, I listened to live stuff. Specs mentioned using Humph's place. Not pretty. I've set up a Word doc., sort of a dictation copier. Each word's recorded and typed. Fill in the recognised names later." Chris bore a wide grin.

"You never cease to amaze me. All this tech stuff is beyond me. Can't keep up with it at times."

"Anyway, how's Harley?" Chris asked.

"Better ask how his old man is. His face when Harley walked to my office was priceless. No pic of it. He paled as if a vampire sucked him dry." Pockets' grin proved his dislike of the DCI.

"Can you get him here tonight? Joanne's back in a few days so I would like to get things sorted. In other words, I don't want verbal diarrhoea in the pub from them pair. Pete will be here. George is back from a business trip so almost a full house in GNC."

Fran looked at Chris. "One more."

Chris tilted back and shook his head. "Douglas."

"So, he stayed longer. That would be a good thing," Pockets said. "Douglas could see faces he has on record. Seeing Harley here too would whet his appetite to use his phone more."

Chris slapped Pockets' back. "What a cop, eh."

79 THE BAR BUZZED

Chris chatted with customers in the beer garden and bar reminded him why he worked hard to transform it. Alice, Rory, and Kumar were run off their feet behind the bar. A fortieth birthday party had the bar buzzing on a Thursday night. It was rare occasion allowing Duo to perform.

Lanky DS Harley King arrived with Pete. He was widely welcomed due to most knowing he was nothing like his corrupt father. They sat near George as Mike moved up. Not much room left at the GNC.

Rory shook Harley's hand. "Long time no see."

"Wow. Your still here." the DS said.

"Manager now," George threw in.

"Well done, mate." Harley released his hand. "Can I have a bitter and whatever Pete is having."

Rory nodded and went to the taps.

Pete recognised Chris's head gesture and followed him to the beer garden.

"Pockets told you about tomorrow?" Chris asked.

"Yeah. How did you manage that? You a P.I again?" Pete tapped his shoulder.

Chris puffed. "Hard work. Pockets filled you in on everything so please, not a word to George."

"This is really mind-blowing stuff. Your best pal? And the Humph guy. Who would have thought that all this has converged on your place?"

It was a valid question, but Chris didn't answer immediately. He leaned to Pete. "Douglas Cartwright is the central point."

"Don't worry, Harley has been told all. We are here for a few pints, laugh and chat."

He saw Chris's quick concerned glance to a woman.

"Shite. Ilsa has seen Harley. Now I bet she's getting in touch with Joanne," Chris said. "Go back and tell Harley to please be good. I'll deal with her."

Pete returned to the bar as Chris tipped Ilsa's shoulder.

"Chris." She acted surprised.

He watched her trying to hide a phone. "Don't text her."

"What's wrong with you?"

"Joanne is on holidays. Returns home in a few days so let her enjoy them. Loads of time to tell her when she comes back." His eyes pleaded.

"What's Harley doing here?"

"Temporary training before promotion I believe. A week at most. He knew Joanne wasn't here that's why he chose to visit."

Ilsa read his face. "Okay, Chris. You're right. I do like him and care for Joanne's wellbeing."

"You're a star."

"And you're a charmer."

She linked an arm, and they walked back to the bar. Ilsa stopped.

Chris shrugged and smiled as Fran came through the bar.

"I like her," Ilsa said. "Oh, whose idea was it to stop smoking out front?"

"The new manager of course. He knew he would have to clean it up."

**

Nobody paid attention as Alan and Douglas entered the pub passing Raz and Marge, except Chris.

He stood at the pillar, a calming smile across his face. "Hi Marge, Raz. All good?"

Marge spoke for them. "Yes, Chris."

Raz leaned to him. "Thanks for telling me about bodies. Hard to take but I'll leave it all to you."

Chris patted his shoulder.

"Agnes rang. Said you dropped in for lunch with another," Raz said.

"Yeah, me and Pockets were on the way to that site. Couldn't tell you at the time—you know." He bent to Raz's ear. "That guy with Alan is important to Pockets' investigation. He could be the one that found out about the bodies and contacted families anonymously."

"Little wimp, eh. Just Alan's type—ow." He felt Marge's elbow.

"He is," Chris confirmed.

"Jesus—you pair stop it." Marge tittered.

Chris turned and caught Rory's eye. The manager understood the on-the-house signal for the couple.

**

Harley and Pete played their part. No shop conversation. They continued with small talk above the music and singing. Fran sat beside Ellen and Ilsa. She noted George had gone onto whiskeys early.

Steve had trouble avoiding giggling from the two lovebirds to his right. He interrupted them. "How long have you known each other, Douglas?"

"Yonks. Over twenty years." His eyes smiled to Alan. "He wouldn't join Cambridge uni boxing club with me. Did you know that Alan preferred running?"

Steve eased back looking at the much smaller man. "Sorry, but you wouldn't think that you boxed."

"Amateur. Our sporting preferences interrupted our studies somewhat."

"Yes. Douglas was a tough one. Then our jobs came first. We drifted apart socially but kept in contact." Alan's mouth appeared open to reveal all.

"And here you are—together again." Steve's smirk was obvious to Chris.

Although not working the bar, he maintained an eye on all conversations and body languages. A habit developed since childhood. He observed Steve irritation with Alan and Douglas's whispered chats. George too had quietened, not the usual joker of the pack. Ilsa and Ellen's exchanges about fashion brought a smile to Chris. Vince's future bride had conformed to his wishes regarding Joanne.

While passing the bar collecting empty glasses, his eyes caught Douglas's rapid hand movement on an object in his loose trouser pocket.

Oh, he's good. Recording the conversations.

Chris had no problem with it. He had set up his system to download all devices related to each person of interest.

He bumped into Pete as the DS went to the Gents. "I want you and Harley to hang back after closing."

"She's great." Pete grinned.

Chris jerked back. "What?"

"Fran. Don't let her go."

Chris' eyes followed him until he opened the gents door.

Fucksake.

He looked to Fran. As if being called, she turned her head and shrugged a question. With Mike's assistance, she climbed off the stool.

"What's up?" she asked Chris.

"Having a chat with Pete and Harley after closing."

He saw George breathe deep and sway. Looking around, his pal slithered away through the side door.

Chris noticed Douglas watching George's exit.

"Back in a minute, Alan. Have to make a call." Douglas zipped through the throng out a front door.

80 THE ALLEY

There were no witnesses. With a couple of clicks on an object, Douglas had disabled the archway camera before grabbing drunken George by his left arm. He pulled him back to the alley. The smaller man's kick surprised his left knee, felling him to the stained, grey concrete. Shoes and punches rained into his stomach, head, and legs. In less than a minute George was unconscious and robbed.

Douglas brushed himself down as he walked through the bar as customers sang along with Duo. He sat unperturbed beside Alan.

"Kumar, can we have another two drinks, please?" His Cheshire cat grin still disturbed the barman.

"Are you okay, Douglas? You're breathing heavily," Alan noted.

His hand rubbed Alan's arm. "I'm fine." It dropped to Alan's knee and slowly moved up.

"Wow. Later. Not here please." He reddened.

**

Chris turned to see Pete come from the Gents.

He looked to an empty stool. "Hold up—where's George?"

"He was here a couple of minutes ago," Harley said.

"He went out the side door. Looked pissed," Vince told them.

Customers waited for a drink as Chris squeezed past them toward the door. "Just checking that he's okay."

Douglas paid attention.

**

An alley lamp highlighted a heap near the far wall of the arch. Chris rushed over and lifted George's head.

"Christ."

He fumbled in a pocket and took out his phone. "Yes. Can I have an ambulance to An Fáilte Tavern, Lower Clapton Road. A man has been beaten and is unconscious. — I'm Chris Freeman, owner of the Tavern. Okay. Yes, he's breathing but slowly. There are cuts to the head. Eyes are covered in blood. Of course, I'll stay here. Hurry."

Chris hung up and called another number. "Pete. Keep calm. Go to my office and get the medical kit and there's a blanket on top of the filing cabinet. Come to the alley through the side door *alone*."

Within a minute Pete was assisting Chris with George.

Pete asked earnestly. "What the fuck happened?"

"Jumped on. His watch, phone and wallet are gone." Chris looked up. "Bastards. My camera is off. The only thing that's not connected to my private security."

Pete looked up. No flashing red light.

Sirens howled closer and soon blue lights flickered through the Tavern's windows.

**

It was a sad ending to the night. Although the music played on, concerns of a violent mugging the main topic of conversation.

George had never married, lived alone. He depended on a housekeeper attending to his upmarket apartment and offices on Clapton Square.

Chris and Fran waited in Homerton Hospital's reception area. He and George were well known for their patronage. The latter's company was on the hospital's list of architect consultants.

Chris lifted his head and eyed the wall clock: 02:23. His mouth tightly closed.

"This was Douglas," he said.

"No way. That little guy?"

"He recorded the bar conversations. Turned off my cameras and attacked George during celebrations." He looked to her. "I saw George leave and Douglas went out seconds later."

She was speechless.

"But he slipped up." He managed a grin and took out his phone. "Watch. It's not nice."

He had logged on to PP bookies cam aimed directly across the road to the archway. Since Specs comical bullyboys attempted disruption, he used the camera as back up to his security after evening racing finished.

They watched George struggling to walk after he had checked that the side door was shut. Douglas moved quickly from the right entrance, grabbed George, laid into him with a few body punches but mostly kicks.

"Jesus. You wouldn't think that the little runt would be capable of that." She shivered.

Chris turned the phone off. "I have to get Pete and Harley to pop into PP's later to ask about camera footage."

A white-coated Asian approached the couple. "Excuse me, Mister Freeman?"

Chris stood. "Yes."

"I'm Doctor Rahman. Mister Inglis is stable. His face is swollen but no major cuts. Five ribs are broken, and his left knee was dislocated. He's asleep at the moment."

"His head looked as if it had been constantly kicked," Chris said.

The doctor breathed heavily. "We took a brain scan and there are no signs of damage from the attack."

"Great. Eh, you have my contact number and I presume a constable is outside George's room."

"Yes. But I understand it was a mugging."

"Well, there could be more to it." Chris shook the doctor's hand. "Thank you again. Any changes, let me know."

81 THE EXPERTS

Douglas had 'enjoyed' Alan for a week. The researcher had always played the subservient role with Douglas. Although towering over him, Alan almost melted in his company. The smaller man had magnetic charm to entice bigger men but surprised them with his domination under the sheets.

He had that way with business performances also. He could control A and B into deals with C thinking their funds would grow. However, he merely moved their accounts around, creaming off the top from Specs and other underground enterprises. His expertise of adding just enough profit to their accounts posed his business as legitimate, showing smooth half yearly growth to impress investors.

Specs paid him well for information gathered and hacking of security systems. The middleman was in great demand. But was nearing an end. A sharper, more enterprising dealer had suddenly appeared.

Chris Freeman.

He had set up his links for the process of fund reduction; illegally.

82 THE TEAM AND LISTENING

Friday July 20

Pete and Harley carried tech gear into the Den. Four monitors were set in line on a portable picnic table next to the breakfast counter. DC Ursula Sharee, an eager tech trainee, had been recruited by Harley. Her husband was a colleague in Hendon.

The team were ready to legally begin tracking the next day.

"Good to have you on board, Ursula," Pockets said. "All informal here. It's not an office."

"Thank you, Guv. I hope you don't mind but I don't like your regular nickname. So, I'll stick to 'Guv'—Guv." Ursula smiled.

"And me too, Guv," Harley told him.

"Lick arses." Pete's remark earned laughter.

"So, Chris here is the real 'Guv' here. Anything he asks you to do, do it." Pockets acknowledge Chris's nod. "Newington and some closed shops had a bad history of bent coppers. That's why, thanks to P.I Freeman, we've been granted permission to set this up here." He turned. "My fav DSs—how did you get on with the cam footage from PP's?"

Pete nodded to Harley, his junior.

"Well, surprisingly one camera had moved facing the pub and arch. It was definitely Cartwright that attacked George. We've sent copies to central crime," Harley said.

"Yes. Chris thought it best that we don't get involved. Let local handle it but advised them to hold back awhile. Puts unexpected pressure on Cartwright from another source when he finds out," Pete explained.

Chris thumbed-up. "Well done you two. You have a couple of personal issues, Harley?"

"Yes. Guv Chris—sorry, couldn't resist." Harley laughed.

"Like the sound of that. *Guv Chris*. Has a ring to it. Ouch."

Fran smiled after elbowing him.

He rubbed his 'injured' arm.

"Chris has offered me the top room from tomorrow—attic. Great layout. So, I'm taking it while here. My dad won't come near the place. Also, Joanne will be told that I have to concentrate on promotion," Harley said.

"Yeah, he's engaged," Ursula said. "My hubby told me."

"Congrats. But now I've to put up with your ex's moans." Chris winked to Harley.

Fran stood from a sofa. "Although I don't know Joanne, I'll help with diverting her."

"Great stuff. That's what I like, teamwork," Pockets said. "Right, c'mon. Leave these two to—whatever and we'll meet here at—" He looked to Chris.

"I'll be easy on my team. Ten bells. Fran will let you in through the side door. From now on, when working here, use that door coming and going. And the upstairs ensuite. Not having all you Plods upsetting my castle. Oh, and I'll be logging on with my password. It'll be linked to all monitors."

**

Chris hadn't waited for the Saturday start.. He and Fran sat with earphones connected and listened to phone recordings.

"Whoa. Too much info, Alan," he blurted out.

"Jesus, Chris. Lucky you didn't plant a cam in his bedroom." She laughed. "Turn him off."

He switched to another phone recorded conversation.

"What the fuck are you doing here?"

"Calm down, George. I'm just visiting an old pal. Me and Alan go back years. He looks better now with all that lovely extra body."

Fran cringed at Douglas's laughter.

"You're too close. Bring him somewhere. Get a room, fucksake. Talk about being obvious."

Chris tipped Fran. "That was last night. George was in the beer garden. What was that? Was that Alan talking to Douglas?"

"Yes. I'll play it back."

She pressed the back arrow and listened.

"I've had enough forget about him. Just leave or I'll tell Alan why you're really here."

"Now now, sweet thing."

"Who's that you're talking to?" Alan's voice distant but audible.

"Fuck, Douglas put his hand over the phone," Chris said.

The conversation continued between Douglas and George.

"Now you listen. Don't threaten me. I have loads on you and your backhand dealing. Just because he can't pay you, Urban does deserve that shopping mall complex," Douglas blasted.

"He must have gone out front," Chris suggested.

"No fucking way. Are you kidding me? Look at your earnings. Just watch this space—I've records too." George's phone went dead.

"What time was that call, Chris?" she asked.

He perused the logs. "Quarter past nine. Just about the time George was less chatty with Pete and Harley."

"Yes. He started on the whiskey."

A ring tone alerted them. They looked at the numbers. Their widened eyes displayed delight listening to the latest live conversation.

"You fucking idiot." The familiar high-pitched voice of DCI King said. *"On camera—fucking camera."*

"I honestly don't know what you are talking about, lover."

Chris and Fran stared wide-eyed.

"You're on camera beating the shit out of George Inglis down the alley."

Fran and Chris waited open mouthed for the reply.

"I–I turned off the pub's cameras." Douglas' voice quivered.

"The bookies across the road caught it all. From the time you left and worked over Inglis to when you left with lover boy later. Even Freeman spotted that his cameras were off. You've fucked up. And you enjoyed it. Smiling and saying something to him as you laid into him."

Another short silence.

"What? No more smart-arse chat from you. Finally got caught out. Take a holiday—like you told old Fowler. Did you shove him down the escalator too? I think that there may be some truth about poor old Marcus being pushed in," King bellowed.

Fran squeezed Chris's arm.

"No. I don't do kill. I leave that to you boys. Specs and co. What about that Professor, eh? He did more than fuck you. Why shouldn't you have him knocked off. An accident indeed," Douglas returned to him.

"I can't be placed there, fuckface. Well, that's what you like, eh." King's sigh was clear.

Fran put a hand to her mouth.

Douglas hit back. *"Oh, there she is. Little Miss Bitchy. What colour panties are you wearing at your desk today, honey?"*

Chris squirmed and held his laughter.

"You're dead, tow rag—fucking dead." A long break, then. *"Hello, huh."*

They had hung up.

Chris eased back on his chair rubbing his face.

Fran scratched an ear still not heeding her mother's advice again.

They were deep in their own thoughts. New revealing visions of what may have been going on for years.

He looked at Fran. "Are you trying to imagine King in panties too?"

Laughter exploded in the Den.

Chris wiped his eyes. "Drink?"

"Oh, I need one after that," she said.

"Tell you what. Let's go out for early dinner. I'll call Bill in the

Pembury to hold a table in case it fills. Good grub."

"Somewhere different I suppose."

**

Fran had headed home after the meal. She lacked clothes at Chris'. With more free time, he got stuck into Douglas's four bank accounts: three under presumed names. It was easy for Chris.

He opened new accounts in three names under an umbrella company called Christian Blessings. A bogus charity organisation supplying food supplements and vaccines for underprivileged families and orphans. The company's credentials were excellent and validated by high-ranking authorities throughout the UK and Europe. It was a work of art. A genius.

How wonderful people are. So generous when it's needed.

The money flowed slowly for the first hour. Then over a period of three, even Specs' cohorts began to see the light and offer funds to the charity.

Every little helps.

Alan began to send funds and, even from his comatose state, George's amount more than generous.

Fuck him. Time to have them accuse each other.

Chris maneuvered money between their accounts. One thousand to Alan from Douglas; five to DCI King from Specs. Douglas then paid Meyer the Chemist seven grand. The Chemist paid King two thousand who gave Alan another two. Money was flying around like tickertape at Mardi Gras. All transactions showed up in their online bank statements.

Christmas has come early.

83 THE SET UP

Chris enjoyed his freedom in the bar. Though being a Friday night, he was relaxed more than ever. Even sitting beside Mike. Though the headaches still occurred, they arrived at times of stress along with inklings or perceptions.

Kumar had taken over from Alice for the night shift with Rory. The bar lacked its usual banter because of the previous night's party.

He talked with his boss during a slack period. "I like Fran. You two looked a couple when I saw you first," Kumar said.

"Thank you, but too early for a raise yet." Chris played with his Pils bottle.

"Boss, I—"

"You have loads to learn, young Kumar," Mike offered. "And you're in the best pub in Hackney to learn."

Chris's phone was active in a pocket. He had it on low vibrate but kept the ring tone on normal.

"How's George?" Kumar asked.

"I rang around seven. Still asleep. But he's breathing okay."

"Any leads to the bastards that did it?" Mike asked.

"Nothing yet. Constables searched the alley, rubbish bins. No wallet found. I bought him that watch for his fortieth. Bastards." Chris acted as the caring best buddy.

He looked at Mike. *Sorry for tapping your phone.*

Pete had suggested it as a link to the killers of the guard. Chris had urged Mike to dig deep into their background, but nothing was found. The most interesting link was DC Tony Bell.

Chris's brain flashed an alert.

"Mike, just a quick word about the gym. Bring your drink to the office." Chis heard a door squeak. "Kumar, work." He thumbed-up Rory.

**

Mike sat and sipped before talking. "This about the guns?"

"The shite is going to hit the fan because of George's mugging. Can't you see it?" Chris said.

Mike quickly understood. "Specs coming here. Something about Kumar. I'm not blind. Humph's accident and this Douglas nutter. Gay as Christmas and not afraid to show it." He took another sip. "Poor Alan. We know his preference, but he never announces it openly. Fucking Douglas nearly had his hand on Alan's cock at the bar."

"Jesus, I didn't know that."

"And talking on the phone before he went outside."

"Driving me mad, all this. Did you know that DC Bell is dirty?"

Mike sat straight. "No way? Did Pockets tell you?"

"He's deep under Kings wing. Must be bent. Pockets thinks that's why he joined your clubs. Keep an eye on you and guns."

"Bastard." Mike took a longer mouthful. "I'll terminate his membership."

"Not yet. I've a plan to get him to become anti-King, with Pockets' blessing," Chris lied.

Mike paid attention.

"I bought two similar watches and gave one to George. I'm going to drop into see how he is in the morning. Place his fingers around my watch and give it to you to pop into Bell's locker." Chris beamed.

Mike drank then breathed heavily. "Jesus. That bad, eh. So, Pockets want's to stir the shit between King and Bell."

"In a nutshell, yes. You see, it's all a game with those bastards. They believe that they are masters of it and no one else can join in. Send in a tiddler to catch the big fish."

"Bell for King and Specs. As a sort of middleman."

"Correct. And he'll be off your back."

Mike stared at him.

Chris eased back. "Not blind, Mike. The guns, on the phone more than usual in off season. Specs gang coming here."

"Yeah, it's been heavy. Some members haven't renewed their memberships. I rang a couple of them. They told me the same story. Specs Morgan's crew jumping queues for equipment. Harassing members."

"You owe?"

Mike nodded with a tight grin then opened for another mouthful.

"It's becoming a confessional in here," Chris quipped. "So, yay or nay?"

"I'll do it."

**

Mid-morning Saturday, in the gym office, Mike took out a master key and went to the changing room. A mixture of sweat and heavy deodorant wafted between the aisles of lockers. He wasn't spying material and flustered as voices chatted and guffawed in the room. Tony Bell's locker was in the third aisle. He looked left and right before opening a grey door. Holding a tissue, he removed the watch from a plastic bag carefully placing it in a trainer. He locked the door and returned to his office.

84 THE TRAVELLING MONIES

The Den, Saturday July 21

Harley had settled into the apartment. The fun continued in Chris's Den as he logged in his password for the team. Initially slow, but fingers worked the keys, pens jotted down notes followed by sharp remarks. The team hadn't noticed Chris homing in on bank accounts.

Their faces expressed surprise throughout the morning and early afternoon. Many of the persons of interest were not happy.

Ursula let out a large 'F'.

"Something good?" Harley asked before he said similar. "Fucking hell." He looked to Ursula. "Money?"

"Yes. Are you getting the same, Pete?" She turned to Chris. "You have to hear this."

Chris picked up an earphone. "My God. They're at it hard."

"You took my fucking money. Bastard. You're fucking dead, ponce," DCI King roared to Douglas.

"No way. It wasn't me, lover."

Harley's eyes widened. "What the fuck."

"You're the only one capable to do it since you knocked off Fowler," King blasted.

"I told you I had nothing to do with his death." A short pause. *"Christ—someone's taken money from my accounts. Alan gave me money and then it went to the Meyer."*

"Don't believe that the chemist can pay me money. Had to be you moving it." King paused for a reply.

"Douglas hung up, Guv Chris," Ursula said.

"He's sussed it," Chris said.

"Hey, you there?" King shouted.

"Here's another one. It's Alan," Harley announced.

"Yes, I'm calling about my account. There appears to be money put in it then given to two other accounts—eh, one is named 'Christian Blessings.' I didn't pass money to these accounts and don't know where the deposit came from." Alan's voice remained calm.

"Mister Bradford, all appears legitimate. The charity is a worthy one. I'm looking at the other accounts—yes, they're not offshore based. Do you want me to contact the fraud department?" the bank clerk said.

"Yes, please do."

Chris pressed keys on his laptop and smiled.

"Mister Bradford, you have donated another five hundred to the charity just now. Hold on—And now you have received a thousand."

"Oh, please stop all transactions immediately."

"Jesus, someone is messing with their accounts. But how is Alan involved with all this, Chris?" Pete said.

"Douglas. They're great pals and—well, you know." Chris logged off his laptop.

Ursula interrupted them. "Specs is going ape at your dad, Harley."

Harley listened in.

"What's your game, mush? The chemist told me he gave you money. Now I see from my accounts, that large sums have been transferred to a charity that has our names on the board of directors," Specs fumed.

"What you on about? It's Douglas. Money has been transferred from my account and some has been paid in. He's the only one capable of doing it now," King said.

"Bollocks. He's collected the briefcase."

"Did what? You fucking mad?"

"Must find out what's on it. We have to sort this out. Meet later at the usual place. Bring Bell." They hung up.

"The one missing from evidence?" Pete asked.

"Yep." Chris smiled.

85 THE MIDDLEMAN

Wednesday July 25

Chris pottered around the Den after the team finished for the first few days. He called Fran on speaker while preparing his dinner explaining some details of findings thus far.

"How did you do it?" she asked.

"Okay, I admit it. They needed an extra push. Now all parties, except Alan, are blaming Douglas. Even a phone call from a person known as the Chemist, was shouting at Specs." Chris laughed stir frying. "I've tapped his phone for reference."

"Does Pockets know?"

"Yes, love. I tell you this. Got Mike to plant a watch in King's DC Bell's locker at the gym. The shite will really hit the fan then. Either Bell will come clean to Pockets or confront King, especially after the large amount he received from Douglas in his account."

He turned off the gas under the wok and dished out the sizzling food onto a waiting plate.

"You're loving all this. Playing detective. I don't like that Douglas man. He's sly; therefore, making him dangerous." She sighed.

Chris's eyes narrowed. "He and George were involved in the hit and run. As I said, he likes to boast, and I found an email to a car rental company in Lanzarote dated two days before it happened."

"No way."

"The same car hired by him for another person. So, he wasn't the driver."

"And George hired Douglas."

Chris drew a long breath. "Yep. Seemingly, Douglas is a bit of a blackmail merchant. Finds things out, passes the info onto those interested and uses both parties. Though a clever middleman, I do believe he's narcissistic."

"Does the team have all that information on him?"

"Some. I don't want to be part of that investigation. Mary is regrettably gone." His voice croaked. "I don't need remembrance of the event."

"Are you okay, love?"

"Yes, Fran. I'm glad you came into my life."

"Chris, I don't know how it happened or who's fault. I've always been a loner. But we seem to have swept each other off our feet."

He broke into laughter and wiped unseen tears. "I love you, Fran Wakefield."

"And I love you, Mister Chris Freeman. Are you sniffling?"

"Hay fever." He sniffed again. "Are you here tomorrow?"

"Staying over at brother Gerald's tomorrow. Barbara, his wife, it's her birthday tonight. When he breaks out his wallet, he really goes all out."

"You enjoy. Look forward to meeting your sis and brother soon."

"Do you want to come?"

"Can't. I won't give password to the team."

"Understand. Call me if anything exciting happens. Bye, love."

He switched the phone off and enjoyed his dinner.

Feet up after and listen in again. Rory can lock up.

86 THE SHOTS IN THE DARK

Abbey Place, Chertsey

On Thursday, Douglas shut down all communications. Efforts to rectify his depleting bank funds had proved impossible. It had distracted him from Humph's briefcase.

"I assure you that I did not change my password," he shouted to a bank manager over the phone. "No, I can't stop the funds going from Billy to Jack. You do it. — What do you mean 'how do you know it's me talking'? You've a mole just below—aha. Now you know. Stop all monies flowing. I'll drop in tomorrow. Thank you."

He made three more similar private calls to other managers. Fists pounded his desk. In his rage, Douglas had written an account in ink on paper and placed it in an envelope addressed to the newly named solicitors, Chadwick and Darling. He squinted as the late evening sun hit his eyes when leaving his bungalow. A traditional red post-box stood yards away. He gave pleasant waves to neighbours of the Penton Park holiday estate when pushing the envelope through the slot.

**

In a marina, a river craft sounded a horn. A noise heard on an island fun park across Fleet and Abbey Lakes over half a mile away.

Thorpe Park resort remained under maintenance. According to a sign at the main entrance, it would not open for another week. The large entertainment area stayed eerie during the setting sun period. Normally, throngs of people would be heading for their cars departing the family orientated park. Now, only a blue uniformed 'maintenance' man lay watching from a thirty-metre-high *Colossus* rollercoaster. A McMillan Tac-50 high powered rifle was aimed at a white bungalow yards from a post-box.

A red Toyota parked on a cobble-block drive right of the house. The 'maintenance' man glanced at his watch.

Won't be long now.

An elderly woman stopped walking a dog to talk to a man.

Come on—move.

He re-checked the silencer and sight. Ensured the light wind was compensated for.

The chatting couple went their separate ways. Again, Abbey Place became silent. A light in the bungalow from the right window and curtains pulled closed. Shadows stretched from a streetlamp on a small roundabout.

Consideration of Tragedies

The distant call of a fox to a mate the only sound.

Nothing stirred on the humid night. Maintenance man switched on a red target-finder. With pinpoint accuracy assured, he pressed a button on a hand-held device. A car's alarm disturbed the peaceful night.

Lights appeared from houses and doors slowly opened.

Number four opened abruptly.

Douglas rushed down three steps towards his car. The force of a bullet to his head sent him over a low front garden wall. The second thudded into his neck.

The assassin watched as two people went to assist Douglas. Presuming he lay dead; they looked left and right. One ran to his home next door.

Five minutes later, the 'maintenance man' climbed into his car on the other side of the island theme park. He headed to the Staines/London Road.

Blue flashing emergency services and police cars passed by.

87 THE RECORDINGS

The Den

Chris dried off after a late shower. His phone sang a familiar tune.
 He pressed the speaker button, "Yes, it's late. Gone midnight."

"Pockets here. Where are you?"

"Having a shite. Fucksake."

"Sorry, no I mean were you out tonight? See anyone hanging around?"

"I wasn't in the bar. Took night off and relaxed." He draped his Arsenal bathrobe around himself and sat at the counter. "Something happen?"

"Douglas was shot at his home in Chertsey."

"No way."

"Local reckon he was dead before he hit the ground."

"Does that mean we're fucked?"

He heard Pockets' heavy sigh. "It's a setback. There must be something on the recordings. I wonder did King tell Specs of his suspicions of Douglas?"

"Hold on, I'll look at the logs." Chris thumbed through pages. "How did we miss this? He called the solicitors—hold on." He read the brief message. "He told them contact King and Specs telling them to buy loads of burners. Listen, I'll call you back after I check."

"Okay. Hold on—so, it's still possible that Specs suspected Douglas of moving money?"

"And king threatened Douglas." Chris hung up.

Browsing through Chadwick and Darling's calls he had found the recordings. He listened to them, and a few other calls.

He saw Alan's last email to Douglas:

Someone's taken money from my account and another put money into it. What did I do on you? I know you're responsible. It was your thing. Showing off. You won't answer my calls. Don't reply to my emails. We haven't seen each other for years yet we enjoyed each other's company for over a week and then you do this. It's the final straw after Cambridge. You slut. I let you off before but not this time.

Chris called Pockets. "Hey. The solicitors told Specs about getting burners. There's loads more calls. I'm knackered but will trace all solicitors calls. I think they believe they're safe. Found an email from Alan Bradford to Douglas sent this evening."

"Good stuff, Chris. Get some sleep. I'll join you tomorrow."

88 THE PHONE CALLS

Early hours Friday 27

DCI Travis King poured another three-fingers of whiskey into an empty glass. He pressed a name on his phone and paced his livingroom waiting for an answer.

Harley was on speaker. "Dad, I don't want to talk shop at this hour."

"Why are you back here? Don't give me bullshit," Travis called out.

"I'm due for promotion. I was told to gain some more experience in fieldwork."

"Bollocks."

"What's wrong with you? Jealous again of someone getting promotion the proper way?"

"Listen here, my boy. I—" Travis steamed and waved a fist at the phone. "What are you on about? You're no son of mine. Your mum was a whore." He stared at the quiet phone then tossed it across the room.

DCI Travis King was losing it.

**

Specs Morgan's bulk turned in his bed to pick up a buzzing phone.

"What the fuck part of 'don't-call-this-number' did you not understand? I don't fucking care if someone was shot—" He listened. "Douglas? — Jesus. Hang up. I'll call you back."

He hung up, grabbed a burner, and pressed a button. "Listen, don't talk. Buy burners. Distribute them. Get the lads together at the warehouse for eleven. Make sure they bring all their phones and get tooled up. Collect whatever food the Chemist has before the meeting." The phone went dead and pulled apart.

He shifted his large body off the bed, donned a Japanese style bathrobe and went down to his livingroom. Switching the light on, he went to a desk and opened a laptop. Placing glasses on, he one-fingered his password and opened 'email compose'.

Douglas dead. My boys will be calling at your lab tomorrow. Have all available product ready for transport to the warehouse. No questions and don't call my number. We need to find out about all this money transferring and sort it out.

89 THE WAREHOUSE

In the Den, Pockets poured coffee from the hot pot. "Want one?" he asked Harley.

"Yes, Guv, cheers." Harley sat beside Ursula. "My dad's fucked."

His statement stopped all movement.

Chris walked back into the room.

"Heard that. Is that your point of view or wishful thinking?" Chris took his 'Boss' mug from a cupboard.

"He called early morning wanting to know what I'm doing here. Sounded really pissed off,"

"Guv," Ursula called out. "There's an email from Specs to the Chemist."

The team peered over her shoulders.

"Pete, Harley get down there now just to observe," Pockets said.

"Here." Chris took his car keys from a bowl. "Use mine. They'll know yours." He tossed them to Pete.

"You sure?" Pete easily caught the keys.

"Yeah. Filled it this morning, so plenty of gas." He went to his laptop and opened it. "Call me when arriving. I can then cross-link to their burners if they use them."

Ursula turned. "How can you possibly do that, Guv Chris?"

Chris smiled and waved a finger. "Trade secret."

**

Rotherhithe

Specs associates stood around chatting in the warehouse near printworks. Their phones formed a pile on a dusty table beside small bundles of product.

Belch and Mouse handed each member four burners.

"Listen up," Specs shouted. "Your phones are off limits. They can be collected when this crisis has been sorted to my satisfaction." He waved a hand to Meyer, the chemist.

The snow white-haired man nodded with a nervous smile.

"Your burners have three names in them—mine, King, and Meyer. No call will be longer than ten seconds and they are not to be used for social. No texting. They are business phones only." Specs' eyes widened. "Is that clear?"

Muffled groans of 'yes, boss' and 'okay, boss' echoed.

"There are one hundred bundles on that table. You will each take six.

I'll hold onto the rest for certain clients," Specs said.

He pulled a Havana from a pocket.

Specs had been hit hard and his reputation fading. Douglas had maintained all his contacts. The ultimate middleman. Specs had no direct dealings with 'merchants'. He just pottered around his large Shoreditch roof garden acting the humble friendly neighbour. An unconvincing disguise in a neighbourhood once famed for outrageous violence. But in the warehouse he attempted to salvage a failing empire.

**

Pete and Harley watched while in contact with Chris.

"We're parked not far from the warehouse. There are seven cars." Pete said over the phone. "He'll send you the regs soon. — Okay. Let me know if you managed a connection to at least one. We wait for the shit to hit the fan."

Pete hung up.

Harley looked through a single scope at the parked cars. "Well? What you reckon? Do you think Chris can connect?"

"He told me that Pockets suggests that you call your old man. He can get a link via his phone." Pete managed a tight-lipped smile.

Harley turned his head. "Joking?" He saw Pete wasn't. "Fuck. I suppose he won't get rid of the job phone. Look, here's the car regs—I'll call the old man while you send them to Chris."

"Put on speaker," Pete advised.

Harley smiled and rang King.

Almost ten seconds past before he heard his dad.

"What do you want?" King whispered.

"Where are you? In a convent? No—a church confessing your sins," Harley said.

Pete put a hand to his own mouth.

"What the fuck do you want?" King asked.

"You heard about a shooting in Staines?"

"Yes. No details yet. Why? Listen. I'm on the job with DC Bell—"

"Now it's you and him?"

Pete thumbed-up Harley.

"Listen you fucking bastard of a son—"

Harley hung up and looked to Pete.

"He deserved that. Chris has the regs and logged on to all the burners. Love to have his technology. We've to let them know when they're leaving." Pete sat straight. "Ah—here they are."

He called Chris on speaker. "They're just leaving now."

"Grand." The phone clicked off.

Harley watched the large group walking sporadically from the warehouse. He jerked back.

"Fuck—Pete. Someone's been shot."

Pete took the scope from him. He witnessed mayhem as gang members dived for cover or jumped into cars. A man lay prostrate at DCI King's feet.

90 THE 16TH FLOOR

On the sixteenth floor of Anglia House, Limehouse, north of the Thames, something stirred. A red light darted from a McMillan Tac-50 high powered rifle. No finger held the trigger. No hand adjusted the sight or assured that the silencer was secured. Another device on the weapon watched the action outside a warehouse almost two miles away.

One by one they left the building towards parked cars. A snow white-haired man nodded to a thin man at his side. An almost silent thud. Blood and bone fragments splattered DCI King's white shirt as the man collapsed beside him. He stood, fixated to the sight of a body with half a head. Brain and red bone fragments clung to King's hair and mouth. All around gang members looked for cover.

**

The car phone rang. Pete pressed speaker.

"Hello, DS. Are they gone?" Pockets asked before Pete spoke.

"Pockets—Meyer the Chemist has been shot. King was beside him." Pete stopped talking. "Harley, where you going? It's not your dad."

Harley stopped halfway from getting out of the car. He moved back to the passenger seat, slamming the door.

"What's going on?" Pockets shouted.

Pete looked at Harley. "All good here, but mayhem at the warehouse."

"Okay. Get back here. If it's not reported then we see what to do next?"

Distant sirens raced towards Rotherhithe Business Park.

**

Alone at his laptop, Chris managed to connect with ten burners in an hour as gang members split up to deliver their goods. Specs and King had disappeared before a squad car arrived at the warehouse.

"So, DC Bell wasn't with him at the warehouse," Pockets said.

"No, Guv. His call came from Orpen's Gym," Ursula replied.

Pockets glanced over his shoulder. "Chris, any noise about the shooting?"

"An ambulance was called for and back up arrived," Chris said.

"I should call the station." Pockets went to the hall.

"There are loads of emails to banks, Guv Chris. The solicitors haven't abided with Cartwright's advice and are still using landlines and mobiles." Ursula jotted down times.

Chris didn't reply. His eyes focused on the monitor and fingers worked the keyboard. He turned as Pockets came back to the Den.

"There's unrelated reports of police at a block of flats in Limehouse."

Ursula typed. "Yes. Three squads have blocked off a tower block."

"Any news, Pockets?" Chris asked.

"A shocker," he said.

Chris and Ursula faced the DI.

"DC Bell has asked to speak with me." Pockets grinned.

Ursula rechecked the phone call timetables. "He called King, Guv, but got no reply."

Pockets looked at Chris. "What did you do?"

Chris rubbed his chin and eased back. "Me?"

"Yes, you."

A smile grew before talking. "I'm missing a watch and thought it might turn up eh, say eh, at the gym."

Pockets' brow raised. "Would that watch be similar to your pal George's?"

"Wow." Chris's eyes widened. "Brilliant. As a matter of fact, yes." He smiled to Ursula. "Stick with this DI and you'll learn loads."

Pockets grabbed his unfashionable jacket. "I'm off to the nick. Keep me informed. The other pair should be back soon."

"Guv, I just got a message from Harley. He and Pete followed a gang member to that block of flats."

"Okay, anything urgent, give me a bell."

**

Harley and Pete met with a constable at a fragile blue and white ribbon barrier.

Pete flashed his warrant card. "What's up?"

"We got a call that someone was screaming blue murder on the top floor earlier. Turned out to be a false alarm. But the door of number sixty-eight was broken. We found an automatic rifle," the constable said.

Harley shrugged.

"It really was automatic. Remote-controlled."

The detectives looked at each other. Without a word, they trotted to the entrance and lifts.

On the sixteenth floor, they flashed their cards at another constable then entered the two-bedroomed flat. White overalled SOCO took photos, dusted for fingerprints, and examined all the rooms.

"Sarge," a DC said. "Strange one this. Never saw the likes before. Look at the small screen on top."

Consideration of Tragedies

They stared at it. They saw another SOCO crew working the Chemist's shooting scene almost two miles away.

"Fucking hell. This was well planned," Pete announced. "And left to be found."

Harley glanced over the rifle. "Looks like it. Would cost a bit." He turned to the DC. "Who lives here?"

The DC looked through his notes. "A Mister Ambrose Wright. Apparently not a social type. Rarely seen since he arrived here over a year ago."

"I noticed no photos about the living room. Any description?" Pete asked.

"Various, Sarge. Between five ten to six two, dark fair or reddish short wavy hair, tight beard, and glasses. Positive with the beard and glasses. Polite. As one neighbour in sixty-five told me a type of professor voice but not posh."

"You need to get an artist impression of this man ASAP. We were casing that warehouse for an ongoing investigation when shots were fired. We couldn't interfere at the time—but now. Fuck." Pete kicked a door.

"Fucking old man." Harley blasted.

"Wright lunched sometimes in The Prince Regent opposite the tower," the DC said. "I was going to ask questions there when finished here."

Pete nodded to the DC. "We'll chat to the landlord and customers of the Regent." Pete handed him a card. "Call me later and I'll give you anything new. But get that artist up here pronto. I doubt if any of these people will drop into your nick. Oh, and get him to the Regent too."

They nodded to the constable when leaving.

"What a mess, Pete. Do you reckon the chemist was the real target?" Harley pressed the lifts call button.

"That was a real assassin job. You can relax. It wasn't meant for your old man."

**

The sketch artist wasn't needed. The landlord of The Regent had Mr. Ambrose Wright on the pub's CCTV camera. Full facial recognitions along with screenshots of him walking around the bar, coming, and going. He had been in the pub on five occasions in a four-week period.

As they walked to Pete's car, Harley said. "Funny thing is that Wright never hid his face. In fact, he appeared unaware that the cameras were there."

"That's true. Now why would an assassin walk around a local pub in clear view? I mean, we even saw the colour of his eyes." Pete unlocked the doors. "He was showing off."

They climbed in, closed the doors, and belted up.

"What did that punter say? 'He was a great laugh in a poshy way.' Back at the shop we should run a check on him." Harley called the information in.

The engine purred into action and the car rolled smoothly along Salmon Lane.

"Give the team the info first. I think Chris's tech is better than ours."

91 THE INTEROGATION

Stoke Newington police station, Friday late afternoon.

Specs' phones were more than burners, they were on fire. The team called numbers sending gang members to bogus addresses. In rival gang areas, Specs' *firm* were attacked and robbed of product.

In Pockets' office DC Bell fidgeted. "Guv, I didn't put that watch there. It was planted."

Pockets eased back in his chair; eyes fixed to the DC. "Though you had the guts to bring it to my attention, you do know that you're fucked either way. Where's the briefcase from evidence?"

"Know nothing about it, guv."

"A hospitalised victim's watch turns up in a copper's gym locker with two sets of prints—his and yours. And you're sorry?"

"It was Douglas Cartwright. He attacked George Inglis, guv."

Pockets' fist pounded his desk. "I'm aware of that. But how did his watch end up in your fucking locker?"

Bell paled.

Pockets leaned forward. "Listen, son." His voice softened. "You may still have a career in the force. Who shot Cartwright? Where's the briefcase? What's your cut for the robberies?"

Pockets enjoyed this sudden interview. The no-good bastard's time on the upper floor neared an end.

"Have you done him other favours—you know, down alleyways on dark nights?"

"No, Guv. He's not like that—no way me neither." Bell wasn't hitting the right notes.

"Well, I have reason to believe that your superior has been involved with some dark sexual deeds involving younger."

Bell's hands hid his face.

"Do you recognise any of these voices?"

Pockets played the recording between King and Cartwright acknowledging the attack on George.

Bell shuffled uneasy. Sweat dripped from his forehead.

The tape stopped.

He wiped his stinging eyes.

"And there's more." Pockets played the next.

The DC shook his head.

Pockets studied each of Bell's nervous movements and distorted twitches at each sentence.

"And here's another." He clicked the play button again. His dimples deepened.

The young man breathed heavy. His head continually shook.

Pockets' eyes penetrated the DC. He stopped the recordings. "Did I hear your name mentioned at the end, Ding?"

"Money was sent to my account from the chemist and Cartwright. Specs always gave cash. Someone had to be messing with all accounts, guv. I didn't kill anyone." Bell shivered and sniffled trying to hold back tears. "Please, guv. You must believe me."

"The two men that gave you money are dead. In the real world, you know, on TV—you still wouldn't be believed," Pockets shouted.

Bell's head shook. "Guv, please, I—"

A hard knock on the office door disturbed the heavy interview.

"Come."

Pete and Harley walked in recognising Bell.

"Oh, sorry, guv," Pete said.

Pockets waved a hand. "Close the door and sit." He looked around his compact office. "If you can find a place."

They both fixed eyes on the DC.

"What you find out?" Pockets asked them.

"We found the weapon. Apparently similar to the Cartwright shooting," Pete said.

Pockets eyes shot at Bell. "DC Tony Bell, where were you between the hours of eight and midnight last night?"

Bell shook as he looked around at them.

"And where were you between the hours of ten and twelve this morning?" Harley added.

No time to answer.

"Why did you join the gun club? C'mon—guns went missing recently," Pete bellowed.

Bell's head was all over the place; back, left, right, forward. Confusion reigned about him.

"How can you afford to suddenly arrange a wedding?" Pockets yelled.

"She's not even working."

Bell twisted to Harley.

"Who told you to take the briefcase from evidence?" Pete's pounding a surface had Bell turning again.

"King—" Bell's hands brushed through his matted hair.

Fists thumped desk, cabinets, and slapped chairs.

Pockets' chair flew back as he stood. "Answer the fucking questions."

"Specs got the guns from the Orpen's gun club. DCI King." Bell looked up at Harley. "He knew there were bodies in Waterbeach. He gave Cartwright info on the Jewellers and Ostofman's so he could manage the security on both."

Pockets pulled his chair back and sat. "Are you willing to make a statement for the record and sign it?"

"Yes, guv." Bell sat straight.

Pockets nodded to Pete.

"DC Bell, you are entitled to representation during the interview. You are not currently charged with a crime, but do you wish to have representation?" Pete asked.

"Yes, Sarge."

92 THE SEARCH FOR AMBROSE

Saturday July 28

With DC Bell turned and the description of a new suspect, the arrows on both sides of the white board were more confusing than a map of London's underground system.

Mr. Ambrose Wright's image was broadcast on early evening news on all UK TV stations. Interpol and Europol had been contacted to distribute copies to all airports, main travel ports and train stations.

It was open season on the suspected assassin.

In the Den, Chris and Ursula had searched the internet for information of the alleged hitman. Ordinary sites like Google proved useless. They stuck to his search engine.

She came up with a suggestion that perhaps Wright had operated before but not in the same fashion.

She was good.

"That's his only address. And no driving licence. Has a passport. He must have lived somewhere else. Try ordinary travelling," he said.

She punched keys, shaking her head at negative results. "Perhaps it's not his real name which will make it harder for us."

"Possibly. Go back further. Airports, starting with UK, then Ireland before trying Europe. This guy isn't a ghost. I'll work on Asia," he advised.

They stared at the results by year, 2018 back through to 2011. Nothing. Then a simultaneous cheer.

"Found him."

They laughed.

"You first, Ursula," he said.

"Okay. A Mister Ambrose Wright was on a first-class flight from Gatwick, May third, two thousand and ten to Kisumu airport, Kenya." She smiled.

"Brilliant. And he was on a return flight from there to Gatwick on the eighth of May. Now, bring up any news reports, deaths or accidents that may have happened during his stay in Kenya." He rubbed his head.

Her fingers appeared on automatic. She stared at the tens of windows on screen.

He watched as the web pages changed her colour tone.

"Bingo." She turned grinning.

Chris joined her reading a report of a boat accident on Lake Victoria three days after Wright had arrived.

Their eyes clicked.

"Hotels." She typed again.

"Stop." He leaned forward. "Look, The Pinecone is near Dunga Bay. Eh, I can check that."

Her eyes widened as he held a finger to his lips. "Shush."

Within seconds his personalised software had found the registration of Mr. Ambrose Wright.

"As Pockets says, 'I don't believe in coincidences'."

Their claps echoed in the Den.

93 THE OOPS

When Chris had revealed new information to the team, he called time for the evening after their Chinese dinners.

Pockets enjoyed the comfort of the sofa. "A good day's work. Proud of all of you."

Mugs and cans of non-alcoholic beverages were raised.

"This is what I want," Harley said.

"You're a born copper." Chris raised his Boss mug again.

"Your old man will do time. Pension out the window. Disgraced," Pockets warned.

"He really fucked things up." Harley breathed heavy.

Chris eyed the group. "Listen, I know it's Saturday night, but c'mon down to the pub—on the house." He saw their doubts. "I can afford it. Sit in the garden or anywhere you like if you want to discuss stuff. But at the GNC—nada."

They nodded, smiled at one and other.

**

Chris shuffled around the pub spreading himself between the team at the GNC and customers. Alan hadn't showed up. Mike kept his usual smartarse remarks to nil when in the company of the Old Bill.

Chris suddenly winced and touched his temple. The easy conversations and light-hearted banter was soon to take a different route.

As a door squeaked, Rory looked up from pulling a tap. His eyes widened to the GNC. "Oops."

Joanne Leigh, showing a real tan on face, arms and legs, strutted towards the bar.

Harley felt Pete's gentle nudge and turned from his conversation with Mike.

She froze. Her shoulder bag slowly slipped off to the polished floor.

Chris *wondered* at the sudden silence and turned from his chat with Ursula. He stood and walked quickly to Joanne.

"Welcome back, Joanne. No phone calls so you had no problems with the bungalow." He kissed a cheek. "Good time?"

It didn't work.

She walked to Harley and a slap echoed.

He grabbed the offending hand, preventing a second strike to his face.

"Joanne," Chris shouted. "Give it a rest. Harley's working." He held her arms and took her towards the beer garden door.

A finger waved in her face. "Stop it. Loads have happened since you went on hols. Real heavy fucking stuff. Harley is due for promotion. He needs fieldwork, Pockets offered. Now calm down, give him an apologetic kiss on the cheek and have a drink on the house."

She threw her arms around Chris' neck. "I'm sorry. It's just the shock of seeing him here." She released him and stood back. "Thank you for the bungalow. I have made more possible clients around Matagorda."

Chris raised a thumb to the bar behind her back.

At the bar, Joanne managed a smile and pecked Harley on a cheek. "I'm sorry. Good to hear that you may be promoted." She coyly stood back, collected her bag, and sat near the hatch beside Ursula.

Chris introduced them. The atmosphere grew lighter.

He went to Harley. "Gently tell Joanne. Ursula has sense enough not to mention things out of line. Best advice—bring her to the beer garden when she's settled, then explain."

Pockets nodded to Harley.

Chris sat between Pockets and Mike, alert to the feminine conversation near the hatch.

Something is wrong with me.

He leaned to Mike's ear. "Cheers for what you did for me. It means a lot." Chris's index finger circled.

Rory began the next round of drinks.

Pockets rubbed his hands.

"Do they miss their trouser comfort zone or are you itching to buy a round, Guv?" Ursula asked.

Amongst the laughter, Joanne managed, "She's good, Pockets."

Pockets shifted on the stool. "When is your review coming up, DC Sharee?"

**

As closing time approached, Pockets took Chris aside. "I know I've remarked before, but without your tech skills and the judge's unusual 'honour' on you—the special detective thing, we wouldn't have gotten this far."

Chris squinted. "You're not getting a freebie."

"No, listen. What you have done wouldn't have been possible at Newington." He looked towards the bar. "See Ursula, well her hubby is with fraud now and has had whispers of 'Where is Pockets and Harley most of the time?' He had spotted Bell, before his turn-over, glued to his computer. He heard Bell ask a tech can coppers be monitored. If we did all this at the nick, Specs and co. would know."

"I'm not signing up for a course."

Pockets laughed.

He placed an arm around Chris' shoulder. "You're a good un. I'm proud to sort of working under you. Without your knowhow, this would've been impossible. At least the investigations are legit now."

"You're still not getting a freebie."

94 THE RAG JOURNALIST

Tuesday July 31

Kumar remained polite and witty to whom deserved it. His boss appeared to have taken him under his wing. Chris had a welcoming aura about him; easy to talk to. The young barman had become aware of most of what was happening in the Den. He had signed a statement revealing his eyewitness accounts of the 'parties' in Cambridge and Waterbeach.

His cousin and another young man had come forward after a meeting with him and Fran on Monday afternoon. Both gave statements corroborating Kumar's tales.

Pockets advised the team to curb back with reports and gather all the evidence for presentation to the Crown Prosecution Service. The team noticed that after a few days off work, DCI King was relieved his bank account had been sorted out. As were all accounts that had been hit with a 'virus'.

"Good lad," Pockets said to Chris.

"Well, it might have fucked things up for your lot if they found out." Chris stood to stretch.

"They've released more info on the bodies and local have asked for help with records." Harley turned to Ursula. "What about that sensationalist journalist, Purcell?"

Pockets looked around the Den hands out wide. "Who's he?"

No one answered.

Ursula reopened a recently found report. "Yes, Guv. He claimed in a magazine to know of underage sex parties that had been rife in the Cambridge area." She scrolled down with the mouse. "Ah, Mill Road." She looked around. "Wasn't that the place that—"

"Yes, young Kumar has done a great job." Pockets interrupted and looked at her monitor. "How the fuck can that tow rag reporter get that info?"

Chris's ears twitched. "Humph was interested in him too. He mentioned him on one of his recordings." He shifted in his chair. "In fact, Alan subscribes to magazines containing his 'scoops'."

Pockets paced the room, hands firmly in their comfort zone.

He stopped at the breakfast counter and turned to the team. "Go back and—"

"Guv? Really?" Harley said.

Pockets' eyes told him to quieten. "Go back and see if there are any connections between this Purcell character and other stories. See if similar names come up and—" He spotted Chris's raised hand.

"He wrote about my Lanzarote accident." Chris opened a window. A gentle breeze hit his face. He breathed deep. "Fran knows of him. Her family sued Purcell for claiming an article he wrote was his when in fact she wrote it. He moved words around."

The room was silent for seconds.

He turned from the window. "We definitely need to get all this together. Pockets is right. But we have the day off tomorrow here so you can do leg work."

Pete tilted back in his chair. "Why? You going somewhere?"

Chris eyed the ceiling shaking his head. "Funeral."

"Ah, sorry." Pete stood. "Forgot."

95 THE DECISION

Wednesday August 1

Marcus Devereux's cremation was a small affair. A few locals from the Prince of Wales, the emergency services and Chris's staff paid their respects.

Fran hugged his arm when walking back to his car. "That was nice of you—what you said."

"Ah, well. Doesn't please anyone to speak ill of the dead. It's done now." Chris waved and smiled politely to passing mourners.

He opened the passenger door for her.

Fran climbed in. "I gave Sir Patrick an update."

Chris shut the door and was soon behind the steering wheel. "All buckled up?"

"Yes. He likes the idea of collecting everything and wants to see DC Bell."

"Mmm. Interesting. Must want to move on King and Specs."

"Any normal person hates anything affecting underage, but Sir Patrick explodes when reading cases like that."

"Well, why shouldn't he."

"Yes, but the loop holes them fuckers find to get off." She turned to him. "He never married but adores his family and the younger ones treat him as the best uncle. When he told me that a grandnephew had disappeared many years ago, I cried hard at home. Even now thinking of a poor defenceless twelve-year-old alone out there."

"Jesus, no wonder this is a sort of campaign."

Fran hadn't replied. Silence reigned for minutes as the car moved along Leytonstone's A12. She appeared hypnotised, deep in thought watching a grey brick wall speed backwards.

Chris glanced to her. "I must tell you something."

She broke from the window. "What's up, love?"

"I might sell up—The Tavern."

She rubbed his arm and breathed in air from the open passenger-side window. "No way. Why?"

"Pissed off. What I could do is offer a short-term lease to Rory. I wouldn't hurt him." He flashed again to a smile. "You vixen. You had an idea I was thinking about it."

"Sort of. After that night—the fight and all that's happening now."

"I've visited a few places before you showed up." He turned and smiled.

Fran shifted to pay attention.

"Brentwood way," he told her.

"No." She hugged his arm. "What does Pockets say? I don't believe in coincidences."

Chris knew she was right and stared tight lipped at his lie drifting away. "You're right. I checked them out two days after our first night."

They laughed.

His time in Clapton was up. This woman had woken him again. Something he had thought would never happen since losing Mary. He wouldn't find true happiness again living as he was. Working all hours. Living on the job, constantly aware of the goings on downstairs and growing tension throughout the community.

96 THE PRODIGAL RETURNS

Friday August 3

George had been released from hospital early Friday. His knee needed a small reduction operation and was placed in a brace to prevent slipping until set.

Late afternoon, the Tavern doors squeaked, heads turned and clapping echoed.

"Hey, hey, Hopalong. Welcome back," Vince announced.

George smiled shaking the nearest hands. He coped well with the single crutch under his left arm.

Alice pressed a button under the counter. "Afraid to ask what you're having, George."

Soon, Chris walked into the bar. "Give him a Guinness on the house."

The two pals hugged. A pretentious embrace from Chris.

He peeled back. "Your swellings' gone down a treat."

"Yes, mate. Ribs still sore though." George looked down. "And of course, the knee. Heard your uncle's funeral was this morning."

"Yeah. Quiet enough. Dropped Fran off her sisters place in the city."

Hiding his inner hurt proved hard for Chris. Worse was holding in the urge to throttle George.

He sat on a stool beside his 'pal'. "In case you see some different things here, Rory is manager and I'm dropping my working hours behind the bar. Kumar is fulltime and Alice will be when he goes to college."

"What about her other care job?"

"The woman she mainly looked after passed on Monday. The elderly man is waiting for a permanent old folks home."

"Cheers, Wonder," George said.

Alice placed the pint on a beer mat.

George took up the glass and enjoyed a long creamy mouthful. "Ahh."

"You heard all the news, I suppose?" Chris asked.

"Yeah. Alan and Steve came up. I believe you were there for most of the time when unconscious."

"Don't like hospitals as you are well aware." Chris looked at him. "Why did Douglas attack you?"

George momentarily stared into his pint. "No idea. Alan was all concerned about that too."

Chris tilted back. "Should I be worried about you and Alan?"

"What? Fuck off."

"I mean could've been a jealous attack." A subtle hint dropped.

"Now, Chris, you know me a long time and never had that sort of interest."

"Yeah, I know. But Douglas wouldn't have known."

"True—anyway, that tow rag got his, eh. Any suspects?"

"Probably linked to the chemist shooting. Similar weapon."

"Good—good." George drifted off for a few seconds. "I've signed off on my recommendation for Steve's Tender."

Chris tried to work George's thoughts. Steer him to reveal something. "Really? That's brilliant. You know he can do it. And being cleared of that accident will be the tonic he needs. A bonus. Well done."

"I was threatened you know." George sipped.

Chris sat up straight.

"Funds started leaking for no reason. I wouldn't offer the contract to a company Specs has a hand in. The money flowed back to my account soon after the Cartwright character was shot."

Chris was bursting inside.

It's only a loan, fucker.

"Hey, you sure of not having a connection with that bloke?" Chris' nose wrinkled.

George's cough had him wincing and holding his side. "Never met him before. Think he mentioned Alan while kicking me."

"Maybe he thought you were really eyeing up Alan." Chris gave a gentle nudge.

His pal cringed.

"Oh sorry, I forgot. You okay?" Chris didn't forget.

"I'm grand."

George had dug his hole deeper.

Chris realised that his old pal was in league with Specs and co., but not the sexual end. The new information about the building firm will open more lines of inquiries.

**

Chris met up with Fran and returned from an evening meal. He had driven George home earlier, maintaining an on the surface friendliness they've known since school days.

It was early enough to claim stools at the end of the bar. Pete had gone on holiday to Lanzarote thanks to Chris' low price for pals and Joanne's travel agency.

"Good din, boss?" Rory placed their preferred drinks on the bar.

"Cheers, Rory—superb. Quiet so far here." Chris lifted his Pils.

"Yeah, suppose so." Rory turned to serve another customer. "Oh, boss. Guess who's visiting?"

Chris' lips tighten in a grin. "You know I don't like quizzes."

"Marty."

A heavy sigh blew across the bar.

Rory looked at the faces. "What? He's a nutter, but gas."

'Hey Girl Don't Bother Me' interrupted the banter. "Pockets—what's up?" Chris still wore a painted smile. "No way." He leaned to Fran. "Another body was found in the small outhouse in Waterbeach. A child."

97 THE WINE TASTER

London City, Monday August 6

News media had struck a blow to the team's discreet investigations. A rag journalist had announced in a magazine in his familiar sensational manner of complicity between the Met, Cambridge University, and a secretive Masons'-style justice society.

Traditionally, though dangerously close at times, he hadn't the real facts.

Sleeping operatives were asked to reply ASAP if tasks asked of them would be accepted or not. Others had been urged to complete backdated assignments ensuring all possible links were cut and leaks sealed.

Julius Sigerson walked into The Fox wine bar off London Wall, Moorgate.

A bespectacled smiling manager, arms wide open, came from behind a small bar. "Mister Sigerson. What a pleasure it is to see you after all these years." He extended a hand.

"William." Julius shook it. "It's a pleasure to see you and the old place again."

A few heads turned or eyes lifted from various interests, but quickly returned to their previous settings.

Julius released his hand and slowly turned around. "You did some work but good to see that you still display rows and shelves of fabulous wines and spirits."

A half-mirrored wall opposite a large window front extended the Georgian kitchen style wine bar. A gap at the opposite end of the bar led to stairs up to a larger lounge. Three rectangle tables stood along the window. Two couples sat separately at tables. A man tapped away on a laptop at the other.

William had always addressed wine connoisseurs by their surname. He bowed as if Julius was royalty. "Don't tell me, Mister Sigerson. A bottle of Luis Montfort, cheese, and crackers." He clapped once.

"Well done you. Yes. I'll stay here at the bar."

They talked of old times and new between glasses of wine and the manager's serving customer duties. Behind him, small talk continued along with the annoying clicking of keys on the laptop. Sometimes bar-side laughter drew the man's attention. Julius casually glanced to the mirror at the stubbled face character. He watched his eyes widen and constantly move ensuring each line of script was perfect.

The man raised a hand to the bar. "Excuse me, William. May I have another glass of Albarino Verde, please."

The manager acknowledged with a smile and slight nod. He turned, reached for a bottle, poured red liquid into a large wine glass, and placed on the bar.

Julius pointed at a high shelf to his left. "Is that a bottle of *Emilio Moro Tinto Ribera del Duero?*"

William was temporarily distracted.

Julius's right hand waved discretely over the glass of wine.

"It is. Hard to come by but 'I know a man who knows a man' as they say." William chuckled. He took the till receipt then picked up the man's glass.

Julius watched through the reflection.

William placed the glass on the man's table.

He didn't look up from his typing and continued tapping the keys. "Hum. Thank you, William."

The manager returned with a scowl and leaned to Julius. "A rag journalist."

Julius nodded.

98 THE EXPLOSIVE MEETING

Tuesday August 7

Julius had moved around on the first two days of his return to London City centre. His next visit of importance was Cambridge, a place he knew well. Mid-morning, he knocked on the second-floor door of Chadwick and Darling, solicitors of law.

"Come in," a crackly voice said.

Julius entered and smiled to an elderly clerk.

"Yes, sir. How may I help you?" he asked.

"I'm Julius Sigerson. I have an appointment with Mister Chadwick."

The clerk looked over his glasses, then to a small appointment book. "Ah, yes. I was told to send you straight in. The left door, Mister Sigerson." His smile added more cracks to his face.

Julius knocked and opened the oak-stained door. A stale library smell greeted him from hundreds of thick leather and cardboard bound tomes. A rotund, small man struggled to stand behind a desk.

"Mister Sigerson, I presume. Please, sit. Excuse me—a touch of arthritis." Chadwick settled back into his high-backed leather chair.

The visitor sat opposite and placed a hard black briefcase at his right leg. They shook hands over a new looking white blotting pad.

Chadwick perused papers in front of him. "Now, I believe you wish to talk about an inheritance you feel you have been wrongly left out of."

"Yes, rather a sticky situation." Julius chuckled.

They had discussed the possible case for over thirty minutes.

When finished, Julius stood and shook Chadwick's extended hand. "Now, don't you worry, Mister Sigerson. We will get in touch with your cousins' solicitors, and I am sure we can sort all this out in your favour without going to court."

The visitor's right foot edged the unopened briefcase at just about the right angle further under the desk. "Thank you, Mister Chadwick. You have my card, so call me anytime." He smiled and walked slowly to the door.

His right hand slipped up his shirt sleeve. He opened the door rubbing the handle, closing it the same way. He nodded to the creaking clerk and opened the office door, shutting it in the same manner.

Everything timed to perfection. Julius stepped over a resurfaced pavement. A sign displayed it had recently been laid by gas company workers. A glorious sunny day, no schools or colleges meant less people and cars about.

Walking past and empty bus shelter and through a park opposite, Julius called a number. "Hello, could you tell me if both Mister Chadwick and Darling are in the office today? — They are? Wonderful. There's a package at the front gate for them— Yes. Would you be so kind and collect it for them? I'm actually in a wheelchair and I believe you don't have a lift— Thank you."

He hung up and stopped at the park's central lamp post. He focused on the front door opening. The clerk looked around but there was no sign of a wheelchair bound person or package.

Julius's left index finger compressed a button in a pocket. The force of an explosion from the second-floor office felled the clerk. Glass, timber, and brickwork flashed across the road landing short of a bus stop. Frantic screams from grass-grabbing patrons as they belatedly coiled for safety in the park.

A cyclist collapsed beside Julius.

His quick reaction saved her hitting the path. He assisted the young woman to her bike and smiled. He nonchalantly walked south to the Gonville Place exit of the park. Sirens soon sounded towards the scene as flames reached the empty third floor.

99 THE BOSS MUG

Wednesday morning before breakfast, Chris finished off his diary notes:
Those bastards. The peados and pushers. Who's worse? Their connections produce evil beyond imagination. The drugs are the stimulus, and the abuse of the poor children is the result. Wish I could do more. But we are getting there.

He rubbed his head and logged off.

**

In the bar, just after opening time, Pockets entered the Tavern, his hands free from their usual zone.

Chris sat quietly at the end of the bar watching him approach. He recognised the DI's unusual posture nearing the empty bar.

"Something's up." He put down a pen.

"Sorry for disturbing you from your bookwork, but the shit has really hit the proverbial fan." Pockets leaned on the bar to sit on a stool. His face red; not fuming red, the blood pressure kind.

"I've been to Fran's place and on a bit of biz in her area—so what's happened?" Chris looked at him. "I think you need a short."

Chris went behind the bar and poured a Jameson. "Here—take it slow."

Pockets stared at the glass on the bar. He breathed heavily and took a sip.

"That journalist, Purcell, has died. Poisoned apparently and then—" He took another sip of whiskey. "Humph's old partners have been blown up. Building almost destroyed."

Chris sat back. "Fuck me pink."

"Indeed. Apparently the company was the only occupier. And wait for it, there's more. A retired judge died in a car accident—collided with an on-coming train at a crossing. Another Cambridge Don high dived from Christ's College." Pockets turned to Chris. "What the fuck is happening? All this since we started our investigation. Oh, here's the killer, no pun. Fran's judge pal, it was his grandnephew found at Waterbeach."

Silence.

Pockets saw another side of Chris.

His right arm swished across the bar. Books and Boss mug flew along the bar before the arm struck the pillar. His face swelled in anger. He stood, easily lifted a stool, and threw it to the enclosed fireplace.

Pockets did nothing.

Chris stilled, closed his eyes, and breathed slow. Mind closed. His hands waved in rhythmic form as he turned on one leg, breathed again. He lowered his palms towards the floor.

Eyes opened, fixed to Pockets. "I'm done."

His phone sang. He looked at the caller's name. Fran.

"Hi love. — Yes." He walked to the office. "Pockets just came in and told me. You okay? Have you talked to Sir Patrick? — Okay, I understand. I've just done a *Hulk* in the pub. Went mental. — Oh really? I was told that too. Listen, come up for a few days. I'll get the team together and finalise this shite. — Okay and between you and the office, I'm breaking their bank accounts." He hung up and moved back to the bar.

"Changed my mind. But do it my way or I walk." Chris's eyes flared at Pockets.

The DI drained the glass. "Bankrupt them?"

"Yes."

They shook on it.

"Here's your mug." Pockets slid Chris's Boss mug back. "It's tough like you."

100 THE SAD JUDGE

Chambers

In the judge's study, Fran hugged Sir Patrick's plump body then slowly released him.

"I've obeyed the law all my life. Ensured that nothing was overlooked at trials." The judge flopped into his easy chair. "I've ensured everything was to the letter of the law, albeit for justice or the unfortunate release, under law, of obvious guilty parties."

"I know, Sir Patrick." She wiped her tears.

"You two have done well gathering the evidence. It's unfortunate a few have got out the easy way." He breathed heavily. "Your man, Chris." He stopped when seeing her wide eyes. "Well, isn't he?"

She smiled. "We are close."

His eyes narrowed. "Well, he must be something to have woken your womanhood, Tomboy." They had earned their laughter after sad news. "As I was about to say, Chris must dig deeper. Get them, excuse me, get them fuckers on the run. Have them slip up."

"I believe he has a plan. We are all meeting tomorrow to finalise something and put all present facts together." She zipped up her jacket. "Chris is thinking of buying a public house near me."

"You must have really got to him. He's a good catch, as a man. I'll let you into a little secret before you go."

She saw his playful smile.

"I met his mother, Margaret, many years ago. Oh, around two thousand, I think. Dashing woman and Ben was a fine man. Still is. I was invited to a bit of a do down Cheltenham way. A long-lost relation had returned. Went missing when caving apparently." He looked to the ceiling for confirmation. "Yes—anyway, they had never met before the do and thinking about it now, they chatted for ages. Then she cried and hugged him. Years later, at her funeral, I asked Ben about the man and why she cried."

He shuffled in his chair. "And it's funny I recall this now—he said Phil, the man, told her that he could cure her cancer. Ben never said how he could do it. She refused and believed in their company's research. Isn't that strange? He's a multimillionaire too. Must be a family thing. Ask Chris of him." He moved to stand.

Fran went to him. "No, you stay. I'll do that. I don't know how it happened—something about Chris drew me to him. He said the same about me. Anyway—" She bent forward and pecked his cheek. "I'm off and promise we will get those bastards just for you."

He smiled. "I thank you and the way you two connected, I have no doubt that you will get them."

A few minutes after Fran had gone, Sir Patrick pressed buttons on a red office phone.

"Hey, Auld Fella. How's the British weather?" a cheery voice asked over the speaker.

"As hot as yours in the shade. Well, I presume you are in the Canaries."

"Damn right. I am sorry to hear of the death of Robin. Only twelve—bastards. Are you sure you don't want me to take care of them? I can zip over and be back in no time." The voice had lost its cheeriness.

Sir Patrick sighed. "I know. But we must stick with our protocol. I have mentioned you in conversation with Fran; therefore, you realise that this present crop must come to an end." His marbled voice filled with regret. "The recent tasks were welcomed under the circumstances."

"We chose a good crew and they have served us well. I will start the ball rolling my end. I'll probably pop by soon." Laughter from the speaker brought a smile to Sir Patrick.

"I thought so. Her ladyship's up to date with events. Well, she is close. We will pencil in a conference call for this Saturday."

"Okay, Sir Paddy. *Adios, mi amigo.*"

101 THE CBCT

Wednesday evening Fran arrived with an extra bag. Chris sat in his office and heard the side door open. "Welcome, love."

She poked her head in. "Watchya."

"Fuunny." He stood, held her then kissed. When breaking for air, he asked, "How's he taking it?".

"Broke up. Never saw Sir Patrick like that. He really wants us to get them." She moved to the stairs door. "I have a feeling that he wants them anyway we can."

His brows raised. "Really? I'm starting a program tonight to disrupt their accounts. Pockets is aware but not the rest of the team yet."

"Great. How are you after what happened?"

"Calmed."

She looked at him while opening the door. "Okay and I want to ask you something." She disappeared up the stairs.

**

Chris got used to being away from bar work. Although not attending Arsenal's winning pre-season Charity Shield match, he felt anew in the Den. Back to his researching mode and reliving the experience of internet technology. Much of which he had been part of anonymously.

Now that Douglas Cartwright was out of the way, he set up new algorithms to disrupt known accounts. The Christian Blessings Charity Trust (CBCT) had become official with new sponsors and trustees. Four stood out: Mr. Hugh Morgan, DCI Travis King, Mr. George Inglis and Mr. Alan Bradford.

Alan had dirtied his bib with Chris. His drinking habits had become irrational. Instead of his usual sipping of bitter, he was taking large mouthfuls and ordering the next pint within fifteen minutes. His verbal diarrhoea of past events began to spread to those that shouldn't be concerned with what was happening upstairs.

Chris leaned back in the chair.

Fran rubbed his arm. "I don't know what you did but I see eight windows of data—numbers flickering up then down and back again. Money deleted then added to another page."

He moved an arm around her bubbly waist and looked up at her. "Alan has been a very bad boy but money from two of Specs' accounts will be filtered to his and then transferred to CBCT. In the meantime, George will send money to King also transferred to CBCT. But the money will be passed to Specs. They may be all aware if their banks contact urgently in the morning."

She pressed up against him. Her ample breasts moving gently. "But they'll get an alert now."

"Nope." His hand slipped to her behind. He rubbed slowly. "I press a button in the morning. All transactions will happen simultaneously. What you see on the monitors are—mmmmm. Stop rubbing them against me. They're a distraction."

"Don't you dare take your hand away. Hurry up and tell me before I go crazy on you."

"I've lost track—oh yeah. That is a model of what is going to actually happen in the morning." He smiled to her.

She went crazy on him.

102 THE NERVOUS MAN

Although Alan recovered from the initial shock of learning about the death of Purcell, he remained concerned over what the rag journalist was going to print next. Realising he had said too much to Chris about knowing both the recently departed judge and Don, he was left without options. He knew that Pockets didn't believe in coincidences; therefore, Alan's latest necessary trips to Cambridge could be suspiciously linked to their deaths.

He waited patiently for his call to be answered. "Ah — *Guten tag. Sprechen sie Englisch?* — Great. I am Alan Bradford — Yes, thank you. I sent you an email yesterday and I am wondering could we bring our meeting forward to Monday twentieth rather than the Wednesday? Okay." He waited while the woman checked dates. "Yes, still here. You can't? Okay, we will keep to the original appointment. — Pardon? — Oh, I will arrive early in Hanover around ten a.m. Fantastic. See you then." He hung up.

"Fuck it."

103 THE WEIRD CALLS

Fran and Chris enjoyed a snack at the breakfast counter.

"Tell me what Alan told you," she said.

"He's an idiot with drink but a cute whore when sober." He poured another coffee in their mugs.

Fran sat straight. "He's on the game?"

"No. My dad said that a lot. Means a clever person—well up on things but not eager to pass on info unless he gets there first. Anyway, he blasts all over the bar that he knew the judge and the Don that 'died' the other day. So, an email of his pops up to *Kerner Pharmazeutika*. He's applied for a job there—doing a runner."

She took a sip from her mug. "Well, you realise that Humph had him on his 'Link list'."

He puffed. "Yeah, but, oh, I don't know. Him and his magazines. Always poking around old cases as if searching for something or maybe hoping his name is not in print." He sipped coffee.

"I thought he was cute but when seeing the email to Douglas—wow. A hidden Alan came out." She stared at him. "Do you think that he could have shot them?"

He laughed. "No way. The guy they want must be well on the run." He stared at his Boss mug. "Although I believe he is a good shot. Anyway, I won't let on to Alan that we are aware of what he has planned."

"Change of subject. Sir Patrick wanted me to ask you of a relation of your mother. Phil?"

"Wow—where did that name come from?" He moved back on the stool.

"He met your mother at a party years ago and came across this Phil character."

"Phil Carmichael-Devereux. I haven't seen him in a while. Hardly bumped into him on Lanzarote. What a character. A very strange but charismatic man. There are two things about him—you either like or detest him."

"Something like you then." She tittered.

"The former means he connected to your head and trusts you." He drank again.

"What? He's a mind reader? Sometimes when you're talking with someone, you look straight into their eyes."

"Suppose I do. Anyway, there are many tales of what happened to him in caves somewhere around Gloucestershire." He wiggled his fingers. "Scary stuff."

"Fuck off. You're acting weird."

He raised his palms. "Hands up, true story. He got me my first place in Lanzarote and—well, you know. He's probably living there fulltime now or maybe Majorca or back in France. He's very secretive. He and his wife Chelle own a company. They make exclusive jewellery—and wait for it—swords."

She rubbed his back. "No way."

"True. Ceremonial." He stared at the cooker and American-style fridge. "I had a dream a while back. Slipped my mind."

"You said you had something to tell me. Was it that?"

"It was bizarre—not scary bizarre, pleasing like. When you first came here and talking to Alan. I was about to walk up the stairs. Mary suddenly flashed into my head. The door shut behind me and then I saw them, smiling—Mary, my mum. It was so real. They smiled at me. They looked so happy, peaceful. Really weird."

"It's just a dream, love."

"Didn't think of it until yesterday while looking at the wedding photo."

Tears suddenly rolled down his cheeks. He was a man of many emotions. His hard exterior was being invaded.

She hugged him.

He brushed away the tears. "Would you mind if I leave just one photo of Mary here? I mean, it is probably hard for you, though you've never brought them up."

"It's your place, your photos of family. I like looking at her—not jealously. You made her happy and I hope I feel the same way."

Was that a hint?

They kissed and moved to the sofa. Slowly they made love, forgetting about time and relations.

Fran energetic, more it seemed than Chris. Was his thoughts elsewhere? Troubled by the vison-type dreams.

He nodded off after a while.

She smiled to his peaceful face. "You need the rest love."

104 THE BOUNCING ACCOUNTS

Thursday August 9

The team were ready for probably the final couple of days of investigations. Chris punched in his unit password, and they were set.

"Now, what you'll see is not legal. But we've been given leeway of sorts to make these fuckers—fuck up." He looked to Pockets.

He just shrugged.

"Okay." Chris tapped a key. The action began on the screens.

Nobody said a word as numbers moved and jumped from one account to another and back again.

Ursula concentrated on phone calls.

Harley watched the frantic emails.

Pockets couldn't keep up with the speed of transactions, calls, and mail.

"Cute," Chris said. "King withdrew cash and closed his accounts yesterday. Lucky man." He laughed. "Perhaps we could sell his house."

"We could try that," Pockets suggested.

His phone rang. Pockets indicated silence to the team as he answered it. "Hello sir — Yes sir, I am busy at the moment. That would be fine. I don't mind if you put a team on them. — Great idea, sir. No, DCI King is not aware of the tracking. We don't know how Specs got the briefcase back. Bell perhaps. I doubt if they will use the same warehouse. — Okay, can I get back to you if we find out where? Thank you, sir." He hung up. "The Commander. — Harley, dig up Specs warehouses for possible meets."

Seconds later Harley had the information. "Specs has a storage facility in the Beavertown Brewery complex in the Hale, Guv. Morgan's Furniture."

Pockets returned the Commander's call. "Hello, sir. The best place is the Beavertown Brewery complex, eh, Morgan's Furniture warehouse. — Okay, sir. Let me know. Yes, sir. We are finalising our information. — Thank you, sir." He hung up.

Chris looked to him. "Was that 'Sir'?"

Pockets turned to Chris. "Funny. Get Mike to go straight to his gun club and check that it hasn't been broken into. Weapons have just been loaded into a Specs car."

Chris made the call to Mike from his bedroom.

When returning to the Den, he gave a thumbs-up.

"Mike said he'll let me know ASAP one way or the other. I didn't tell him about Specs. Just that I *heard* a rumour about another possible robbery," he told them. "Will I sell your old man's house, Harley?"

"Yeh, go on." Harley smiled and clapped. "He'll have to give me something out of it."

Minutes passed as Chris worked his magic.

"Guv." Ursula turned. "DCI King's bank called him."

**

Four gang members stood outside a small warehouse in the warm sunshine as things grew hotter inside.

"I thought your boy was taken care of," Specs bellowed at King. "Now Ding has been moved to Pockets' department. How fucking convenient. That fucking laptop is locked. God knows what Barrington had on it."

King wasn't taking things lying down. "You're done. I don't care about your boys here. They're not fucking bankers or accountants, but I can guess that your bank money is almost gone. I withdrew mine. So, fuck you."

Specs paced. "Must be a glitch. How the fuck can hundreds of thousands be transferred to a charity. I tried to call it—CBCT. No answer. I ran a check and it's legit—so legit, I'm a fucking director, as you are, King. That fat fucker Bradford and Inglis are too." He stopped pacing in front of the DCI. "Don't you think it strange that connections to the Tavern are directors of the charity?"

"Couldn't give a monkey's. I'm taking early retirement, selling up and moving to the coast." King's phone rang. He raised a hand. "Need to get this."

King walked yards away and answered the call. "Hello — It is. That's a coincidence. I was thinking of doing that. But how — What? Hold on, I didn't say I'll drop in to sign the deeds over. No way — stop it now. Don't draw up any paperwork. No. A charity? I'm on my way — No, do fuck all." He hung up.

"I've to go." King waved a finger at Specs. "You get them two sorted out—Bradford and Inglis. It must be one of them or both together. No matter, do them."

He raced to the exit and car.

Specs Morgan had aged over the last few days. A greyness matched his hair. Now he was losing for the first time. Tales from his cohorts of continued attacks had drained him. Even his usual comforting Havana had lost its flavour.

His eyes flamed and looked at what remained of his loyal band. "Do them. We'll see if that will stop the rot. And hurt whoever has connections with them. They robbed me; I'll pay in kind."

105 THE DAYLIGHT ROBBERIES

The Den, Friday August 10

Mike had ensured Chris that all was good at the gun club. As Pockets and Harley were called for 'ordinary' policework, this left Ursula to man the pumps alone. She had familiarised herself with Chris's unique tracking methods and had picked up on vital conversations. Each gang member was designated a letter to represent their names.

"Guv Chris. Trouble is brewing," she said.

Chris attended to the coffee machine before moving to his laptop. "Okay. Let's look and hear." He paid attention to the two short conversations. "Are they really that dumb?"

"Do you think you should warn Inglis and Bradford?"

He rubbed his chin, sat back, and ran fingers through his hair thinking. Taking deep breaths, he looked to the ceiling for answers.

"No. How many calls have there been relating to George and Alan?"

She patted the keys. "Three, and as Specs' gang is thinning out, I reckon two members, eh—" Ursula read notes. "D and L will work together with a driver."

Chris didn't reply at first. He stood and poured a coffee for both. He placed Ursula's mug beside her and returned to the counter.

"Thanks, Guv Chris."

He didn't answer. Deep in thought, he stared out to the sunshine.

If Alan gets to Germany next week, he'll be safe. Fuck him. What about George though?

"Do you think that D and L can be set up for a crime; therefore, getting arrested?" he asked.

"Hold on." She ran their rap sheets. "Both have been done for extortion and armed robbery."

"Addresses?"

She was astute and smiled. "You're planning a plant."

"Say no more. The less you know." He winked. "Okay. I'm going out for a while, type of house hunting. I'll call you later when I have found the suitable abodes. Carry on DC. Great work." He grabbed his car keys. "Fran should be on her way soon to help out."

**

Chris parked his car on Farleigh Road near Hackney Downs Park. Looking around, he entered a house unnoticed. Minutes later, he walked along Amhurst Road towards Mare Street.

Consideration of Tragedies

Chris phoned Stoke Newington police station and waited seconds. "Hello." He breathed purposely heavy. "My car has been stolen — When? I'd say within the last five minutes. Chris Freeman. Yes, the very same. Yes, parked it on Sandringham, went into cleaners and gone when I came out to get my wallet. No cards in that one but driving license, ID, cash. — Anyone suspicious on Sandringham? Are you having a laugh? — Sorry, it's a mid-grey Subaru Legacy, reg is LD sixty-seven, yes LD sixty-seven, PJK. Correct. I just collected my wife's—" a pretentious choke and cough. "Sorry, yes—collected her necklace from repairs. The catch was broke—pearls with two opals. I know—I'm an idiot. Hopefully, it's not seen between the front seats. My number is O-one-four-two-three-five-two-five-one-two-O. Thank you so much. Yes."

He smiled as the Cheshire Cat. He continued walking further towards the Pembroke Tavern and entered.

"Watchya, Chris. You're almost becoming a regular," Bill the landlord said.

Chris held an arm guiding Bill to the end of the bar. "Listen, do you mind if I use your phone. I know it's not on the directory."

"Yeh, of course mate. You know where it is."

Chris winked and went behind the bar to the office.

He pressed numbers and cleared his throat. His voice changed dramatically. "'allo, that Newington nick? Cushtee. Listen, I'm not a grass buh saw these two geezers in 'oods. — Yeah ski fings, init. They got owt of this cool car, right and ran into this 'ouse real quick like — rapido like, on Farleigh. Yeah, numbah one 'undred and ten — Yeah, near the Downs. Fowt funny — one dropped this necklace on the steps, man — shouhin' all sorts. When? Jus nah. Well, 'eard abouh that jewellery robbery fing awhile back, so two and two, know whah I mean? Nevah saw the car on the road before — Fink it's a watchymacallit, eh, Subaru, yeah. Grey, silvery, init. My name? John Green — live in Blitz Court looking owt me windah — Nah not getting' me numbah. 'old on, is there reward? Okay later, yeah."

Chris hung up and couldn't prevent laughter tears. Wiping his eyes, he walked through the bar. "Bill, give us a pint of Extra Pale, please."

Seconds later, Bill placed it on the bar. "On the house."

"Cheers, mate." Chris took a long mouthful. Phoning was thirsty work.

"So, how's tricks? Ready for the new season?" Bill asked.

"Not really. Took a pass on the Shield match. Don't fancy our new manager. We'll see what the next era brings, eh."

106 THE GOOD AND BAD RESULTS

Saturday August 11

In the Den, Chris bore a huge smile.

Fran saw it. "What have you done?"

He said nothing; just hummed a tune and checked the coffee.

The team sat staring at him.

"What?" he asked.

Pockets opened. "Where's your car?"

Chris waved his arms about. "Somewhere, anywhere."

"Would it happen to have been reported suspiciously stolen outside a cleaners?"

"Now—there you go. What a copper." Chris quipped.

"And would it happen to have been seen in Farleigh Road outside D and L's number one hundred and ten, Guv Chris?" Ursula joined in.

"That would be great." He looked at their unimpressed faces. "It wasn't—was it?" His eyes widened.

Harley laughed. "Warrants are out for their arrest for robbery and car theft."

"Brilliant." Chris clapped. "Who's for coffee?"

**

The threat on Alan and George remained outstanding but temporarily postponed. Intel confirmed the arrest of two suspects for car theft. Chris had got his 'stolen' items and car back all undamaged. A good result for the team, albeit semi-illegally.

However, there was one thing that the team didn't see coming. Forensics had proven that a fire at Mike's gym had started in a locker. The building left as a shell and thankfully nobody was injured. His staff had always checked security, alarms and ensured no one was left inside when locking up at around 8 p.m.

His army pension lump sum was used as a down payment. The loan had another year to go. Although the club paid for itself, there wasn't a large profit after each month.

Mike hugged his pint glass. He welcomed condolences from the Tavern faithful. Steve and Vince stayed with him and forwent their usual times to leave for dinner.

Chris watched them, cursing all that has happened recently.

He had set up two fund boxes at each end of the bar. Clapton lacked reasonable places to keep fit, some were outlandishly priced for a common working-class area. Chris had sponsored new items for children to use in the gym.

Fran hugged his right arm as they sat at the hatch. "How did that get under our radar?"

"No idea," he said.

The GNC reached full capacity bar.

"Look. That's friendship—even with George hobbling in." Chris puffed.

George managed to pat Mike's back. "Really sorry, mate. How are you keeping?"

Mike breathed heavily. "Hasn't hit me. Need to think what to do tomorrow."

"If you need any help, let me know."

"Cheers, George." Mike's shoulders remained heavy.

Chris eyed the GNC. He turned to Fran after acknowledging George. "They haven't checked their bank accounts."

She sat back. "Wow. How much has moved?"

"Percentage wise each, sixty. George has a personal account and separate job one. Alan only has one direct account and mortgage."

Fran nodded to George. He sat too close for anymore secret chatting. "Hi, George."

"Hello, Fran. Awful about Mike's place."

"Sure was. One can never be too careful," she suggested.

Chris sipped his Pils watching all around him, studying their faces as if designed to. He was oblivious to Fran and George's general chat.

A nudge disturbed his thoughts.

"Sorry, Fran, miles away."

"It's late for cooking," she said. "Will I call some food in?"

"Yes, good idea." He pecked her cheek and looked towards a squeaking front door. "Oh no."

**

GNC looked around. Muffled groans and shaking heads *welcomed* a man walking to the bar.

"May your God be with you. Guinness, young wan please. And usual for my sis and bother-in-law," he said.

"Oh shite." Chris let loose. "You're barred." He stood and walked to the man. "This area is only for Arsenal Nutters." Chris hugged the small priest and lifted him. "Not real ones like you, Marty."

"Fucksake, sis—help." Marty's feet were returned to the floor.

Fran's eyes widened at the scene.

Chris did the usual finger twirl for on the house for Marty and company.

Marty stood back and stared. "I never said it before, but you remind me of someone." He threw his hands up. "Anyway, great to be here again. How's the Auld Fella? Still enjoying Florida and whatever?"

"Missus M—Tom, next time bring a leash for this nutter." Chris brought their drinks to the pillar as Marty's Guinness settled. He waved to Kumar to come over. "Now, sit Marty. This is Kumar, my newest staff. You would be pleased to know that Rory is manager."

Marty sat. "How do you do young man." He spotted Kumar's cross and chain. "And do you go to church?"

"Say nothing, Kumar. He's very observant and hasn't even had a drink—yet," Tom said.

"Kumar will be looking after you tonight as long as you behave, Marty." Chris tapped his back.

"No *problermo*. Ah, this better be good." Marty lifted the glass to his lips. "It will do."

Chris shook his head walking back to Fran.

"So that's the infamous Marty," she said.

"Oh, you better believe it." He finger-twirled again for him and Fran.

Marty's arrival has changed the mood of GNC. He constantly moved from the pillar to chat with patrons as if he had known them all their lives. Mrs. M and Tom merely raised their eyes each time he went a-rambling.

107 THE DISCOVERY

Chris had felt uneasy in the pub and at dinner in the apartment. As they snuggled on a sofa, Fran knew it.
"You did well today love," she said
"A month."
Fran looked up from his lap. "What do you mean?"
"Getting out of this in September. Made up my mind. Going off tomorrow to finalise the one I want near your place." He looked down to her tempting lips and more than enticing breasts. "And we can then fuck off to Lanzarote for a month."
She looked down to her attractions. "So, you think I may not be a distraction on the beach?"
"Beach? My place is in the mountains. No beach for you girl—work on the *bodega*."
"What's that?"
"Vineyard."
They kissed and moved to the bedroom.

**

Fran got out of the bed pre-alarm and went to the ensuite locking the door behind her. She belched, lifted the toilet seat and dry-reached. Breathless, she managed to stand and gazed at her dishevelled appearance in the mirror.
"Oh no."
Leaning on the sink, her eyes shut tight, belched again, and hung over the toilet bowl. Her wet eyes blurred and continuously heaved.
A shiny round object drew attention behind the outflow. Her fingers stretched to drag it to pick up. She moved to the sink again and ran water over the coloured thin object.
A hazel contact lens. Chris must have had someone staying here and lost one. But why a colour?
She dried it and went back to bed.

**

Chris felt the extra warmth beside him. "Are you okay? Heard moaning in the bathroom."
She lay on her back holding the lens. "I'm grand. Do you know anyone who wears contact lenses?"

He stared at the curtains and rolled over to her. "No. Why ask?"

She held the lens to him. "It's hazel."

Flashes of his past pained him. Researching details. Ensuring alternative escape routes were in place. Trusting his instincts and ability of reading people.

All this shite going on and can still figure out I actually love and trust her. Fuck it—here goes.

His hands dropped from his eyes. "It's me."

She turned and wrapped a leg over his. "You don't wear glasses, never mind contact lens."

He gazed to the ceiling. "I killed them. I'm Ambrose Wright."

They breathed together slowly—calmly.

Chris realised what he had just revealed.

Her head moved in with rhythm on his chest. "I won't ask why but tell me how." She rubbed the contact lens.

She's unusually calm.

He took a deep breath. "I've fished on Lake Victoria too."

She punched his stomach. "You're a very clever man. I don't know why I'm attracted to you."

She caressed his chest.

His throat was dry and gulped air. "I was back around midnight after shooting Cartwright. I felt nothing. No sweaty hands, eyes were dry and focused. Everything was perfect. I modified the rifle later for remote control in the tower block." A deep breath then he exhaled. "Bought the two-bedroom flat two years ago to keep the odd look out on the warehouse. Perfect clear view within a span of eighty feet. Went back and forth, seldom noticed until the warehouse was visited more." He looked to her.

"I knew Cartwright was involved with Mary's accident but didn't know why." His hands softly stroked her pale torso.

"I could have done him hundreds of times. It was left up to me, but others had an interest in higher things. Asked me to wait. Killed me it did. Now, glad I did." He kissed her head. "But I was a tad shocked to learn of George's connection, thanks to you."

She moved up, letting her head rest on his shoulder. "I-I don't know what to say. Why aren't I screaming and ranting at you? Or running to the door as if in a movie trying to get out?"

"Because you know it's justice done the right way."

She rubbed his furry chest. "Please don't do anything to George, love. Let the law handle him." "I won't or touch Specs or King, they're not on my, eh, list." He kissed her curly head. "But, if I discover that either of them had anything to do with Sir Patrick's grandnephew, I'll hurt them."

"You kept up the pretence very well." She squeezed him. "What list?"

"Oh dear. Fowler accidently tripped down the escalator. I slipped a special pill into his water before he left after meeting Cartwright. Wouldn't be detected. Could have done him there too." He didn't flinch. His eyes focused on the ceiling. "I know Mum will forgive me about Marcus."

She slid quickly away from him.

"Is this the film moment?" His eyes remained fixed to the ceiling.

"Jesus, no. How could you do that to your own flesh and blood."

"That fucker was drunk on duty in Lanzarote." He sat up quickly. "He was temporarily head of the emergency services. If he had been alert, the ambulances would've arrived fifteen minutes earlier—enough time to at least given Mary a fighting chance. She died before they arrived."

Fran slapped a pillow. "But that's vengeance not justice, Chris."

He ignored her comment. "He was also responsible for delayed response to a fire in an orphanage on La Palma. Seven children died and many suffered burns."

He managed to turn to her. Tears rolled to the pillow as he shook.

She wiped them but they kept flowing.

Sixteen years of holding the pain inside had erupted. Telling her had released the grief. His somewhat cold heartedness removed with each reveal. Indeed, the tasks were performed robotic style. No emotion outside personal related acts.

Through the tears, he resumed. "Ursula was working away at her monitor as I focused the rifle on the warehouse via video link."

She held him closer.

"We sacked that fucker, Meyer, when discovering he had changed and weakened a formula of tablets just before production. They were sent to Uganda for treating children with a river blindness. More were to be produced for other African countries, but we found out in time that the tablets enflamed the bowels."

He shivered in her arms.

"Tens died but we were blessed not all the tablets had been used. Having tested them, we knew who was responsible." He moved away and looked at her through wet eyes. "Justice."

They kissed gently.

"I'm here for our child. I couldn't manage that without telling you what I've done." He rubbed her stomach.

"I know there's more. Tell me everything."

"I'm an operative for a secret Society of Justice. Don't know how many others are in it and never met anyone related to it. I've randomly received written tasks that needed to be performed in a manner left to my judgement." He breathed heavily. "Due to my availability to travel anywhere, and what I went through during rehabilitation, I suppose they drew me in." He puffed.

"I've seen horrors in China, India even Moscow. Everywhere I went, what I saw and did, I recorded in my online diary. I've outshot snipers in Afghanistan, Ukraine. Assassinated a U.S supremist during a rally in Hoover, Alabama." He saw no response from Fran.

"I've been told that some operatives may cross each other's path—sort of work within another's area relating to similar incidents. The last notice arrived recently." He paused for a reaction.

None came.

"I've been made redundant and must tidy up. Fowler, Cartwright, the Chemist, and Marcus had been marked years ago. You see, all are justified accidents and assassinations. I wouldn't have done them if I thought different. The only way I can be caught is through you now." He stared hard, reading her eyes.

Her irises enlarged.

She wasn't going to report him. Fran waited for more.

He stayed silent, breathing calmly.

She grinned. "I'm pregnant."

Chris' eyes widened. He stiffened. "So, that was the noise." His only words.

He turned his head slowly to her.

I'm awake.

His head moved closer, and they kissed.

They broke away; tears dripping for their eyes.

"What you want for breakfast?" she asked.

He smiled and wiped his dampened eyes. "Just cereal and toast. Tea. I love you Fran Wakefield and vow when this is over, my secrets will be told to you."

Her eyes widened as she rose out of the bed. "I used to like bedtime stories but now the morning ones are better. If you do have, as you say, a 'task' to finish, I really don't want to be compromised and leave you to get on with it." She pushed her petite feet into flip-flops. "And oh, I love you too. Did I tell you I'm pregnant."

108 THE TUDOR STYLE PUB

Sunday August 12

Chris and Fran discussed his endeavours after the big reveal. He showed her some of the tasks he performed in Asia, Africa, and the US. He turned down tasks in South Africa and South America. He believed they should be left to those directly affected. Drugs is a worldwide problem.

Chris wanted her ideas on moving ASAP.

During his conversation with Bill at the Pembroke, a pub for sale came up near Stapleford Aerodrome. Fran agreed to view it with him.

They stopped for lunch at the Ongar Arms on The Street, High Ongar. The countryside pub had everything a 'townie' required. Peace and quiet. The landlord, widower Jonas Shepherd, and his sons had no interest in retaining the once family run pub.

Chris had enough. Though An Fáilte Tavern was his baby, turning it around as a profitable local, his time was up to move on with Fran.

"I love the range-type fireplace and the Tudor design interior," Fran expressed.

Jonas smiled. "It's a listed building and dates from the mid-eighteenth century."

Chris looked to her. "We are not spending our time cooking. I hope that the food here is franchised."

"Oh, I assure you I'm not the kitchen type and have the same people looking after the food end of the pub for seven years—no complaints." Jonas read their doubt. "Well, within reason. The customers' bills are two tiered and combined—food and drink. This how it works. You enter ask for menu, one of their staff comes to you and one of mine for drinks. Separate orders, separate bills."

"And of course, percentage on each," Chris suggested.

Jonas bowed to his knowledge. "Of course."

"Nice one." Chris stood. "Would Tuesday be okay to sign all?"

Jonas, bent and sore, leaned on a walking stick. "Much obliged. I can see this'll be in good hands."

Outside, at the back of the large beer garden, Fran stalled.

She held Chris's arm. "Are you sure about this?"

He looked down at her. "Yes, love. I've probably done it all, but without children in a nice environment away from *my* mayhem, it means nothing. I want a normal family. It's all your blempt." He kissed her smiling face.

109 THE ATTEMPTED ASSASSINATION

Monday August 13

Chris had been busy. He registered the charity organisation. After a chat with Marty, he announced the priest as the CEO. He agreed on the position with the assurance that the alleged criminals' names be removed ASAP. As far as the Team knew, Specs Morgan's stashed cash was all he had to depend on. CBCT had generously received almost a million from him.

Chris continued delving into accounts. Mike received a large sum from him as part compensation for the fire in lieu of the insurance. Steve Urban agreed to rebuild the gym as soon as London Fire Brigade had completed their investigations.

Fran more 'huggy' than usual as they walked to the Cricketfield Road exit of Hackney Downs. His revelations hadn't damaged their growing relationship. While ambling in the warm August evening, they talked of new beginnings outside of London.

"What if we keep the manager and staff for the present. Let the pub run as normal and slowly bring in our upgrades?" Fran asked.

"'Our upgrades'? Nice one." He smiled and kissed her head. "Nothing indicating real football interest and there's a few golf clubs west of High Ongar. Might start something on them lines. Throw up a pic of me and Wenger."

"You're really up for this—getting away from Clapton."

"I am. And I don't want to be stuck behind the bar. Plan 'A', get it up and running, buy another in Matagorda, Lanzarote. Give Rory the lease on the Tavern for five years." He stopped walking and looked down to her. "Let him and Alice have the upper floor. No way is he getting my place yet."

"Lanzarote?"

"Yep but won't do so if you don't want to." They walked on.

"What about junior?"

"Oh, school here. But living in both places, he'll pick up both languages."

She hugged his arm tighter.

As they walked along Clarence Road back to the Tavern, she missed the kerb and stumbled.

Chris bent forward still holding her. A windscreen of a black Audi parked in front smashed. He was quick and turned Fran to the ground behind the car as another shot hit the car's front wheel.

Two passing children screamed.

He leapt from behind the car and grabbed them to safety beside Fran as a third shot hit the pavement.

He peeked over the bonnet and saw a head move from roof railings of a block of flats on the opposite side.

"Stay here, keep down," he told Fran.

She hugged the two girls.

**

Chris ran to the Staplehurst block entrance. Sirens sang in the distance as he reached the only stairwell of the four-story block, waited.

The assailant wasn't going anywhere unless ducking into a flat.

A Honda motorbike rushed towards Chris. A single shot zipped past him.

He quickly turned for cover behind a wheely bin then shoved it at the speeding bike.

The rider skidded, crashing into a parked car.

Two screaming squad cars entered through separate gateways.

Chris held his hands up as they screeched to a stop.

The officers cautiously climbed out of the cars.

"The shots from the roof. He hasn't come down yet. And that guy is with him."

"Okay, sir. I want you stay there. Get on your face," one called out.

Two more went to the biker as another kicked a gun away. More arrived outside the gates blocking entry and exits. Within minutes Clarence Road was blockaded by police vehicles. On the pavement, Fran and the children were led to safety.

Chris was joined by an officer. "Chris. Fucksake man, why didn't you say who you are? Get up." He assisted him. "You okay?"

"My partner is outside looking after two kids." He looked at the block. "I want him." Chris started to the stairwell but was dragged back.

A man walked down the stairs; his hands held high.

"Stop where you are," an official shouted.

Two armed officers ran up the stairwell to apprehend the shooter.

"Two minutes," Chris pleaded to the officer beside him. "Give me two minutes. He *fell down the stairs*." His eyes hard, flamed in anger.

The biker was cuffed and escorted to a squad car. They were slow. Chris' roundhouse kick connected with the biker's head, grounding him and the two officers. Another held Chris from doing any more damage. Throngs of people peered over balconies shouting and cheering his actions. The sniper was led from the stairwell.

Chris recognised the man and broke free. "He's one of yours."

In one swift motion, he leaned back, left knee raised and the front kick to the sniper's chest felled him. He stood over him, fist loose but ready.

The officers ran to him.

More heavy footsteps rushed into the estate. Pockets leading them. "Stop, you fuckers."

Six plain clothed armed officers joined him. Guns aimed.

"Them two." Pockets pointed to the men beside Chris. "Put them in cuffs."

Harley aimed his Glock 19 at the two officers escorting the biker. "On the ground now."

Chris stood back shocked.

Pockets patted his shoulder. "Fran's okay."

Chris side-kicked a guilty officer's knee as he passed. "Cheers, Bert."

"Sorry, we're a bit late. Did you notice how quick these fuckers responded?" Pockets said.

Chris said nothing as they walked toward the entrance.

"One came from Clapton Square. The other was in the estate at Perrywood House. You have to thank Ursula's talents. She spotted something odd last night just before finishing up at the Den. She didn't want to alarm you but hadn't realised the danger until her partner mentioned doing overtime today. Said he was to keep watch on you for the drugs squad."

Chris listened and waved to Fran with the girls across the road.

"Harley decided to listen in today and heard the codes for a strike—on you."

He stopped walking. "Where's King?"

"He's clean. No connection via phones. Nothing."

"Gimme one of them—anyone. I'll make a connection to King." His eyes narrowed to Pockets.

"Love to, Chris, but we need this legal."

"So, trying to get me and Fran was legal because they're coppers?"

"Don't play silly buggers with words. You know what I mean. It's nearly done." Pockets threw up his arms. "But Specs has gone to Spain—Alicante."

Chris walked out to the road.

When reaching Fran and the girls, he bent down to the children and smiled. "Thank you for looking after my friend. You are very brave."

He stood and looked to a WPC. "When getting them home, will you get back to me. The DI here has my address."

The policewoman nodded and led the children away. The girls stopped, turned back to Fran, and hugged her.

110 THE STRANGE GUINNESS

News of the Clapton shooting brought extra customers. Fran and Chris were the topic for the night in the Tavern. Hugs and handshakes from all had them worn out. Rory had to close one door to restrict entrance to regulars only.

Chris did a walk-about in the pub.

George had turned up. He had had a few and all smiles talking with Fran.

"How lucky were you two, eh. And daytime too. Wow," George said.

"Scary is right, those children froze. Chris was remarkably quick to grab them before the next shot." She fiddled with her glass as the memory hung.

"He can be. The way he floored that biker and went for the shooter. Wow. Those Taekwondo kicks and him with a bad leg." He took a sip from his pint of Guinness. "Amazing."

Fran stiffened, suddenly uncomfortable. She stared at her drink.

How did he know how fast Chris floored them? He only told me what happened.

**

A poke to an arm interrupted Fran's thoughts.

"Another, love?" Chris asked.

She jumped. "Eh, yes. I'll be back in a few minutes. Have to go upstairs—" She leaned to him and patted her stomach. "Junior."

He nodded tight lipped, eyes smiling.

"How you doing mate? Bit of a Sweeney out there today," George remarked about the old TV series.

"Crazy man." Chris signalled Rory with his twirling finger. "Never saw anything like it before—for real. Fucking scary. All those coppers flying around us, even though we were the victims."

Rory placed the order in front of Chris. "On the house."

"*Funny*. I could promote Alice to manager. Love you man. You're a good bloke." Chris raised his glass to the manager. "Give George another Guinness."

"Cheers, mate." George drained his glass ready for the next one.

**

A tenor tone sung from a pillar. Marty had a wonderful voice and drew many high swaying hands during the chorus of 'Fields of Athenry'.

Fran helped behind the bar soon after returning from the apartment. Kumar was on a break. She placed another Guinness in front of George. She needed more practice for the future bar work.

With her stint done, she sat beside Chris. Rory placed another round of drinks for them on beer mats.

"Cheers, Rory." George paid for the drinks and took a sip. "He's still a nutter—Marty."

"Damn right there, mate. But his heart is good. That's why I asked him to be CEO of a new charity organisation." Chris grinned as he raised his glass.

George said nothing. He took another drop of the creamy pint.

Fran realised Chris's motives. "He's perfect for it. Only met him twice until tonight and must say—hic, oops, excuse me—that he's a real gentleman." She slanted to Chris. "I hope you put me down for a few shillings?"

Chris saw her pretentious rolling eyes.

"Number one contributor, darling." He kissed her head.

George took a long mouthful.

111 THE TRUTH

In the early hours, George Inglis laid naked and pale on a slab as a pathologist cut a Y shape opening into his chest. His sudden tumble outside the Tavern after closing time on Saturday night had stunned many. One minute, him and Alan sang, linked together preventing each other from stumbling. The next, George pulled his arms from his fellow drunk, clutched his chest, and collapsed with a thud to the kerb. Blood oozed from his head on impact.

The examination was necessary. He didn't have a heart or blood disorder. Yet a fit forty-two-year-old suffered a major heart attack normally associated with an obese person in his fifties.

**

Fran and Chris sat in silence at the Den counter. Both phones waiting to vibrate with news beside their almost empty breakfast plates.

He raised his arms and broke the silence. "Who would imagine that over eight weeks ago I was talking to some nosey fucker called Humphrey Barrington. Then, due to his death, a gorgeous woman walked into my pub, solicitors get blown up. I killed four bastards. Get shot at and now my so called bestest friend hits his head outside my pub and dies. Could only be made for Hollywood."

She said nothing. Her fork maneuvered the last piece of sausage on a plate and finally placed it to her mouth.

He watched her eyes. They didn't look to him though felt a need to. He let a utensil rattle on his plate to remind her he was there.

She looked up.

Then he saw it. That moment of guilt.

"'Let the law handle him.' That's what you said about George." Chris tilted his head and eyes widened.

Her silence broke. "Yes—well, things happen." She shrugged.

"No, they don't. They're caused. Oh—" He leaned back. "What does our bestest DI say?"

She mumbled. "Coincidences I don't believe in."

He drummed the counter. "Exactly. Let the law handle him. You killed George." He smiled in triumph.

She shivered.

"I found this minute black pepper-type powder in the bathroom." He placed a small plastic bag on the counter. "In my pharmaceutical experience I discovered it's odourless and dyed to merely dissolve unnoticed in say—" He angled. "Guinness."

Fran remained silent.

"I mean—there's me blabbing my guilt to you and all along you planned to kill George. Let the law handle him and you from a law family."

He stood and walked around the counter.

Fran's head buried in her hands.

He slipped an arm around her. "I still love you, Fran Wakefield."

"I'm retired too. Got a letter before we met."

He turned and jumped about clapping.

She shook chuckling over her plate.

"Guess what?" he said. "I struck you off my list."

"So did I."

She lifted her head. "Only joking."

He stood beside her and kissed.

He broke free, rubbing egg from his lips. "So am I. You used sodium fluoroacetate."

"*Okay*. Can cause cardiac arrhythmias, leading to a stroke. Larger amounts can be on the spot fatal," she admitted.

"And virtually undetectable if not looking for it." He stared hard at her. "You minx. You rinsed that pint glass before putting it into the dishwasher."

"We best change our ways before junior comes along."

He had reached a new level of release from grief.

"Oh." Fran rubbed her stomach. "I've a scan tomorrow. Want to come?"

He smiled. "Don't like hospitals."

112 THE INTRUSION

Alan relaxed in his easy chair. The doorbell disturbed him. He looked at his watch.
Wonder who that is?
He pulled the hall door open and stiffened.
"Alan Bradford, a word if you please." DCI King flashed his warrant card and squeezed by the rotund man.
Alan's hand stayed on door lock after closing it.
"In here will do," King shouted from the livingroom.
Alan moved to the doorframe. "What do you want?"
King pointed to a sofa and threw magazines on the coffee table.
Alan walked in and sat without a word.
"Do you know a journalist—Brian Purcell?" King took out a packet of cigarettes.
"Sorry, you can't smoke in here."
"Open a fucking window." King lit the cigarette and tapped the magazines. "Answer the question." He looked around. "Oh, got an ashtray?" He sneered.
Alan stood, opened a window, and brought a saucer from the kitchen.
"Thank you."
"I don't know him." Alan sat. "I only read his articles."
King pointed to the top magazine. "Page seven."
Alan's hands shook as he thumbed to the page.
"Interesting, eh. 'Alan Bradford told me' et cetera." He blew smoke across the table. "Page four on the next one. Quickly now."
Alan took it up, turned to the page. His eyes blurred.
"You were in Cambridge and had a thing with a Doctor Brotherton or Prof as he was locally known." King stood and placed a finger further down the article. "Is that the same Vince in the Tavern? The postman."
Alan jumped across the table and fell on King. Fists rained into his face and stomach. The older but fitter King shoved him off. The larger man was on his back as the DCI landed kicks and punches to his side and groin.
He stood over Alan. "Would you believe it. The Gay of Clapton has bottle. I bet your pal Vince would love to know what you were up to before he arrived there. And with the same Prof. Filthy business."
Alan leaned to the sofa to stand groaning. "What about you and Douglas?" He grinned through the pain, collapsing to the sofa holding his jewels. "He used to whisper in my ear when behind me. 'King's panties wouldn't fit you, fat boy. Too tight to pull aside.'"
King lashed out with two fists.

Alan spat out blood and a tooth.

"You're fucked, fat boy. That article can be used to have the boys around to question you officially." King picked up his cigarette from the floor and crushed it into the table. "Don't think of going anywhere."

114 THE BRUISED ALAN

Tuesday evening was quiet in the Tavern. Raz and Marge sat with Mrs. M, Tom, and Marty around a pillar. The baker liked Marty, but the priest asked many questions. He told him a strange tale that appeared not to be right.

"Marty, I don't know how you could've come across Noel in Chelmsford." He leaned to the priest's ear. "He was found recently in a ditch. Buried with others. He's supposed to have been there over seven years."

Marty was stunned. "Well, I never. Fuck me."

"Marty." Mrs. M slapped his knee.

"Sorry. But Raz, I was talking to Noel, and he made me breakfast in Rose's Café. Said he was going to Paris." He was relentless.

Chris happened to be passing collecting glasses. Raz tipped him.

"Hey, nice company, Raz," Chris said.

"Marty's insisting that he saw and talked with Noel well after—you know."

"Maybe the year is off," Chris said.

Raz grinned and nodded defeat.

**

Alan walked to the bar claiming his stool.

Kumar held a pint glass. "Alan, what happened to you?"

"I fell—a few times." He lisped.

Chris stood beside him. "Who did that?"

Alan shook his head. "I fell, right. Can I have my usual please, Kumar."

Chris said nothing, went to the office and used his phone.

**

Pockets joined Chris outside Alan's apartment holding a small black bag.

"You sure about this?" Pockets asked.

"Positive."

Chris looked left and right before opening the door.

Inside, they moved to the livingroom. Everything in place. Clean as a whistle.

"He was attacked here. I'm sure." Chris insisted.

"Okay. I'll check the bedrooms. You do here and bathroom." Pockets stopped walking up the stairs. "Alan doesn't smoke."

Chris niffed the room "Yeah. Someone was definitely here." He looked down and saw a stain. "Here, there's a burn on the coffee table."

Pockets joined him. They read each other's eyes. "Waste bin."

A brown tipped butt stuck out from under a paper towel in the bin. Taking tweezers from the carrier, Pockets removed the butt, and dropped it into an evidence bag.

He twisted to Chris. "King's brand."

"Can we put it back? I mean if Alan makes a complaint, someone will drop in, interview—"

"Too late, he's already tidied up."

"Thought this would crack it." He was despondent as they walked out of the apartment.

"We'll get him."

115 THE INFILTRATION

The last pieces of the puzzle were slowly being carved to fit into place. The Society of Justice had been infiltrated and operatives needed to disperse. A younger generation was already being identified as possible rebirths when the current group had fully retired, along with new committee members.

In his study, Sir Patrick pressed the phone on speaker. "We can talk now, Phil. This is a secure line."

"Great, Sir Paddy. I know, I designed it. I saw that Fran had taken the bait. Those too are made for each other," Phil Devereux said.

Distant waves echoed in the study.

"At Harry's Bar again, eh. Is the Pocillos promenade busy?"

"Not really, was very hot today but now people walking around to restaurants."

"I agree about Fran and Chris. They and others have received their last notifications. It is well that we close our present group. After all, they have lives to rebuild too."

"Too true. I heard Specs Morgan has fled to Majorca via Alicante, so I'll be having a couple of days in Calpe before dropping him off somewhere in Hackney."

"Brilliant. How's Chelle, and the children, Ric and Eadlin? They must be big now."

"All well. Ric is fourteen and Eadlin eleven. Even I felt the years fly by. Okay. Going to hang up now and will defo pop in to see you when dropping Specs home." Their laughter echoed with the backdrop of the waves.

116 THE REAL EVIDENCE

Chris had returned to the Tavern unnoticed. Having earlier called Fran, she waited for him in the office.

She saw his concern. "What did you find?"

"It was King. Pockets found a cig butt in Alan's waste bin. Poor idiot tidied up too well. Can't prove fuck all now. But—" He grinned. "Pockets reckons we'll get him."

"Alan's in bits at the bar. Joanne and Harley are trying their best to comfort him. If that young man finds out it was his dad—well."

He took her to him and kissed. "I know, love. C'mon, let's change the subject in there."

He breathed a sigh of relief seeing Raz and Marge had left. Marty was doing his regular walk about. Chris saw Mrs. M's signal.

"Get them in, love, back in a sec," he said to Fran.

At the pillar. "Yes, my love?"

"Hubby wants a word." Mrs. M ticked to inattentive Tom.

Tom leaned forward. "I saw the state of Alan. I need to tell you that DCI King left Alan's place earlier today when I was walking the dog. He's a right boyo."

"Really—King was in Alan's place?" Chris looked to the bar.

"Yes. And he was marked. Cuts on his face." Tom took out his phone. "Look." He showed them King stumbling at the gate holding his stomach and wiping blood from his brow.

Chris' chin dropped along with Mrs. M's.

"Did he touch the gate?" Chris asked.

Tom played the thirty second video back.

"There." Chris clapped. "And there's a time on it too. Send it to me. Don't move, stay here for another." He looked at Marty approaching. "And for him."

Chris went to Alan extending a hand.

The big man sat back and shook it. "What's up?" Alan stared at him.

"I hope you didn't wash your clothes yet." Chris squeezed his hand. He whispered. "We can get King if you want to press charges. He left blood on the gate, so I reckon you and he have left stains on your clothes."

Alan pulled his hand free.

Chris looked at the reddened knuckles and smiled.

Just what I needed.

He went to Fran at the end of the bar. "We have him."

She sipped her drink. "Who?"

"Tom has a vid of King leaving Alan's place in bits. Alan gave him a

smacking too."
"No way. Good for him."
"I'll call Pockets to leave the ball in his court."

117 THE FRONTS

Wednesday had started bright on the weather front. Conditions changed throughout the day as people busied themselves. However, a thunderstorm brewed around mid-morning altered the plans of many.

Fran went for the scan alone.

Chris called into his solicitor to draw up papers for the new public house. He had grown uneasy when Fran was away. Getting use to her and due to their revelations to each other, his concerns worsened. The weather was so severe, he changed his mind about following her to Sir Patrick's.

He typed into the diary:

Amazing, the two of us working for that crowd. Solutions must be near. What about King and Specs though? The fucker in Spain.
Must tidy things up. Write out reports for Pockets to present to the CPS.

**

Alan had rung in sick, although leaving for his German planned appointment on Wednesday week, he didn't like missing work. He typed into his laptop, read the screen, and sent an email.

On the police front, Pockets and two constables arrived soaked at King's house. The abode had been saved recently from being sold. There was no reply to their constant banging on the front door.

"He didn't say he was taking leave, Guv," a constable said.

"He's not answering his phone either. Fuck him. C'mon back to the shop." Pockets' shoulders bent more forward than usual to the car.

He looked back to the house; a curtain shivered but no windows were open.

118 THE FRIENDS BRIDGE

Fran had rung Chris earlier telling him Sir Patrick was fine and optimistic.

Chris sat at GNC looking along the almost empty bar. He glanced at the clock; nine-forty-five. He saw Alan's head dropping a few times, only waking when the door squeaked.

"Oi, Alan. What did I warn you about?" he shouted to him. "You're getting on my tits."

Alan jolted awake again and his eyes strained. "Sorry, Chris."

Chris signalled to Kumar.

"Yes, boss?"

"I've had a hard day. Will you get him home if he falls to the counter again?" Chris nodded in Alan's direction.

"What about the bar?"

Chris waved his hands. "I still know the biz."

Kumar flustered. "I didn't mean—"

"I know. You're a good kid." He took up his Southie and downed it.

Kumar realised his boss's actions and heavy eyes. He was drunk.

**

The rain returned after midnight. Thunder followed lightening producing a humid uncomfortable night.

However, Alan Bradford snored in his car as it reached a single trail at the end of Millfields Road near Hackney Marshes. The car continued left along a wide footpath. The downfall pounded the roof like hail stones as the path twisted and turned towards Friends Bridge over the River Lea.

A gloved driver stopped and got out. He dragged dozed Alan's bulk from the back seat. He 'walked' the heavy load along the remaining path onto the narrow pedestrian bridge.

The body rested against the railings.

The driver went to the car, opened the boot, and removed a garden rake. He held an almost new coiled mooring line with a carabiner attachment and returned to the bridge.

Pulling Alan up, leaning him against galvanised rails, he looped one end of the line around the still body's neck. It jerked tight.

A sleeping groan came from Alan.

The driver wrapped the other end under and over the top rail three times then secured with the carabiner.

He edged the torso up onto the top rail. Firmly holding a shoulder, he groaned when lifting Alan's legs to rest along the four inch wide handrail. Looking left and right, he pulled the shoulders back allowing the legs to dangle over the water. He checked the mooring line at both ends. Easing Alan up to a sitting position, he placed the rope into Alan's gloved hands. The driver shoved hard over the low end of a curved, red-painted steel reinforcement. The crack of the neck almost unheard as lightning brightened dark clouds.

The killer returned to the car trailing the rake over Alan's footprints. He walked to the rail through his own tracks as the body swung slowly feet above the water. He strode over another pedestrian bridge towards a towpath to the Prince of Wales carpark.

He opened a car boot, removed the same make of shoes as Alan's from his feet, and slipped into another pair. He placed the rake and soiled shoes into a large black refuse bag and put it the boot. The rain persisted as the thunder and lightning drifted off into the early dark hours. The driver climbed into his car and drove off.

119 THE KING IS DEAD

Thursday August 16

Harley King stood emotionless over his father. SOCO had completed their initial examination of the scene and body. They bagged a fallen glass, an almost empty bottle of whiskey, pack of cigarettes and plastic pill container.

"No note about, Sarge," a DC said. "You okay?"

"Strange, but yes, I am," Harley returned. "I'll look in his pockets, but I doubt he left one."

He bent down and fingered through the wet trousers and jacket pockets.

"If there was a note, the suicide victim would leave it in plain sight." He stood. "No forced entry—nothing appeared wiped, no extra glass. His conscience caught up with him I guess."

Harley went to an overalled female pathologist. "What's the time frame? Just in case something turns up."

"Well, definitely after one a.m. He must have been out in that awful weather. Death wouldn't be instantaneous, so dead about—" She looked at her watch. "Nine now so, five hours."

He breathed heavily. "I don't know. Two suicides the same night barely a mile apart—and knowing each other. What about those scrapes and cuts?"

"Probably a day old. Not related to this."

"Okay." Harley looked to the DC. "Anyway, this is yours. I'm getting over to the Lea. I'll read the reports later."

He took a last look at his father.

**

At Friend's Bridge, Harley showed his card to a constable and ducked under white and blue tape.

He arrived just as the body was maneuvered over a trolley on the bridge. "Christ, this is a mess."

Pockets, with hands shoved into his trousers, looked on.

Two white overalled pathologist assistants carefully lowered the cadaver. The hoist belt removed, a constable slackened blue mooring rope from the neck and railing, placing it into bag. A junior SOCO primarily examined the limp body as others tentatively inspected the rail for any tell-tale signs and prints.

"This is a waste of time," one uttered. "Fucking pissed all night."

"Well?" Pockets impatient as always.

"Straight forward suicide, Inspector." The junior stretched to his full height and looked to the handrail. "Easy to climb—even for a man of his build."

Pockets leaned over the rails. "Did he stand or sit? It wouldn't take much of a jump to clear that part of the bridge."

"I don't really know. There doesn't appear to be any scuff marks and it would be logical to assume he wouldn't have managed to stand on the rail," the junior suggested.

Harley stood beside Pockets.

"You okay, Harley?" Pockets looked the river.

"Yes, Guv. The old man may have done himself in. He must have been out though. His jacket and trousers are wet."

Pockets strained his neck around, mouth screwed. "I don't believe in coincidences."

"My feelings exactly, Guv."

They watched as SOCO examined the body and distorted face.

Harley bent forward. "Fuck. It's Alan Bradford."

Pockets attention grabbed.

"I was with him Tuesday night in the Tavern. Apparently he's been drunk loads lately," Harley said.

"Okay. I'll have a word with Chris. You stay here, take notes. Find out where that rope came from, and we'll meet up at the lab."

Pockets called to an officer. "Bring me to the Tavern. I'll make my way from there to the lab later."

**

Mrs. M emerged from the Tavern.

Pockets climbed out of the squad car.

"A bit early for you, Bert."

"Love your Irish wit, Missus M. See you."

He held the Tavern door open.

Behind the bar, Chris had recognised his voice. "We're shut."

Pockets closed the door and walked, head low, to a barstool. "Take a seat." He noticed Chris's scowl. "I insist."

Chris threw a damp cloth to the sink, walked around the bar, and sat.

"Two strange deaths were discovered this morning not more than a mile apart." Pockets sat straight staring at him. "They're piling up."

"And you're telling me this why?"

"Alan Bradford and DCI King."

Chris hung onto the bar counter taking deep breaths. "How and where?"

"King at his home and Bradford dangling from Friends Bridge at the

Marshes."

Chris puffed. "Jesus."

"King was found on the floor and presumed self-inflicted poisoning. Bradford's car was found past the cricket club near the bridge. Perfect night as no one would be out in that storm."

"I suppose. Fucksake, he was drunk again last night. I made sure Kumar got him home." He looked up from the bar at him. "Alan was too drunk to drive."

"What time did he leave at?"

"Suppose about eleven. I let Kumar off early. Rory and Alice weren't on—wasn't busy." He rubbed his face. "Alan—Jesus. Oh, I forgot to tell you. Well, not really, I was waiting for you to drop in."

"Like now? Tell me what?"

"It was defo King at Alan's place and had a fight. Missus M's Tom has him leaving the Court on phone vid."

Pockets sat straighter. "You don't say? I can't imagine Bradford fighting."

"He had cuts to his fists, above his eyes and lips. Missing a tooth too. The vid shows King stumbling against the gate and bloodied." Chris took out his phone turned the vid on. "Here, look."

Pockets stared at the short video then took out his own phone.

"Harley, get someone to bag any bloodied clothes of your old man's. Then meet me with SOCO at Churchwell Court ASAP." Pockets hung up without waiting for a reply. He called another number. "Get two cars to Churchwell Court. Cover the exits and don't let anyone touch gates." He moved off the stool. "I'm heading around there now."

Pockets walked to the exit and waved without turning.

120 THE AULD FELLA'S VISITING

Chris closed the Tavern out of respect for Alan. His phone busy. He contacted Fran, Rory and all GNC members.

Kumar had arrived as requested.

"Lock the door and stick this to the widow." Chris held up a sheet of paper and tape.

Kumar did so without reading and walked tentatively back towards him. "Is there something wrong, boss?"

"Saw you coming so the Guinness is freshly poured." He shoved the pint glass to a coaster.

Kumar sat on a stool staring. "A bit early. Did I do something?"

"Take a long mouthful." Chris nodded to the pint.

The young barman did so.

"There has been two serious incidents overnight." He raised a hand for Kumar not to speak. "DCI King was found dead early morning." He read his face and continued. "And Alan was found in the Marshes hanging from a bridge."

The young barman slipped off the stool.

Chris was unusually slow. "Fuck."

He gently lifted Kumar's head up. "Are you okay?"

"I'm sorry, boss"

Chris moved his hands under the barman's arms and hoisted him back to the stool.

"You're going to be visited by Pockets. You tell him the truth. What Alan was like before you left him home. How was he there. The time you left his place. Et cetera. Drink. We're shut for the day. Fran will be here soon."

Chris drank more coffee.

Kumar almost drained the pint after two mouthfuls. "I—I left Alan at the gate. He kept telling me to go. 'I'm finished' he said."

"It's okay, Kumar. It's okay."

The way Chris had taken him under his wing proof he cared about most people. Nobody is faultless; everyone has secrets. It was brave for Kumar to announce his. Chris had seen the change in the young man. Was it him or the patrons that broke the young man's edginess or perhaps both?

"Get yourself another one. Pockets knows you're here but he's up to his eyes in policework. God knows when he'll be here, but he promised to call first."

Chris's phone sang and vibrated on the bar. He shrugged and picked it up. "Dad? What's up?" He signalled to Kumar while getting off the stool.

"Tomorrow? Really. Jesus. There's some heavy shite going on here. — No, the two of you stay here. Marty would be pleased to see you. — What you mean am I trying to put you off?" His laugh brought a smile to Kumar. "What time? Oh. Want me to pick you up? — Okay. Give me a shout when you've landed. See you when you two come here. Oh, I won't say a word to anyone bar Fran. Promise. — Yep."

His eyes rolled to Kumar. "Pour me a Southie, please."

"Sure, boss. I won't say a word."

"You think Marty is nuts? Wait until you meet the Auld Fella. I think I'll close until he's gone home—maybe both of them."

A door closing behind alerted him. "Here's Fran." He put a finger to his mouth. "Shush."

She walked in and removed her helmet. "Hi, Kumar. So quiet."

Chris went to Fran, took her helmet, and assisted with the jacket. He kissed her head. "Closed for the day."

"I understand." She leaned to him. "Twins."

His eyes widened along with a smile. He took a long slug. "Fuck me pink."

They kissed.

Kumar turned embarrassed.

"Sorry, Kumar." Chris looked at Fran. "Pockets will be here later. Kumar has been put up to speed about being interviewed."

"It's terrible what's happened, Kumar. I won't ask or say anything as I'm sure Boss here has done it all."

"Yes, Fran, you want your usual?"

"God no." She looked at Chris.

"Give her the usual."

Kumar laughed realising Chris's stare.

"What?" she asked.

Chris shrugged. "Auld Fella and Gloria are arriving tomorrow. Staying here."

"Fantastic," she said.

121 THE TRUTH AND NOTHING BUT

Kumar sat in the beer garden with Pockets and Harley. Chris had ordered food for all. He sat at the bar with Fran. "Where were you, love?" He chewed into a double beef burger with cheese.

Fran still chuffed at her news "After the scan, I went to see my brother Gerald." She crunched her chicken salad.

"Yeah, okay." His kiss left ketchup on her cheek. "Sorry." He wiped it off.

Her eyes widened. "You don't think I did King?" She looked around to the beer garden door.

"The news of having twins, love." He winked.

The forkful hung at her mouth. "Did you?"

"What?"

"Chris Freeman, you said you're retired."

"Loose ends." He dipped a chip into mayo. "The hardest thing, well, not really—was 'assisting' with Alan's drop." He raised a brow before dipping another chip.

She froze. Her mouth gaped; tongue glued.

He stared at his plate. "Alan was my first given task. Sorry—" Chris held up a chip before it disappeared smartly into his mouth. "Well, second task really." He looked to Fran. "Take a drink."

She did and stayed silent.

"Fucking hated him."

"Jesus—Chris."

"Alan Bradford was head of research in the cancer department of Ostrofman. He signed off on many projects, in other words, he was the main man before actual production. All tests on a certain drug had ninety three percent certainty of slowing down the rate of ovarian cancer. Thereby reducing death when caught in the early stages." He took a sip of Southie.

"How in the name of God did we think that it would take the place of chemo? But he said it would eventually work out. We stopped production within weeks. A few women had died, and millions lost. When I found out that he had personally used my mother as a guinea pig, it was too late for her. That fucker killed my mum."

Fran rubbed his arm. "You've bottled all this up for years. You moved here for him."

"I most certainly did." He emptied the glass and slammed it on the bar reverberating.

He read her eyes. "Believe it or not, Bradford was actually doing some fine research. He led a team, so, for the sake of the public, I delayed his end.

Consideration of Tragedies

For years that Purcell fucker played on his mind. Reading all of his crap. Something in my head said 'wait'. I did more research on Bradford."

She rubbed his shoulder. "Why did you wait so long?"

"Though brilliant at his job, I found he lacked confidence and easily led. Was there someone behind him? Why would he interfere with tested drugs? When I found the Douglas Cartwright connection, I let Alan be. I suspected there's something bigger here. Then of course Cartwright turning up as he did. And hey presto, look what we all dug up—literally. The time was right."

She fiddled with her glass. "He was responsible for my mother's death too."

He placed an arm around her shoulder.

"She was one of the first that died. I wasn't joking about my list." Her stare revealed what was coming next. "I was given names of those that could lead to Alan. I accidently found a file belonging to Humphrey Barrington. I was going to return it, but me being curious, read it. Mentioned Alan, cancer research, you, your dad, deaths of women that had used Ostrofman's drugs. I reckon someone left it for me to find on the train." She straightened. Her hand slipped over her mouth. "Oh my God. Someone that looked like Marty had sat opposite me."

He shook his head gazing at his glass. "Jesus, no way. Now that would be a coincidence."

"I guess so." She smiled. "The day I first met you, I had a feeling that you had another life. For the first time I was afraid of someone. You." Her eyes teared. "I remarked many times that you're a clever man and what you have just told me proved I was right." She bent sideways and kissed his lips. "I love you, Chris Freeman. We have been brought together for a reason. Perhaps it was destiny."

He sat silent. Waiting for something. She was correct. He turned to her.

"Don't worry. I know you didn't do King—I did." Her grin tight lipped.

Chris clapped once. "Ha, ha, ha."

Her brows raised. "You are well aware of the research we do first, and he a creature of habits. Never smoked in the office so I swapped the cigs in his car earlier that day. They won't find anything." Fran sipped from her glass. "I watched later as he struggled home in the rain. I entered through the back garden and replaced his cigs, left the tabs, et cetera—as you would say."

Chris stared at her for what seemed ages.

She's incredible.

"That's brilliant. They will look at the pills and whiskey."

"I was only concerned about the treatment of Kumar. Nothing to do with Alan."

Chis stood and went to the Pils fridge. "You mean, King was an 'extra'?"

Her wide smiling eyes gave him the answer.

"What a pair we are." He opened the bottle, took a mouthful, and sat. "And Bradford topped himself. Coincidence after King? Nice one." His hands raised. "As soon as Kumar left. I locked up. Got changed and took my special route to Churchwell. Was well pleased seeing Bradford alone almost passed out on the steps. Got him into the backseat of his car to 'sleep off the drug'." He took another sip. "I had already parked my car at the Wales earlier. Got a bus back to Clapton Common. The torrential rain helped loads." He played with the bottle. "I fucking hated him. Serving drink almost each day." His eyes watered. "Putting on a face every time. Going to matches and him in my private box at the Emirates."

He patted the tears and raised the bottle. "For you, Mum." He sipped and turned to Fran. "We've known each other for two months; you're expecting our children—" His eyes still watered. "Fran Wakefield, will you be my wife?"

She threw her arms around him. "Yes, yes, yes. And I knew this was it for me."

They kissed passionately.

Pulling away, Fran said, "When will we announce?"

122 THE PRE-POST-MORTEM

Friday August 17

Harley and Pockets arrived at the lab the following day for the pathologist's preliminary reports on both bodies. At the victims homes, soiled clothes were removed in evidence bags. In Alan's apartment, SOCO had found minute samples of blood and dusted for prints. Outside at the gates, smudge bloodstains and prints were taken for examination.

Alf Parsons hadn't yet cut into Alan's body. "The neck broke on the fall." He pointed to a screen. "As you can see, the rope burn is V shaped. You see the redness and position of the head—he wanted to prevent strangulation. Wanted it over quick—a finality so to speak. I wouldn't be surprised if you find reading material at his home relating to accidents and killings."

Harley went to the corpse. "As a matter of fact he loved unsolved crime mags and he's a member of a gun club. Why this way and for what reason, Guv?"

"Your old man and Mister Bradford were involved in an altercation. And as you know, he was doing a runner to Germany. So, something was afoot." Pockets clapped once. "Get back to me after you cut him open. Make it thorough, Alf. I want to rule out interference."

"As always, Bert. Let me know your thoughts of the DCI's report."

Harley stalled. "Alf, what about the rope?" He took out his notebook. "Boatmen were interviewed, and one reported mooring rope was taken off his houseboat that night—" He perused a page. "A spare 'navy blue pre-spliced three strand polysoft mooring line' to be exact. Almost brand new—his words."

Alf scratched his chin. "Yes, that would be the type removed from the body. It wasn't frayed, so possibly new. Oh, fragment of the rope fibre was taken off a glove. We have to compare though."

"Okay," Pockets said. "We need to re-interview the boatmen. Find out did any see or hear something out of the ordinary."

"Guv, it was coming down buckets last night," Harley noted.

Pockets rolled his eyes.

**

Late afternoon, in Pockets office. The Bradford preliminary report was open on his desk. "Only one set of footprints from the car. Though partially washed away, they match Bradford's." Pockets pointed to the photos in the file.

"What's that?" Harley asked. "Alan was particular about appearances." He noticed his superior's stare. "Okay, why should he care before this. But look—there are scuff marks on the back of the shoes. Scrapes even."

Pockets took a closer look. "Hum." He scratched his head. "Dragged perhaps? Could've happened when climbing the rails or sitting contemplating whether to jump. Maybe had his feet between the rails steadying himself before jumping. They're very slight."

He looked to Harley. "See the knuckles and cuts over the eyes?"

"Yes. So, he was with someone."

"I told you that he and your old man had fisty cuffs at Bradford's apartment. Your dad's prints were found there. Bloodstains on the stairwell and gate outside match your dad's. A cig burn to the coffee table."

"Shit." Harley had opened DCI King's file. "Says here that bloodstains found on his shirt were not all his. His clothes were probably wet due to the rain. They're waiting for further tests."

Harley sat back. "You reckon that Alan would have the bottle to do the old man and then did a dive off the bridge?"

"He was a recognised chemist. Now they're considered self-inflicted deaths. But as you well know—" Pockets smiled tight lipped.

"You don't believe in coincidences." Harley nodded.

"And Bradford was wearing gloves when jumping. None of his prints at your old man's."

Harley took out a notebook. "Ah—yes, Guv. Alan had met up with that Doctor Brotherton and had been reported for sexual misconduct in Cambridge Uni." He looked up to Pockets. "Shit—Dad knew of Kumar. How did we miss that?"

"Kumar is innocent. A victim. He left Alan at the stairs. I reckon Alan was aware of all this via Douglas Cartwright. Hence him hitting the bottle more. It's all connected. That Humph guy really opened up a can of worms." He sat back. "I'm sure your old man would have covered his arse—no pun."

"The mooring is confirmed to be the one taken from the houseboat. The rope fibres matched the fragments from Alan's gloves. The boatmen never moved outside after securing the barges at around seven due to the storm."

"Okay. Anyway, your old man will have notes, records somewhere. Get Bell in here."

**

DC Bell entered Pockets' office when hearing his guv's permission to do so.

"Sit." Pockets indicated to a spare chair.

"Yes, Guv." Obedient as a puppy.

"You drove DCI King all over the place until recently. Anywhere we are not aware off? Bank or PO deposit boxes?" Pockets asked Bell.

"No, Guv. But we did pick up a large metal box months ago after he got some builder to redesign his shed," Bell announced.

Pockets and Harley stared at him.

"What?—Guv?"

"I asked you to give us everything and you forgot about that." Pockets smiled and clapped once. "Harley, find out about the builder and then you two get over there. There will be a warrant on its way within the hour. Only coz the house will be yours now. Don't do fuck all until you have the paperwork."

123 THE AULD FELLA AND GLORIA

Saturday morning at An Fáilte Tavern.

Chris watched Fran from his Den desk. Were they really meant for each other? Yes. Had they been purposely led to each other?

Fran poured coffee into two mugs. "I can feel your eyes again, love."

"And why not." He tilted his head.

She picked up his 'Boss' mug and left it on the counter. "I won't be walking around like this in your shirt after today."

"You don't have to wear anything. I don't mind." He closed the laptop and went to the counter.

"You know what I mean. What time are they arriving?"

He sat and took a sip of coffee. "Landing soon. So, over an hour's drive they'll be here in time for a cuppa with Missus M."

"I'm nervous."

"Why. Don't tell me you're going to put something in the tea."

They laughed.

Would it last? Who knows?

**

While Fran caught up on writing in the Den, Chris stacked shelves with bottles.

Mrs. M hummed a tune out in the beer garden as she finished the floors.

"Did you get your hair done, Missus M?" Chris shouted.

She waddled back in. "How would you notice if I did or didn't?"

"Ah. You know the Auld Lad is coming this morning."

She patted her hair. "Go away with ya—ya eejit."

A car on the security monitor caught his attention. "Here they are pulling up in the alley. You got your lipstick ready?"

"Jesus—let me at ya."

He went to the side entrance and opened the door.

Ben Freeman stepped from the back of a hired limo as his son opened the other back door.

"Gloria, looking gorgeous as usual." Chris smiled and extended a hand for her to hold.

The late forties short haired brunette eased out. She stood in front of her stepson reaching to peck a cheek.

"Still the same old Chris."

He turned to his dad. "Looking good, Dad."

Ben shook his hand. "Cheers, son. Thanks for the limo."

"No bother. Come in the pair of you. Bar or Den?"

Ben's brow rose. "Is she still here?"

Chris nodded smiling.

"Bar."

Gloria linked her shorter husband as they walked through to the bar.

"There she is. The one that got away." His Dublin accent clearer.

"Oh no. Like father like son," Mrs. M cried out. "Ben, ya old fecker—and Gloria. You two look great, permanent tan and all." She gave them both a hug.

The driver opened the boot.

Chris directed him to leave two suitcases and small holdall in the office. "Cheers." He handed him a fifty note.

The driver's eyes widened. "Tha–Thank you, sir."

"I'll guide you out of the alley."

**

They gathered at GNC.

"I'll have the young fella make tea. Surely you're not having something stronger," Mrs. M said.

Ben looked at his watch and to Gloria. "Tea, please Missus M."

Chris walked in. "I heard all that. You got your hair cut since Dublin, Dad."

Ben rubbed his hand over his snow-white two blade cut. "Yeah, too warm for my bush."

"How about coffee? Have the machine on."

Mrs. M's eyes stared at him. "I suppose so."

He pressed a button under the bar and took down four mugs. His eyes widened at Mrs. M.

She grinned.

Pouring the fresh brew into the mugs, he twitched to the sound of the stair door closing. All eyes stared at smiling Fran.

Ben and Gloria looked to Chris as she walked to them.

"Dad, Gloria—this is Fran," Chris said.

His face beamed. The last weight eased off his shoulders. They didn't have to ask why Fran was there. The look on the lovers' faces said it all.

Ben politely stood, hugged, and kissed her cheek. "Thank you," he whispered.

She pulled slowly back. Head slightly cocked and looked at Chris.

Gloria stood beside her husband and hugged Fran when he let her free.

"Have I missed something here?" Mrs. M asked. "Don't tell me that you didn't tell Ben that you two were—you know," she said to Chris.

Consideration of Tragedies

Chris jerked back. "Were what?"

The group laughed.

"It is good to meet you two." Fran sat beside Gloria.

Chris looked to Fran.

She nodded.

"Eh, something to tell you. We're getting married." Chris smiled.

"Ah—" Mrs. M hugged Chris. "I had a feeling." She then embraced Fran.

Ben shook his son's hand then kissed Fran's cheek. "Fantastic. I'm so glad for you both."

Gloria held Fran's hands and looked to her face. She pecked both cheeks and smiled.

"Twins," Fran blurted out. "Were expecting twins."

More hugs and wet eyes.

During the coffee-break the chat generalised around Chris and Fran. No crime or deaths mentioned. Even Mrs. M had understood 'mum's' the word when in his company. She remained ladylike. Say nothing unless asked.

"I believe the nutter is here," Ben said to Mrs. M.

Fran sat straight and looked to Chris.

"Oh, he is and now you arrive. It'll be Mass twice a day and confession to try to get back to normal when the pair of ya are gone." Mrs. M kissed Ben's cheek.

Chis smiled to Fran. "Told you. It's a long, long story."

124 THE GRAB

Calpe, Spain. Sunday morning August 19

From his holiday home roof top overlooking the *Reial Club Nàutic* marina, Calpe, Phil Carmichael-Devereux sipped a small cup of his regular Columbian brand coffee.

He turned from the balcony railing to the opened livingroom. "Do you want to come later, Chelle?"

"Yes—that would be nice. As long as you stay out of whatever is happening over there," his sultry wife said.

Chelle maintained her shoulder-length dark hair. She wrapped a floral kaftan around her voluptuous body. Though approaching sixty, the ex-supermodel retained the looks that continued selling her husband's designs.

"Tempting me again, eh."

"You wish." At the rail, she linked him.

They turned to the sea view.

"Is this the end of the society?" she asked.

"For the moment." He pecked her cheek. "I'll be off soon."

"Your hat." Chelle pointed to his Stetson on a chair. "Give them a hug from me. Tell the nutter I'll join him for a song soon."

"Jesus. If anyone can break that man's priesthood, it would be you. We'll see him together." They kissed. "Love you."

**

Santa Ponca, Majorca Sunday afternoon.

Phil climbed out of his hired *Seat* outside a high dark-grey gate on *Via Cornisa*, east of Santa Ponca, Majorca. His sudden arrivals didn't surprise anyone. Locals in the taverns often remarked, '*Parece aparecer de la nada.*' (He seems to appear from nowhere).

He pressed a bell on the security intercom of the villa overlooking the bay.

A harsh voice answered. "*Si?*"

"Hello, Yes is Mister Morgan available, please?" Phil's Spanish fluent.

"Yes. Who are you and why do you want him?"

"Phil Devereux. I have the package he is waiting for." He was good at bullshitting.

A camera whirred above the Stetson-wearing delivery man. "Ah, Senor Pheel. I see now."

Phil waved to it.

Consideration of Tragedies

A minute later, two bolts sounded, and a latch turned. The wide gate slowly pulled back to reveal a short white-shirted man.

"Senor, Pheel. You arrive again. But why have you a package for Senor Morgan?"

"I was at the post office, chatting—you know what I'm like."

The man dipped his lips and nodded. "Oh, si si. Always helpful."

"I mentioned I was heading this way and was asked to give this to a Senor Morgan at this address." Phil rubbed the package.

"You are really well liked, Senor Pheel." He extended a hand to the bundle.

"No, Miguel. Though I do trust you, I must give it to him personally."

He walked past without leave to do so.

Miguel stood blankly.

Phil followed sounds of splashing water down steps to a pool area.

As he climbed out of the pool, Specs squinted at a shape approaching. He donned his glasses.

"Who the fuck are you?" His gruff manner evident.

"A messenger." Phil extended the package to him. "Here. Specially delivery from the post office." He smiled and rested a hand on Specs' left wrist.

Specs stared at the package, held it, and jerked as a small needle penetrated his wrist.

**

Shoreditch, London Monday August 19

Phil piloted his own Cessna Citation CJ4 landing at London City Airport. Two team members assisted a drugged body from the plane to his hired car. He made his way to an underground carpark of an exclusive apartment block in Shoreditch.

Phil's age didn't prevent him from carrying bulky Specs to a private lift. Pressing 'P' button for the penthouse, the door slid shut.

The lift smoothed to a stop and the door opened.

Phil stepped out with his cargo. "Nice place you have here, Mister Morgan."

He dropped Specs on a highly polished floor.

He stirred and stood, still in swimming shorts, in the livingroom of his Charterhouse Square apartment.

"Do you mind if I make a phone call?" Phil asked.

"What have you done to me? I'm numb."

"Is that a yes? Okay." Phil took out his phone and waited. "Ah, hello. There is a disturbance in an apartment block off Charterhouse Square,

Shoreditch. — Pardon, oh, I don't know. Think his name is Hugh Morgan." He hung up and waved to Specs. "See you, bye."

**

Specs was glued to the floor. The drug hadn't worn off. He turned realising the familiar room. He shook his head awake.

"Where did you go? Where's the package?" He tried to walk. "How did I get here—you bastard. I'll fucking kill ya."

Sirens grew louder.

"Bastard, fucking bastard. Where did he go? Fuck. I can't move."

Minutes later, loud movement outside his apartment, then shouts. "Police, open the door."

Specs couldn't. He laid on the floor.

The front door burst open.

His time was up.

125 THE METAL BOX

Monday midday at Stoke Newington police station, Pockets had collected DCI King's keys from evidence. After examining the bunch, deduced the newer one fitted the metal box lock.

Harley had accompanied its transfer from his father's back garden shed under warrant. The two by one-foot grey box sat on his desk waiting for the key to be injected into the lock. Pockets gave Harley the honour of opening it.

The lid creaked open to reveal a recorder, files, and notebooks.

"He must have learned how to keep records from that Humph geezer," Harley dryly said.

"Get some gloves on and we bag after looking through them." Pockets suggested.

They sat almost in silence sifting through the box's contents. List of drug deals, money exchanges, details of raids and robberies overlooked by police. A mention of high ranking officers. Photos of children with MPs and a bishop. Names and ages on the back had Harley retching. King's name conveniently missing from all the evidence of child sexploitation. However, because of Kumar's detailed stories, the DCI was easily identified as the hooded man.

"Got him." Pockets clapped once. He turned to Harley with the file. "Look. Your old man really covered his arse. Specs with Lens and a young lad. Though not there, I reckon he got this from Cartwright. Oh, here's a DVD." He stared at the DS.

They turned to the computer and slipped the DVD into a slot.

Silence. Harley put a hand over his mouth as the horror played.

Their eyes told what was on their minds.

"Shoot 'im. Go on, son," Specs shouted to a boy.

A young lad quivered and sobbed. A gun too big for one hand.

"No—hold it with two hands. That's a good lad."

The scene shook to a large man kneeling facing away from the boy. Noel Peters, gagged, blindfolded, and trussed up. He struggled knowing what was happening behind him. The camera zoomed to the boy's welled-up eyes. Lens was ordered to assist in holding the weapon.

"Fucking do it," Specs roared again.

The boy jolted.

The shot echoed through the derelict house.

"Good lad." Specs raised another gun and blasted away at his brother.

Lens couldn't react; nor could the boy as a stray bullet hit his head.

"Fucksake, Specs," the cam man said.

Pockets punched the stop button.

Harley turned to a waste bucket and brought up yellow bile.

The DI shoved a box of tissues towards him as his phone rang. "Hello, DI Macken here." He wiped his wet eyes. "No way. You don't say. When did he return? Fuck off — He said he was just dropped home? He's looking for the funny farm. — Okay. Get him to the nick, let him get a brief." He hung up "Harley, get yourself togethen—tidy this up and bag the lot. Specs has been arrested at his gaff."

Harley wiped his mouth and disposed of the tissue. "When did he come back?"

"Apparently someone dropped him off at his place in his swimming shorts. No matter. We get this to the CPS before his brief has been, eh— briefed."

126 THE SON AND DAD CHAT

Chris and Ben sat alone in the bar after midnight.

"I'm delighted for you and Fran, Chris," Ben said.

"Meant to be, Dad—my headaches are getting worse. They occur before something happens or certain people enter the bar." Chris sipped his Southie. "Like a premonition—warnings."

Ben stared at his Guinness. "Your mum was like that. Your Granny Devereux too. I was always getting the paracetamol."

They laughed.

"Now I'm having weird dreams." Chris' mouth tightened momentarily. "Mary, Mum. Driving me mad."

"You have a lot on your mind. This case. Uncle Marcus. Fran, of course. You need to slow down."

"Okay. Try this for weird. Specs was suddenly brought back from Spain and dropped off in Shoreditch." Another mouthful of Southie eased down.

"That was Uncle Phil. He's Interpol."

Chris sat straight and stared at Ben.

"True. Has been for years. Mostly undercover and works alone. You're like him. A tech genius. Pilot's his own plane too."

Chris sipped his Southie. "Maybe the dreams were aimed at him and Specs. A kind of foresight."

Ben drank the Guinness and wiped his lips. "Son, you went through hell after the accident. We thought you would lose the leg. But it healed quickly. I recall you telling me that the headaches returned about two thousand and eleven."

"Yes. Around that time when we were thinking of selling up."

Ben shook his head and turned to Chris. "No. After your mum died."

Chris rubbed his face. "Forgot."

"You'll be grand."

"Buying a new pub. Getting out of this place."

Ben smiled. "She's good for you, son. A new life with Fran and a family is just what the doc ordered."

"Eh." Chris played with his glass. "There's something I need to tell you. Really heavy stuff."

Ben breathed heavily. "Son, it's late. Coping with what you have told me is enough for one night, if you don't mind?"

Chris lowered the remainder of his drink. "You're right, dad. Cheers for the chat. You go on up. You need a good sleep before flying to Dublin tomorrow. I'll tidy up."

Ben eased off the stool, patted Chris' back and left him alone.

He didn't tidy up. He poured another Southie into the glass.

All of a sudden too many coincidences. Dad, Gloria, and Phil arriving. He an Interpol agent. There's a connection somewhere—I can feel it.

He rubbed his aching head.

127 THE GANG CHAT

Specs Morgan was locked up after being formally charged on various accounts of criminality and refused bail. He recruited a renowned law firm to represent him. Claud Hands had a reputation of winning the most outlandish of cases. His specialty being undermining prosecution witnesses and producing client alibies if paid well. A problem Specs would have to overcome quickly.

From inside, he had organised a series of robberies throughout the Midlands and Wales. The monies was needed for Claud to begin his work.

Belch and Mouse were out on bail due to being incapable of performing heavy criminal duties. Belch hardly spoke. His wired jaw proving to be at fault.

Mouse was almost as bad. His broken arm healed slowly but after the kicks, his jaw remained sore. Owing to the many attacks suffered from small-time thugs, the only functioning parts of their bodies, on low battery, were their brains.

They sat at greasy table in a low-life dockland café.

"You fink that the guys can do the next two jobs?" Belch — belched.

"Credit banks are small," Mouse said. "Though no visible security, you can bet at least one is behind an office door. Boph will 'av loads of cash." He rubbed his arm. "Fuck."

"We 'ave to take care of the uver problem." Belch picked at his pie and mash.

"We do that after the jobs are done, eh. We need two of the guys to 'elp us—distraction. Easy as that pie."

"You fucking joking? That Freeman is a nutter."

"That was some punch though."

"Lucky, that's all."

"Yeah right."

128 THE NEW MOB

Stoke Newington Thursday August 23

Chris remained free again to visit with Pockets and catch up on the investigations.

"When is George's funeral?" Pockets asked.

"Saturday. Ben and Gloria will travel back from Dublin tomorrow."

"Good to see Ben again. She's a nice woman."

"Cheers, yes." Chris appeared distracted.

Some words were spoken but not heard until Pockets tipped Chris' Shoulder.

"Oi—Chris."

"Sorry. Miles away." He shifted in a chair opposite Pockets' desk. "These robberies, are you sure they're Specs' related?"

Pockets opened a file and removed a blown up CCTV photo. "That type of rose tattoo on the neck indicates only one person."

Chris picked it up. "Josh Mackenzie."

Pockets eased into his chair. "Oh, you do remember him."

"A pox bottle. Threw him out of my pub soon after it opened. Remember?"

"I sure do. He and Mouse were trying to sell drugs. You did well keeping them out." Pockets shoved another two photos to Chris. "Mac has been seen in the company of these two. They're new to the manor. Travelled via Alicante and your hometown."

"Fuck me pink. Specs can't be serious letting these two into his fold. Paddy 'Bruiser' Mulligan and Gary 'Nosey' O'Dwyer."

"Yep. Specs can pick them. They have been ostracised from Dublin's Kennedy mob. Serious people."

Chris stared at the pics. "They boxed. Dirty fighters. Though Mulligan was well hard." He tossed the photos on to the desk. "Never made the grade. Just like Mac. Nosey's not bad though. Bit of chancer more than dirty low life. Good organiser. Probably why Specs hired him."

"Specs has hired Claud Hands for his defence. So, we expect more robberies to pay for his unworthy reputation." Pockets stood and paced. "He will get to witnesses. Search for the deepest secrets to undermine their worth." He scratched his head. "Something else."

Chris' eyes followed Pockets worried look.

"There's CCTV of Specs arriving back to his apartment. Must be a glitch but it is weird and may be used to get him off." Pockets returned to his seat and pressed a button on a laptop. "Watch."

They both looked at the screen. Chris opened mouthed. Pockets tight lipped.

"Oh fuck." Chris jumped up and paced rubbing his head.

Pockets turned the footage off. "That's your uncle with Specs."

He still paced cursing quietly.

"Specs said he was just dropped off to the apartment and couldn't move." Pockets brow furrowed. "Chris?"

Chris breathed heavily and sat. "Has Hands got a copy?" He realised the DI's tight lips.

"Your uncle will be looked into."

A clap echoed in the office. "Forget to tell you. He's Interpol."

"What has Interpol got to with the CCTV?"

"No." Chris smiled. "Uncle Phil is an Interpol Inspector. Undercover mostly."

"Okay. That would give him the right to bring Specs in under the European warrant."

Chris' face beamed further. "He didn't need to bring him to a station. The fact that local arrested him is better and less complicated."

"That's true. But your uncle must appear in court to give his full report of how he brought Specs back."

"I'll look after that."

Chris turned and left the office in a better mood.

129 THE INTERPOL CONFIRMATION

Thursday evening, Pockets read through more robbery files while waiting on a return call from Interpol's UK office in Manchester. He was worn out. Rubbing his unshaved chin and yawning more than usual. It has been a tough case. He had expressed concern of the many coincidental deaths to his superintendent.

His phone's tone disturbed his recapping. "Hello. Ah yes, Chief Inspector. Thank you for getting back to me. — You don't say? Really? Yes, that is fantastic. So, Inspector Devereux does tend to do things in his odd way." Pockets laughed. "And good to know. — I hope so. Goodbye." He clicked off just as a 'ding' alerted him to incoming email.

He stared at the link results. Specs popping in and out of shot on numerous occasions. Belch and Mouse appearing and suddenly disappearing at different times over a period of days prior to the shooting of Douglas and Meyer. The dates and times in the bottom left corner confirmed Chris' tech genius.

Pockets eased back and clapped. "Brilliant."

130 THE FUNERAL

Saturday August 25

From a pulpit, Chris had put the past behind him to honour happier times of a long friendship. The packed mourners stood and clapped after his often funny recollections of George Inglis.

Special permission had been granted for George to be buried with his parents in the old graveyard of St. John-at-Hackney Churchyard. An apt resting place for a local and less than a hundred yards from the Tavern. The small, picturesque, enclosed park was filled with friends, relatives, neighbours, and George's work connections. Passers-by occasionally stopped at the black railings as if trying to spot a celebrity or two. Some shops close by had shut during the morning service for staff to attend.

Chris and a close older cousin of George, Robbie Inglis, had organised the funeral. Though his friendship with George had been blown apart, a buffet-style gathering immediately after the service was held in the Tavern. The doors had to be locked after verified mourners gathered in the open bar affair. Robbie had shouldered the cost of the catering and bar tab.

The guests mingled, chatting, and laughing in remembrance but perhaps more had rekindled many years of not seeing each other. The GNC members ruled their corner as normal. Two stools remained vacant in respect to their normal occupiers. Framed photos of George and Alan in Arsenal attire sat on the bar in place of their pints.

Alan Bradford's cremation was delayed until Wednesday.

Pockets signalled to Chris. They managed to manoeuvre to the office with a few taps on the back and smiling 'hellos'.

Chris closed the door as Pockets sat.

"You two did a great job of this—you and Robbie." Pockets placed his pint on the desk.

"Cheers. Never had any time for the man. Always creeped me when around at George's after school. Wasn't surprised to learn he had divorced only after a few years of marriage." Chris shivered. "I guess you want to tell me something else." He twirled his glass of Southie.

Pockets eased back. "Why don't you enter the police academy as a tech? Your abilities are amazing. I don't want to know how you did it, but the 'cleaned-up' CCTV clips have convinced the CPS to go ahead with Specs' prosecution." He took a slurp. "They are currently organising experts to verify the footage."

"Sorry, are you accusing me of something?" Chris smiled.

"Funny man." Pockets raised his glass in a toast. "And would you believe that your Uncle Phil still holds an Interpol Detective Inspector rank. It was confirmed he does have uncommon methods—but legal. What is it with your family?"

"I thought that he might have attended today." He took a sip of Southie. "Just a weird feeling."

"You must tell me about George's cousin sometime." Pockets folded his arms.

"Perhaps. But I thought you knew everything." Chris shuddered.

**

By four o'clock all that remained in the Tavern were GNC members, staff, the team, a few of George's work colleagues and cousins. The frequent old lads managed to maintain their customary Oval window seats along with a handful of regulars scattered in the beer garden. Fran had been made an honoury member of the GNC but sat mostly with Ben and Gloria throughout the day. Though the football season had started, TVs were banned. This was a celebration of George's life, no matter how it turned out.

Mrs. M insisted Marty be barred for the rest of the day. He was when bursting into a rendition of 'Come Out Ye Black and Tans'.

Chris looked around his pub from his GNC stool.

Another few weeks and gone. Going to miss it though.

A peck on his cheek broke the thoughts.

"You look knackered," Fran said.

"I'm grand." He emptied his glass and waved it to Kumar for a refill. "Would you believe that's only my third Southie." He helped her to 'George's' stool. "Has to be used sometime."

"Thank you, love."

Kumar placed Chris' drink down and a soft drink for Fran.

"Do you think I should recommend a rise for this barman?"

"You better." She picked up her glass.

"Cheers, boss." Kumar's phone vibrated in a pocket.

"Go on—answer it. And that's your last serving. Get going, you deserve it. See you tomorrow night."

"Really, boss? Cheers."

Arrows from Rory and Alice's eyes alerted Chris.

"Close at six." He smiled to them.

He nudged Fran and nodded to where Ben and Gloria sat with Mrs. M and Tom.

"They go back a while," he said. "So I was told by Marty."

"That was funny her leading him out of the pub to a taxi. The way everyone booed her actions and him waving and bowing." Fran took a sip.

"Fuck."

She leaned back and stared at him. "What?"

"This may be weird—but what if Missus M and Tom's grandson didn't just fall into the lake?"

"Chris. Really? Take the day off."

He breathed heavily. "Sorry, love." He kissed her cheek.

"Pockets left early. I like him but it appears that he's working all the time."

Chris raised his glass to Ben's company. "He doesn't stop."

"See you, boss—Fran," Kumar shouted from the private door.

"Bye," they both replied.

"Boss, boss."

Chris got off the stool a walked to the door. His face dropped.

131 THE ATTACK

In the sound proofed Den, Chris ranted at Phil. "Fucking tell me when you are arriving. You drop Specs off at his place without telling anyone that you are still Interpol. Pop in as if you're next door. Give me loads of bullshit." Chris paced holding his head. "Why are you here with your family?"

Phil sat calmed at the counter focusing on his nephew's rage.

"Sick of this secrecy. It's all down to you." Chris stared at him. "What's all this about you taking care of me years ago? Hanging around my hospital bed. You're hiding something from me."

Phil sat up. "I'm here for you—always have since the accident. Under your mother's orders. I never break a promise."

Chris openly cried. Everything seemed to come crashing down in seconds. Thoughts of the accident and Mary, his trauma in being studied by consultants hadn't given answers to why the headaches. Now all this; Specs, George. Thank God for Fran. Tension released. His hands rubbed his eyes.

Phil hugged his taller nephew.

Chris nodded as they broke away.

"We have both been through our own hells." He tapped Chris' shoulder. "I'll tell you about mine one day. Now, let's get down to the bar. This travelling is thirsty work."

"Piloting your own plane—yeah, right."

"True. A Cessna Citation CJ4. Thought you had a licence."

"I do, but, well, mine is a bit bigger."

How can I calm so quickly? Is it Phil's presence?

**

Fran stirred when Chris approached the bar. "You two must have had some chat."

"We did, Fran," Phil said. "Ah, Rory. *Conas tá tú?* And Alice."

"I'm fine, Phil. Welcome back." Rory took a glass out of a fridge.

Alice waved. "Hi, Phil."

Chris looked at his actions.

He certainly had an effect on people.

"When did he arrive?" Fran brought Chris back to real conversation.

"This morning." He jolted. "He must have thousands of air miles."

"Well, did you learn anything new?"

"Tell you later. All fine." Chris smiled and waved to Ben's table.

"I'll leave you two alone. Have to chat with your auld lad." Phil took up the handled glass. "Ah. Missus M and Tom too. Marty must be drunk again."

Fran leaned back as Phil went to the table. "He's a strange man." She turned to see Chris looking around the bar. "You okay? Chris?"

Phil turned quickly; brows raised.

"Sorry, love. My mind was elsewhere," Chris said. "We had a great chat. Do you know Uncle Phil is an Interpol agent?"

Fran tilted to him. "No way. So that's why he has been floating around. Ah—he brought Specs back."

"Yes. In a sense. He holds an honoury Detective Inspector ID. But he is fully operational in times of emergencies."

"Wow. What a strange family you are turning out to be."

His world had been turned sideways in a good way. He drifted from the conversation and thought about what had happened. He instinctively knew it would take seconds, but his mind flashed through the pub.

Chris' ears pricked and his brow furrowed. He quickly focused to the oval window.

Without warning, he jumped from his stool, grabbed Fran to the floor. "Get the fuck down."

Phil realised his nephew's action and pushed Ben and company to the floor.

The oval window shattered as shots whizzed past the bar.

Rory leapt over grabbing Alice.

Together Chris and Phil rushed to the old lads. Too late. Coloured glass scattered over their heads as some shards entered skin.

"Nooooooo." Chris roared.

Regular GNs, Mike, Steve and Vince plunged to the floor with partners safely covered by their bodies.

It was over in seconds.

Chris saw the dark van pull away towards Amhurst. He stood, bloodied, brushing off glass and checking for holes. The bullets missed him. But others weren't so lucky.

He sat cradling Joanne's lifeless body. His tears fell onto her bloodied hair.

"No, no, no, no." Chris' head shook as his voice blasted louder than the multiple shots.

Fran crawled to him. Other's began to rise helping those that struggled to their feet.

Phil assisted Fran before attending to his nephew.

It was then Chris saw the greatest damage and bleeding bodies at the oval window.

He and Phil walked to the front then outside.

Stunned commuters on a stopped bus gradually looked through the windows. People began to get to their feet on the pavements. Others emerged from their places of safety, behind parked cars and shop fronts. PP punters took a gamble and came out of the bookies to view the mayhem.

Chris breathed calmly. *Phil again.*

Phil patted his arm. "You better come back in. it's not good."

132 THE SUPERINTENDENT

Armed police had cordoned off the area. Ambulances waited to take the injured to hospitals. Chris, his face still bloodied, and Ben sobbed openly. An old lad was carried out in a black body bag. Throngs of onlookers, held back behind barriers, watched paramedics attend the injured. Detectives interviewed those that were able to comprehend what had happened. White overalled SOCO personnel worked the exterior and interior scenes.

Superintendent Weybourne, in full ranking uniform, surveyed the scene with Pockets.

"I know you were here earlier, and you have had a few, Bert. Leave this. It's a day off," Weybourne advised.

"Sorry, sir—can't do that. This is connected to my case." Pockets stared at the body bag being loaded into an ambulance.

"Okay. But let the juniors do the interviews." He sniffed. "And take a mint or two."

They walked to Ben and Chris.

"Chris, this is Superintendent Weybourne."

Squatted against an outside pillar, Chris managed to look up to Pockets then to Weybourne.

Chris helped Ben to his feet. "Hello." He shook Weybourne's extended hand and shivered. "This is my father, Ben."

"How do you do? This is a mess. Never before have I seen this type of violence." Weybourne's voice wasn't of the street.

He had risen through the ranks via the old college pals scheme.

Ben still shook. "I played dominos with old Jack back in the day. How can this happen? I mean a seventy-eight-year-old enjoying a laugh and pint with his best pals."

Chris moved an arm around his auld fella's trembling shoulder.

"Your son and the other man—" Weybourne looked to Pockets.

"Phil Devereux, sir. An uncle," Pockets said.

"Yes, of course. The Interpol Inspector. They have done well. We will get to the bottom of this and—"

"The bottom of this is awaiting trial." Chris's eyes flared at the equally tall Superintendent. "That fucker needs the noose."

Pockets' stare warned Chris.

Weybourne puffed. "I understand." He looked at his watch. "I have to make a statement. Perhaps we can meet later when this has quietened down."

Chris nodded.

Pockets stayed with Chris. "We know this is down to Specs. We have him and his lot will pay legally."

Chris shook his head. Thoughts of Joanne ran through him. Her helping hand when needed. The unlucky in love travel entrepreneur he had helped bring back from self-destruction over a younger man. The leggy woman now stuffed into a body bag in an ambulance. His mind momentarily drifted amongst the gathered crowd.

I can sense their anger. Their community has witnessed another shoot up. What about those bent bastards that tried to gun down me and my future wife? Where are they? Probably under house arrest having a fucking laugh.

"Phil." He waved for his uncle to join them.

Phil detected something as he approached. "I'm really sorry for you lose. I realise Joanne was there for you. How are you now?"

"Weird. Not sad—annoyed." He stared into his uncle's eyes. "I'm sure he's bent—the superintendent."

Phil watched as the high ranking officer climbed into a car. "Jesus. None of us—I mean, didn't know."

Chris twitched.

**

After they were interviewed, Chris and Ben stepped over glass and debris inside. SOCO had completed their interior investigation.

"I think I'll get away with a small packet of filler."

Chris' sarcastic remark about the few bullet holes earned a smile from Ben.

Besides the oval window, the pub was lucky to escape serious damage. A few tables had been broken. Bottles and glasses took most of the rifle fire. But the focus remained the dead, Jack's two injured pals and another injured local.

Jack's pals received wounds to shoulders whereas he was hit in the head. He hadn't suffered.

Chris and Ben walked through to the beer garden joining the remaining customers and staff. Mike stayed visibly shaken. The muscular man had a hard time since the guns used in a robbery were linked to his club. Along with the firing of his gym, it was no wonder he thought the bullets were intended for him.

Fran remained strong and attended to minor wounds while Alice ensured coffee and tea were available. Kumar sat with his parents who had arrived soon after the incident hit the radio and TV news. Ben joined Gloria, Ilsa and Vince.

Chris went to Alice. "He'll be grand. You are best being here instead of worrying in A and E."

She sniffed. "They wouldn't let me into the ambulance with him. No room. Rory looked bad, Chris. And poor Joanne—why?"

"She was a good friend and great listener." He hugged her. "Listen, what I was told makes me proud to have Rory here. Jumping over the bar and grabbing you. Wow. Okay, he has a broken leg and tens of cuts from glass." He released a shaking Alice. "But he's in good company. Missus M and Tom will put a smile back on Rory's face."

She looked around the destruction.

"We leave all this until tomorrow. I guess there are a few surviving glasses." His laugh brought a smile to Alice. "You can go whenever you want. Won't be opening for a few days, so enjoy extra hols in the sun."

Alice pecked his cheek. "You're the best, boss."

He raised his brow. "I know." He managed a smile.

133 THE BOOKING

Wednesday August 29

Chris, Fran, and Kumar worked hard for days refitting An Fáilte Tavern. A type of distraction from what had been part of his life lately. Fran and Chris both relieved the babies checked okay.

Steve had replaced the door, oval window, lettering, and all, and restored the damaged seating area.

Flowers, dominoes, and cards decorated the pavement outside the pub in remembrance of Jack and Joanne. The normally busy area had a solemn emotional quietness as passers-by paused to either add to the growing arrangement or read the cards. Cars and buses slowed more than usual around the turn in sombre respect.

Rory had been discharged from hospital in time for Alan Bradford's cremation. Chris took a back seat this time. His feelings had been drained over the last week.

The same church was packed showing respect to a man locally known as Sherlock. His awkward walk, research interests, and outwardly lovable character was announced from the pulpit by two cousins. When the mixture of laughter and tears ended, a standing ovation continued until Alan's coffin entered a waiting hearse.

Fran pulled in Chris' arm. "You okay?"

Chris nodded. He stared as the hearse door closing. He had refused closeness to perform his tasks. But he had a real future to look forward to. Fran, a family. A chance to like and trust people again instead of years of supressed pretentiousness. His true character could be revealed. The coldness of his tasks was not him. He realised the Society planned his meeting with Fran. But how much did they know of him? How did they understand his mind?

The couple walked in silence from the church grounds towards the closed Tavern. Chris stopped abruptly at the arrangement. He stared at the flowers and remembrances.

Fran rubbed his back.

He turned to her. "I'm not going to the cremation. Alan's gone. That's my part played. It's been many years since, but I'm going to get pissed."

"Yeah. Let's."

They walked under the arch to the private entrance. Inside, the fresh smell of varnish and paint had replaced the aroma of alcohol. That would soon change.

She sat at the bar while he organised their favourite tipples. The weather remained in the mid-twenties. He undid his annoying tie.

Consideration of Tragedies

They small talked. Taking time-out from investigations and Specs.

Chris' phone sang. He placed it on the bar, speaker on. "Hi Chris, Phil here."

Fran's brows rose.

"Hi, Uncle. Bad timing. We just returned from a funeral."

"Oh yes. I forgot. Won't keep you long. I want to book your conference room for a Friday evening."

Chris stared at Fran. "For why?"

"A conference. I have a list of guests and can guarantee they'll all show up."

"Would you be looking for catering, drinks?" Chris said.

Fran shrugged.

"No, just water. Don't want full mouths during the chatter. Is Fran with you?"

"Yes."

"Hi, Uncle Phil," she called out.

"Fran, you are a star to Chris. A shining light bringing him back to life."

She stiffened. "Why thank you, Chief Charmer."

Chris smiled. "Okay. Let me know in good time."

"Sure will."

Chris logged off. "Want another drink?"

"Are you giving me more than our normal measures? Our juniors may like alcohol too much. Just orange for me, love."

"Told you I wanted to get pissed." He moved from the stool and refilled their glasses.

Why have a conference here?

134 THE LONG-AWAITED TRIAL

Old Bailey, Monday September 10

Chris secretly monitored Hands' growing bank accounts. Robberies continued outside the Met's jurisdiction. He had become Specs' new middleman. Mulligan and O'Dwyer soon had control of the East End gangster's operations, on Specs' behalf.

I have a sneaky suspicion that they are working for someone else.

The CPS were ready for the trial of the century, in Clapton terms anyway.

During the first two weeks in the courtroom, Specs often wore a hopeful grin. That slowly changed to furrowed brows and head shaking. What was to be the final week, he fidgeted throughout, calling a brief over many times. His eyes shot at the jury and Chris.

Pockets was spot on with some witnesses suddenly becoming 'doubtful' and their statements torn to shreds by Hands' team. The main evidence the Crown depended on were CCTV, phones, and emails. The defence council tried their utmost to undermine the prosecution's experts in those fields.

However, Phil Devereux's statement and credentials paved the way for the main expert witness. They had not welcomed Chris Freeman's absolute tech know how. He held the jury's attention when showing the details collected by the Team. The defence failed at every turn to undermine his capabilities.

Chief Justice Swan remained in awe of his expertise and presentations. His pen busy trying to keep up with Chris' demos and explanations of how this and that worked.

Chris held 'court' for three days due to the defence throwing everything at him. But he was relentless even when Hands insisted that old camera footage should be thrown out. It wasn't. Speech analysts agreed on the phone callers and background voices in the Waterbeach shooting.

The public were removed from the court when the footage was played and replayed for the jury. It was hard for them not to show emotion. Some openly cried, a few men lowered their heads and a woman juror fainted. The trial recessed until she was well enough to return an hour later.

Pockets had ensured that the jury were safely sequestered. They had no phones, papers or any media that may have influenced their judgment. Even the superintendent had no idea where they were. Spec's gang had been foiled at every avenue to find out who the jurors were. Cameras were strictly forbidden during proceedings and the twelve secretly ushered away immediately after the court adjourned for the day.

Wednesday September 26

The day had arrived. The jury took merely six hours to deliberate. The court resumed as the public whispered excitedly inside. Outside, media jostled for best positions anticipating some faces to shove their recorders and mics towards.

The court stood when asked as emotionless Chief Justice Swan took his seat above all. He nodded. Silence was deafening as the usher went off to bring the jury back in. Their eyes focused on the seats as they reached them. The silent court gazed at them trying to determine the outcome.

The judge remained stern faced. "Foreman of the jury, have you reached a verdict?"

A well-dressed middle-aged woman rose unsmiling holding papers. "Yes, My Lord."

"On what counts have you reached a verdict?"

"All, My Lord."

The court clerk collected a paper from the foreman and handed it to the judge. Again, silence reigned as fingers twitched and some elbows nudged people next to them.

Chris stared, reading Swan, and smiled. He turned to Specs then winked.

Swan looked to the clerk.

"Will the accused please stand."

Spec's tried an unconvincing pretentious smile as he stiffly stood, chest and chin out. He buttoned his well-filled two piece aptly named *Boss* dark blue suit.

Still standing, the foreman listened to each count read out to her by the clerk in alphabetical order:

"Assault with weapon with intent to rob, attempted murder, causing a child to engage in sexual activity, conspiracy to murder, gross indecency between males where one is twenty-one or over and the other is under sixteen, kidnapping, manufacture and supply of scheduled substances, murder, offences in relation to proceeds of drug trafficking, possession of firearm with criminal intent, possession of firearm with intent to endanger life."

They all carried a unanimous verdict of guilty. Victims, witness, and police sighed and managed smiles after each verdict.

Specs had to be assisted to remain standing.

The judge gave his submission to Specs. "Hugh Morgan, AKA Specs. You have been found guilty on all counts. A verdict which I agree with.

You will be—"

"Bastards all of ya," Specs yelled. "You did this, Freeman. And you, Pockets, will get yours."

"Silence. You will be held in custody until a hearing for sentencing is arranged. Take him down now," Swan ordered.

It was over.

Fran hugged and tipped-toed to kiss Chris's wet cheek. He visibly shook as if tension had been extracted from his body.

Pockets, Pete, Ursula, and Harley received handshakes and pats on backs. Kumar cried with his pals and parents. The brave boys, men now, joined them. An emotional wave breezed over the court as Chief Justice Swan disappeared to his chambers.

135 THE SUPER'S ROUND

The semi-refurbished An Fáilte Tavern had reopened during the trial without fuss or ceremony. Chris had been given photos of Joanne and Jack enjoying the pub in years past. Taking the most appropriate, along with one each of George and Alan, he placed them together on a wall near the entrance.

The afternoon of the verdict in the pub was like a Saturday night without music. All hands, including Rory, manned the pumps except Kumar. He enjoyed the company of family and friends in the beer garden. The team joined members of GNC. The mood bounced between sombre and laughter.

Behind the bar, Chris tapped Fran's shoulder. "It will ease off."

"I wish. Juniors and I are starving." She nodded to another thirsty customer.

Chris watched glasses slowly lowering to last mouthfuls. He grinned while unashamedly listening in on some conversations.

"Yep. I'll get ready to clean the few tables." He walked from behind the bar to the main seating area opposite.

Small talk with punters before leaving was interrupted by a familiar song. He took out his phone.

"Hello. — Ah, Uncle Phil. *Cómo estás*? What? How did I know? The sound of the waves. — Yes, great news. Sentencing will be sooner rather than later." Chris laughed at the reply. "That's okay. Six? Yes and I'll have everything ready. Great, see you then."

His smile still held while bringing empties back to the bar when a tall character walked in.

Chris nudged Pockets. "Here's trouble."

The Team looked around.

"I hope you do not mind me joining you, DI Macken," Superintendent Weybourne said.

With an obvious puff, Pockets said, "Okay, sir. Your round."

Chris laughed while placing the empties into a dishwasher tray. "Mine's a large Southie. Fran will have a soft drink." He leaned on the bar. "Cocktails, ladies?"

"Oh, yes please," came a unanimous reply from Ilsa, Ellen and Ursula.

"And the gents will have double of their favourite tipple. Thank you, Superintendent." Pockets grinned triumphantly.

Weybourne's eyes widened. "You all deserve it. A huge release for all that have been infected by Specs and co."

As the staff looked after the large order, Chris winced.

Consideration of Tragedies

What's that smell?

He placed the doubles and their mixers in front of the men. He spotted minute traces of white crystalline powder under Weybourne's manicured fingernails.

Chris left a half pint of mild in front of him and extended his hand.

Weybourne shook it. "That is some grip you have, Chris."

"Thank you—and thank you for your support. I am sure the community would welcome a tour from you soon." Chris withdrew his squeeze.

His damp hand had collected what was needed.

"Fran, I'm popping upstairs for something. Are you okay here?"

"Yes, love."

**

Careful not to use his right hand on any surface, Chris scraped the few minute crystals onto a saucer. Beside his desk, he opened a large, locked cabinet, removing what was needed, placing them on the kitchen counter.

I have a funny feeling that this is Fussol. But how could I smell it? It's supposed to be odourless.

He set up the mini-lab. Wearing latex gloves, he dissolved the samples in 1.5ml of 'heavy water' containing sodium trimethylsilylpropanesulfonate. Undissolved solid filtered through a Pasteur pipette fitted with a cotton plug. The liquids were then heated over a Bunsen burner to remove the solvent. The result showed a presence of fluorine.

Definitely Fussol. What's the superintendent up to? Why would he have a poison substance on his hand?

He removed small containers of chemicals from the cabinet and measured samples of each and mixed the clear concoction. One hundred mg of Dimaval, Sodium bicarbonate and flumazenil.

This should be enough antidote if needed.

He tidied up, washed his hands thoroughly and returned to the bar.

**

The pub thinned out as 6 p.m. approached.

Only Fran had missed him. "All done, whatever it was?"

"Yep." Chris stared at Weybourne.

The superintendent shivered.

"I know that look," Fran said. "You're up to something."

He pecked her cheek. "Just some emergency research."

A door squeaked. All GNC turned as if expecting Alan or George to walk in. A biker approached the bar. Helmet under an arm, a large brown envelope in a hand.

"I'm looking for the owner," the tall messenger said.

Chris waved from the bar.

"Here you are, sir. I was just told to deliver this. No signature required." The biker turned and left as quickly as he had arrived.

Silence along the bar.

"What? Nosey lot. Okay, I'm expecting specifications on a project. Go drink." Chris laughed. "Did I hear another round called by our generous Superintendent?"

Weybourne shuffled uneasy. "What? No. Eh. Okay. Same again please."

Hoorays and clapping welcomed the offer.

136 THE LAST TASK?

Early hours Thursday September 27

Chris had a restless night. It wasn't due to Fran's snoring. He looked at the bedside clock. 03:24.

Damn.

He moved quietly into the Den. Turning the desk light on, he sat, opened the envelope, and removed its content.

Fuck. Not again?

Hello Friend,

It pains us to inform you of a task refused by another operative due to family matters. Due to only recently discovering the actions of the subject, we remain shocked. However, being the source of the leaks to media personnel, the subject must be attended to in whatever manner you deem fit. There is no need to place an add because this is not a task open for refusals.

We have learned of your enterprises thus far. You deserve happiness and we vow you will not be called upon again.

We wish you all the best. Enjoy your family in the future.

God bless you.
Mors meritas (MM)

Chris perused the information. He shook his head when seeing the photos and reasons for the attention.

Unbelievable. My suspicions were right.

Taking a lighter, he lit the envelope and papers. They fell into a metal waste bin at his feet.

Soft padded footsteps behind caught his attention.

Fran stopped and stared at the blaze. "No way."

Chris puffed and showed his palms. "No relation, friend or local."

"That's a relief. I won't ask when, how or why." She kissed his head then straddled him.

Her shirt not fully buttoned.

He buried his head between her inviting breasts. His tongue and lips caressed her pale skin.

She felt him growing and slipped his Arsenal bathrobe open.

137 THE CONVERANCE PREPARATION

An Fáilte Tavern, Friday September 28

Chris once again called all hands on deck due to the expected conference that evening.

"I'm leaving the side entrance unlocked for them to arrive. I don't know the exact numbers, but I've placed all the chairs at the long table," he told Rory.

"What about catering?" The manager asked when serving Vince his Guinness.

"Uncle Phil said water will do. Must be an important meeting to hold it here. Anyway, none of my business."

Vince signalled Chris. "Oh, forgot to thank you for the nosh up after our win against Everton last week. Though being in the box is cool, I still prefer the stands."

"It was a good break from the shite. Fran enjoyed it too." Chris went back behind the bar and took a Pils. "Anyway, we all have many things to look forward to." He raised the opened bottle in a toast. "Up the Arsenal."

"Ooooh to be a Goonah."

**

Chris and Fran laid out the mahogany table in the large room with mats, upturned glasses, and bottled water.

"What time is it?" he asked.

"Just quarter to six. Any word from Phil yet?"

"Not a whisper. Probably pop in again."

A familiar ring tone. "Speak of the devil." He took out his phone and placed on speaker. "Uncle Phil."

"Hey, nephew—hi Fran."

"Hi." She raised her brow and mouthed. "How did he know I'm here with you?"

Chris shrugged. "We just finished organising the room. The side door is on the latch. So, you on your way?"

"Not too long. Can you please ensure that we are not disturbed? I'll call you if we need anything. Oh, hate to ask. Can we use your spare apartment facilities instead of the bar's?"

"Yes to all. I'll leave a key on the table. By the way, how many are expected?" Chris winked to Fran.

"Including me, twelve at first but expect a couple more later."

"Great. And would you all be spending a few bob in the bar afterwards?"

Chris thumbed up.

She tittered.

"Oh, I am sure we can release a few shillings as a thank you. See you two later."

"Bye, Phil," Fran said.

Chris hung up.

Weird.

**

Phil walked into Chris' office at 6:05 p.m.

"Uncle Phil. What a surprise."

They laughed.

Chris gave him the key to the conference room. "I'll be pulling the curtain across the bar entrance and be out of your hair in a few moments. Nobody will see anyone coming through."

"Fair play to you, Nephew." Phil played with the key. Something on his mind. "I realise that the bar gets packed on weekends, but would it be at all possible to reserve the oval area for our group?" Phil read Chris' doubt. "Now before you make up your mind, we all won't be sitting there."

"Well, I rarely reserve any tables, but will make an exception tonight. You will have to buy the regulars who sit there a drink though—or two."

Phil beamed. "Done."

He trudged upstairs to the conference room as Chris tidied up the office.

Fran said when coming out of the apartment. "Uncle Phil. All is ready. Hope we see you later."

"Yes, Fran. You are looking rosy," he said.

"Go away. Too many charmers in your family."

138 THE SOCIETY OF JUSTICE

Chris sat on his barstool beside Fran and looked towards the bar clock. "Just after seven. Not a sound of anyone coming or moving about."

"Soundproof is working." Fran sipped a coffee.

He stared to the oval window. "Weird. Never place reserved at the front of the shop before."

"It's hard, love. I know I've only served Jack a couple of times, but I do miss him." She wiped an eye.

He kissed her cheek.

"I noticed you haven't left the pub at all today."

Chris grinned. "No. Nothing happening yet so don't even be nosey about it."

"Just wondering." Her titter brought a smile to him. "Hope whatever it is, it's the last."

"Shite." He twitched and took the phone from his shorts. "Uncle Phil—really?" Chris furrowed a look at Fran. "The two of us? Do you want drinks or something? — Okay."

He hung up. "We're wanted upstairs."

"Why?"

"He wouldn't say. Just come up and join them at the table."

They stood.

"Rory, we'll be upstairs. Please, no problems."

The manager thumbed-up.

**

Although he owned the building, Chris politely rapped on the conference room door.

"Come," an unrecognisable male voice said.

The couple stepped in as if expected at an interview.

Chris let the door shut automatically behind them.

They stared stiffly at many familiar faces.

After seconds, in his straight to your face mode. "What the fuck is going on here?"

A grey-haired elderly man stood at the head of the long table. "Chris—son, the two of you sit and you will be told all."

"How the fuck did you all get here without me hearing—" Chris eyeballed a smiling Phil.

His uncle continued to smile as the couple sat on the nearest empty chairs. They gazed at each person.

"Missus M, Tom, Gloria. What the hell is going on? —Sir Patrick, Superintendent Weybourne. Really? No way—I don't believe it—Marty. This is too weird." Chris' hands moved through his hair to the back of his neck.

Fran sat opened mouthed.

"Son. We *are* the Society of Justice."

Chris' eyes shot to Phil again. His fist thudded on the table. Water sprouted over glass rims.

Fran shivered.

Ben sat, Mrs. M and Gloria rubbed his hands. His face appeared older; drained. "Son. For years you and others have performed unbelievable tasks in the name of justice. Fran too has done her part in surveillance and acts of justice. We commend you both."

Chris remained fuming. Silent.

Phil recognised his nephew's doubt and unbalance.

Ben continued. "Your role was necessary after the death of Mary. We increased membership. The committee grew as we reached out to other departments and foundations unjustly wronged in many ways. Too many to recite here. Courts let the obvious guilty go with false statements from witnesses. Children continuing to die due to profit making politicians and their suppliers like Specs. Greedy, uncaring individuals working on the weak minded to bring them into their fold—" He stopped, visibly shaking. "The likes of Meyer and Bradford turning their backs on working for the common good and world health for gain. Bastards, all of them."

"But why me in the first place? Why reveal all now?" Chris' head shot to Weybourne.

Something isn't right.

Beads of sweat formed on the superintendent's brow.

Chris looked at the table. Folders and pens had been prepared in front of each member, him, and Fran.

What's this really about?

"Ladyship, can you explain to our young operatives part of what was done?" The marbled voice of Sir Patrick brought a smile to Fran.

"Well, young fella," Mrs. M began. "When our grandson disappeared and our son—" She stalled as Tom held her hand. "Well, you know—" Her pronunciation and dialect had changed.

Chris stood glaring at his favoured Mrs. M. "Hold on. Without any more fucking about. How come your accent has gone posh?"

"Son, just fucking listen." Ben's sudden outburst stunned Chris.

He sat and listened as a child without questions. Each one explained their reasons for heading the society.

Chris and Fran held hands as individual tales revealed.

He already knew of some of Phil's accidental disappearing and returning yarn.

Tom Mooney revealed that the woman known as Mrs. M was of noble birth. The Right Honourable Lord O'Brien of Kilfenora was the Lord chief justice of Ireland in the late nineteenth century. Mrs. Theresa Mooney was a direct descendant.

Marty had brought the news of child abuse and sex to his sister after the loss of her son. Ben's story obvious when his daughter-in-law had been mowed down. Of course, when Gloria accidently found out Ben's secret, she jumped on board.

Sir Patrick Royston suspected child sex was progressive in Cambridge and other university towns. Along with known criminals getting off because of misspelled words and unreliable police evidence, he was perfect for the society.

Other founder members' varied reasons for committing to the cause. Drained children funds destined for third world organisations were top of their agenda. Religious hierarchies using charity resources for their own comforts. Industrialists not adhering to research codes for necessary medical needs. The list endless.

"I sat on the fence, Chris," Tom said. "When hearing of your family tragedy, I empathised with you. Oh, how I wish I could have performed the necessary tasks."

"I realise how easy it was to recruit me. My short temper, tech skills." Chris squeezed Fran's hand. "You somehow used Mary's memory every time. This bought you assurance that at least I may consider the tasks. Mental blackmail, Dad." He opened the water bottle and drank. "I should've just killed the German fucker first and end of—got out."

He turned to Fran. "That fucker—the George connection. It took major planning. Driving for months to the continent. Disguises. Poor Toplan. A genuine employee. I was amazed that he never recognised me."

Ben brushed tears from his eyes.

Chris stared at the table. "The first. Did you know that I had a few Southies before choking the life out of that bastard in Paris? Needed Dutch courage. Don't know why I took the credit cards. I chucked them in some bin."

Fran looked at him as he told the tale of throttling an African diplomat. He had transferred much needed children's charity funds to finance child trafficking.

Chris took a long mouthful of water. His audience quiet. At last, he could release all that had maimed and troubled him for almost fourteen years.

"I was enjoying the match when that eejit Vogel decided to go to his meeting early. Pressed the button and boom—gone into the water. But I would have like to have met Herr Müster socially. He made me laugh."

"So, you knew then of Douglas?" Fran asked.

"No. My head wasn't right yet. Doing that German for Mary's death released something in me. Later, I began to research all the subjects lined up for punishment. You are all aware of Lake Victoria."

Mumbles and sips from glasses echoed.

"He was my fav character—Ambrose. But Noel was the hardest. I never baked in my life. Took classes under another name. Looked up his family. Visited Raz's shop as Julius. Learned the dialect. Man, it was hard going." Chris took another sip of water. "Put on natural weight, not like Brownlow. All padded and wig, but beard was real. I'm fluent in Spanish, German, French and Italian, so that was easier than character pretentiousness." He looked to Fran. "I was really concerned about John Carr. All was perfect. None of my tech left for forensics. All disintegrated after use. When you mentioned Carr, I choked inside and looked at the paintings. It still didn't click about George.

"Coming back to my natural weight was hard. Jogging, martial arts training. Took almost a year to lose it all."

"We were aware of that. Hence the gaps for your tasks. You were constantly monitored. Bradford being your main target along with side tasks, including, regrettably, Marcus," Ben admitted.

It was like a friendlier mode of the Inquisition. The committee were sitting in thankful judgement of Chris' deeds. Perhaps without vilifying their existence.

"The one I do regret was Humph." Chris realised Fran's concern.

She jerked back. Eyes widened. "What?"

He managed a tight grin. They unashamedly kissed.

"Young fella. Really."

"Missus M, you're not wearing your pinny now. Behave."

After some polite chuckling, Chris continued. "I felt invisible at times during the tasks. As if carried or assisted by someone. Humph was easy to read. Gooner, me hole. Setting up the three apartments was easy too." He rubbed his head. "Each time I met him; my head was on fire. Like a bad migraine."

He saw questions in many faces.

"I armed the digs he stayed in. Just in case. Sitting at a high table in Brady's, Dublin, I watched and listened as Humph viewed each place. I ran out of patience as Dad and Gloria were due. So, I pressed a button."

He read their unconcerned faces again. They appeared to appreciate the summary of his expertise.

"Did I enjoy any of the assassinations? Loved the planning and watching the outcome of the accidents. But shooting Douglas and Meyer I really enjoyed. Knowing that Ambrose was to 'disappear', it was a delight to leave evidence." More water passed his lips. "The solicitors were dodgy. Finding out they were the legal end of a 'sex orphanage' made it easier for me. The force of the blast was aimed left and right ensuring not too much escaped through the windows."

Fran's hand covered her mouth.

"But doing Purcell was personal due to your connection, love." Chris pecked her cheek. "The stuff that fucker stirred up and gave to Douglas. Bastard. Alan, well—it took a long time to plan. Getting to know him. Douglas played a part. His arrogance proved too much for Alan and he fell into the bottle. Made my mind up to carry it out." His mouth was dry, and he took another mouthful.

Fran, still holding a hand, felt his tension lessen. His breathing slowed to a normal pace. Heartrate down. "Did I feel guilt after each one? Kind of. I revisited the subjects' past. I realised a sort of 'yes, I really did the right thing'."

He eyed each one waiting for responses.

Nada.

"You lot are colder than me." He emptied the bottle. "Meeting Fran, whether it was planned by you lot or simply destiny, has brought new life to me. When finding out she too was an operative, I was released. The guilt of thinking 'Is it only me?' lessened. And now, having revealed as much as I can recall, I must tell you that I'm letting the Tavern out." He smiled at Fran. "We're to be married and moving to a new premises. But I suppose you lot have been aware of our relationship. But listen hear now—" His fist thudded the table again. "We'll refuse anything that comes to our door. If I see another 'Hello friend', even a Jehovah's Witness, the literature will be burned without reading."

Phil stood and began the handclap. Others followed his lead. Soon the room filled with the sound akin to Spanish castanets.

When the adulation eased, they all sat.

"Okay, thank you, Chris. You are to be commended." Weybourne wiped his brow. "There is a file in front of each of you."

They were opened almost simultaneously.

Chris sniffed the air.

"To finalise the closure of the society, and membership, we must sign the documents in the files. Doing so will bring to an end to the many unfinished contracts out there. The police, at least here, have their streets and community back and—" Weybourne recognised Chris's raised hand.

"Before you sign anything, I happen to have a crate of Luis Montfort in the cellar. Perfect for celebrating this occasion." He held Fran's hand.

"And as we are having twins, how say you?"

The members stood and clapped.

"Me, a granddad." Ben went to his son and hugged them.

Chris smiled. "Now. Don't touch a pen. I don't want any of you jumping the queue." He laughed when leaving the room.

nine text here. Insert chapter nine text here. Insert chapter nine text here. Insert chapter nine text here. Insert chapter nine text here. Insert chapter nine text here. Insert chapter nine text here. Insert chapter nine text here. Insert chapter nine text here.

139 THE BOTTLES

First, Chris rushed to the apartment for vital materials before heading to the bar.

Scurrying to the cellar brought enquiring eyes towards him from staff and punters.

He pushed the first syringes into the corks of eleven bottles. The liquid mixed with the alcohol. The marked twelfth received a different concoction.

Can't be too careful.

He shoved the crate up to the bar floor. And climbed out.

"Alice, Kumar—grab those trays and put fourteen wine glasses on them. Rory, take the grate up to the landing please. I'll manage from there. Cheers."

Great staff.

**

When the trays were placed on top of the bottles outside the door, the staff returned to normal duties.

Chris knocked on the door.

Phil opened it and took a tray in, placing it on a side table at a window.

Chris followed with the crate of wine.

At the side table, they turned the glasses onto their stems.

"Blast." Chris raise his hands. "Forgot the opener. No worries. Have two in the apartment. Back in a jiff."

He was and opened two bottles.

Phil began pouring wine into glasses directed by his nephew.

"Uncle Phil, will you start handing the filled glasses while I open more bottles."

"Of course." He started at the head of the table.

Chris ran a hand over a glass and poured from the marked bottle. Three more were filled from another bottle. He placed each in front of Weybourne, Marty, French Commissioner Mademoiselle Lavelle, and Fran. He left himself and Phil last before sitting.

"Superintendent, may I suggest that before they sign the papers, you make the toast." Chris bore a smirk.

Fran gazed to Chris' gleaming eyes.

"Of course. Would you please raise your glasses," the superintendent said.

They stood.

"To the past success of the Society of Justice and the future of a law abiding world."

"Hear, hear," echoed.

They drank long mouthfuls. Plenty more available.

Thirsty Marty raised his glass. "And to Chris and Fran. Congrats."

Glasses lifted again.

"Now. We sign." Weybourne grinned.

The fourteen clicked their new member-pens and scribbled signatures on five papers each. All done, the files closed, and glasses raised again.

Phil directed his to Chris.

He bowed winking.

After a few refills of wine, chat and laughter, the room emptied.

140 THE AFTERS

Some of the society hadn't previously been in the bar. Mademoiselle Lavelle happened to enjoy a casual smoke, but being polite, she sat with Mrs M and company. None smoked. The two Africans, the lone Asian and Sir Patrick sat at the oval window with Phil.

Most GNC regulars, what remained of them, had not arrived at that time. Chris and Fran sat with Ben and Gloria along the main wall. Weybourne was seated with Pete and Mike at the bar.

Chris placed a trayful of drinks down.

"What were you up to?" Fran asked.

He looked around then back to them. "You'll all be grand. There may be some discomfort for a day or so, but don't worry."

Gloria sipped her lager before talking. "I like Luis Montfort, but it was probably a tad warm."

Fran's eyes widened. "You put something in the bottles." She scratched a thumb.

"Don't do that," Chris warned.

"It's itchy."

He took her hand and sank the thumb into his Southie. "Rub your thumb over your fingers then dip the other one."

Her mouth screwed but did as asked.

Ben realised what was happening. He dipped his left then right thumb into a Jameson and Gloria followed.

Chris nudged Fran to look at the society members.

She did.

"Is this a ritual?" She returned Phil's wave.

Chris laughed. "Na—no love. We've all been poisoned."

"What?"

Heads turned to her loud question.

Ben titled forward. "Shush, Fran. I assumed the antidote was in the wine, Son?"

Chris managed a nod while still laughing. "Ouch."

Fran withdrew her fist from his side. "How? With what?" She sat straight. "The pens or papers. So, cleaning with alcohol."

"Both." Chris took a mouthful of his favourite tipple.

"But who did it?"

"Well, knowing the ex-operator, I would hazard a guess that we may find out later if we all stay," Ben said. "This being his grand finale. A public execution of sorts."

He raised his pint of Guinness to Marty at the pillar.

"It wasn't Marty?"

"Fran, just drink." Chris read her before she asked. "And no, our juniors will be grand."

141 THE LAST BASTARD

The holiday season had cut back on many regulars in the pub. Although remaining lively for Friday night with chatter of football ruling the GNC conversations, Duo entertained all. They announced their last set just after 12:15 a.m.

Marty had almost been tied to his stool by little sis until once again his favourite song was announced.

"Here we go. No holding him back now," Chris said.

But he wasn't the only one. On the second line of 'The Fields of Athenry', Ben rose to join his old pal in the centre. The pub erupted into an arm waving, chorus singing euphoria. Even society members let their hair down joining in as best they could.

Only one person appeared not to fully join in the fun. Superintendent Weybourne tried his best to utter a few words of the ballad at the bar.

Chris grew interested and looked over.

Pete and company sang along not realising a head slowly swooned beside him.

Weybourne's shoulder jerked. With one hand fixed to the bar, the other holding his stomach, he placed a foot to the floor. His behind slipped off the stool, forcing it to buckle under him. He doubled over and collapsed.

Marty and Ben sang the final line. When finished, hugging each other, they bowed to rapturous applause.

Chris thumbed-up Phil.

**

Weybourne never recovered from the fall. He died two days later. According to Pockets, nothing was found in his system to suggest foul play. The superintendent had a record of seizures for few years. It was suggested his unusual robust night out, with more drink than normal, was the cause.

Chris had learned that society members had a variety of unsettlement, ranging from sore throats to doses of diarrhoea. He had saved their lives and put an end to operations.

142 THE LADY THERESA

Monday morning, Lady Theresa O'Brien-Mooney, AKA Mrs. M, pleaded to be kept on at An Fáilte Tavern.

Chris looked up from his bookkeeping at the bar. "I don't know. I mean you'll have me bowing every time you enter from the beer garden or the toilets."

"Go away with ya—ya eejit."

"Even that has lost its tone. It's too 'marbled'." He caught the wet cloth. "Well, at least you haven't lost your aim. I may have to reduce your pay though."

"Okay. Only if you let me wear my tiara."

"Really?" Chris stood; eyes widened walking to her.

"Jesus. Not by itself. Stay away."

He grabbed her, kissing her cheek. "You are amazing, Missus M. And Tom— oh, forgot about Marty. My extended family. I love you all."

"We have known you for years before you came here. Tom remarked how like your mother you are."

He released her and stared opened mouth. "Now I know what Dad meant by 'the one that got away'. You lot have known each other long before this all started."

"We met again after years in late nineties. Then Phil returned out of the blue. He was presumed dead in Gloucestershire mines. Took us ages to realise his influence on people. He avoided me and Tom for a while." She sat at the bar. "He confessed later why. He knew our grandson would drown but could do nothing to stop it. Phil is a good man but can be cruel. His ability to read people, know the good from the not so good was important to the society. But he could never interfere with what was to happen."

He sat. "You mean he really can see things."

"I think there's something else about him. But he's closed. As if he'd only tell someone close—very close, about what he's about."

He looked at her. "I need to see a specialist. Dad is still holding back stuff. I reckon he knows why certain incidents and feelings bring on the headaches."

"You are a special one, Chris. You were somehow groomed but mostly left to your own advancement. Uni, sports and the like." She caressed his hand. "Weybourne never knew of Phil's foresight. His reading of people was a blessing to the Society of Justice. Keep your enemies closer. We knew Weybourne 'buried things'. How do you think King was fast tracked to DCI?"

A radio continued to play softly.

"Fuck me pink." He stood, took down a bottle and poured Southie into two glasses. "Ice?"

She looked to the clock and shrugged. "Two cubes, please. Don't you dare tell Marty."

They talked of Phil and Ben. The private jet always brought Mrs. M and Tom on holidays. Marty had been mentioned. A real living saint, she called him. Chris learned how he had brought the society's attention to the child sex ring.

"He loved Cheltenham. We had an uncle there. Raised a family. Marty often stayed there when attending seminars in Cambridge." She took a sip. "That's where he saw the first episode. He wasn't a bishop then, the priest he saw with two children. Marty started drinking that day. Uncle Leo found him huddled soaking wet on his front porch." Mrs. M sniffed. "Our uncle talked him out of leaving the priesthood, telling him to fight and help the boys. Marty went back to Ireland, did missionary work in Africa. That really—excuse me—fucked him up."

"My God. Missus M."

They laughed.

"He contacted Ben. What they saw disgusted them. Children dying due to lack of funds that were supposedly sent but not received. That was the foundation of the society."

"Marty and my Dad. Wow." He finished the glass, went behind the bar, and poured again.

"Jesus, young fella. What you after?" They laughed again in their old style.

"Cheers to Marty and Ben." Their glasses clinked.

"Ben contacted Phil, Commissioner Lavelle, she's a cousin of his, of sorts. And a business acquaintance, Adedayo Mfume. You met him and his wife. They really enjoyed Friday night. Anyway, when discovering the whole truth of missing funds, child, and drug trafficking, they set up a network of information collectors. And that was it."

"How could Dad have kept that secret all those years?"

"When Mary was killed, that was it for him. Phil was in full mode. Popping up all over the place using his Interpol ID. He found that German, Vogel, drinking beer in Costa Teguise with George two days later."

He remembered Phils' words. 'Calm, stay calm.'

She rubbed his back. "Weybourne was added to the society well after you were recruited. We needed a high ranking police presence—you know, to gather information. Look how that worked out." She swallowed again. "Phil's felt he shouldn't be told too much. But we learned yer man Barrington was given some false info about a woman, Bryant, dying due to taking a drug."

"Chris sat straight. "You mean, Dad set that up?"

"Oh yes. Your dad is very astute. Barrington believed he could earn big for his company if claiming but he messed up and went alone. His partners sacked him. We were finished." She took a swigged. "We needed to ensure that them having fingers in the so called *orphanage*, we could link all with the drugs and African exports. We wanted this to be public. Be done legally. Due to Barrington's greed, we lost the chance. He found a small link to us, fed Purcell. Then, as you know, you were brought in then Fran."

Chris leaned over and hugged her.

She kissed his head. "I was given the task to tell you all now. You know Phil trained you somewhat secretly, mostly."

He sat straight.

She smiled. "He would sometimes visit you when you slept in hospital. And another, he didn't say who, was with him. He knew you would learn to control your hot temper—sort of. It would help you open your mind. You have bottled up the memory."

He sat quietly pondering what was just revealed. Rubbing his chin, he picked up the glass and sipped. His eyes fixed to the range of bottles across the bar.

Fucker. Sixteen years he knew of George. Stay calm. Football matches. Calm. Drinking. Take it easy. Holidays. Sixteen years. Stay calm.

"I just thumbed-up to the van driver—thanking him for stopping at the crossing. Mary was merely a step ahead of me chatting to a group of tourists. Gloria." He breathed heavily. The memory hard on him. "A hand." His eyes shot to Mrs. M. "Someone pulled me. No—tipped me sideways."

He blinked as if recording the event.

She rubbed his back.

"The car didn't swerve to avoid. I felt the side of the bumper hitting me and a wheel going over my leg. It ploughed through Mary and the group. So sudden. Less than a second. My head hit the ground. Nothing. No more memory when waking up in hospital." He took a long mouthful.

"Phil told us as much as we should know. Marty is the one who receives 'guidance' sometimes—but he's a priest." She picked a tissue from the box and gave it him.

He wiped the deluge as his shoulders shook.

She moved an arm around his waist. "All will be well. You were saved somehow. It wasn't your time."

He calmed. A nod and then a smile grew. "Thank you, Missus M. This is going to be hard to take in."

"It's good you are leaving this behind. With Fran, you will re-build your life—well, hers too."

He didn't reply. The glass touched his lips again and he drank.

Paul Brady's 'The island' played on the radio.

Chris shook to the sound of the stair door shutting.

Fran walked to the bar and stiffened. "Really? At this hour." She looked at the guilty silent faces. "What's wrong?"

"I'm sacked." Mrs. M winked. "Well, I will be when I tell Chris this."

He stirred. "More? Are you for real?"

Mrs. M. smiled. "Marty knew that you played the part of Noel Peters." She looked to Fran. "And he left the file for you to find on the train."

"I thought I had seen him before," Fran said.

Chris drummed the bar.

"Marty suggested to the society that you would be perfect for those tasks, and he could keep an eye on you at the café."

He hugged Mrs. M and planted a sloppy kiss on her cheek.

"Lucky you are here, Fran. God knows what he would be up to next after all these." She shook her glass.

Fran sat beside her.

Chris and Mrs. M retold the morning tale.

143 THE FUTURE PLANS

Days later

The big news was Hugh 'Specs' Morgan's life sentence without parole. A few were unhappy. They sat huddled around a table in The Bird Cage pub, Shoreditch.

"What's goin' to happen now?" Belch asked.

"Well, let me tell yez," Nosey O'Dwyer opened. "He's fucked. Unless we can break him out or he appeals."

Mouse rubbed his stiff jaw. Lost at Nosey's suggestion. "Appeal what?"

"The conviction, stupah." Bruiser Mulligan took a slug of whiskey.

"I fink Hands knows more than he's telling. 'eard him whispering on 'is phone. But I fought 'Specs has no kids'. He never married or nuffing." Harris hears all, but does fuck all, Specs once remarked of his nark.

"Watchya on about, Harris?" Mouse still slow.

"Well, Hands said 'your dad' a few times to someone. Then said 'Specs'."

"Nah. Specs has no kids." Belch agreed.

Bruiser eyed Nosey. "Very interesting, pal."

An opening door permitted daylight to highlight a brown beer-stained carpet. Their attention drawn to a tall figure.

"Watchya, mates. What's occurring?" Robbie Inglis and another strode to their table. "We need to make plans. You all know Mac here."

**

The Den Friday October 5

Phil had dropped by with his family for a couple of days. On the local front, Pockets had been promoted to superintendent, under protest, bypassing the natural progression to DCI. There were no other candidates. Pete had gained his inspector's pay while Harley secured a permanent place in Stoke Newington. He had introduced his wife-to-be, Ruth, to GNC.

Chris and Fran cuddled on a sofa in the Den. "The last week here." He kissed her head.

"You're going to miss this—I mean the pub."

"At first. It's only natural. Had some great times here. Love the locals. Hearts of gold—most of them." He cuddled tighter.

"Mmmmm. I was thinking about leasing my house when we move to Ongar." She flashed her long lashes at him.

"Great idea. I mean there's four bedrooms in the new place. A new Den. Loads of room for starters. You know, before juniors arrive if anyone wants to visit. And a garden." He rubbed her stomach. "Putting on weight, girl."

Her hand covered his. "I'll write a book about the misconduct of universities regarding covering up the kind of things we discovered."

He stayed silent for seconds.

"What if I open a P.I office? Hire permanent staff."

Fran looked up. "Really? I would've thought you'd had enough."

"Nah. I'll never stop the research game. It's in the blood. My mum's." He shifted. "Just ordinary investigations. Nothing heavy like the stuff we've been through."

"Hire Pockets when he retires."

Chris chuckled. "Great idea. Hates desk work. But first, family. Don't forget, Lanzarote next Thursday—"

"Oh yes, Vince and Ilsa's wedding."

"And we can look at a possible places there, a holiday home—watchya think?"

"Yes. I love you, Chris Freeman." She sat up.

"And I love you, Fran Wakefield."

They kissed.

**

The End.

Consideration of Tragedies

ABOUT THE AUTHOR

Pat Kane's *Consideration of Tragedies* is his first book. He was born in East Wall, Dublin in 1954. His family moved to Hackney, London when he was 3-years-old. Not finishing his education, the Kane family returned to Ireland at the end of 1969. In Dublin 1970, frustrated with missing life in Clapton he began his painting and decorating apprenticeship in June of that year. Met his future wife Margaret that same year and they married in 1975.

He and Margaret gave their four children a good education and family values. Pat admitted he lacked education, missing out on a better career path. He entered an adult education course in his workplace, Dublin City Council. When retiring at 60, he took up a creative writing course and progressed to Maynooth University earning a BA degree in geography and history in 2018.

During his renewed interest in education, he began to write short stories. Then progressed to composing a historical novel. This has grown into a saga that still waits to be completed. He subscribed to Scribophile, an online writing site for beginners. Placing his historical novel up for critiquing, he took a break from his favourite genre and delved into crime writing. Remembering his Clapton upbringing and love of Arsenal FC, he drew on memories of a working class area and researched to compose *Consideration of Tragedies*.

So, from a simple background, bounced between Dublin and London working class areas, this is his first book.

Printed in Great Britain
by Amazon